MW01490533

# WHEN HOPE DIES

FOLIANT

BOOK 2

MIKE KRAUS

MUONIC PRESS

WHEN HOPE DIES
FOLIANT: TWO

By
**Mike Kraus**


www.muonic.com

www.MikeKrausBooks.com
hello@mikeKrausBooks.com
www.facebook.com/MikeKrausBooks

# CONTENTS

## WANT MORE AWESOME BOOKS?

Find more fantastic tales at books.to/readmorepa.

---

If you're new to reading Mike Kraus, consider visiting his website (www.mikekrausbooks.com) and signing up for his free newsletter. You'll receive several free books and a sample of his audiobooks, too, just for signing up, you can unsubscribe at any time and you will receive absolutely *no* spam.

# SPECIAL THANKS

Special thanks to my awesome beta team, without whom this book wouldn't be nearly as great.

Thank you!

# CHAPTER 1

**The O'Brian Family**
**Los Angeles, California**

The dead city stood silent around them, the penetrating darkness of night interrupted by probing, blue-lit illumination as the police car's lights continued their even strobe. Alongside the Los Angeles Police Car, a uniformed officer rested prone on one shoulder, lifeless, one corpse in a city filled with millions of them. His dead body remained partially in shadow from a nearby sedan, its own exterior scarred and maimed by an earlier collision.

Jason O'Brian stood next to his wife Samantha, twins Eli and Sarah huddled nearby, all of their attention fixed not on the dead, but on the living. They'd come across countless corpses since the mysterious events at the onset of the crisis in downtown L.A., but they'd run into very few survivors. Three of those survivors stood before them in red jackets, clutching pistols, all three weapons pointed directly at the four O'Brian's.

Jason raised his hands, palms outward, his voice calm, but edged with steel. "We're just passing through."

The lead man was lean, his jawline shadowed in stubble and he grinned wide enough to show teeth. "Nah."

Silence stretched for a few moments, the men illuminated in pulsing, even rhythms by the slashing strobe of blue lights. Kale barked loudly from within the RV, a frenzied chorus of angry, warning yowls. Beneath the shadow of stubble, the lead gunman's jaw tightened, his teeth clamping together. His pistol didn't waver, his grip never loosened, his arm ramrod straight as he turned slightly, looking down the barrel of the weapon in his hand. The wreckage of the earlier accident surrounded them: a battered police car, a mangled sedan, a wide, sprawling carpet of broken glass, fuel-soaked pavement, and debris from the vehicles' impact.

All of that fell into the blurred background of Jason's narrowed vision, a tunnel forming on the three men holding weapons. The lean one in the middle gently twitched his index finger, sliding it from the trigger guard with the most subtle of motions. Broken glass crunched beneath the sole of Jason's boot as he shifted the position of his hips, inching to the right, still twisted in the direction of the eight-story building ahead. Its shadow was thick and deep, a darkened stretch only broken by the three armed men who stood before them in their red jackets.

Stale fuel and the coppery tang of spilled blood tugged at Jason's nostrils as he turned back toward the O'Brian family RV, still a fair distance away, too far to make a run for it. Blue lights slid across the darkened roadway from the crashed police car to the right, a mangled sedan pushed up against the edge of another nearby building. Littered glass reflected the spill of blue illumination, revealing etched cracks of worn pavement beneath their feet. For the briefest of moments his gaze and Samantha's caught in silent acknowledgement before he faced the armed men again, fists clenched, and spine steeled.

In the front seat of the RV, Kale, the O'Brian's German Shephard, lost her mind, barking in a raucous fury of wet snarls, her claws hammering at the half-rolled-down window of the passenger side. For the narrowest of moments, the armed man in the center of the trio diverted his attention toward the sound of the family dog and Jason moved. All at once, he charged to the right while Samantha wheeled around, both of them springing apart in swift coordination. Jason threw himself toward the twins, arms spread, colliding with them both in a forward tackle, knocking them from their feet and sending them sprawling backwards. As a trio they struck the hard ground and tumbled awkwardly toward the rear of the police car until they skidded to a stop, the vehicle separating and blocking them from the armed men in the shadows.

Samantha lurched toward the dead police officer, throwing herself from her feet in a clumsy, head-first baseball slide. She struck the officer's corpse as she hit the ground, rolling across his body and behind the sedan as the armed man in the center of the trio finally pulled the trigger. Flat claps of pistol shots tore through the night, bright muzzle flashes combating with the blue rotating of police lights in a bizarre fireworks show. Sparks danced from the exterior of the sedan as Samantha flattened against the ground, cheek pressed to concrete close to the lifeless body of the uniformed officer. Jason's throat tightened, his pained knee digging against more shattered glass alongside the police car.

"Eli! Sarah! Are you okay?" Twisting away from the incoming fire, he took measure of the two children.

Eli huddled a few feet back, slowly crawling upright from where his father had knocked him down, while Sarah remained on the pavement, eyes wide in shock, reflected in the momentary glow of bubblegum lights on the roof. Her mouth was open, her pale face temporarily awash in blue. Eli jerked his head into an uncertain nod, but Sarah remained stock still, just staring blankly back at her father.

"Sarah!" Jason hissed. "Nod back if you're okay!"

Sarah bobbed her chin up and down, the color removed from her taut expression. Detritus along the pavement dug angrily at Jason's knees, not just the shards of broken glass, but chunks of torn metal, ripped asunder from the impact of the car accident surrounding them. Samantha ducked her head low, a clatter of bullet ricochets dancing from the blunt end of the trunk a foot from where she crouched, digging at the duty belt of the dead police officer. Her fingers clawed at his holster as the trio of men fired in her direction. Window glass erupted from a volley of rounds, spraying into the air, more bullets slicing above, piercing the darkness and blasting chunks of brickwork exterior from the building next door.

Jason poised by the rear of the police car, body coiled like a spring, ready to launch in his wife's direction. Bullets chopped at the pavement between the vehicles, hacking up chunks of broken asphalt. Finally, Samantha clawed the clip of the holster open, fingers grasping the handle of the pistol as she wrenched it free, then ducked back, more weapons fire crashing around her. She clutched the pistol in two hands and pushed gently up into a crouch, one shoulder pressed against the rear of the vehicle she hid behind.

Voices shouted from the shadows of the nearby building, and Jason sprang forward, scooping a fistful of debris from the road, gathering glass and metal shards into his cupped palms before twisting back toward the opposite side of the police car.

"Dad? What are you doing?" Eli reached out a cautious hand.

"Stay back!" Jason crept forward, head low.

As gunfire converged on the other vehicle, Jason dipped out from behind cover and pitched his handful of shrapnel in the gunmen's direction. A glittering rainbow of metal and glass scattered about the trio, forcing one of them to recoil, turning away from the spray of unexpected projectiles.

"Gun 'im down!" The man in the center stabbed his pistol

barrel in Jason's direction, ejected his magazine and slammed another one into place.

His two friends directed their next volley of fire in Jason's direction, forcing his hasty retreat. Jason threw himself backwards, heels catching on the uneven pavement as he sprawled toward the cover of the police car, rounds flying just ahead of where he'd been. Bullets crashed into the police car, a rapid fire *thunk thunk thunk* of bullet impacts on metal, followed by an outward explosion of safety glass as the passenger side window blew out. Samantha lunged upward and swung around the rear of the vehicle she was using for cover, fingers coiled around the handle of her weapon.

Her finger pumped the trigger three times in rapid succession, punching three rounds into one of the shooter's chests. Lurching backwards, his head pitched, his mouth opened in a silent scream as he went down, hitting the pavement with a hard thump. Shifting her weight, Samantha jerked the weapon left, firing again, though the other two shooters were already turning back in her direction. Her bullets sliced a neat path between targets, spinning off into the shadows as muzzle flashes illuminated, sending yet more enemy fire crashing into the vehicle she was using for cover. A thunderstorm of weapons-fire chaos swirled through the neighborhood, the persistent flash of blue police lights interrupted by muzzle flashes until a stray bullet hammered into the light bar and blew it apart in a gleaming shower of broken glass and colored light.

"Heads down! Heads down!" Jason waved his hand frantically at the twins, both of them drawing further back, up near the sidewalk, knees sharply bent, and heads lowered.

Kale continued to lose her mind, barking furiously, a cascading chorus of feral snarls as she slammed against the half-rolled-up window time and time again. Her snout extended through the opening, flashing pale fangs and dark, black lips, spittle flying from the aggression. Samantha took cover, pistol held low as the men in red jackets fired upon her once more. She swung around the rear of the vehicle, firing back, though struggled to get a good angle, her ammunition swiftly dwindling.

Jason scanned the ground for more shrapnel and scooped up another fistful, then uncurled his fingers, looking helplessly at the gathered shards in his palm. Gunfire echoed as he inched toward the side of the car. Behind him, Kale's barking reached a fever pitch, her howling snarls reverberating from within the RV. There was a muffled crack, Jason twisting his neck around as Kale took one more leaping charge at the passenger's side window. Her large body struck, smashing into the half-opened slab, blasting glass fragments into the air outside the vehicle. Kale's aggressive forward momentum carried her through the broken window and out into the air, bringing her to the ground where she landed, claws skidding on glass-scattered pavement.

She wheeled left, back claws kicking glass fragments in twin rooster tails as she sped forward, a brown blur of motion, racing toward the pitched conflict. Jason lunged toward her, hand outstretched, dropping the glass fragments from his opened fingers.

"Kale!"

The dog continued on, roaring past, paws slapping the pavement, her pumping legs carrying her forward at top speed. A swift smear of brown motion hurtled toward the gunmen firing upon Samantha, the angry chorus of aggressive howling leading Kale's way. Jason slammed his palm on the back of the police car, pushing himself upright, legs coiled to spring forward in pursuit of the racing dog. Kale moved quickly, bearing down on the two armed men before Jason could close the distance. She snarled again, a roaring, wet growl of rage, one of the men stumbling toward the dog, weapon coming around. He was half a step too slow, Kale already launching airborne, throwing herself from the pavement. Teeth bared, Kale latched onto the gunman's arm, closing around the limb in a splintering clamp, teeth sunk into flesh, ripping at muscle and tendon.

He howled, one leg buckling and lost his balance, trying to yank his arm back in agony. Kale released for a moment, landing on her paws, then launched forward again, carving at his arm with gnashing teeth. His pistol tumbled loose from his fingers, crashing to the pavement as he wrestled desperately with the aggressive German Shephard.

"Don't just stand there! Shoot the freaking thing!" The gunman half-knelt, clutching his arm while the second gunman spun the pistol barrel toward the frenzied animal.

"Stop!" Jason ran headlong into danger, his legs pumping rapidly, his voice caught in his throat, coming out a squeak more than a shout.

The pistol centered on Kale's chest, everything moving in slow motion, caught in a perpetual cycle, every second drawn out into perceived hours.

"No!" Samantha leaped out from behind the car to Jason's right, grip clutched firm around her pistol. "Kale! Heel!"

Kale went rigid, whipping to the right and darting away, following her master's direct orders. Samantha unleashed a swift torrent of gunfire, tugging the trigger in rapid-fire motion, sending several rounds downrange. The gunman recoiled, his pistol jerking away from Kale, his shoulders whipping around toward Samantha's vocal cry. Ducking his head, he stumbled backwards as Samantha adjusted her aim slightly and fired again, two more bullets screaming past the shooter's left shoulder. Nearly falling over, the gunman stumbled as he ran, the shadows of the eight-story building shrouding his retreating form. The second gunman followed, fumbling clumsily with his pistol on the ground, wounded arm hanging loose before spotting his retreating friend and taking off in pursuit.

Their footfalls faded into the distance, the runners swallowed by the darkness, leaving the O'Brians standing in the center of the intersection. Samantha kept her weapon trained on their vanishing bodies, barrel centered between the shoulders of the nearest escaping shooter. At the last minute, she jerked her weapon up six inches and fired twice, sending bullets into the air just above the sprinting men. They shouted in unison and moved more quickly, soon completely swallowed by the surrounding blackness. Jason expelled a swift breath of gasping air, bending slightly as he studied Kale, back legs still tensed as if she might spring.

"Kale!" His voice was a rasping breath. "Stay!" His back bent, his palms pressed to his thighs.

Kale whined and tilted her head, but reluctantly obeyed her master.

"Are you okay?" Samantha crouched next to him. "Eli and Sarah?" She pushed upright, she and Jason both turning toward them simultaneously.

Despite their stress-fueled exhaustion, they sprinted toward the police car, Kale following behind them, ears perked. The trio approached, Jason curling around the police car and shouting into the shadows.

"Eli! Sarah!"

"We're okay." Eli melted from the darkness, crunching over the splintered remains of the shattered police light bar.

He held up his hands, scraped raw, blood welling at a series of shallow gouges in the tender flesh of his palm.

"Can you run into the RV?" Samantha glanced in Jason's direction. "Grab the first aid kit?" She knelt by her son, hands clasped around his, turning them over in her hands. "Come here, sweetheart." She gestured toward Sarah who joined them, holding her hands out as well.

Jason jogged to the door of the RV and scaled the steps, pushing through the lingering pain stabbing his thighs. Swallowed by the momentary silence of the RV's interior, the echoes of the gunfight reverberated loudly within his mind. His fingers clutched the nearby seatback as he gathered his breath, stopping for a moment so the world would stop spinning. Steadying his posture and the uneven intake of air in his lungs, he pushed himself forward, slipping down the aisle and into the rear sections of the vehicle. Walking through the kitchen, he sped toward the narrow alcove that made up the bathroom and slid the door open. He crouched into the bathroom and opened one of the modular cabinets, then lifted out the slender first aid kit, tucking it under his arm and spinning back to the front of the RV.

As he passed through the kitchen he plucked a flashlight from the table and slipped it into his pocket, then trotted down the steps and back out into the smoke-filled city. Samantha led the kids toward the RV with Kale in tow and Jason thumbed on the flashlight, then handed the first aid kit to Samantha, who took it and cracked it open on faintly squeaking hinges.

"Let's take a look at this." She beckoned Eli over first, Jason shining the beam of the light down on his son's upturned hands.

They were scraped raw from road rash, a few glittering specks of broken glass caught in shallow wounds on the surface of his skin, glimmering in the flashlight's beam. Samantha pulled a pair of tweezers from the first aid kit and leaned in close to Eli's palms, pinching the tweezers around a scatter of various thin glass slivers. One by one, she tugged them free, dropping them with soft *tinks* onto the pavement. After freeing the glass slivers she could find, Samantha set aside the tweezers and found a wet wipe antiseptic pad. Tearing it free of its plastic wrapper, she used one of the wet wipes, brushing it across Eli's skin, wiping free some of the stray blood and dirt. Eli sucked in a breath and started to withdraw his hand, but Samantha gripped his wrist and held it.

"Stay still, okay? I know it stings." She applied more antiseptic and gestured for Jason to lower the flashlight, then examined him more closely.

There was scattered road rash on his arms and his left elbow, but mostly superficial. She nodded to her son and gently patted his back, then gestured for Sarah to come closer. Tweezers plucked again at slivers of glass fragments as Samantha leaned in even closer, positioning her head not to block the glow of the nearby flashlight. She tore open another wet wipe and worked it up and down Sarah's hands and her right arm, cleaning the two of them as best they could.

"If any of those start bleeding again, let us know. We've got bandages, but I don't think you need them at the moment." Samantha stood, closing the first aid kit, the trash bunched up in one fist.

She strode toward an overstuffed trash can on the sidewalk nearby and fed the garbage into it. Samantha handed the first aid kit to Jason, then walked toward Kale and crouched alongside, running her fingers through the long, brown fur. Probing and applying pressure, she checked for any signs of injury, but the dog stood firm, not shying away from her touch. She cocked her head and studied her master's face with rapt attention, tail slowly wagging as Samantha finished her quick examination.

"Eli, Sarah. Take Kale in the RV, okay? Your dad and I will be there in a minute."

"What are you going to do?" Sarah asked, gently rubbing her road-rash littered arm.

"We're just going to look around for a few minutes. Go on in the RV, lock the door and we'll be right there."

"Okay, Mom." Eli whistled for Kale, joining Sarah as the three of them disappeared into the vehicle, shutting the door behind them.

"Are you okay?" Jason gently touched his wife's arm, his fingers brushing her bare skin.

She exhaled again with a curt nod. "I'm okay. How about you?" She turned toward her husband, reaching out to touch his bicep.

"Holding together. Wasn't expecting that."

"Who would have?" They stood shoulder to shoulder, the chaos tossed around them, a spoiled giant's playground of discarded toys.

One of the shooters lay dead in the middle of the intersection, bent awkwardly on the pavement, motionless. Samantha stood facing him, her spine straight, her jaw set firm, a scattering of loose hair brushing her left cheek.

"It was self-defense," Jason said, putting his hand on his wife's back.

"I know it was," she replied. "My children were in danger. I'd do it all again."

"Without hesitation," Jason agreed.

He took a step away from her and approached the shooter, sprawled on the pavement, the Roman numeral "5" showing plainly stitched in the fabric of his red jacket. As he approached, his foot kicked the discarded pistol, and he crouched, scooping it up, the weapon pressed against his palm. Jason slid it into his pocket, then unfastened the jacket of the gunman and opened it, searching briefly for anything of value. A spare magazine sat laden in the man's inside pocket and Jason pulled it out, shoving it in a secondary pocket of his jeans before standing again. Samantha was already approaching the dead police officer, so Jason joined her, the two of them crouching low and going through the man's duty belt.

"It was just a matter of time before something like that happened." Samantha's attention focused on the belt as she worked a couple of spare magazines free for the pistol she'd already taken from the corpse.

"No doubt. I figured we'd have more time before the city turned into a warzone."

"I don't think those were just ordinary guys." Samantha turned her head toward the darkness in the shadows of the nearby apartment building. "Those matching jackets were the same ones that other group was wearing. It's not a coincidence."

Jason tugged a baton loose from the officer's duty belt but found little else of value and the two of them stood, walking toward the police car itself. Samantha leaned into the opened door of the cruiser and fumbled around inside until she popped the latch for the trunk, the slightly dented rear hatch lifting up on squeaking hinges. The trunk stopped partway, and Samantha gripped it, forcing it to rise further, exposing the interior.

"Do you think the kids are doing all right?" Jason peered over Samantha's shoulder and into the trunk.

"Physically they seem fine, besides some bumps and bruises. Mentally, we'll have to watch them." She turned back toward the RV, then met Jason's gaze. "Dealing with stuff like this at their age..." she shook her head, her jaw clenched. "No teenagers should have to witness what they've witnessed in the last twenty-four hours alone."

The interior of the trunk was crammed full of supplies, four nested traffic cones filling up a large chunk of the real estate along the left edge of the compartment. A rectangular weapons locker was pressed to the rear of the back seat while a canvas black duffel sat on the floor between the locker and the trunk door. Folded alongside the duffel was a ballistic vest with LAPD stenciled in a fabric square stretched over the plate nestled into the plate carrier. A megaphone rested, speaker-side down in a small section of trunk alongside the duffel, a set of thick, black pouches wrapped within a molle pouch strapped to the interior of an organizer panel.

Jason stepped around his wife and pulled the ballistic vest free, holding it with two hands before he slung it over his shoulder. Samantha leaned into the trunk, immediately going for the weapons locker, which she unclasped and opened with a skillful swiftness, her fingers working precisely with the latching system. The AR-15 within the locker slid out with ease, balanced in

Samantha's hands with innate familiarity, an extension of her own body. She bent and rested the AR on the rear bumper of the police car, then reached back into the weapons locker, freeing and removing some spare magazines for the weapon.

"Jackpot," Jason said, nodding appreciatively at the treasure trove they'd found in the trunk of the police car.

"Let's hope we never have to use it." Samantha handed the magazines to Jason, and he slid them into pouches on the ballistic vest, then lowered it to the pavement near his feet.

Samantha opened the black duffel which contained several road flares, a collapsible fire extinguisher, a few tactical flashlights and a thick, Kevlar helmet with a face shield that could lower. Passing these items aside, she slid across the trunk toward the molle sleeve, tore free Velcro straps and removed the thick, black pouches from within, holding them up for a better look.

"Individual First Aid Kit," she said with an approving nod. "A lot better than the one we had in the RV. It'll be good in case we need something a bit more robust."

The IFAK was compact but sturdy, marked with a white cross stitched onto its surface. She unzipped the bag, the sound of the zipper loud in the eerie stillness, the pouch opening into two neat panels, contents held in place by elastic and mesh designed for rapid deployment. The first thing inside the IFAK was a tourniquet, tightly coiled and marked with instructions printed on the black nylon strap. Beside it, a pair of chest seals for treating gunshot wounds were tucked into a transparent pouch, a reflective label glinting in the low light.

In another loop sat a roll of compressed gauze, vacuum-sealed in clear plastic, next to a packet of hemostatic gauze, which bore a bold warning about its powerful clotting agent. She touched the edges of the packet, as she nodded at the items contained within, lips moving in silent inventory of the kit's contents. A pair of trauma shears with rounded tips and black handles was secured in a side pocket, their blades sturdy enough to cut through fabric or even seat belts. Next to them was a nasopharyngeal airway, its green, rubbery tube packaged with a small packet of sterile lubricant designed to be inserted into the nose when no other airway was available. Samantha grimaced, her teeth clenching as her chin dipped slightly, her fingers moving skillfully through another section of the kit. In a smaller mesh compartment, she found several sterile gauze pads, adhesive bandages, and a compact emergency blanket folded into a shiny, rectangular package. There was also a pair of nitrile gloves, bright blue and slightly powdery to the touch, and a small bottle of saline solution rested in the bottom corner, the clear liquid sloshing faintly as she picked it up. Lastly, she found a portable suture kit sealed in a clear, thick bag, unopened with all of its contents intact.

Her fingers lingered on a small instruction card tucked into one of the loops, outlining basic steps for handling trauma including bleeding, airway management, and shock prevention. She barely read the instructions at all, quickly closing the kit and zipping it back up with practiced efficiency before she stood and turned to Jason.

"It's got what we need. If someone gets hurt, even potentially seriously, we should be covered."

"Good," Jason replied. "Let's hope we don't need it."

As Samantha had been going through the IFAK, Jason had located a few tear gas grenades in the black duffel which he'd removed for future use.

"I'd say we did pretty good here." He gathered up the vest and the grenades as Samantha lifted the IFAK and the AR, the two of them returning to the RV, loaded down with the police car's contents.

As they approached, Eli unlocked the door to the RV and let them in, Jason climbing the steps first, Samantha close behind. Eli stood stock-still, frozen in place as Samantha entered the vehicle, the AR in her hands, the IFAK slung over one shoulder. Jason made his way around the rear of the driver's seat and rested the ballistic vest against it, then stashed the tear gas grenades in a compartment built into the wall.

"Don't get too excited." Samantha read the shocked expression on Eli's face as she placed the rifle in a small alcove alongside the center console, putting it in arm's reach of her in the passenger seat. "We're all hoping we never have to use it."

"We're stealing that stuff, too? Just like we did with the food and dog treats?" Sarah's arms were wrapped around her body, her hip pressed against the kitchen table.

Samantha took two steps toward her and placed a calming hand on her shoulder. "I know it's a big adjustment, and I love your sense of right and wrong. But getting out of the city comes before anything else right now."

Sarah nodded unevenly, chin lifting up and lowering in a jerking, unsteady motion.

"Tell us the truth," Jason said, crossing his arms as he took up a position just behind the driver's seats. "Are the two of you holding up okay? That was a dangerous situation, there's no shame in being scared."

Kale whined softly where she lay in the kitchen, her tail sweeping back and forth across the smooth floor. Sarah knelt by the dog, gently stroking her fur-covered head, diverting her attention to the German Shephard.

"I'm okay." Eli lifted his narrow shoulders in a soft shrug. "It wasn't like the movies."

Samantha turned toward him and grasped his arm gently with her fingers. "You're right. It never is. It's important for you to realize that, and I'm glad you did." She leaned in closer. "Are you holding up?"

"I'm fine, Mom. Honest."

"Okay. I'm just checking." From where she stood, her hips swiveled so she could face Sarah. "Sarah?"

"I'm okay," Sarah replied, her voice barely a whisper. Her

fingers continued to claw at Kale's fur-covered scalp in a comforting, repeated rhythm.

"Good, because we need to get as far away from these apartments as possible." She strode toward the passenger seat and Jason was already settling into the driver's side, squeezing in behind the large, circular steering wheel. "Being this close to all of these tall buildings makes me uncomfortable. There could be other survivors."

Jason turned the key in the ignition and started the engine.

"If the two of you need to grab some shuteye, that's okay. It's late."

"We should all try and get some sleep at some point," Samantha echoed.

Jason touched the accelerator, pulling the RV forward and inching it past the wreckage of the vehicles they'd nearly lost their lives trying to move.

"That sounds like a luxury we might not have." Jason's grip tightened around the wheel as he navigated the widening street, steering around a scatter of corpses that lined a nearby storefront. "We can take watch rotations if we need to. You and me, anyway, I want the kids to get as close to a full night's sleep as possible."

"Agreed. We definitely can't just stop anywhere, especially not with all of these tall buildings around." He leaned over the steering wheel, squinting into the surrounding shadows, the RV's headlights carving a pale path through darkness. "Honestly, our best bet might be to find a wide-open area somewhere. We'd be pretty visible, but whoever was on watch would also have a good field of vision to make sure nobody was sneaking up on us."

"That's not a bad idea."

Jason guided the RV around the smashed remains of another collision, two cars hammered together into a tangled mass along the left sidewalk. One of them had been pushed broadside into a light post, buckling the metal and making the post lean at an almost forty-five-degree angle. Spires of tall buildings remained around them, stretching up into the Los Angeles night sky. The city was still, empty roadways and alleys caught within the splash of their headlights, revealing scattered trash, more dead bodies, but little else. Samantha brushed aside a lock of her hair and unfolded the hand-drawn map on the dashboard, pressing her finger to their approximate location.

"Who would have thought our lives rested in the hands of tent city occupants and their hand-sketched map of the city." Jason laughed softly.

"They haven't led us wrong yet." Samantha rotated her shoulders as she leaned back in her seat, allowing her eyelids to settle closed for a handful of seconds.

Buildings emerged on the outer borders of the RV's headlights, then fell away as they continued navigating the city streets, moving slowly and precariously, narrowly avoiding the corpses and stalled vehicles along the way. Jason gritted his teeth as they approached another intersection, several pedestrians spread out in a wide fan around the spot where the streets met. Two cars sat askew in the center, they hadn't collided, but their drivers had evacuated during the chaos and left their vehicles behind. He cranked the wheel right, riding the sidewalk along the right side of the intersection, bones crunching beneath the weight of the driver's side tires.

"I'll never get used to that sound." Jason steered back into the middle of the road on the other side of the intersection, easing down on the accelerator and picking up speed.

The next city block was still littered with buildings, though most of them were two and three-story structures, not the tall monoliths of apartments they'd passed through moments earlier. Jason slowed as he was forced to weave through another stalled clutch of traffic, then accelerated again, leaning left to peer across the two-lane street. To their right, an office complex stood, wrapped around the corner of a pair of side streets, its parking lot spread out beyond it in a wide fan of pavement.

"Check out that parking lot over there." Jason gestured toward it, steering with one hand. "Pretty big and I only see cars parked in the front half, closest to the building."

Samantha leaned over the dash, squinting into the darkness. Los Angeles was softly lit, moon and stars filtered through layers of smoke and underlying smog. Everything was edged in a slightly yellowed haze through the beam of RV headlights.

"I think you're right."

Jason was already starting to steer toward it, guiding the RV at an angle across both lanes. Rather than search out the entrance, he brought the RV straight forward, bumping up the sidewalk that separated the road from the parking lot. Steering left, he merged onto a narrow perimeter road that surrounded the lot, passing by rows of parked vehicles. Bodies were fewer, but still present, occasionally caught in the outward splash of headlights as Jason followed the bend of the access road around the office park.

The rear of the parking lot was empty, nearly a hundred spaces marked by even, white lines filling the massive section of vacant pavement. A few squat buildings rode the far edge of the lot, none of them over a story tall. Jason steered the RV toward the center of the wide-open section of lined pavement, drawing back on the accelerator, then stopped completely in the center of the lot, surrounded on all sides by empty parking spaces.

"We're stopping here?" Eli inched forward on his seat, craning his neck to try and see through the windshield.

"We're hoping everyone might sleep a little better if we're stopped."

"Everyone? You guys, too?" Sarah asked.

"We're going to take a watch rotation. One of us will stand watch while the other sleeps, then the other will wake up and take over. Half a night's sleep is better than no sleep at all."

The twins nodded their agreement as Jason turned off the engine, both he and Samantha standing from their chairs and stretching their arms above their heads. Kale sensed a change in routine and sprang to her feet, head whipping around curiously as her tail twitched.

"Come here, Kale." Samantha gestured toward the dog. "We should take you out before we all crash for the night." She nodded toward Sarah and Eli. "Do your bedtime routines, get in your PJs and crawl into bed, okay? It's time to get some sleep."

Neither child argued or protested, they only nodded wearily and retreated deeper into the RV, following their mother's instructions. Samantha led Kale down the stairs and pushed the door open, stepping aside so she could sprint out onto the parking lot, claws clicking on the pavement. Jason followed, the two of them shoulder-to-shoulder as Kale sniffed the ground eagerly, tail wagging. Samantha stood rigid, her muscles taut, never standing completely still, head swiveling as they took up their spot outside the RV.

"Almost like we're behind enemy lines."

"It is a familiar feeling," Samantha replied, "a little too familiar, if you ask me." A few feet away, Kale found a suitable area to do her business. "I'm okay taking first watch." Samantha reached out and touched Jason's hand with hers. "You should get some sleep."

"Both of us could use some sleep."

"I'll get some. You know me, I can sleep almost anywhere."

"You've got lots of practice."

Kale stood again, scratching her back paws along the pavement before she continued sniffing, making a lazy circle, her nose pressed to the surface of the lot.

"I was looking forward to driving through L.A. believe it or not." Jason lifted his face toward the smoke-filled sky.

"I think we all were. Now, all I want to do is get out of here as fast as humanly possible."

"First thing in the morning," Jason promised, laying his arm across Samantha's shoulders. "We'll get out of the city and on our way. We just have to hope the roads between here and Oregon are less dangerous."

Samantha leaned her head against his shoulder and said nothing, the two of them standing quietly as Kale finished her own bedtime routine.

# CHAPTER 2

**The Vineyard**
**Silverpine, Oregon**

The guest bed upstairs was just small enough to be uncomfortable, though the events of the day had been enough that despite his discomfort, Benjamin had dipped soundly into sleep. It was rare that he slept through the night, always getting up once or twice to take care of the normal things men of his age needed to take care of in the middle of the night, so when the light scuffle of footfalls dragged him from a deep slumber, it took him a moment to locate himself. A rattling snore caught in his throat as he stared up at the darkened ceiling. Benjamin had his own tiny house at the far edge of the property, so it was rare when he took advantage of the upstairs guest room in the vineyard's main building, but it had been decided that everyone should stay close together, given the situation.

He'd grumbled as he'd scaled the stairs, bothered by the disruption in his normal routine, but that bother had been swallowed quickly by much-needed sleep. So, when the hinges squeaked and the door eased open, he bunched his fists, clutching the cotton sheets between tightly clenched fingers, his teeth gritting. A shadowed figure crept into the small side bedroom, the narrow silhouette barely exposed by the starlight shining through the nearby window. Benjamin shot upward as a hand reached toward him, his legs whipping around. A female voice gasped, the approaching figure stumbling backwards as Benjamin reached for her, fingers clutched around her narrow wrist.

"It's me! It's Brandi." Her voice was a hushed, desperate hiss and Benjamin immediately unclamped his grip.

"Sorry," he breathed, then bent over, arms resting on his thighs, his displaced sheets bunched up around him. "Not used to middle-of-the-night visitors.

"Darryl told me to come find you."

"What's wrong?" Any hint of tiredness evaporated at the insistent tone of her voice.

Before she even replied, he yanked the sheets aside and stood, a cool brush of air washing over his bare chest. Benjamin usually slept only in boxer shorts, though the previous night he'd at least worn a pair of flannel pants, much to his own and to Brandi's unspoken relief. Turning toward the bed, he clawed for the spot where he'd hung his shirt and started to yank it loose of the post. His previously sluggish movements had turned crisp and purposeful.

"Darryl's been keeping watch, and he heard an engine running a few minutes ago. He was watching out the window and headlights appeared."

Benjamin swore under his breath, tugging his shirt over his shoulders and hastily fastening a few of the buttons. "Where is he?"

"He's in the other upstairs bedroom. Just across the way." Brandi gestured vaguely toward the front door.

Benjamin stormed toward the door, pausing momentarily to

slip his bare feet into a pair of hiking boots, then lifted a shotgun from where it leaned against the wall just inside. Gripping the weapon in two hands, he nodded, then followed Brandi out into the hallway and toward the opposite side of the upstairs level. His heavy steps thudded on creaking floorboards, the two of them navigating the dimly lit hallway. Benjamin stepped ahead of Brandi, guiding her down the corridor with familiar expertise, closing in on the opposite side bedroom in a matter of seconds.

Without even announcing himself, he passed through the opened door and into the other bedroom, clutching the shotgun tight in his fingers. Both guest bedrooms were set up similarly, with a double bed, a squat, four-drawer dresser and small attached bathroom. The sheets from Darryl's bed were piled in a heap on the floor, his own pants and shirt laying askew nearby. On the far side of the room, he crouched by the backlit window, fingers tugging back a curtain so he could get a better look. He wore basketball shorts and like Benjamin had been, was shirtless, his messy hair draped along the back of his skull.

"What's going on?" Benjamin asked as he stomped into the room, kicking aside the discarded denim pants near the bed.

"You tell me," Darryl said, inching to his left to make a little room for Benjamin to approach. "Heard the engine before I saw the headlights. It's rattling something fierce. Sounds like a dying bear."

"I've never heard a dying bear that sounded like a car engine before." Benjamin crept toward the window, angling down to peer through.

"Heard a lot of dying bears?"

"This seem like the time to crack jokes?" Benjamin pulled aside the other half of the curtain for a better look outside.

Darryl didn't reply as he stepped aside a bit to make more room for Benjamin, who was pressing himself tight to the glass, shotgun still clutched in one hand.

The rattling engine approached from a far distance, followed by a persistent low, metallic scrape, like a snow plow across bare ground. Faded headlights shone in the distance, pale against the dark night, the sounds and sight emanating from the end of the access road, though slowly approaching. Headlights swerved slightly as they made their way slowly down the road, angling right, then dipping left, the vehicle approaching in a drunken lurch, something scraping the ground as it made its way closer. For a handful of seconds Benjamin just stood watching, staring through the glass, his already tight grip tightening more around the handle of the pump-action shotgun.

"Is it coming here?" Brandi leaned to peer between the two men.

"Can't tell," Benjamin replied.

Suddenly, he stepped away from the window, twisting back toward the door that led out to the hallway.

"What are you doing?" Darryl followed Benjamin's motion with a soft turn of his head.

"Going downstairs. If you want to put some pants on and join me, you're welcome to."

Darryl rushed around the bed and gripped the pair of jeans he'd left on the floor, quickly pulling them up over his legs. He tugged a T-shirt over his shoulders and then stepped into a pair of sneakers, quickly lacing them up. The moment he'd finished tying the second sneaker, Benjamin started down the hall, his steps even heavier, thundering across the worn wood as he stalked toward the stairs leading to the main level below. Darryl moved around Brandi, putting himself between her and Benjamin, lifting a hand and guiding her to move in his wake.

Benjamin had already reached the base of the stairs when Darryl started jogging down, the two of them reaching the main level a few heartbeats before Brandi.

"Stay behind us, okay?" Darryl spoke in a low whisper to the young woman.

"I will." She bit her lip, her gaze dancing toward the front of the main vineyard building. "Who do you think it is?"

"No clue," Darryl replied honestly. "Could be almost anyone."

"Whoever it is," Benjamin said, "they're going to learn quick this place isn't a refuge."

"What if they need help?"

"Don't much care if they do. We have ourselves to worry about."

The narrow, darkened hallway ran around the perimeter of the main restaurant and the three of them followed it, moving quickly in the darkness. Instead of making his way toward the front door, Benjamin led them down a branching maintenance hallway, heading toward the western edge of the vineyard building where a side door opened up on a section of gravel left of the main entrance.

"Don't you think Doug and Sheila would want us to help them?" Brandi darted a quick look toward Darryl, then back to Benjamin.

"Mr. and Mrs. Tills would want us to protect their property and ourselves. And that's what I intend to do." Benjamin lifted the shotgun, barrel pointed toward the ceiling as he neared the door that led toward a small storage area alongside the side exit to the property.

Using his broad shoulder, he pushed the door open and moved into that same storage area, holding his position so Brandi and Darryl could file out behind him. The small room was lined with shelves carrying various tools, building and maintenance supplies, with a few lengths of PVC pipe for irrigation repairs resting against the far wall, just inside the door that led outside. Darryl strode directly toward the collection of PVC, silently measured it, then lifted a three-foot length of two-inch pipe, brandishing it like a club, fingers closed around it, testing its heft.

"I'll take the shotgun, thanks." Benjamin closed his fingers around the doorknob, turned it and pushed it open, leading the other two out into the cool Oregon night.

A soft wind rustled through the nearby trees, cooling the air, bringing with it the lingering scent of pine, lavender and a sweet hint of grape vines from the vineyards out back. The soft, soothing wind and the pleasing aroma might have been relaxing if it wasn't for the rattling metallic grind of the approaching engine and the clawing scrape of metal digging at gravel as the vehicle drew nearer. The soft glow of approaching headlights swerved, moving from the road to the driveway itself, gravel crunching beneath the tires of the vehicle. It wobbled as it navigated the narrow dirt road, inching left and right, the headlights slightly askew against the backdrop of nighttime darkness.

The persistent scraping sound followed, coming from underneath the driver's side as Benjamin lowered the shotgun from his shoulder, gripping it in two hands, the barrel pointed in the general direction of the nearing vehicle. Darryl twisted his hands around the pipe as if choking up on a baseball bat, holding it low as he stood to Benjamin's right, torquing his waist like he might swing for the fences. Brandi, weaponless, lingered back, a few paces behind them, not far from the side door they'd exited.

Benjamin inched forward, shoulders partially turned, the shotgun held across his body, barrel right between the twin headlights. One boot moved forward, crunching on loose stone, an oily, exhaust smoke stink wafting from the direction of the vehicle. Headlights brightened as the vehicle meandered its way toward them, weaving slightly, metal scraping until its rear tires skidded to a halt, kicking rocks out from beneath. It halted several feet away, the engine snarling into silence, the headlights cutting to dark as the soft tick tick tick echoed in the wake of the dying motor.

Benjamin's lips parted as he took another broad stride forward. "You best stay inside, whoever you are!" His voice was a deep, guttural bellow, loud and throaty enough that even Darryl flinched alongside him. "Identify yourselves right now!"

Despite Benjamin's request, the driver's side door eased open, hinges protesting the movement, a darkened figure emerging from behind the steering wheel.

"I said stay in—"

"Benjamin?" The female voice was a wet gasp, an unsteady tumble of words, the figure supporting itself by gripping the top of the opened door.

Benjamin's own voice ceased at the sound of the woman, his shotgun lowering further.

"Benjamin?" The voice came again, the silhouetted figure inching her way around the opened door.

Darryl freed one hand from the PVC pipe, fished a flashlight from his pocket and shined the beam on the opened door of the vehicle. Sheila Tills was caught within the sudden backsplash of light, flinching as she recoiled, putting a hand up to shield her face.

"Mrs. Tills?" The entire tenor of Benjamin's voice changed, dropping as abruptly as the shotgun barrel had lowered. "Sheila is that you?"

"It's me. It's— it's us." She framed her words carefully, crossing in front of the Jeep, using the hood to help her move.

"Hold this." Darryl handed Benjamin the flashlight and he took it, the PVC pipe clattering to the ground as Darryl rushed toward the vehicle.

Brandi sprinted forward as well, the two of them converging on Sheila Tills, one of the owners and operators of the vineyard.

"What's going on? This isn't Los Angeles! What happened?" Benjamin let the shotgun hang at his side with one hand while he clutched the flashlight with the other.

Darryl stood alongside Sheila, the two of them making their way around to the passenger side as Brandi joined them. Letting

Brandi remain next to Sheila, Darryl separated, opening the passenger side door, then stepping back in alarm.

"Mr. Tills! Are you okay?"

"What happened?" Benjamin marched onward, his light broadening across the hood, windshield and roof of the Tills' Jeep. "Mrs. Tills, what's going on? We weren't expecting you for days. I-I could have shot you."

"We didn't mean to surprise you," Sheila replied, picking up her pace as she followed Brandi around to the opened passenger door.

Together, all three of them bent low, leaning into the car and working together to hoist Doug Tills out of the passenger seat and to his unsteady feet. Darryl slung Doug's arm over his shoulders, pressing hip-to-hip to keep him upright, Doug nearly collapsing against his support.

"Things were okay for a little while." Doug's face briefly contorted in the splash of Benjamin's flashlight. "Roads started out relatively clear."

"They didn't stay that way," Sheila continued, positioning herself on Doug's other side so she could assist Darryl in helping him stand. "We made it all the way to Salem until things went completely sideways."

"Sideways how?" Benjamin flinched a bit, as if he might help the others, but then drew back, giving them room.

Doug was pinned between Sheila and Darryl with Brandi fishing their bags from the back seat of the vehicle, Benjamin standing idly by, providing illumination and little else.

"Tractor trailer was jack-knifed across all lanes. Almost wiped us out totally." Doug shook his head and winced, heavily favoring his injured left leg.

Benjamin lowered the light a bit and a thick strap of fabric was wrapped tightly around Doug's thigh, his pants caked with dried blood.

"And you turned back?" Benjamin asked.

Doug and Sheila exchanged a brief, knowing glance, then Doug shook his head, directing his gaze up toward the vineyard building. Together, they moved across the gravel path, slowly, tentatively, as a gathered group all at once.

"It wasn't just about the jackknifed truck." Sheila blew out a long, exasperated breath. "Beyond the truck there were cars everywhere. A mass of stopped traffic as far as the eyes could see. We could smell smoke and gas..." she darted another brief, shadowed glance at Doug. "Other things, too."

"Other things?"

"Smells we couldn't identify," Doug finished for his wife, "but if someone asked me what death smelled like, I might say that's what it was." Doug hobbled forward, supported by Sheila and Darryl, as Brandi shouldered one of the bags from the car and Benjamin followed, lighting their way with the flashlight.

Benjamin turned back toward the Jeep, momentarily bringing the flashlight around in its direction.

"Jeep doesn't look like it's in horrible shape."

"It made out better than I did," Doug replied weakly. "The blown-out tires were the worst of it."

"Doug managed to get the spare on one of them," Sheila continued, "A little donut, but it was good enough. Helped us limp our way back home."

"You hurt your leg in the accident?" Benjamin once more illuminated the path forward as they all closed the distance toward the side maintenance door.

"I did. It's not broken, I can say that much, still hurts like a son of a gun."

"We'll get you inside and check it out."

"Solar still holding things together?" Doug peered over his left shoulder and Benjamin nodded his answer.

He picked up his pace, circling around to the left of the others so he could make it to the door ahead of them. He swung it open and stepped inside, giving the trio space to maneuver through, then waited for Brandi as well before following them all inside, closing the door and locking it behind them. Already Darryl and Sheila were leading Doug down a branching hallway, footfalls echoing as they moved deeper into the vineyard building. Rather than following the perimeter hallway, they turned sharply left, cutting through the kitchen as they made their way toward the restaurant itself.

"Get him in a chair somewhere. Here. Over here." Brandi dropped the bag on the floor and stepped around the trio, grabbing one of the dining room chairs and sliding it out, turning it toward Doug.

Darryl and Sheila lowered him into it, moving gingerly, then stepping away once the weight was off his foot. Lifting his chin, Doug blew a sharp breath into the air, his lids closed against the soft glow of a lantern as Benjamin flicked the switch.

"Can you grab us something to eat and drink?" Sheila crouched near Doug's injured left leg, glancing briefly in Brandi's direction.

"Sure." Brandi nodded her head jerkily and retreated from the restaurant, making her way back into the kitchen.

"Here." Sheila stepped toward Doug and offered him her shoulder, and taking the hint, Darryl did the same from the other side, the two of them working together to help him stand. "Drop your pants."

"Excuse me?"

"We have to check that leg."

"Sheila—"

"Don't be so bashful. You've got boxer shorts on, just drop them."

Doug grumbled, color flushing his cheeks as he fumbled his belt apart, then lowered his pants, settling back down into the chair with a wince. Sheila moved back around, running her fingers along his leg, cradling his knee at first, then probing his calf and finally his ankle. Thick, purple blotches bruised his entire thigh, a clotted wound running a jagged, angular gash just above his knee. More bruising colored his calf and shin in clouded purple, the darker color edged by an almost jaundiced yellow shade.

"Darryl, can you get some bandages and rubbing alcohol? If you head down that hallway there should be a bathroom on the right."

"I know which one."

"There should be a first aid kit mounted on the wall in that bathroom; stand at the sink and turn around." Sheila remained focused on Doug's leg, still moving it gingerly as she ran her thumbs along the muscular contours of his thigh.

"On it." Darryl hustled off.

She cupped his ankle in both palms, then moved it gently left and right. Doug inched back in the seat, sucked in a breath, but didn't shout. His muscles tensed, fingers curling tight around the perimeter of the chair he sat on, his shoulders bunching like clenched fists.

"Did that hurt?"

"Yes, it hurt."

"Scale of one to ten?"

"Five or six."

Sheila nodded, gently releasing his ankle. "You twisted it pretty badly, but it's not sprained."

"What's the plan here, Sheila?" Benjamin crossed his arms, face pointed down toward her as she continued examining Doug's leg.

"I'm not sure what you mean."

"Are you going back to Los Angeles? Sticking around here?"

Sheila bit her lip and swallowed audibly, applying pressure on both sides of Doug's swollen ankle.

"Here's some— oh my!" Brandi twisted away from Doug, her cheeks blushing red, holding a bottle of water and a bowl of pasta in each hand. "I'm sorry, I didn't realize—"

"They're just boxers," muttered Benjamin, walking toward

Brandi, then retrieving the food and drink from her. "Nothing worse than a bathing suit." He made his way back to where Doug stood and offered the bottle of water, which Doug opened and took a swig from.

"To answer your question," he said, "We talked about that a fair bit on the way back and we don't know what the plan is."

Darryl re-entered the restaurant, a first aid kit tucked under one arm and a bottle of hydrogen peroxide in his opposite hand.

"We only saw a small section of highway between here and Salem and it was completely impassable. Cars off the road, others crashed into each other. Even more just empty. Doors open, their drivers gone, people just up and leaving their vehicles behind. It was total chaos, or it had been at one point."

"We were lucky we missed the worst of it. That's the only reason we were even able to make it back." Sheila lifted a hand and took the peroxide from Darryl.

Benjamin lifted a folded napkin from a nearby table and handed it to Sheila as well, so she poured the peroxide across the clotted wound, much to Doug's dismay. He sucked in a breath and tensed again, his thigh bulging as his muscle firmed. Dried blood began to loosen as the liquid was poured gently over it, foaming on impact as Sheila wiped it with the napkin, then applied some direct pressure. She pushed the napkin hard against the wound with her palm, nodding toward the first aid kit under Darryl's arm.

"Grab me a few bandages out of there, please."

Darryl fumbled with the kit, prying it open and removing a box of bandages. He opened it up and slipped out three of the flesh-colored strips, then pressed them into Sheila's palm. She gingerly lifted the crimson-colored napkin, which had started absorbing the flowing blood from Doug's wound, then she tore one of the bandages from its wrapper, applied a little pressure, wiped away the peroxide and thumbed the adhesive bandage in place. She went through that routine twice more, using all three bandages one right next to the other, to cover a length of the gash which had started slowly seeping once more.

"Give me one more?" She held out a hand and Darryl gave her a fourth, which she pressed into place before resting back on her knees.

Doug straightened, shaking his head. "We'd love to get the kids," he said softly. "We need to get our kids. But the roads are just impossible to travel. Even the small towns we passed seemed to be the center of their own little pockets of chaos. Smoke trailed through the trees, whether in big cities or smaller residential areas. I have to believe it's just as bad no matter which direction we go."

Darryl's face lost its color, his lips parting as his breath stilled. "Is it really that bad?" His voice was barely above a whisper, the first aid kit clinging to his fingers as his hand hung by his right thigh. The kit trembled slightly as if it might slip from his grasp and Sheila reached up, taking it from him and setting it on the floor.

"You were only gone for a few hours." His hand free of the first aid kit, he brought it up and crossed his arms over his chest, fingers clenched to each opposite bicep as if shielding himself from an unexpected chill.

"That's all it took." Doug shrugged as Sheila wiped away another stray streak of blood.

"The ankle's not sprained or broken, so I don't think we need to get you a splint or anything. Just try and stay off it as much as you can."

"Have you seen everything that needs doing around here?" Doug pressed his palm to the seat of his chair and stood, grunting as he bent low and inched up his pants, one leg at a time.

Brandi's face shadowed an even deeper crimson, and she turned fully around, her back facing them.

"Plenty of muscle around to help." Benjamin fixed him with an impassive stare. "That's what me and Darryl are here for."

"Brandi and I are fully capable of helping, too," Sheila reminded them.

"Wouldn't dream of saying you weren't." Doug cinched his belt around his waist and gingerly tested his weight on his left ankle, leaning into it as he grimaced.

"You haven't eaten anything yet." Brandi lifted the bowl of pasta from a nearby table and held it out.

Doug finished clasping his belt, then pushed the chair closer to the table and settled into it, scooping up a forkful of pasta and chewing it down.

"Sheila. You, too." He gestured toward his wife with his fork, and Sheila dragged her chair out from the table, taking a bite of her pasta as well.

Silence settled momentarily throughout the restaurant, her shoulders sagging slightly from the weight of everything that had happened. She fixed her gaze on the white tablecloth neatly tugged over the top of the table, her mouth slack.

"Sheila?" Doug leaned, swallowing his mouthful and looking up into his wife's vacant expression.

"We can't leave them there, Doug." Sheila's voice choked as she turned, her clamped hand supporting her against the back of the chair. "We can't just leave them there."

"Sheila." Doug set down his fork and planted a palm on the table, hoisting himself upright. "The roads—"

"The roads? I don't care about the roads!" All at once, emotion clawed at her, drawing her neck into taught cords, squeezing her words out in a gasping sob. "What do you think *they're* dealing with? Salem was a disaster zone, so what does Los Angeles look like?" She shook her head with vigor, releasing the chair and twisting away, burying her face in her hands. "What kind of parents are we? We're just going to leave them there?" Her words were muffled by her palms, her shoulders gently shaking.

Doug slung an arm around her shoulders, squeezing her to him. "We're going to do everything we can," Doug promised. "I'm just... I'm not sure what else..." an unusual uncertainty set a slight waver into his words.

"What about the tracker?" Benjamin cleared his throat, his mouth only slightly open, a bit of color in his cheeks. "You were following them on the tracker. They're still moving aren't they?"

Sheila sniffed hard, turning her hand over and rubbing her eyes with her knuckles. Doug released his grip, and she made her way toward the bag that Brandi had brought in from the Jeep, crouching and unzipping the main flap. Sheila removed the tracker from the bag and stood, holding the power button until it flickered back to life.

"Doug checked it just before we got back into town," she whispered, blinking down at the faintly illuminated screen. "They'd been stopped when he checked it, though they were steadily moving throughout the night."

The device wavered in her grip, a pale, green light coming softly to the square-shaped screen. Sheila gripped the device with both hands, clutching it like a lifeline as Doug moved toward her, each step a teeth-gritted plod.

"They moved!" Sheila's gaze brightened, color returning to her cheeks. "Doug! They're still going!" She stumbled toward Doug, and he intercepted her, both of them leaning on each other for support.

Benjamin approached as well, angling his neck to peer at the illuminated screen where the tiny beacon glowed from the center of a sparse, open area surrounded by thickly grouped city blocks.

"They were further south the last time we looked." She lifted the screen toward Benjamin.

"Maybe they've stopped for the night." Doug's arm was draped over her shoulders as he looked down at the tracker.

"Important thing is that they're still moving. They're clearly still doing fine. It might drive you crazy to not be with them, but it sure looks like they're handling things on their own."

Sheila and Doug shared a nod as she shut down the tracker, the screen fading into darkness.

"If we can't safely get to them now, then we should really batten down the hatches here and prepare for the storm that's coming. When things calm down again, we can re-evaluate. See if we can try again. But getting yourselves hurt or worse trying to reach them isn't going to help them or you."

Sheila lowered the tracker, then crouched and returned it to the backpack. Leaning on each other, she and Doug headed back toward the table where Brandi had set another bottle of water at Sheila's place. With Sheila's help, Doug lowered back into the chair, and she pushed hers back again, settling down into it.

"It's nothing fancy," Brandi said, almost apologetically. "Just warmed up the stuff we had earlier."

"It's lovely, Brandi." Sheila took an eager bite, chewing and swallowing the mouthful down swiftly. "I apologize for being unladylike." She scraped her fork through the bowl with a renewed enthusiasm and within a few moments, the bowl was nearly empty, and Sheila was dabbing at the corner of her mouth with a napkin.

Brandi scooped up the two bowls and retreated back toward the kitchen as Darryl walked slowly toward the row of windows overlooking the sprawling orchard. He stood at the glass, peering out into the darkness, stepping left, then right to get better angles on the surrounding property.

"Darryl's been taking watch so far." Benjamin nodded toward Darryl, who stood rigid by the windows, staring intently. "I was supposed to swap with him in about an hour or so." Benjamin glanced at the watch strapped around his left wrist.

"We didn't mean to stir things up." Sheila sighed and took a drink of her water.

"It's your place, not ours. We're just squatters." The corner of his mouth lifted, though both Doug and Sheila's expressions remained stoic, lost in a myriad of thoughts. Benjamin cleared his throat again. "We've all had an eventful night. Darryl, I'm going to go ahead and swap out watch with you for the rest of the night. You and Brandi should help the Tills get the rest of their gear out of the Jeep and then get ready to grab some shut eye. The best thing we can do for our own mental wellbeing is to get as much rest as possible."

Sheila stood and stretched, arching her back as she raised her arms over her head. As Doug struggled to stand, she intercepted him and gave him some assistance rising to his feet.

"Brandi, do you mind helping the Tills out? Getting Mr. Tills up to the master bedroom?" Benjamin stabbed a thumb toward the door leading to the outside parking lot. "Darryl and I are going to empty the Jeep. We probably shouldn't leave that stuff in there overnight."

"We can manage," Sheila said, a renewed smile creasing her lips.

"I'll just grab the backpack and follow you up." Brandi walked to where the backpack rested on the floor as Benjamin and Darryl walked to the front door.

They stepped back outside into the cool darkness, the persistent breeze whisking some of the sweat from their skin. The Jeep stood parked in the driveway straight ahead, and Benjamin fished out the flashlight once more, using it to guide their way.

"I suppose there could be some good news in all of this," Benjamin said as they neared the Jeep. "The harder it is for us to drive out of town, the harder it is for others to drive into it."

"You sure we're going to run into those kinds of problems?" Darryl raised a skeptical eyebrow, his normally happy-go-lucky tone darker.

"Absolutely. That's our biggest threat, if you want my honest opinion. If the big cities are burning like the news says they are, people will start converging on the smaller neighborhoods and rural communities. That's us." He turned and gestured toward the building and the acres of vineyard beyond. "We're a pretty big target here. That's good in some ways, plenty of resources within arm's reach, but it also puts a big old bullseye on our backs."

"Well... I, for one, am glad the Tills have what they have, and that they're sharing with us." Darryl shrugged. "It'd be a whole lot more difficult without them."

Benjamin nodded and opened the rear door of the Jeep, pulling out the jerry cans of gasoline they'd loaded up before the Tills had taken off for Los Angeles. There was still weight to them both, liquid sloshing from within, and clutching one in each hand, he walked toward the side maintenance room door as Darryl continued unloading the rest of the supplies. Benjamin set the cans down on the floor of the storage room just inside the door, then Darryl joined him, bag slung over his shoulder and the PVC pipe he'd discarded earlier clenched in his other hand.

Stepping into the storage room, he set the items down, then the two walked back outside, locking the maintenance door behind them. Boots crunching on gravel, they made their way back to the Jeep and Benjamin gave it one a once-over, passing the beam of his flashlight along its scuffed-up exterior. There were a few minor dings and dents, and the spare tire was clearly smaller than the other two still-intact tires. The remains of the wheel that had been without a tire were small, the metal having been ground down to the nub over the miles that the Tills had driven back to the vineyard.

"You know what struck me the most about what the Tills said about their short trip?" Darryl crouched and ran his fingers along a series of ragged, discolored scrapes.

"What's that?"

"They didn't say anything about law enforcement or emergency services. No signs of rescuers or anything."

"We'll have to ask them about that. But my guess is that the biggest dangers are in the cities right now. That's where most of the dead are. I'm sure that's where most of the rescue efforts are, too." Satisfied that the Jeep had been emptied, Benjamin began walking back toward the front door.

"That means we're even more on our own out here."

"Exactly what I've been saying. Nobody's coming to help us." Benjamin shook his head firmly. "But don't go spinning that yarn to Brandi, okay? She's a tough kid, but the last thing we need is her spinning out. Or any of us spinning out for that matter. Most important thing is keeping our heads on straight."

"Couldn't agree more."

They both walked back into the building, following the short hallway before they returned to the restaurant. Sheila and Doug were gone, but Brandi poked her head out of the kitchen when they stepped inside.

"The Tills get upstairs okay?" Benjamin checked and double-checked the deadbolt on the front door.

"They did." Brandi nodded, her dark hair spilling loose over her left shoulder. "You have a knack for making them feel better."

"Must be my cheery disposition." Benjamin stopped and scrunched up his face, sniffing the air. "Is that coffee?"

"It is. Thought it might help you stay awake while you're on watch."

"Oh, you brewed some for the old curmudgeon but none for me. I see how it is." Darryl snickered good-naturedly as Brandi approached him and punched him lightly in the shoulder.

"Maybe if you're not a jerk, Benjamin will share some with you."

"No chance." Benjamin shook his head firmly and made his way to the kitchen, leaving Brandi and Darryl gaping at him, unsure if he was joking or not.

As he approached the door, Benjamin turned and glanced over his shoulder.

"After I fill my thermos you can have what's left. Don't drink too much, though, you need some shut eye."

"Don't we all?" Brandi replied, muffling a yawn with her fist.

Benjamin nodded and stepped into the kitchen and made his way toward the soft burble of the coffee maker.

# CHAPTER 3

**The O'Brian Family**
**Los Angeles, California**

The night stretched long and quiet, an uneasy silence that pressed into Samantha's ears like wads of cotton stuffed too deep. She sat cross-legged on top of the RV, her newly acquired rifle sitting beside her, its barrel gleaming faintly in the sparse moonlight. Though the sky remained thick with smog and smoke, the stubborn glow of the moon persisted, working its way through the gray haze and offering its scant illumination. In the distance, the Los Angeles skyline rose dark and skeletal, its usual vibrancy replaced by a hollow stillness. No lights blinked from office towers, no hum of traffic rumbled below, and no distant sirens wailed to punctuate the night. It was a city unrecognizable, a vast necropolis that bore the faint scars of its downfall.

From her perch atop the RV, Samantha had a clear view of the surrounding office complex and the empty, vast expanse of parking lots around them. The buildings, once hubs of corporate energy, loomed like silent sentinels, their windows dark, a few of them propped open or shattered. Silhouetted forms were spread across the surrounding grass and walkways, huddled corpses a stark reminder that though the city was dead, it was not empty. A few stray pieces of paper skittered across the pavement, carried by a soft, inconsistent breeze. Somewhere in the distance, a car alarm chirped faintly before falling silent again, as if the city were still trying to remember its former rhythm.

She scanned the horizon, shoulders tensed, one hand resting on the roof within reach of the rifle they'd taken from the police car. They'd come across far more dead than living, but the survivors they'd run into so far hadn't exactly been friendly. Shadows shifted along the edge of the lot, and she slid slightly, touching her fingertips to the hard, smooth surface of the rifle. Leaning right, she closed her fingers around the handguard and slowly dragged it close, but before she could lift it, the darkness clarified into a tree, branches of leaves moving in the ocean breeze.

Blowing a long breath of air, she leaned back on her palms, her arms rigid from shoulder to roof. Jason would be up soon to relieve her, but until then, she had to stay sharp. She rubbed her eyes with the heels of her hands, exhaustion clawing at the edges of her focus. Sleep was a luxury neither of them could afford to indulge in for too long. She shifted slightly, the metal roof of the RV cool against her jeans. Above her, the faint pinprick of stars through smoke sprawled across the sky, scattered but more numerous than she might have expected. Samantha stared up at them often, searching for familiar constellations from childhood. Struggling to pick them out through the haze, her chin lowered. Samantha's gaze lingered closer to the ground once more, tracing the jagged lines of the skyline and the empty highways that criss-crossed the horizon like veins in a withered leaf.

The twins were asleep inside the RV, curled up in small beds nestled within the rear compartment of the vehicle. At thirteen, they had adapted to their new reality with a resilience that both amazed and terrified her. Though their vacant stares held an all-too-familiar distant look, they'd insisted they were fine and from time to time had acted almost normally. Just before bed, Samantha had caught Sarah sketching quietly in a notebook, a childhood habit she'd mostly given up in time for her thirteenth birthday. They'd packed the sketchbook for her as a way to cope with the inevitable boredom during their long trek down the Pacific Coast Highway, though earlier was the first time Samantha had seen her using it.

Eli had focused most of his attention on Kale, playing awkwardly with her as they prepared to bed down for the night. Jason had warned him not to get her too keyed up right before bedtime and thankfully, she'd joined Eli in falling asleep relatively quickly, curled up on the floor, evenly spaced between both twins' fold-out beds. After Sarah had closed her eyes for the final time, Samantha had leafed through her sketchbook, settling on the most recent page, a stark, black-and-white drawing of the RV. Lost within the shadows of the vehicle on the paper were demonic looking silhouettes, ghoulish figures surrounding them, pinprick eyes visible where their faces should have been.

Samantha's chest tightened and she wrapped her arms around herself, suppressing a chill that wasn't a result of a dip in temperature. The moment she'd seen that drawing, she'd fought the urge to wake Sarah up again, to hug her tight and rock her to sleep, but she'd battled against those motherly instincts, promising herself that she'd talk to her in the morning. The breeze picked up slightly, carrying with it the faintest hint of salt from the ocean, tinged by the lingering acidity of smoke. It was a strange juxtaposition: the sharp, acrid tang of burning city that marked the incident and the clean, briny scent of the Pacific. The two smells didn't belong together, and yet they coexisted in the ghost of a city that had once been so alive.

A faint rustling caught her attention, unlike the blowing leaves on the trees and her hand instinctively moved to the rifle. She froze, every muscle taut, her fingers clamped around the weapon, drawing it slowly toward herself. The sound came again, soft and irregular, like a plastic bag caught in a weak gust. She checked the perimeter of the parking lot again, heart pounding, until she spotted movement along the edge of the sidewalk. Her grip tightened on the rifle as she swung around, rising up onto a knee, facing toward the right side of the parking lot. A coyote, lean and mangy, slinked out from the shadows of the nearby office complex, roaming tentatively and with cautious apprehension. Its ears perked as it sniffed the air, filtered moonlight reflecting in its gaze with an eerie glow. It padded cautiously across the pavement, pausing now and then to glance around, searching for food like everyone else.

The coyote stopped near a discarded fast food bag, nudging it with its nose before losing interest and moving on. Samantha relaxed slightly but kept focused on the animal until it disappeared into the darkness. Predators, both human and otherwise, were a constant threat, and she'd learned the hard way never to let her guard down. Her grip had tightened around the rifle, one hand around the grip, the other around the handguard, the barrel pointed at a downward angle near the roof of the RV. She glanced at her watch and registered fifteen more minutes until Jason was scheduled to take over before allowing herself the briefest moment to let the cool night air wash over her, salt and smoke twisting within her nostrils.

The RV creaked softly beneath her, a familiar sound that reminded her of the first few nights of their trip south from Oregon. Her parents' RV had been a symbol of freedom and adventure, a way to escape the grind of daily life. Since the incident in downtown Los Angeles, it was their lifeline, a fragile bubble of safety in a world gone mad. When she lifted her face again, the skyline darkened further, as if the city were slowly fading into an abyss. Los Angeles had once been a sprawling metropolis teeming with life, its streets alive with music, laughter, and the endless hum of activity. Standing before and around her was a graveyard, its bones picked clean by the catastrophe that had claimed it.

Faint footsteps on the nearby ladder rungs made her turn as Jason's head appeared through the door in the roof, his face illuminated by the soft glow of a flashlight. He gave her a weary, uneven smile as he climbed up, stepped out of the roof hatch and slunk his way to her side.

"Anything?" he asked, his voice low.

She shook her head. "Just a coyote."

"A coyote?" He arched one eyebrow.

"Probably came down from the Hollywood Hills or something."

They sat in silence for a moment, staring out at the empty city until Jason nudged her gently. "Go get some sleep. I've got it from here."

Samantha hesitated, lingering on the horizon, a dark, shadowed shape looming just beyond the trees where she'd seen the coyote. The entire city was cloaked in various shades of gray and black, a stoic wall enveloping that sparse parking lot where they spent the night. Exhaustion soon won out and she nodded, squeezing Jason's hand before standing.

"Kids still sleeping?"

"Like two little logs. Three if you count Kale. Almost seems... normal."

Samantha hesitated at the top of the ladder leading down into the RV. She placed one foot on the rung and the ladder creaked softly, shifting to the right, but holding in place.

"I sure hope this isn't our new normal." She shuddered and descended the ladder, slipping back into the RV and easing the roof hatch closed behind her.

Jason bent his knees, pressing the soles of his boots to the flat roof of the RV as his weary gaze drifted across the pavement surrounding them. His muscles were leaden, his back slightly slouched, and his mind still clouded with the after-effects of the early alarm. Exhaustion weighed on his eyelids, and he forced them open with an aggressive rub from the back of his hand. Somewhere in the darkness, the off-kilter cackle of a coyote call sounded, momentarily clearing Jason's mind and drawing him closer to alertness. The coyote's call faded into the distance, leaving behind an emptiness that sagged with its own dead weight. Jason shifted his position, letting his right leg stretch out while keeping his left knee bent, the rifle laid across his thigh.

Through breaks in the smog, the moon cast long shadows across the parking lot, transforming ordinary objects into grotesque silhouettes. A shopping cart, abandoned near the office building's entrance was a twisted metal skeleton. Scattered papers danced across the asphalt in the occasional breeze, ghost-white against the dark pavement. Each time they moved, Jason's stare snapped to follow them, his fingers tightening instinctively around the rifle's grip. Thick silence was broken only by the soft whisper of wind through dead leaves and the occasional distant crash of something in the city. The sounds drew his arms taut, the rifle easing closer to his body as his gaze darted in the direction of the faded sounds. When they'd first entered Los Angeles, the frenzy of activity had been chaotic to the point of overwhelming, a sensory overload of sounds, lights and movement. Less than twenty-four hours later, the penetrating darkness and ocean-deep stillness was somehow even worse.

Pre-dawn hours were always the hardest, when fatigue pressed most heavily, and the shadows of night were most absolute. To stay alert, he began a ritual of counting the visible windows in the office building across the lot that glinted in the faded moon. Thirty-two on the side facing him, spread across eight floors. Most were dark voids, but something inside one on the fourth floor reflected a hint of moonlight, creating the illusion of life where there was none. Along the far side of the lot, darkness swallowed the eastern horizon, the combination of smoke and night concealing what lay beyond from view.

The breeze shifted, bringing with it the medicinal smell of eucalyptus from a nearby tree, momentarily overshadowing the omnipresent scent of smoke. Jason inhaled deeply, grateful for the brief respite. A flash of light in the distance drew his attention from the direction of downtown. It could have been anything from survivors sending signals to a fire catching something reflective, or simply his tired mind playing tricks. He watched the spot intently for several minutes, but no further illumination appeared, that momentary flash consumed by the darkened pitch that surrounded it. The city remained a dark mass of geometric shapes, its famous skyline now just a jagged tear in the night sky.

The first hints of pre-dawn began to lighten the eastern horizon, a swirling acid mixing in Jason's guts. Slowly, the night began its retreat, but Jason braced himself, anticipating that the added light might also make the survivors bolder. Jason adjusted his position again, muscles protesting after hours of stillness, and methodically scanned the perimeter of their temporary sanctuary. His brow furrowed as his gaze focused on an area of starker shadow that gradually illuminated as the sky brightened on the cusp of dawn. The sun's rays punched through the still smoke, lifting layers of settled smog and added some much-needed clarity to their obscured surroundings.

Skeletal shapes along the Los Angeles skyline slowly came into view, more distinct and purposeful than their geometrical mass from overnight. At the far end of the parking lot, darkness lifted, a large, familiar structure opening up before him as the sun illuminated the world, moment by agonizing moment. Where there'd only been darkness earlier that night, a building emerged, tall and broad, a stoic sentinel that rose across the wide expanse of the far side of the parking lot. Jason's furrowed brow eased into softness, recognition loosening the taut lines of his clenched jaw. The familiar form of the Los Angeles Convention Center threw off the blanket of night and stood stark and solid before him, familiar, yet also alien, considering the desolate remains of the city around it. For several long moments he sat on the roof, staring at the convention center, his mind using it as a beacon with which to navigate.

Jason lost track of how long he sat staring, almost hypnotized by the slow revelation of the cityscape around him. A muffled clatter of noise from the RV beneath him yanked him from his daze, murmured voices following the noise and even a chorus of young, soft laughter. Blinking away the weariness and approaching sunlight, he shifted where he sat, turning his body toward the hatch that covered the pull-down ladder into the RV.

Jason's stiff legs protested as he worked his way to his feet, grabbing the rifle by the handguard and lifting it with him. He strode toward the hatch, crouched down and lifted it open, then scaled the ladder into the belly of the RV, closing and locking the hatch above him. Once he reached the floor, he pushed the extendable ladder back into its narrow storage compartment, then turned toward the kitchen where both twins were fully awake and preparing food for breakfast.

Kale sat perched in the center of the narrow section of kitchen floor, back straight, nose scrunching with the chorus of various aromas. Her tail swished across the floor, her ears perked in excitement, though not enough excitement to tempt her to leave the food fixing place.

"You're awake." Jason bent his head slightly to stretch his neck.

"Shhh," Eli said, putting a finger to his lips. "Mom's still sleeping."

There was a small alcove in the RVs kitchen, complete with a small stove top. Two small camp skillets were on the stove top, one of them sizzling with slices of beef jerky, which rested in a shallow layer of cooking oil. Eli shoved the dried meat around with a fork, flipping it to heat it more evenly while Sarah babysat a second skillet filled with yellowing eggs.

"We were hungry," Sarah announced, stirring up the egg mixture. "There were a half dozen eggs still in the fridge which we figured we should use up."

"We heated up some of the jerky we found at the gas station yesterday, too. Probably as close to bacon as we're going to get. Look." Eli stepped back and pointed a fork toward the torn open wrapper on the small sliver of counter. "It's even pork jerky."

"So, it is." Jason chuckled and stepped into the kitchen, crouching so he could scratch Kale behind the ears.

"There was some juice left, too. Do you want some?" Eli held up a glass of orange juice, then took a sip.

A gentle smile turned Jason's lips as he drew his fingers through Kale's fur. Both children moved with an almost carefree purpose, grateful to have tasks to accomplish and something to do. Sarah used a spoon to toss the scrambled eggs together, mixing them up as they slowly lifted wisps of smoke from the skillet.

"What's that smell?" A thick voice came from the rear bedroom of the RV and Jason peered toward it as Samantha extracted herself.

She blinked, shaking loose the last clutching tentacles of sleep. Standing in bare feet with a pair of basketball shorts and a tank top, Jason couldn't stop staring at his wife, his smile showing no signs of faltering.

"What are you looking at?" Samantha asked, narrowing her gaze.

Jason stood and stretched, Kale's head lifting in anxious inquisition, her dark gaze staring at his fingers which were no longer scratching.

"Not a thing. Good morning. Eli and Sarah decided that eggs and bacon sounded good."

"Eggs and bacon? Since when did we pick up bacon?" Samantha's voice slurred at first, but quickly clarified as she took a step forward.

"Pork jerky," Eli replied with a shrug. "Same thing."

"Not even remotely." Samantha shook her head, though her face creased into a crooked, almost appreciative grin.

Hooking her fingers into the sliding door, she tugged it open and stepped inside, closing it behind her. A rush of water ran from within the bathroom and Jason stepped from the kitchen and into the narrow corridor. Already the water had ceased when he reached the door, then rapped his knuckles softly on it.

"How are we doing on water?"

There was a moment of silence from the other end before she replied. "Okay. Ish. Potable tank is pretty full, over three quarters. Fifty gallons or more, which should be okay for a few days."

"What about the gray water?"

The faucet ran again very briefly and then the door slid open, Samantha emerging as she dried her hands on her shorts and turned back toward the bedroom.

"Gray tank is about a quarter full. I think we're a little ways from needing to empty it, which is a good thing because I don't have a clue where we'd find any RV hook-ups in downtown Los Angeles." She disappeared into the bedroom, her voice fading. "Though I don't suppose we really *need* a hookup to dispose of it, do we?"

"Probably not. Feels like we should ration a little bit if we can help it."

"Yep. The more we conserve the longer it'll last," Samantha replied, returning from the bedroom, dressed in a T-shirt and jeans, her bare feet padding along the smooth floor of the vehicle. "We're not in crisis mode – not even close – but if it takes us a long time to get out of the city, things could get a little hairier."

Food continued to sizzle in the small skillets as Eli and Sarah finished making breakfast. "It's ready," Sarah announced, and opened a cabinet, removing a few plastic plates.

She and Eli worked together, piling the various food on the plates and slipped them over onto the table nestled within the small dining nook of the RV. Samantha slid close to the window and Jason sat across from her, accepting the plates and a fork for each of them. Sarah gingerly placed two glasses of orange juice in front of them, smiling and nodding.

"Great service." Samantha lifted a glass in toast to her daughter, then took a quick swallow.

Jason carved off a chunk of warmed-up pork jerky, combined it with some of the eggs, then took a bite, chewing purposefully.

"Delicious. My compliments to the chef."

"Thank you." Eli took a mock bow.

"All you did was heat up some jerky. I'm the one who made the eggs." Sarah stabbed playfully at Eli with her fork and the family shared a soft chorus of laughter.

On the floor nearby, Kale sat ramrod straight, tilting her head, nose sniffing dutifully. For a few moments the only sound was of silverware scraping plastic, the four O'Brians eating their breakfast in relative silence. As he separated another small pile of eggs, Jason lifted his gaze toward Samantha.

"You'll never believe where we are," he said, chewing what was already in his mouth.

"Where we are? You mean, besides Los Angeles?"

"Of course, we're in Los Angeles, I mean where we are *in* Los Angeles. I recognized it this morning after the sun rose." Samantha scraped another forkful of eggs into her mouth, but said nothing, just stared expectantly at Jason, brows lifted. "The convention center. You know, where the president was holding his rally, the one we drove past right before everything went sideways?"

"Yeah?"

"It's right over there." Jason turned in his seat and pointed his fork toward the rear of the RV. "I could see it from the roof after sunrise."

"Are you kidding me?" Samantha set her fork down. "The convention center?"

Jason nodded and scooped up the last forkful of eggs, then stuffed it into his mouth, stabbing a final chunk of jerky and scarfing it down directly afterwards. Clutching his glass of orange juice, he drank another long swallow, then nodded at Eli, who had sat between him and the aisle. Eli stood and retreated, giving Jason room to slide out while Samantha finished her plate as well, then squeezed past Sarah.

"Where are you going?" Eli's voice was muffled by half-chewed eggs.

"Just right outside. We'll take Kale, too, so she can do her business. I just want to show your mother what I'm talking about." Jason patted his thigh and said Kale's name in a singsong voice, drawing her to follow them to the front door.

They all stepped through, out into the cooling, smoke-tinged air of Los Angeles, the sprawling pavement of the parking lot extending in all directions. As Kale circled a section of asphalt, searching for a place to relieve herself, Jason and Samantha made their way toward the rear of the RV.

"See? There it is." Jason gestured toward the looming building in the near distance, just beyond a section of trees that lined the far side of the lot.

"How did we miss that last night?"

"It was dark. All the smoke and smog, it's tough to see through, especially in the dark."

Samantha crossed her arms and leaned back against the RV, staring in the direction of the convention center.

"What's on your mind?"

"What do *you* think is on my mind? You know me well enough by now, Jason."

"I know, but I don't agree. You want to check out the convention center, don't you?"

Samantha nodded. "Something was going on there. Something

that sparked all of this." She gestured vaguely in the air. "Plus, you remember that convoy, right? The military convoy that was tearing through traffic?"

"I'll never forget it."

"There was something about the convention center they were heading toward. Maybe even something they were trying to stop."

"Like this attack."

Samantha shrugged. "We're not even sure it was an attack. But whatever it was, the convention center is in the middle of it."

"Which is exactly why running straight toward it is a bad idea." Jason shook his head. "Things are dangerous enough without willingly heading straight into the belly of whatever beast did this."

"Whatever happened already happened. It's said and done."

"How can you know that?"

"Just listen." She cupped a hand to her ear and turned her head.

A gentle breeze continued rustling the nearby trees, lifting scattered paper from the pavement and sending it spinning like tumbleweed in an Old West movie.

"The city's dead, Jason. Whatever was happening there isn't happening anymore. But that doesn't mean we can't learn something, or maybe grab some resources."

Jason blew out a breath.

"Hon, you saw the vehicles in that convoy." Samantha leaned into her argument, detecting Jason's weakening resistance. "The way they were smashing through that line of traffic, they might have something there that could help us do the same. If we get our hands on it, it could make getting out of the city a whole lot easier."

"You want to steal a military vehicle?"

"Is it stealing if the driver's dead?"

"I think I'm supposed to say 'yes' to that question." Jason stuffed his hands in his pockets, his hip slightly cocked as he scanned the far edge of the parking lot. "But I don't mind the idea."

Samantha lifted one eyebrow.

"Using one of those big armored vehicles to make a path could make getting out of the city a whole lot faster and easier. And the sooner we rid ourselves of this place, the happier I'll be."

"The happier we'll all be."

Jason nodded, then gently stroked his chin, rough with unshaven stubble. Kale trotted over to where they stood, tail lifted, ears perked in silent inquiry.

"All done?" Samantha asked, crossing in front of Jason and dropping low, stroking both sides of Kale's upturned face.

Jason's gaze lingered on the monolith of the convention center just beyond the trees. With the sun having fully risen, the patchwork of attached parking lots was illuminated, a vast and sprawling acreage of pavement with the sort of massive capacity the convention center required. Morning sun glittered on the fields of vehicles in the distance, a logjam of steel and glass that separated them from the convention center itself. As the front door eased open, he pulled his attention from the horizon and followed Samantha and Kale into the RV.

Eli was just gathering up the dishes and bringing them to the small sink, his hand extended toward the faucet. Hesitating for a moment, he glanced for silent approval and received an affirmative nod from Samantha, so he turned the water on briefly, rinsing off the dishes, then quickly washing them with a damp rag and some soap. Sarah took the wet dishes from him and dried each of them with another rag, then placed them back in the cabinets where they belonged.

"All it took was the end of the world for our kids to learn to clean up after themselves. Imagine that." Samantha tussled Sarah's hair.

"We clean up... sometimes." Eli hung the rag on a drying rack.

"You do pretty well for yourselves." Jason stood just behind the driver's seat, crossing his arms once more and surveying the kitchen. "Listen up, Eli and Sarah, okay?" The two of them turned hesitantly, their expressions flattening into passive looks of uncertainty. "Mom and I talked about it and we're going to check out the convention center this morning." He didn't offer the statement as a question, merely a matter of fact. "Your mom thinks, and I agree, that we may be able to find a vehicle there that might help make traveling through the city a little easier."

"One of those convoy vehicles?" Eli asked.

"Exactly." Jason uncrossed his arms and put his hands at his hips. "We all need to be very attentive to our surroundings. Eyes open, heads on a swivel, can the two of you do that for us?"

"Sure." Sarah nodded swiftly.

"Yeah, Dad. We can do that."

"It's okay to be worried. It's okay to be scared, if that's what you are, but Mom and I are right here. We won't let anything happen to you."

"We're not scared," Eli replied flatly. "We just want to get out of here, that's all. We're sick of Los Angeles." He glanced toward Sarah knowingly and she replied with a soft downward tilt of her chin.

"We're all pretty sick of Los Angeles." Jason nodded his agreement, then walked along the rear of the seat, before sliding into the driver's seat and fishing the keys from his pocket.

Samantha lifted the rifle and brought it with her before settling into the passenger's seat, the weapon straddling her lap, the seat belt hooked across her chest. With the kitchen clean, Eli and Sarah buckled themselves in as well and Jason slowly accelerated, steering the RV into a wide left-hand turn to guide it back in the direction of the convention center.

"I still can't believe we ended up right next to the center." Samantha shook her head, leaning forward to stare out the windshield.

"To be honest I was a little frustrated when I saw it. I was hoping we'd made more progress than that."

"Some progress is better than none. 'Better is better' is what a book I read last month said."

"Sound advice."

Jason steered to the left, driving toward a section of connecting pavement where one parking lot led to the next. Shadows from the nearby trees fell over them as they passed beneath, the sprawling skyline of the city clarifying through the smoke and smog, backlit by morning sun. As they continued through the next parking lot, vehicles increased in frequency, at first neatly slotted into their designated spaces, but then in heaped tangles of bumper-to-bumper traffic. Several cars had been in the process of coming in or pulling out when the event had happened, and several of the travel lanes between rows of evenly spaced lots were clogged with vehicles.

"More bodies." Samantha shook her head, and Jason followed the direction of her stare.

Corpses were spread about throughout the parked vehicles, lying on the ground between stopped cars and trucks, a few hunched over steering wheels, still trapped within their makeshift coffins. Steering left, Jason moved along the rear of a long roadblock of parked vehicles, moving space by space until a small gap opened up between the rows. He turned into that space, wedging through, once more scraping the sides of the RV against the surrounding vehicles. Crunching and jostling, he pressed the vehicle onward, pushing smaller cars aside, scraping past a box truck, and nudging through a pair of SUVs who had stopped a few feet from colliding.

As Jason veered to the left to work his way around a three-car pileup, they cruised beneath a hanging banner of red, white and blue, celebrating the political rally that had been scheduled to occur inside the convention center. Each light post carried vibrant signage, some of them with the President's smiling face peering out, each of them welcoming him to Los Angeles and congratulating him on his inevitable victory in November.

A long, extravagantly decorated banner hung across the next lane of travel, the words *Vote for America's Future – Vote McDouglas for President* stenciled across the colorful fabric. They passed beneath, Eli and Sarah leaning closer to the window, peering up in the direction of the hanging banner.

"Don't suppose President McDouglas needs to worry about the vote this November anymore." Samantha spoke in a low whisper.

"That's one way of looking at it." Jason nodded. "It would make sense if that's what the convoy was doing downtown, trying to evacuate the President."

"The question is, how far did they get?"

Smoke grew thicker and swirling in the immediate vicinity of the convention center, the sky swarmed by a dark and rising cloud. Jason navigated the RV toward a wide-open section near the far edge of the mass of vehicles and turned right, the convention center looming tall and broad before them. He traveled for a short time before a sudden congestion of vehicles emerged along the right side of the passage, a crumpled mass of olive green and camouflage interspersed with a few jet-black SUVs all twisted into a mangled, uneven thornbush of vehicular impact.

"That's it." Samantha twisted toward the passenger side, angling her neck. "That's the convoy. I recognize the markings on one of the Humvees." The air was sucked out of the RV at her words, their previously whispered voices cutting to silence.

The convoy stretched for a long distance through the parking lot, a grotesque monument to a failed evacuation. Three M1117 Armored Security Vehicles formed the vanguard, their olive-drab hulls scarred black from intense heat, their reinforced tires melted and fused to the asphalt. Behind them, a pair of up-armored Humvees had crashed into each other, forming a V-shaped wedge that trapped a sleek black Suburban between them.

The Suburban's bulletproof windows were intact but clouded, hiding whatever horrors lay within. A massive M977 HEMTT cargo truck had jackknifed, its armored cab crumpled against a concrete barrier, the canvas covering its bed torn away to reveal empty supply crates scattered like fallen dominoes.

Smoke rose in thick, coiling fingers from the wreck, the husks of vehicles blackened by heat and roiling flames. The air stunk of spilled fuel and lingering smoke, all of it resting atop the coppery tang of blood. Dark stains marked the pavement between vehicles, dried to a rusty brown, and tattered bits of uniforms stuck out from beneath the wreckage, digital camouflage patterns incongruous against the urban backdrop. Other bodies were strewn about, figures dressed in camouflage, some of them with gas masks still clutched in gloved hands.

Samantha's jaw tightened, her shoulders hunched as she surveyed the wreckage through the passenger window. Eli inched forward in his seat, as much as his belt would allow and Jason turned toward him.

"You might not want to look."

Eli drew back, chin lowering and slumped against the seat. Kale whined softly, took a few steps toward him and rested her head on his lap. More vehicles were piled up around them, knocked aside from the convoy's charge, or stopping short of it, creating more chain reactions of violent collisions throughout the few remaining travel lanes of the congested parking lot. Their forward passage blocked by wreckage, Jason tapped on the brakes, bringing the RV to a shuddering halt, his knuckles white as he gripped the steering wheel. Samantha reached across her body and unhooked her seat belt, standing from the passenger's seat and taking a step toward the front door of the RV.

"What are you doing?" Jason unhooked his own seatbelt, partially rising, using the steering wheel to help himself stand.

"I'm just going out for a minute to look around."

"You good?"

Samantha held the rifle in her left hand as she took a single step toward the door.

"I'll be fine. I'll shout if I need you." Samantha shoved her feet into a pair of boots that stood not far from where she'd been sitting.

Crouched to one knee, she laced up the boots, tugging them tight on her feet and securing the laces near the base of her ankles. Jason's grip tightened around the steering wheel as he stood wedged between the seat and the console. He was poised, hesitantly, his muscles still and taut, tension humming through them. But Samantha's steely resolve held him in place, and he nodded as she eased open the front door and stepped into the unknown. Setting one foot onto the asphalt parking lot, Samantha eased out into the gray Los Angeles morning, palming the RV's door closed behind her.

Stale gas and a thicker, acrid smoke stung her throat, heat still radiating from the remains of the convoy spread before her, buckled, twisted and burned out. The smell of fuel became almost overwhelming, a pungent thickness that filled the air like morning fog lurking above cold water on a humid day. Tears prickled, her nose flaring and throat raw with the sudden stench of it all. It staggered her for a moment, not just from its sensory overwhelm, but from that strange familiarity, a callback to a past life. Dead soldiers were scattered about the ground before her, some of them consumed by crumpled wreckage, others splayed out in the open, a few of them with their gas masks clamped in tight fingers.

Samantha crouched near one young man in camouflage, his face colorless, wide whites of his eyes encircling twin thumbtacks of dark pupils, thin yellowish drool and copious amounts of blood caked thick to his lower lip and across his beardless chin. Her gaze fixed on the young man's face, a soldier who couldn't have been much older than Eli, his teeth exposed behind a contorted, last-gasp grimace. She tucked her chin to her chest and shook her head, standing once more and staring more intently at the pavement. She took a few steps, studying the hard ground, head swiveling left, then right as her alert, well-trained instincts guided her observation. There were several bodies in her immediate view, some of them with hands outstretched, a few holding their masks, though throughout the entire chaotic wreckage before her, there was something missing.

"Where are their weapons?" She whispered the words softly to herself, her grip tightening around her own rifle.

Stepping over the young, dead soldier, she threaded her way through a section of ravaged convoy. One of the Humvees stood before her, blackened with char, thin, whispered fingers of smoke rising from the skeletal remains. The stink of fuel and smoke was strongest there, and a low, throbbing heat still resonated, the air around the wreck several degrees warmer than the normal outside. She picked her way carefully through the carnage, studying the vehicle remains, checking the condition of a few more bodies, silently evaluating what was left of the convoy that had battered its way through traffic at the start of the crisis.

Inside the RV, Jason stared through the windshield, leaning to the left to stay fixed on Samantha as she stepped in and around the ruined wreckage of military vehicles. There was a purposeful assuredness to each of her movements, a certainty as Samantha crouched down to one dead body, examined the empty ground alongside it, checked how the person's hand gripped the unused gas mask, then stood and walked throughout the wreckage of a crumpled Humvee. Time stretched out and Jason shook off his frustration, opening his fists and striding toward the front door.

"Dad?"

"I'm going to go help your mom." He turned partially toward Eli and Sarah. "Keep your eyes peeled."

"Wait..." Eli took a tentative step forward, holding out a hand, though Jason was already pushing the door open.

He stepped outside, wincing at the fist of pungent stink that struck him full in the face. His boots scraped on the parking lot as he descended to ground level and approached the smoldering convoy, a darkened mass of armor, melted rubber and burned flesh. Samantha crouched several feet away, silently examining another corpse, her arm hung low, fingers clasped around the handguard of the rifle they'd taken from the police car. She glanced in his direction as the door he was easing closed forced open again, Eli and Sarah squeezing out through its narrow gap. They closed the door before Kale could join them, the dog's soft whining cut off as they did so.

Eli stopped short, pressing a hand to his stomach as he surveyed the brutality, and Sarah pressed a hand to her mouth. They steadied themselves, however, and recovered quickly, giving each other a quick, cryptic look whose meaning only twins are privy to.

"Sorry," Jason shrugged at his wife, "I needed to know what you were seeing out here."

Samantha stood, directing her first response at the children. "It's not pretty out here. It's fine if you stay in the RV."

"We're okay," Sarah replied on both of their behalf. "We've... we've seen worse."

It was the unfortunate truth. Samantha turned her attention toward Jason and took a few steps in his direction, then motioned at the scene.

"You see how many of them are holding on to their gas masks?"

"Yeah."

"Whatever kind of chemical agent this was, it came upon them with startling speed. So fast that the equipment they had on hand couldn't be put on fast enough to save them."

Jason shook his head as he stared down at one of the dead soldiers. Eli and Sarah moved around him, walking slowly along the ragged edge of the convoy's wreckage.

"You know how well-trained even the youngest of these

soldiers was, particularly if they were sent to rescue the President."

"Oh I remember the mask drills. The gas chamber – all of it."

"It wasn't good enough." Samantha shook her head, studying the blistered armor and slumped corpses. "You notice anything else?" She lifted one eyebrow, fixing Jason with a curious look.

Jason swiveled his head, looking throughout the damage before them. He stepped slowly forward, pausing for a moment at each dead body, taking in the scene for just a second before moving to the next.

"Their weapons are all missing." He crouched and pointed to a holster on the hip of a young man in camouflage. "Even the sidearms." He tapped the plastic sleeve attached to the drop-leg system.

"Exactly. Someone must've—"

"Mom! Dad!" Sarah's shrill voice called from beyond a section of nearby damage, echoing into the previously silent morning.

Samantha wheeled around, sprinting toward the sound of her voice and Jason charged in her wake, the two of them rushing toward where the twins had disappeared around the curved edge of blackened vehicles. Jason and Samantha came around the edge, spotting Eli and Sarah, who stood stock still, gesturing toward a section of pavement alongside the mangled wreckage of a military transport, its armor blackened, the nose of the vehicle compressed into the rear of a smashed Humvee.

"What is it?"

"More bodies – but they're not soldiers. They're in suits."

"In suits?" Jason swung around the backs of Sarah and Eli, coming around so he could see the section of pavement they were pointing toward.

Just as they'd said, three men in suits were splayed across the rough, cracked asphalt, one of them face up, another face down, the third slung over on his left side, all three of them equally lifeless. The man who lay face up had thick, blonde hair, his polka-dotted tie fluttering gently in the breeze. Red droplets spattered the bottom half of his face, a modern art spray of crimson dotting his flesh like freckles. More red stained the surrounding concrete, the already dark suits thickened and pitch black with dried blood.

"Just stay back," Samantha warned, "don't get too close."

"What do you think?" Jason turned slightly toward Samantha as he advanced on the bodies, one cautious step at a time. "Secret Service?"

"No. No holsters, no earpieces... and – no offense to the dead – their suits suck. That one is a few sizes too big."

"Look at the ground," Sarah said softly, her narrow finger pointing toward the pavement. "Is that blood fresher than the blood from other people we've seen?"

"Looks that way." Samantha took another careful step forward, lifting her foot over the blood pool so she could get a bit closer to one of the corpses.

She crouched alongside the body and pinched the flap of his dark jacket, then slowly began to peel it away. The white shirt beneath was coated with blood, thick, dark and rust colored, an even darker puncture in the center of the wide circle that stained the shirt. She lifted her chin, looking toward Jason, who was kneeling down next to another one of the bodies.

"These people didn't die from a chemical attack. These are gunshot wounds."

Jason leaned, examining the ground next to the body he knelt by. Reaching down, he pinched something from the parking lot and held it up, the sparse sunlight glittering from the brass-colored object between his fingers.

"Shell casing. There are quite a few of them here." He inched forward, examining the ground even more closely, then lifted his face to check the surrounding vehicles. "A few bullet holes here and there, too. There was a gunfight here, no doubt about it."

"And these people were on the losing side."

Still kneeling, Jason turned toward Samantha, a tight heat

suddenly filling his chest. Looking past her, he focused his attention on the RV, then back at Eli and Sarah, assessing the entire scene. Standing, he shook his head and took a step away from the suited bodies.

"This isn't right. None of this is right."

"Hold on!" Samantha lifted a hand, her brow knitting.

Jason hesitated in mid-stride, twisting back toward her.

"Do you hear that?" She stood slowly, turning her ear toward the nearby wreckage of ruined vehicles.

"Hear what?"

Samantha placed a finger to her lips and Jason stopped speaking, silence filling the morning air. From somewhere nearby there was a muffled clunk, followed by a scrape. Jason wheeled toward the noise, spinning around to face the armored military transport that had slammed headlong into the burned-out Humvees. The sound came again, another scrape of noise, the truck itself settling oddly as the clunk of something dropping echoed from within the cargo container. The rear doors were buckled and bent, a narrow seam separating them, keeping them from locking tight.

Narrow fingers slipped between the gap in the doors, one set, then a second, and then they pushed out, forcing the armored doors to open, despite the oily protest of hinges. Gravity took over and one lopsided door swung more swiftly, slicing through the air and hammering against the side of the truck with an echoing bang of metal-on-metal. A figure stood within the opening at the rear of the truck, a man draped in shadow, emerging from the wreckage.

"Stop right there!" Samantha had her rifle up in an instant, practiced hands clutching the grip and the handguard, barrel level at the stranger's chest.

Jason followed her lead, pulling the service weapon she'd taken from the police officer free and pointing that at the man as well, gripping it in two hands. The figure froze, caught within the opened frame of the transport's rear. His face was pale, his eyes clouded and narrow, his unkempt hair a mess. He was well-dressed, or had been, though his jacket was off, his shirt was untucked and whatever tie he'd been wearing had been discarded long ago.

Samantha stared long and hard at the man's face, a strange sense of recognition slowly widening her previously paranoid stare. She fixed her attention on the man for a moment then caught sight of one of the nearby banners fluttering against a bent light post.

"No way," she whispered, her voice so low it was almost hoarse. "No way."

Jason twisted toward her, his weapon still lifted.

"Put your gun down, Jason," she said softly, lowering her rifle.

"What?"

"Put. Your gun. Down."

Jason studied the man's face for a moment, realization hitting him a few seconds later. Slowly, he lowered his own weapon, pointing the barrel of the pistol toward the ground, staring at the man in the rear of the armored vehicle.

"Come on out of there," Samantha said, taking a step forward, extending her hand. "We're here to help."

"Help?" The man stood at the rear of the transport, staring out at the surrounding carnage, his pale face somehow losing even more color as he laughed nervously. "I... it... it might be too late for that."

Still, he ambled down from the truck, favoring one leg, a hand pressed to his side as he navigated the uneven step down toward the parking lot.

"Mom?" Sarah tilted her head, eyes narrowing at the man. "Is that...."

"Sarah. Elijah." Samantha turned toward the two, lowering her voice. "Meet Timothy McDouglas. The President of the United States."

# CHAPTER 4

**Jane Simmons**
**An Undisclosed Location in New England**

Jane sits in the silence of the conference room, exhaustion so deep it settles within the marrow of her bones. The room's wood-paneled walls absorb the early morning stillness, a rare moment of quiet in a space churning with crisis. She sits at the dark, Brazilian walnut conference table, its surface polished to a soft sheen, reflecting the gentle glow of overhead recessed lighting. Around its circumference, eighteen high-backed leather chairs stand in perfect formation, each one empty, a litter of discarded papers strewn about the tabletop with reckless abandon. Various reports are stark white against the deep, rich wood of the conference room table, some of them with bright red block text which designate their level of secrecy.

Morning light seeps through bulletproof windows, casting long shadows across the navy blue carpet, the room rich with understated elegance, but its true power rests in its understated technology. Secure video screens are built seamlessly into the walls, classified communication systems are concealed behind well-hidden panels and discreet cameras monitor every angle. Climate control systems continue to regulate interior temperatures and air quality, humming almost imperceptibly, maintaining a constant 68 degrees with built-in filters to clean the interior air. Four digital clocks mounted high on the wall silently track the time in various locations throughout the world, including Washington, DC, London, Beijing and Moscow. Maps line sections of the wall where screens aren't mounted, the world divided into regions and strategic zones, each a potential flashpoint. Pushpins mark the various locations where attacks are known to have taken place, a countless canvas of colored tacks too numerous for Jane to absorb.

She stares for a moment at the map of the United States, littered with dozens of colored pushpins, each small sphere indicating unthinkable numbers of lives lost. Her steely, yet weary gaze tracks pushpin to pushpin, each one vibrant against the pale paper map, involuntarily drawing her gaze as much as she doesn't wish to look. A subtle scent of lemon-based cleanser lingers in the air, mixed with leather, wood and the underpinning of freshly brewing coffee. A credenza in the corner holds a bronze bust of President Ronald Reagen, its patina catching the strengthening rays of sun that paint golden rectangles on the opposite wall. To Jane's right rest three empty coffee cups, the leftover relics of the previous late-night session, the odor of fresh brew strong in the air. Jane's fingers grow tighter around the stack of papers in her hands, words printed in evenly spaced lines of black ink, mixed with the sporadic inclusion of charts and graphs of various different colors.

While there are other colors chosen to record the data on the charts, the majority of them are consumed by a vibrant crimson, red lines and pie-pieces translating incomprehensible casualty numbers into an almost ridiculous representation of elementary school color. The papers crease within the tightness of her grasp, the colors bleeding together as her vision smears from exhaustion, the strong, pungent smell of coffee even clearer, clawing its way through the fog. She blows out a breath and drops the papers on the table, presses her palm to the edge and shoves back, sliding her high-backed swivel chair away from the colors and lines of text. Jane stands, the chair spinning away as she strides toward the door leading out to the carpeted hallway of the safehouse.

A middle-aged man with a shock of graying hair and broad shoulders turns toward her as she moves from the conference room to the hallway. He wears an impossibly white shirt and a neatly pressed black coat, the familiar twisted coil of his communications device nestled against his muscular neck.

"I just need coffee." Jane lifts her hand and moves past the agent.

"Madame President. We have people for that." The agent pushes from the wall and strides quickly to keep pace, lifting his wrist toward his thin-lipped mouth. "Scholar is on the move. East hallway heading toward the kitchen."

"I can get my own coffee." Jane continues walking crisply, her shoes thudding in swift succession on the carpet.

She slows, then finally turns, angled back toward the agent who approaches in her wake.

"What did you call me?"

The agent clears his throat. "Your callsign is Scholar, Madame President."

Jane rolls her eyes and angles left, crossing the carpet and walks into the small kitchen where the scent of fresh coffee is almost overwhelming. Four separate carafes stand on warmers on the counter across from the door, neatly stacked mugs emblazoned with the Presidential seal resting alongside them. A young woman in an apron gapes at Jane and heads toward her quickly, hands extended.

"Please, Madame President, let me..."

"I can get my own coffee." Jane reiterates the sentiment, plucks a darkly colored mug from the stack, and manages to pour her own steaming cup of coffee.

Warm ceramic presses against her palms as she nods a silent thanks to the woman in the apron and wheels around, stalking back toward the door. The Secret Service agent abruptly follows, whispering something she cannot hear into his wrist mic. Another agent is in the hall, a few feet away and approaching quickly as Jane veers right and makes her way back toward the conference room. Once inside, she closes the door behind her, separating her from the Secret Service, surrounding herself once more in silence, then she settles back into her chair, leather squeaking as she does so.

She lets a long, languid breath slide from her lips, then takes a tentative sip of hot coffee, her bleary vision slowly clarifying. The casualty report on the table is the first thing she sees with clearer vision and she wishes she could be blinded once more. Slowly she reaches out, clamps the stack of paper between her fingers, and drags it across the table toward her, slowly flipping from one stapled page to the next. Knuckles rap on the door, a sudden noise that jolts her from her focus, her head whipping back toward the door she'd closed moments earlier.

"Come in."

The door eases open and a well-dressed woman enters, slides into the room and palms the door back closed behind her.

"Excuse the interruption, Madame President."

"It's okay, Joy." Jane blinks, sets down the papers, then takes another drink, one motion following the next. "What is it?"

"We've got a live feed from Washington."

"From Washington?" Jane sits bolt upright and sets the mug down with an echoing clatter.

"It's a team from the 20th out of Aberdeen who specializes in CBRN, we just got comms up, and..."

"CBRN?"

"Chemical, Biological, Radiological, Nuclear. They specialize in deployments into hazardous environments, we activated the team based on your orders."

"Good. Yes, that's good."

The young woman lifts a remote from a nearby counter and stabs a button, pointing the slender device at the largest screen mounted on the far wall. Darkness fades into soft illumination as the screen crawls to life, soon clarifying on a somewhat grainy image that shows a crew making its way across a sprawling field of grass, flattened by the rotor wash from an unseen helicopter. The team moves in practiced, coordinated unison, the camera's view bobbing slowly as they move forward toward the all-too-familiar building in the near distance. Perched along the far edge of the South Lawn is the White House, a stark sentinel against the gray haze of greater Washington, DC. The first thing Jane notices is an almost serene lack of activity, the normal frenetic rush in and out of the nation's capital brought to a harrowing standstill.

"What am I seeing?" Jane asks and laces her fingers together, leaning just a bit forward.

"Live camera feed from the team lead's helmet cam. There are six of them, boots on the ground with a team of support personnel. It was difficult to put the team together, for obvious reasons."

"What reasons are those?"

The young woman clears her throat as the door opens and someone else enters. He's dressed in military greens, hair cropped close to his head, though his chin is dusted in an uncharacteristic stubble.

"These attacks didn't just kill civilians, Madame President. Our military has suffered numerous losses as well. Not just the dead, but..."

"AWOL, Madame President," the man in dress greens interjects. "There has been an epidemic of men and women leaving their post in the last twenty-four hours. Concerns over family, over what they might be asked to do. To our military's credit, we still have many personnel at our disposal, but it's been a hectic period of time."

"And you are?"

"Colonel Grady, Madame President." He turns toward her with a respectful nod, then leans over the conference table and hooks his fingers around a phone sitting atop its polished surface.

He drags it over, sliding it across, pushing away a stack of papers to set the phone close to both him and Jane. Without hesitation, he scoops up the handset and presses it to his ear, narrow fingers wrapped tight around the receiver.

"Put it through to this line." He nods, listens for a moment, then nods again. After another few seconds of silence, he continues, "putting you on speaker with the President." His finger stabs a button on the phone, and he hangs up the receiver, leaning forward, propped up, palms against table. "Sergeant? Comms are open."

"Yes, sir, Colonel, reading you loud and clear."

On the screen, the squad moves forward in unison, each visible soldier wearing a full-sized hazmat suit with integrated boots, hoods and gloves, colored in stark white. They look less like soldiers and more like actors in a futuristic science-fiction movie. Each of them wears a large, cumbersome backpack, a few of them clutching hand-held devices in gloved hands as they slowly approach the White House, which grows larger with each passing step.

"What are they carrying?" Jane asks, nodding toward the projection on the faraway video screen.

"Broad spectrum analyzers. Handheld devices that scan for a wide range of chemical or biological agents simultaneously. They provide instant readouts on anything from nerve agents to industrial chemicals, military-grade stuff to common toxins. Our latest models can identify over a thousand different compounds in just under thirty seconds."

"Taxpayer dollars well spent." Jane leans back in the chair, her laced fingers folded in her lap. "Have they detected anything?"

"No, Ma'am," Colonel Grady replies with a shake of his head.

Hissing breaths from the response team pass through the speaker of the phone, a steady backdrop of rasping inhalations and exhalations. All six of the team members continue forward, advancing on the White House, angling toward a nearby entrance. As they steadily approach, the grainy image reveals a darkened form on the ground ahead, sprawled between the advancing team and the White House entrance beyond. One of the lead soldiers holds up a fist, silently telling his team to stop, which they all do. White-garbed figures separate, making room for the team lead, who pushes his way past, the helmet cam moving slightly up and down with each measured stride.

He looks down at the body, a young man in a suit and tie, carrying the familiar look of a Secret Service agent. An earpiece has slipped out of his ear and rests on the pavement next to his vacant stare, connected to him by the coil of white cord. Dark stains of blood coat the ear's interior and paint the side of his neck, trailing from where the communication device had fallen out.

"Male. Deceased." The hissing voice echoes from the speaker phone as the team lead reports what he sees. "Age approximately late twenties to early thirties, cause of death unknown." The camera dips lower as the sergeant crouches down to closely examine the body. "Copious amounts of dried blood around his mouth, nostrils and head that appear to have emanated from his facial orifices."

On the screen, Jane can see what the man is describing in full detail. The young agent's eyes are closed, his lips partially open and rust stains his chin and forms a strange, broad moustache between his nose and his upper lip. A secondary figure steps forward, using a broad-spectrum analyzer, waving the device around the corpse, taking a moment here and there to examine the readout on the screen.

"Analyzers are still clear, showing nothing out of the ordinary."

Jane leans forward and touches the mute button on the phone, which earns her a swift sideways glance from Colonel Grady.

"How much do they know?" she asks.

"Enough."

"Have they been briefed that it may be related to Novichok?"

"That information has been strongly compartmentalized. We've revealed what we had to reveal in order for them to do their jobs."

"What can you tell me about Novichok? Half-life? How long it stays active out in the environment?"

Colonel Grady stands and strokes his stubble-coated chin. On the screen, the team lead stands again, the camera pulling back from the dead body as the group begins to move in a different direction.

"Some of the known Novichok variants could last for extended periods in sunlight, while others start breaking down in less than an hour."

"So, if this is a Novichok variant, it must be one of the less stable sorts."

"That is one of our hypotheses." Colonel Grady nods.

"How can we possibly know who dispersed it? How they dispersed it? When?"

"Those are all questions we don't have answers to right now, Madame President. That's what we're hoping these teams will help clarify."

"How can they help clarify it if they can't find any trace of it?"

Colonel Grady flushes, but quickly regains his composure, a quick side-eye darting toward the monitor screen once more.

"We have teams sweeping Denver and Houston as well as D.C and many others. That's exactly what we're hoping to do – gain enough intel to know how it was deployed and who deployed it. Those answers might take time, though."

"Time we don't have. Do we have any reason to think these attacks are over? Or could there be more coming?"

"I apologize, Madame President, I've been focused on analysis. If you're looking for intelligence, you may want to check with Colonel Drake and the Joint Chiefs, they're more focused on the Homeland Security side of the fence. Perhaps Agent Provost can help fill in some of those holes."

Jane untangles her fingers and gently massages her eyes, then lifts her mug of coffee and takes another long swallow.

"I know how frustrating this must be, Madame President. We share your frustration. The world is teetering right now, and we have to step very carefully. We have to measure twice before we cut."

On the screen, the team continues to walk the perimeter of the White House, stopping only to examine other dead bodies along the way. There's a scattering of more dead Secret Service, a couple of groundskeepers, a few nameless men and women dressed in business professional attire. Colonel Grady taps the mute button, once more opening up comms to the team on the ground.

"Sergeant, anything?"

The team hesitates for a moment, a pair of men in hazmat gear lifting their scanners and waving them slowly through the air. "Still clean, Colonel," the voice comes back.

They move forward as a group for a few more moments, then hesitate as they near another entrance into the White House. Jane leans forward and is momentarily captivated by the images on the screen, her palms pressed to the polished table. She hooks her fingers through the handle of the coffee mug and sips as the CBRN team does its work. The feed shows five white-suited figures moving methodically again across the South Lawn, their movements precise despite the bulky Level A protection. The

Capitol dome looms in the background, illuminated against the upcoming approach of morning light.

"Grid Delta-7 clear," a voice comes through with a slight static, echoing through the phone's speaker.

The woman speaker turns toward the team lead with the helmet cam, breath fogging the inside of her mask momentarily. The broad-spectrum analyzer in her gloved hand sweeps left to right, its digital readout reflecting off her faceplate.

"Moving to Echo sector."

Two team members break right, toward the Treasury Building, their suits ghostly in the smoke-filtered daylight. A third member kneels, taking some soil samples near a row of barren cherry trees while the fourth tracks air particulates with another spectrometer, its quiet whirring barely audible over the team's breathing.

"Martinez, tell your two on the east to pull back fifty meters." Colonel Grady speaks into the phone. "Go grid-by-grid."

"Copy that." The Sergeant relays those orders and the two figures near Treasury immediately retreat, their movements quick but controlled. "Newman, what's your reading on the south perimeter?"

"Nothing above baseline, Captain." Newman's analyzer sweeps in wide arcs. "Whatever hit here is long since degraded or—" He stops mid-sentence.

"Or what?"

"Or something we don't have the ability to detect." The camera pans right as Sergeant Martinez turns. The historic fountain sits silent, its water drained weeks ago for maintenance and Newman approaches it slowly, his analyzer working the air as he moves toward it. "Still nothing detected, Sergeant. Air is clear as far as our scanners can tell."

The Capitol building in the background looms over the scene like a stoic watchman, its white dome stark against the lightening gray sky. Martinez's camera pans slowly across the South Lawn, taking in the surreal scene, the empty grounds, the abandoned guard posts, the white suits of his team harsh against the surrounding gray. Jane watches this all with rapt fascination, her shoulders clenched tight, her throat constricting, allowing only the slightest slice of air to pass through. Anticipation claws at her, grips her tense shoulders, carves the bulging tendons of her neck and hammers a bolt through her rigid, upright spine.

On the grainy head cam footage, the team converges on the South Lawn, moving with purpose, scanners testing the air as they cross the green grass. Jane watches as the camera feed bobs with each of Sergeant Martinez's steps, drifting left and right, silently evaluating. They near the blackened bars of the perimeter fence and the sergeant hesitates, staring out upon E Street just beyond. He freezes, the steady forward movement of his head cam comes still, locked firmly on the bustling thoroughfare near the intersection of 15th Street. The road is filled with death, slung bodies sprawled about the pavement in numbers heretofore unseen through the feed. Corpses are visible from left to right, all along the broad asphalt sidewalks and upon both lanes of a road that had been relegated to pedestrian use only in the wake of September 11th.

Jane lets out a short, squeaking gasp, her fingers press to her lips, a flood of chilled air fills her chest and rises up into her throat, bringing acid. Her mouth hangs slack, unspoken words resting on her tongue, words that are insufficient to communicate the depths of what she sees on the camera feed before her. Her fingers hold, half an inch from the curved surface of her coffee mug, the tepid liquid no longer the least bit appetizing. As the response team advances, bodies are visible, squeezed through the iron bars of the fence, desperately crawling for perceived safety. Their faces are stained with tears of blood, their open mouths swallowed by a caked-on crimson mask which makes them look almost demonic, caught in a silent, guttural scream of horror.

Jane presses a hand to her stomach and stands, knocking her chair back, barely supporting herself with her left palm against the edge of the table. She ducks her head, drawing in a deep breath, filling her cold chest with warm breath, though it does little to soothe the churn of boiling bile.

"Cut the feed." Colonel Grady hisses toward Joy, the president's aide, who appears hypnotized by the horrific images on the monitor.

Joy doesn't move, she sits there rigid, pink nails dug into the top of the table.

"Cut the—never mind, I'll do it." Colonel Grady repeats, then lunges left, yanking the remote from the top of the table and stabbing the screen into darkness.

"Colonel?" The sergeant's voice echoes from the speakerphone.

"Continue your perimeter sweep, Sergeant. Gather your reports and have them ready when you're done. We'll reconvene for a sitrep in an hour."

"Yes, Sir." The voice is clipped, then the backdrop of hissed static cuts into silence.

Jane's breathing is heavy and haggard, her left knee slightly wobbling as she leans forward, supported by the rigid post of her left arm.

"Madame President? Are you okay? I'm sorry about that."

Jane closes her eyes, each inhalation steadier than the last, each exhalation a more even breath outward from pursed lips. The bile in her gut settles, her tight throat swallows the burn back down and she allows herself to lift her chin, gaze drifting toward the recessed lighting in the ceiling. Hooking a finger into the collar of her shirt, she tugs gently, loosening it from around her neck, easing her uneven breathing.

"Why are you apologizing?"

"I..."

"Did you not want me to see reality? Those are the streets of our nation's capital!" She stabs a finger toward the darkened screen. "Those are American citizens. Those are *my* citizens."

"Yes. Yes they are."

"Is that what it's like? The whole damn country?"

"It's a travesty. Unprecedented in size and scope." Colonel Grady stands upright, his arms crossed behind his back.

Jane expels a sudden gust of sour air and slumps down into her chair, clawing her fingers into each leatherbound armrest. She stares for a moment at the sheen of the table, the sparse reflection of overhead lighting smearing across its smooth surface. She loses herself in the patterns of light reflections, a Milky Way galaxy swirling within the gleaming wood varnish, then finally speaks after a long moment.

"Talk to me about survivors."

Grady leans a bit forward and presses a button on the phone he'd dragged closer. "Can you send in Provost and Colonel Drake? Our ten o'clock is being bumped up."

Jane grasps the mug of coffee, cooler to the touch, and tips it up, taking a long drink of the lukewarm liquid. "Do we need to wait for Provost and Colonel Drake?"

"I'd rather we did, so everyone's in the loop."

"Why don't you start? Just give me an update from our previous meeting. Rescue and recovery operations, logistics, that sort of thing."

Colonel Grady clears his throat and folds his hands in his lap, leaning back in his chair.

"The hardest hit areas have been the population centers. Big cities and transport hubs, areas of increased activity. We're finding that the vast majority of the survivors are in more rural, remote locations, which makes it very difficult to launch rescue or recovery operations. Of course, the large cities aren't the *only* ones being hit... it's still very much a dynamic, fluctuating situation all around."

A soft knock comes at the door, and a moment later the Secret Service agent is pushing the door open so Colonel Drake and Agent Provost can file inside the conference room. They each walk the perimeter of the table, drag a pair of chairs out on the other side, then settle into place, each dropping a manilla folder on the table's surface with a soft thump.

"Sorry to alter the schedule." Jane nods at them both. "Thanks for coming on such short notice."

"No apologies necessary. We're nothing if not flexible." Provost leans back, a smile playing upon his lips. "You were saying?"

"I was saying," Colonel Grady resumes speaking, "that you have good timing. Happy to hand you two the ball on rescue and recovery. We were just starting to discuss how most of the survivors right now are in rural areas."

Provost leans forward, resting his elbow on the table, "The rural nature of the survivors makes things difficult. When designing rescue efforts, you want the biggest bang for your buck, but survivors are scattered, small pockets spread across vast oceans of real estate. It makes it difficult to prioritize one place over another. Plus we're still finding survivors in urban environments – albeit far less than rural ones – and we have the investigative missions ongoing in those same environments. It's a lot to juggle."

"Let's not get caught in analysis paralysis. If we have the opportunity to rescue people, we need to be doing it."

"It's less about rescue and more about re-supply." Colonel Drake holds up a hand.

"Oh?"

"It's a little of both," Provost interjects. "In some cases, we're attempting to centralize displaced citizens into a single location. Leveraging boots on the ground FEMA resources to set up secure perimeters. Trucking in food and water, transporting any survivors that teams find into those central areas so we can offer protection and regular meals. In other cases, there isn't a good option for building out that infrastructure, so we're looking at air-dropping those same supplies. Food, water, hygiene products, that sort of thing."

"The only problem is that fuel shortages are going to be here before we know it." Colonel Grady lifts a thin stack of paper resting on the table next to him. "Fuel production has all but stopped. Distribution is at a standstill. We have no way to get gas from point a to point b. There are either highway closures, a lack of personnel, or other extenuating circumstances."

"Extenuating circumstances." Jane shakes her head, then glances at the watch on her wrist. "It's been two days since this began, people. Two days. People are going to start dying of dehydration and starvation if we don't figure out how to solve this problem. I don't want to hear about excuses, no matter how good they may be. I want to hear about outside-of-the-box solutions."

"We've got our best and brightest working on this, Madame President," Colonel Drake said. "The Joint Chiefs—"

"No offense, Colonel Drake, but the Joint Chiefs seem to be focused more on who they can launch missiles at, not how we can be best helping our own people."

"One might argue both elements are equally important." Colonel Drake's voice is chiseled from hard stone. "We need to take care of our people, but we need to make sure we aren't going to fall prey to a second attack of some sort."

"If we let our citizens die, then it doesn't matter if it's an isolated incident because our nation will crumble. There will be nothing left for them to attack. If we turn our backs on the people who depend on us, this little shooting match is already over, and we're on the losing side."

Colonel Drake clears his throat, his gaze briefly meeting Grady's across the table.

"We're all working under an immense amount of stress," Provost says, lifting both sets of fingers, as his palms rest on the edge of the table. "But it's more important than ever that we work together. Toward the same goal. If we can't come to an agreement here, we can never hope for the nation to come to an agreement outside these four walls."

"I couldn't agree more," Jane replies and spreads her hands in a gesture of acknowledgement to the people who sit around the table. "Can I take that to mean we agree? Our first priority must remain to our people?"

"Madame President—"

Jane pushes herself upright from the desk, jaw clenching, chin lifted. "Let me rephrase: I want a plan on my desk. Four hours or less. A plan focused on how we provide for our survivors, not which nation state is in our crosshairs. Can I trust the three of you to do that for me?" Her slightly elevated voice resonates within the tight confines of the conference room.

Around the table, Colonel Grady, Joy O'Hara, Colonel Drake and Agent Provost remain silent, fixing each other with lingering stares, as each one waits for the other to speak.

"Four hours. On my desk. Let's hustle, people!" Jane pounds the edge of the table with her fist, the sudden impact urging the meeting attendees to leap upright, pushing back their chairs.

"Yes ma'am." Colonel Grady nods curtly and spins on his heels, swiftly marching out of the room.

Drake follows close behind, with Provost bringing up the rear and as he walks past Jane, he lifts a thick eyebrow in thinly veiled admiration and nods his head with just a touch of subtlety. Soon the three men file out, which leaves only Jane and Joy standing within the conference room.

"That was impressive, Madame President." Joy's mouth is tucked into a thin, pinched smile.

Before Jane can offer her own reply, Joy crosses the room and reaches the door in three long strides. She slips out into the hallway and closes the door behind her, leaving President Jane Simmons alone once more.

# CHAPTER 5

**The Tills Family**
**Silverpine, Oregon**

The tapping was soft and uneven at first, but then grew louder, finally stirring Doug, the repeated drumming reaching into the depths of sleep and tugging him out, inch-by-inch. His shoulders shifted from beneath the thick blankets as the rapping continued just outside the darkness of sleep.

"Doug," Sheila whispered from next to him, a sharp elbow jabbing his arm. "Is that someone at the door?"

Doug drew his arm back, draping it over him and rolled, biting down hard as a fresh surge of stabbing pain raked the entirety of his left leg. The sensation shot him like a cannon out of his sleep, the world erupting into vibrant, painful light. His eyes sprang open upon the master suite of their vineyard bedroom, golden sunlight shining through the surrounding windows. The entire room was cast in a mixture of yellow and gold, the wine-colored carpet in sharp contrast to the golden light, the intricate winding patterns of woodgrain on their dresser carved in deep relief. Everything sharpened as Doug pushed back, bolting upright, throwing the blankets from his body.

The tapping continued from the closed bedroom door, even as he slipped from the bed, wincing as he leaned away from putting weight on his left leg. Sheila remained in bed, her covers pulled up to her shoulders, a long thrust of her hair sprawled across the side of her face. Doug limped heavily and Sheila started to push her own blankets off. He wore a black T-shirt with a logo of their vineyard emblazoned on it and a pair of flannel pajama pants that hung loose around his waist, their cuffs dragging across the carpet.

"Your leg! I forgot about your leg." She blinked heavily and rubbed her knuckles into her eye sockets. "Get back in bed, let me see who it is."

"I'm fine," Doug replied, lifting a hand toward his wife. "I'm already up."

The sun caught her features just right, bringing out a youthful pink in her cheeks, the silver streaks in her hair nearly glistening in the reflection of the morning sun. For a moment he just stared at her, smiling, the rapping knuckles continuing outside his sphere of attention.

"What the devil are you looking at, Doug Tills?"

"Just appreciating the scenery." He flashed her a wink, then turned back toward the sound of the knocking, limping heavily in the direction of the door.

"Mr. and Mrs. Tills?" A whispered voice rushed from the other side of the door. "Sorry to wake you..."

"Not as sorry as we are." Doug grumbled as he swung the door open, revealing Darryl standing on the other side.

"I'm sorry. I'm sure you need your sleep. We were just worried, and Benjamin was surprised you weren't awake yet."

"Worried? What were you worried about? We're over sixty so you think we're going to just up and croak in our sleep?" Doug chuckled and limped back into his bedroom, his uneven gait almost angular.

"No, not at all, that's not what I was saying." Darryl leaned against the doorframe.

"It was a long day, Darryl. A long night, too." Doug pressed his hands to the small of his back and leaned to stretch. "But you're right – we need to get up."

Sitting upright in the bed, Sheila twisted over and lifted the tracker from the end table next to her. She held the power button down until the screen lit up, then stared down at it, blinking.

"You kept that thing next to you all night?" Doug asked.

"Of course. I wanted to check it first thing." The screen glowed a pale green, and Sheila leaned in closer. "They moved! Not much, but they moved."

"Good. They must be up and about this morning. Knowing Samantha, they probably got an early start." Doug wandered over to his dresser and pulled out a drawer, then started to fish out a change of clothes.

His brow furrowed as he shuffled through the neatly folded and piled clothes in the dresser and he lifted his chin, turning toward a nearby window.

"Anyone else hear that?" He slammed the drawer closed again.

From somewhere outside there was an echoing hammer of noise, metal banging hard against metal, a sharp, rhythmic impact, one after the next. Doug walked away from the dresser and limped across the bedroom, putting only the mildest amount of pressure on his left leg.

"What's going on out there, Darryl?"

"I'm not sure. I've been helping out in the kitchen with Brandi all morning. Benjamin had a bur in his saddle about something earlier, but I don't know exactly what it is." Darryl shrugged good-naturedly. "You know how he gets...."

Doug crossed the hall outside the bedroom, reached one of the windows and leaned into the glass, twisting to get a good angle on the front parking lot. Just beyond the outward edge of the main building, their Jeep sat parked, looking the worse for wear as it was illuminated by the morning sun. Paint was scuffed, the metal was dented, the front bumper partially peeled away from its frame. The Jeep was up on a jack, its small donut-sized spare resting on the gravel a short distance away while Benjamin knelt alongside the Jeep, pushing a larger tire into place. A ratchet and tire iron rested near his bent knee, and he scooped up a lug nut, pressed it into place, then started tightening it as Doug watched from the window.

"Is he fixing the Jeep?"

"Oh yeah, and then some," Darryl replied.

Sheila pushed off her covers, revealing her own silk pajamas, then stood, making her way around Darryl to stand next to Doug, staring through the window, shoulder-to-shoulder. Down in the parking lot, Benjamin clutched the tire iron with two hands and grunted, using all of his muscle to twist one of the lug nuts into place. He dropped it with a clatter, then used the back of his hand to wipe sweat from his brow.

"He's going to give himself a heart attack if he's not careful." Doug stepped away from the window and hobbled over to his dresser. "Wait down there for a minute, would you? We'll get dressed and be right out." He glanced over his shoulder and Darryl nodded hurriedly, walking stiffly back through the master bedroom and out the door, closing it behind him.

Doug gathered up a change of clothes, lifted it into his arms and went into the attached bathroom. He went through his early morning routine, forgoing a shower, though he desperately wanted one, choosing to just wash his face and apply extra deodorant for the time being. He exited the bathroom, dressed in fresh clothes, though the tacky sweat from the previous day still clung to his body. Shelia gave him a gentle kiss on the cheek, then brought her own change of clothes into the master bathroom and did her own morning routine, joining him a minute later back outside.

"I'd kill for a shower right now," Sheila said.

"You and me both. Let's get downstairs, though. We can grab showers later tonight."

"I'm just glad we've got a well – and power to run it."

"At least during daylight. We need to get those batteries going."

"Don't stress yourself out, dear. There's plenty to do, and we'll get it done, we don't have to do it all today."

She walked back toward the bed and circled around it, picking up the tracking device and slipping it into a baggy pocket of the cargo pants she wore.

"Never leave home without it, eh?" Doug lifted his eyebrows and she gently pushed him in the shoulder.

"Leave me alone."

"I'm glad you're keeping tabs on them." He wrapped his arm around her slender shoulders and pulled her into a tight embrace.

"I'm... glad we made it back here in one piece. Part of me wants to run off and rescue them again right now, but...." She stared out another one of the nearby windows, looking off into the distance at the dangers they couldn't see.

"We'll figure things out. We always do."

"Somehow we manage to stumble through it." Sheila shrugged, then joined Doug as he moved toward the door.

Darryl was waiting just outside for them and nodded his greeting as they gathered together.

"I'm sorry for waking you, I really am."

"It's okay," Doug replied, slapping him on the shoulder. "Best not to sleep the day away. There's plenty to do."

They made their way to the stairs and Sheila positioned herself next to Doug, though he shrugged off her help, leaning heavily on the banister as he took each step one at a time, sucking in a pained breath with each downward drop.

After a long, precarious descent, they arrived at the base of the stairs and continued onward. A light smell wafted from the direction of the restaurant and Sheila hesitated, stepping into the large dining area before they reached the front door. Brandi emerged from the kitchen a moment later, smiling broadly, a towel slung over her shoulder, a white apron tied around her waist.

"Morning, Mr. and Mrs. Tills. I was just trying to figure out breakfast."

"Dear, I'm going to convince you to call us Doug and Sheila if it kills me." Sheila strode in Brandi's direction, though she hesitated for a moment, twisting back toward the two men. "Can the two of you handle Benjamin on your own?"

"No chance," Doug snorted, "but we'll muddle through."

"I know you will." Sheila disappeared into the kitchen with Brandi.

Darryl stepped closer to Doug, extending a hand to support him as he walked.

"Get away from me." Doug waved the younger man's hand away. "I'll be just fine." He limped toward the door and pushed it open, and Darryl followed him outside.

The air was warm and gently soothed the bare skin of Doug's face and arms. He stopped for a moment and relished that warmth, the lingering smell of the vineyards painting a joyful morning canvas. The constant smell of grapes edged with lavender filled his nostrils, complemented by an entanglement of floral bouquet, both from the vineyards themselves and the surrounding forest. He stood there, hips cocked, weight firmly on his right leg and drew the smells deep into his nostrils, filling his chest with the flowery organic odor of home.

Benjamin muttered a whispered curse and banged against the tire, yanking Doug from his momentary morning reverie. Darryl stepped away from Doug and crossed between him and the Jeep, rushing toward where Benjamin knelt by the tire.

"Let me help you with that."

"You ever changed a tire before, boy?"

"Plenty of times."

Benjamin grumbled his response as Darryl knelt down beside him, helping to hold the tire in place so Benjamin could go back to work on the lug nuts.

"What are you thinking, Benjamin?" Doug shook his head as he limped his way toward the Jeep, grimacing with each labored step. "Doing this work on your own?" He shook his head as he drew near. "Why are you even doing it in the first place? Didn't we just decide last night the roads are too dangerous to travel right now?"

"We need a working vehicle, Mr. Tills." Benjamin spoke through clenched teeth as he twisted the lug nut into place. "Just in case. You never know if we might have to make a hasty exit, and your Jeep is probably the best vehicle out of everyone's here." He blew out a breath, dropped the wrench and stood, using the Jeep to help himself upright. "Besides it just wasn't sitting right with me. This old bird just parked out here, that tiny donut on there and that torn-up stub of a wheel, too, something needing fixing that wasn't being fixed."

Doug hobbled around to the other side of the vehicle and studied the tire, still elevated from the jack. "Where did you get the new tires, anyway? We don't have the right size spares kicking around, as far as I know."

Darryl and Benjamin exchanged a brief look.

"What?" Doug asked, crossing his arms, leaning right to favor his injured leg.

"Darryl and I... we took a walk this morning." Benjamin wiped his hands on his overalls and jerked his head toward the vineyards. "We went out to the neighborhood just before dawn and there were plenty of tires there to choose from." He shrugged his broad shoulders.

"Wait. You stole a couple of tires from one of our neighbors?"

"We *borrowed* a couple of tires. Left a note and everything so they know who to call to get reimbursed. But I'll tell you what, that whole place is abandoned. There isn't a soul to be seen anymore."

"Abandoned. Totally and completely abandoned?"

"As far as we could tell. Didn't see a single person, didn't hear anyone. If you thought it was bad when we visited before, it's ten times worse now. The whole place gave me the creeps, if you want to be honest. Like a ghost town."

Doug considered Benjamin's words, turning his head to look in the direction of the neighborhood, though it was concealed by the vineyards and the trees beyond. "They had plenty of abandoned vehicles?"

Benjamin nodded, placing his hands on his hips.

"Why not just take an entire car? Or a truck? Rather than removing a tire."

"Honestly, that was my first thought. Young Darryl here talked me out of it. Said it felt a little bit too much like stealing."

Doug ran his tongue across his teeth, nodding. "I think I agree. Taking a couple of tires is one thing, but grand theft auto? That might be a step beyond what I'm willing to take."

"At least so far," Benjamin said, a flicker in his steely eyes.

"True." Doug sighed. "I might not be too crazy about the idea, but I guess you did the right thing. Having a working vehicle makes sense, given what else is going on." Doug limped back toward the Jeep as Benjamin crouched by the jack and began to lower the vehicle onto the tire they'd just replaced.

He and Darryl disengaged the jack, folded it together, then set it off to the side with the other tools, gathering them together to return to the shed.

"That's a job well done," Darryl said with a broad smile, "and it's not even breakfast time yet."

"If it isn't yet, I hope it's soon. I've already worked myself up a fierce hunger." Benjamin pressed a hand to his stomach.

"Sheila and Brandi were starting to get some stuff together as we came out. If anyone can work some magic in the kitchen, the two of them can."

Darryl approached the tools, crouching by them and starting to gather them up. As Doug followed his movements, he spotted something resting against the side of the Jeep and took a few limping strides toward it.

"Is that the shotgun?" He gestured toward it, angling his neck back toward Benjamin.

"Yessir," Benjamin replied immediately. "I don't go far without it these days."

"Just be careful. You almost put a barrel of buckshot into our windshield last night."

"You know me better than that, Mr. Tills."

Doug smiled, but before he could smile too broadly, a window from the main vineyard building slid up, the sudden sound drawing everyone's gaze. Sheila leaned out, her arm extended, and gestured toward the men who made their way in her direction.

"We've got a problem!" The urgency in her voice stopped Doug short, though Darryl and Benjamin continued. "Brandi spotted a van at the end of the driveway."

"A van?" Doug asked. "What do you mean a van?"

"It's a white panel van. Brandi was grabbing some supplies and glanced out the window and saw it."

The three men twisted toward each other, a trio of eyebrows raised, a deep, knitted furrow creasing Benjamin's forehead. Doug retreated toward the Jeep, turning and hobbling back in its direction. As Benjamin and Darryl headed toward the near edge of the building, Doug lifted the shotgun from where it rested and clutched it tight, limping as quickly as he could in pursuit of the other two men. Darryl slowed just a bit, giving Doug an opportunity to close the distance, then the three men circled around toward the front of the building.

By the time they reached the front entrance, a run-down, aged panel van was approaching, tires crunching across the gravel driveway as it meandered toward the main vineyard building. A relic of the previous century, the van ambled up the slope toward the main customer parking lot, moving like a bloated whale through still waters. Benjamin stood in the lead, stepping out into the main lot and lifting a hand, placing himself directly in the path of the approaching van. The old Ford Econoline wheezed up the vineyard's gravel drive, its pale-colored paint peeling away in patches to reveal rusty wounds beneath. Its passenger side mirror hung askew, vibrating with each snarling gasp of its engine.

"Vineyard's closed until further notice!" Benjamin shouted, his loud, gruff voice bellowing out across the silent expanse of morning.

Tires skidded as the van eased to a halt a few feet away from where Benjamin stood. Doug tightened his grip around the shotgun, though the barrel was pointed toward the ground. Darryl stood next to him, both of them back a bit from where Benjamin had placed himself. The driver's side window eased its way down, offering a glimpse into the van itself.

Behind the wheel, the driver's nicotine-stained fingers drummed against cracked leather, his face a topographical map of hard living. Deep valleys were carved around his mouth, sloped mountains of scar tissue and weathered flesh across his jaw, which was covered in a scraggly beard, more gray than brown. Beside him, a skinny woman picked her teeth with a fingernail painted a chemical cherry-red, chipped down to bare at the tips. Bleached hair had grown out from three inches of dirty dishwater colored roots, pulled back into a rubber band that barely held the hair in place.

Barely visible in the back, a young man in faded denim leaned forward, trying to get a better view, and as the window opened, the yapping chorus of an exuberant chihuahua barreled free, a raucous shout of sharp barks, one immediately after another, the dog barely kept in check by a pair of narrow arms wrapped around the tiny canine. The dog's false rhinestone collar glittered in the slices of sunlight through the window, its teeth bared with each voracious snarl of its narrow, black lips. The dog owner's own jewelry was plastic and pot metal, but she wore it thick like the crown jewels, bangles clacking with each abrupt bounce of her dog's aggression.

"Hey, man," the driver said, leaning toward the open window. "We're just looking for some water. We've been driving for hours, and these roads are awful. You should see it out there, it's bad news."

"We've seen it. Doesn't change the fact that the vineyard is closed." He lifted his arm and extended a finger, pointing back toward the driveway. "I need you to turn around and go back the way you came."

"C'mon, Eddie. I'm thirsty!" The bleached blonde woman leaned across the driver's chest. "I just need something to drink!"

"Hush up, Becky," the driver hissed, gently pushing her away. He turned back toward Benjamin. "All we need is some water. Can't you spare some?" A muffled clunk from inside the van signaled the interior door handle yanking open.

"I told you," Benjamin insisted, "vineyard is closed."

The driver didn't listen. With a rusted squeak of hinges, the door swung open, and the man extracted himself from the driver's seat, stepping out onto the gravel, tightly gripping the door. Doug lifted the shotgun in anticipation, the barrel drifting left with Benjamin firmly placed between him and potential danger. A scowl darkened the already cavernous lines on the driver's face, and he wheeled angrily toward Benjamin as he exited.

Then, in a blur of motion, Darryl appeared out of nowhere, whipping himself around Benjamin's right shoulder, closing swiftly on the driver. Darryl's hand lashed out, ramming an open palm against the driver's weathered throat. His mouth gaped, his forward momentum shifting into abrupt reverse as he stumbled back, leaning sideways against the driver's seat. Darryl advanced, grabbing the driver's side door and yanking it fully open, then slammed it forward, hammering the metal edge into the driver's head. The sharp crack of metal on bone was still echoing in the quiet morning when Darryl yanked the door back and slammed it again, a secondary skull impact throwing the man fully into the driver's seat with force.

The driver sprawled, his head shooting back, the crown of his skull smashing hard into the bleach-blonde woman's lower face. There was a pistol shot smack of bone on bone and her head whipped, multi-colored hair fanning as a single tooth tore loose and spun into the air, tinking against the windshield. The two of them slumped into their seats, the woman shrieking and clutching at her bleeding mouth, the driver staring out at Darryl with a dazed, faraway look.

Thin, twisting rivers of blood worked their way down from the left side of his face, darkening his hair, following the deep grooves in his weathered skin. Doug hobbled forward in a swift, undulating limp, shouldering past Benjamin, shotgun raised, the barrel swinging up and around to point at the truck's inhabitants.

"The man said the vineyard is *closed*!" Darryl hissed, one fist clenched as he pointed with his opposite hand back toward the end of the driveway.

The driver wheezed, clutching at his throat, which was already colored yellow and purple with newly formed bruising. Gagging and rasping, he coughed and sputtered, shocked gaze still fixed on Darryl. Lowering his pointing finger, Darryl closed his second hand into a fist and took a step toward the van and the driver lurched, grabbing the door and pulling it swiftly closed with a shattering bang. He gunned the engine, a belching cloud of blue exhaust ripping from the rear of the vehicle, then slammed it into reverse. The van leaped backwards, kicking stones in its wake, then swerved wildly left, two of the tires threatening to lift from the driveway with the speed of the vehicle's rotation. It leaned precariously, dangerously close to capsizing, then swung around and hurtled forward, steadying its crooked gait as it roared away, heading back toward the narrow stretch of gravel driveway it entered from. Billowing dust swirled in its wake, blocking the vehicle from view as the engine faded away to nothingness.

Darryl's fingers unclenched, his hands hanging by his side. His whole body sagged and he offered a nonchalant shrug as Benjamin and Doug gaped at him, slack-jawed. He walked between the two men, his stride once more long and languid, a casual walk carrying him back toward the house. Benjamin and Doug turned toward each other, faces drawn and narrow, mouths still hung open. Benjamin wheeled toward Darryl first, catching up to him in two long strides.

"Hey!" He gripped his shoulder gently, forcing Darryl to stop and turn back in their direction. "What... what was *that*?"

"What do you mean?" Darryl shoved his hands in his pockets, glance darting away from Benjamin's steely stare.

"What do you mean, what do I mean?" Benjamin shook his head, then turned back in Doug's direction as he approached in his hobbled limp. "Mr. Tills – what... what just happened?"

"First of all, thank you, Darryl," Doug said, "I didn't have a clear shot and that could have gone sideways pretty quickly."

"It's fine." Darryl shrugged. "No big deal."

"No big deal? Are you sh—*kidding* me?" Benjamin's voice ticked up an octave. "You kicked that guy's ass. He didn't have a chance to even think, much less react. Not that he didn't deserve it, but where did that come from?"

"Does it really matter?" Darryl rolled his shoulders and started to turn away again, his normally happy-go-lucky features turning dark.

Doug and Benjamin followed, Doug's uneven stride causing him to linger slightly behind, though the other two walked slowly so as not to leave him.

"Seriously," Darryl insisted, "it was no big deal."

He quickened his pace slightly, walking back toward the front door, which he eased open before stepping inside. Benjamin caught the door before it closed, holding it open so Doug could limp through, then shut it and locked it, double-checking the deadbolt.

"Darryl, honestly," Doug said, hobbling more quickly to catch up to him. He lifted a hand and touched Darryl's arm, prompting him to turn around. "We're potentially going to be here together for a while. It would be helpful if we knew what each other were capable of."

"We're not being nosy, kid," Benjamin echoed, sympathy etched into his words. "It's just that... I've never seen that side of you before. What's going on?"

Darryl's jaw flexed and he finally offered a subtle nod, exhaling in annoyed acceptance. "Fine. But it's not as exciting as you think."

"C'mon kid, spill it."

"I... used to be a martial artist."

"A martial artist? Like Kung Fu?"

"Judo." Color flushed Darryl's cheeks.

"Judo? For real?" Benjamin raised an eyebrow. "I thought that was mostly throwing and flipping and stuff like that?"

"Depends on what style you follow."

"You said you used to be," Doug interjected, "looked like you still are to me."

"It's muscle memory. Once you learn it, it sort of sticks with you. I haven't trained actively since..." his voice trailed off and he glanced away for a moment. "It's been a while." Darryl put his hands in his pockets again and continued walking down the hallway toward the restaurant.

"That's some kind of muscle memory to still be able to move like that." Benjamin cast a sideways glance toward Doug, who offered little more than a shrug.

"I competed at a pretty high level."

"You competed? Like you fought other people? Like in the UFC?"

Darryl halted, shaking his head. "No, not in the UFC." The color in his cheeks deepened. "The Olympics. Other competitions."

"What?" Both Doug and Benjamin asked the question simultaneously.

"I didn't medal or anything." Darryl turned around again and once more quickened his pace toward the restaurant.

Doug struggled to keep up and Benjamin lingered back so as not to leave him behind. Angling left, Darryl opened a door leading into the restaurant and kept it open so Doug and Benjamin could file through.

"I'm sure breakfast is ready by now."

"Changing the subject. Expertly done." Doug lifted an eyebrow toward Darryl as he hobbled past him.

"Look, it's just not something I like to talk about all that much." Darryl eased the door closed. "I'm just glad he decided to take his lumps and go."

"Absolutely." Benjamin nodded. "Like Mr. Tills said – thank you. You made all the difference out there."

"Yeah, well... we can talk more after breakfast." Darryl shrugged again.

The double doors leading to the kitchen pushed open and Brandi stuck her head out.

"Food's ready!"

Sheila eased out beside her. "And you all best be telling us how you sent that van on its way."

"Let me help you to one of the tables," Benjamin said, offering Doug some assistance.

Doug, for once, didn't protest, his leg throbbing with a renewed agony in the wake of the hectic activity that morning. "Thanks. I'm past due for the ibuprofen."

Darryl made his way toward the kitchen, rubbing his hands

together eagerly, leaving Doug and Benjamin alone at one of the tables.

"Can you believe that?" Doug asked, twisting around in the chair and glancing toward the kitchen. "Where did that version of Darryl come from? Have you ever seen him move like that before?"

"Nope. Your guess is as good as mine. I thought he was a lover, not a fighter, one of those hippy-dippy sixties type of fellas." Benjamin shrugged and settled into the chair across from Doug. "To be honest, I was a little worried about how he'd handle a situation like that." Benjamin leaned in closer. "Don't get me wrong, the kid is a wizard with a tool kit and one of the hardest workers I've seen, but when stuff like this happens, things can get hairy. I figured him a little too 'aww shucks' nice to be of use when that happens."

"Twenty minutes ago, I would have agreed with you about him – and called you paranoid for thinking that something like this would happen so soon. But...." Doug's voice trailed off and he turned in his seat, staring through the window at the driveway outside the building. "I'm worried that van was just the start."

Doug leaned back and ran his fingers through his hair, then looked toward the hanging chandeliers. He silently searched the ornate fixtures for answers, the beams of sunlight dancing among their uneven crystalline shards. Then the door from the kitchen thudded open and Brandi emerged, a tray in hand, smiling widely as she approached with breakfast at the ready.

---

Forks scraped across plates as the group gathered around the table polished off their breakfast. They'd prioritized freezer food first, cooking up a few links of sausage for each of them and cracking a half-dozen eggs to spread amongst them all. Brandi and Sheila had added a dash of spice and some garnish, using up some of their refrigerated reserves of orange juice to drink. Benjamin leaned back, resting his hands on his stomach and staring blankly at the empty plate.

"No seconds, Benjamin, I'm sorry." Brandi shrugged, her expression crestfallen. "We're trying to use up the refrigerated and frozen stuff just in case we have issues with our power, but we're still trying to spread it out over multiple meals."

"It's fine." Benjamin forced a narrow smile. "We've got to make this last as long as humanly possible."

"We've been so busy eating," Sheila said, leaning over her empty plate, "you haven't told us what happened with that van. I looked out the window one minute and you were talking to them and then I looked back a second later and they were speeding away like their rear ends were on fire."

The corner of Benjamin's pursed lips lifted in a half-smirk.

"What?" Brandi crossed her arms and leaned back in her chair. "What happened?"

"Our boy Darryl has a secret." Benjamin jerked his head toward him.

"It's not really a secret," Darryl replied, "it's just never come up in conversation."

"What is it?" Brandi leaned sharply forward, her elbows on the table. "You have to tell us now!"

All eyes turned toward Darryl, whose face shifted to an even deeper shade of crimson, his gaze lowering to his empty plate as he scraped his fork against its surface.

"So, there were four people in the van," Doug said, "they said they were just looking for water, but..."

"It wasn't just water they were after." Benjamin shook his head with a firm certainty.

"Yeah, I can't argue with you there." Doug exhaled and shifted in his chair, moving his left leg, wincing as he did. "When Benjamin told them the vineyard was closed, the driver argued and threw open the door and came out like he was ready to fight."

"What?" Brandi put a hand to her mouth. She and Sheila exchanged brief expressions, then swiveled their heads back toward Doug.

"Yeah. Came out like a tough guy."

"Until Darryl, of all people, sat him back down."

"Sat him back down?" A smile played at Brandi's lips, and she leaned forward once more, cocking her head.

"Throat punch." Benjamin smiled broadly. "Never thought I'd see it in real life." He lifted his chin and pointed to a tender spot just by his Adam's apple. "Right there. Bam! Came out of nowhere. Then he slammed the guy's head with the car door a couple of times and told 'em to take a hike."

"Darryl!" Brandi gasped and Darryl's face deepened an even further shade of burgundy.

"Turns out our boy is a Judo master." Benjamin nodded toward him, smile still plastered on his face.

"I'm not a Judo master," Darryl whispered, eyes averted from the conversation.

"Sorry. He's a world champion." Benjamin offered some air quotes with his hooked fingers. "Competed in the Olympics and everything."

"Get out of here." Brandi leaned back again, staring at Darryl as if she was meeting him for the first time.

"It's not that big of a deal. Really."

"It's kind of a big deal," Doug said. "It saved our bacon out there."

"You were the one holding the shotgun." Darryl waved a hand in Doug's direction.

"And he was closer than twenty feet," Doug retorted. "Goes to show how important that rule is."

"Tell me about this world championship," Brandi said, leaning forward again, ignoring the rest of the conversation.

"It's not important." Darryl shook his head and stood from

the table, gathering up the dishes. "There are more urgent things to deal with right now."

"He's right." Sheila gave him an affirming nod and stood from the table, then leaned over and started gathering up the dishes. "Come on, let's get this cleaned up then we can talk more. And I want to hear about this championship too, Darryl." She grinned at Darryl, who just kept blushing in response.

Sheila pulled the dishes together into a pile and Doug limped to his feet as well, helping her get everything gathered together. Soon all five of them were standing and following Sheila and Doug as they walked toward the kitchen, Doug moving slow and purposefully in his stiff-legged gait. Pushing through the doors into the kitchen, Sheila headed directly for the industrial sink built into the long counter and set the dishes inside. As Doug followed her, she lifted her face and focused her attention on a radio that stood on a shelf just above and to the left of the sink.

Doug moved around her and set the dishes down as she reached up and clicked on the power button releasing two speakers of hissing static. Everyone gathered around, putting dishes in the sink, working together to start washing them as Sheila tracked the station scanner knob slowly across the network of radio stations, all of which were little more than background static. Dishes clattered together as they began to wash them, then the static crackled into loosely formed, urgent words.

"— not a test. We repeat, this is the emergency broadcast network. We repeat, this is not a test."

All other voices ceased, heads twisting toward the small countertop radio.

"The United States of America is under widespread chemical attack. Multiple population centers are reporting mass casualties, and all citizens must take protective actions."

Sheila pressed her hand to her lips, her fingers stilling a trembling quiver.

"If you suspect you are in an impacted area, move to the highest floor available in your building. Seal all doors, windows and vents with plastic sheeting and tape. Turn off all external ventilation systems, do not go outside or attempt to evacuate, do not open the doors or windows for any reason. Shelter in place, above ground level if possible. Military and emergency response teams are deploying nationwide for assistance. Please follow their instructions. This message repeats."

The voice faded into silence again, the five people gathered in the kitchen all standing in shocked silence.

"This is the emergency broadcast network," the voice continued, "this is not a test. We repeat, this is the emergency broadcast net—"

Sheila reached up over the sink and snapped off the radio, the kitchen sinking into a momentary silence. Nobody talked or moved, they all just stood there, pressed together in the kitchen, embraced by the sullen silence that followed the broadcast. Benjamin was the first to make a noise, quietly clearing his throat before he turned his attention to a few of the dishes in the sink.

"Things are bad out there," he said quietly, everyone nodding in agreement.

"The power won't be coming back anytime soon." Doug crossed his arms and leaned gingerly against the nearby counter, taking some weight off his injured leg. "That seems safe to say at this point."

"I'm not sure it'll ever be back." Benjamin shook his head.

Brandi pressed a hand to his back and eased him away from the sink, taking over cleaning duties and Doug turned toward the running water. "We're on a well, so we'll be fine for water at least."

"And we've got those batteries in the barn outside." Benjamin stabbed a thumb over his shoulder. "Don't forget about those." He lowered his hand and shrugged. "One plus of this situation is I don't think we need to wait for those useless inspectors anymore.

If we get to work today, we might have those batteries installed and the circuits switched over in the next, I don't know, couple of days?"

"Count me in," Darryl said with a firm, jerking nod. "I can help however you need me to."

"They're all set up and ready to go, right? All unpackaged and everything?" Doug lifted an eyebrow.

"Yup, all ready to be hooked up." Benjamin affirmed.

Brandi looked over from the sink, her hands dusted with foaming dish soap. "I know we're rationing just to be on the safe side, but we've got a decent supply of food for everyone thanks to that big shipment that came in."

"If we get power going to the freezers all the time instead of just during the day, we'll be in much better shape." Sheila turned toward the group again. The color had left her face, and her jawline was pulled taut in worry, but her words were firm and without hesitation.

"Good. We're good, all things considered." Doug stroked his chin as he considered the words everyone was speaking, deepened lines creasing his forehead.

"What about those jerks in the van?" Benjamin gestured vaguely toward the front of the restaurant. "Not only could they come back, but there's no guarantee other people won't try the same thing. Lots of people know about this vineyard – hell, there are signs up on all the roads around here, and billboards in town. Plenty of folks will suspect we've got a cache of supplies, or just be looking to get drunk."

"And they'd be right," Brandi followed.

"Someone needs to be on lookout at all times," Darryl said. "At least one person in the main building, twenty-four-seven. If someone comes down that driveway, we need to know as soon as possible."

"That means the radios." Sheila snaked through the crowd in the kitchen. "We put them all on the chargers back at the beginning. We'll have to make sure we don't forget to charge them regularly." She looked specifically at Doug, who drew back in mock offense.

"I feel targeted."

"I'm targeting us both." Sheila smiled as she stepped out, the door thumping in her wake.

"While she's getting the radios," Doug continued, "we need to talk about slightly less pleasant matters."

"What's that?" Benjamin asked.

Doug hobbled toward the kitchen door and lifted the shotgun from the wall where he'd leaned it earlier. He held it up, scanning the others in the room.

"Weapons. If things get hairy, like Benjamin thinks they inevitably will, what's our plan for self-defense?"

"You tell us, boss," Benjamin replied. "I know you've got a couple of long guns in the safe. I've got one back at my house, too, just in case the bears got testy."

"I've never been a big gun collector." Doug shrugged, once more leaning back on the kitchen counter. "But, yes, I've got a couple of them in the safe. Ten-round magazines, which isn't much."

"We've got the paintball guns." Benjamin crossed his own arms over his broad chest. "Plenty of paintballs, too from when we had the livestock."

"I remember that," Darryl said with a soft chuckle. "We had a real coyote problem back then, but Sheila didn't feel right about killing them."

"Mmm, let's not dredge up that old argument," Doug said. "But yeah, I remember that, too. Those won't do us much good if there's an actual firefight." Doug rubbed his palm over the slope of his head. "I can't believe we're even having this conversation."

"Better believe it," Benjamin warned, "because this isn't the last conversation we'll have about this."

"You could freeze them." Darryl spoke again. "That would do

more than sting a little. You could really put a hurting on someone that way."

"What?"

"Freeze the paintballs. Make them little chunks of ice."

"What we really need," Benjamin said, turning away from Darryl, rolling his eyes exaggeratedly, "are some more rifles with thirty round magazines. Something with enough spare ammunition that we can defend ourselves against multiple enemies."

"And how do you suggest we get our hands on some of those? We're not in California, but Oregon isn't exactly a bastion of 2A."

Benjamin shrugged, though there was a pensive, bunched furrow in his brow, and he stared at something in the middle distance as if trying to solve a complicated math equation. The doors to the kitchen bumped open again and Sheila returned, carrying five walkie-talkies in her arms. She began to hand them out to each of them, each person taking one, turning it on, then clipping it onto their belt or the waistband of their pants. They decided on a common channel and did some test communications back and forth to ensure they all worked.

"Brandi, do you want to take watch for the day with me?" Sheila asked as Brandi dried her hands with a nearby dishtowel, having finished washing the dishes.

"Sure."

"We need to run some more inventory numbers." Sheila turned her attention toward Benjamin, Doug and Darryl. "There are a lot of fresh foods that need to be cooked up and either frozen or otherwise prepped for long-term storage. Those that can't be frozen raw, anyway. We'll need to make this food last as long as possible, and we don't want any of it to go bad if we can possibly help it."

"Sounds like a plan." Doug nodded his approval. "Meanwhile, Benjamin, Darryl and I will get started on the battery project."

"No offense, Mr. Tills, but..."

"Don't finish that sentence, Benjamin. Bum leg or not, I'm helping. Let's go." Doug limped toward the door as Benjamin and Darryl exchanged an eyebrow-raised look with Sheila before the pair shrugged and followed Doug out of the kitchen.

# CHAPTER 6

**The O'Brian Family**
**Los Angeles, California**

Although the man had been identified, Samantha and Jason's weapons were still held at the ready position, both of them staring intently at the man who stood just outside the military transport. Slowly, the barrel of Samantha's rifle eased downward, her gaze fixed on the man's pale, soot-colored face, and Jason's pistol followed suit. Inch-by-inch both weapons drifted down, until they were pointed at the ground where the three men in business attire were sprawled, their own blood staining the pavement beneath them. Samantha's mouth was dry, her throat parched not just with thirst but with the shock of who they had encountered.

The man eased back a bit, still scrutinizing them with a watchful glare in spite of them lowering their weapons. His face darted left, toward Samantha, then darted right again, passing between the two of them with a tentative mistrust.

"Uh..." the man cleared his throat. "Can I assume that since you have kids with you, you're *not* going to kill me?"

"You really are him, aren't you?" Samantha stepped forward, lifting an eyebrow.

The smell of smoke and spilled fuel still soured the air, the morning sun filtered through a haze of gray. It gave the city a strange, muted color, as if they were viewing reality through a thin, charcoal-colored semi-translucent sheet. The man's hair was a tangled mass, a spot of crusted blood thickening it by his left ear. Some of that blood had run across his cheek and dried there, and other spots of his face were colored dark with soot. He no longer wore a suit jacket or a tie, and his button up shirt was untucked at the waist, halfway undone, his pants thick with grime and the skin below his left knee was exposed by a torn pantleg.

"I... yes, I'm who you said I am." His voice was hoarse. "Timothy McDouglas."

Jason and Samantha exchanged another bewildered look.

"Sorry," Samantha finally said, her voice a touch softer. "It's been a very rough couple of days. Looks like you've been through the wringer, too."

McDouglas ran his fingers through his hair, wincing as his thumb brushed the section of clotted blood. He shook his head, blinking away the lingering effects of shock as he slumped backwards, resting against the rear of the transport.

"A couple of days. Has it been that long already? A couple of days?"

"Is that really the president?" Eli whispered to his father. "Should we salute or something?"

"Eli. Hush." Samantha lifted her hand.

McDouglas sank down, sitting on the rear bumper of the transport truck, leaning slightly forward, his vacant stare settling on the three men in suits spread before him. His breathing was shallow and somewhat labored, his shoulders lifting gently with each inhalation.

"Who did this, Mr. President? Did you see them?"

"Not clearly," the president replied, his voice a soft, strangled sound. "Not their faces, anyway. Red jackets." His gaze shifted into slits. "Red Jackets with a 'V' on them, only I'm not sure it was a letter, I think it might have been a Roman numeral." He lowered his head into his hands.

Samantha and Jason turned toward each other in unison. The president lifted his head from his hands and studied them both.

"You've seen them?" His lips quivered and the sections of his face not stained with soot or blood were bleached white. His voice croaked even further, squeezing through a constricted throat and his shoulders gently swayed, even though he was seated.

"We've run into young men wearing jackets like that twice now, yes." Samantha took a step toward the President and lowered into a crouch, laying her rifle on the ground as she took a close look at him.

Pressing her hand to his shoulders, she studied his face, especially his pupils. With the back of her hand, she touched his cheek, then used two fingers to press to his throat, checking for a pulse. Her head slightly tilted, she counted off the beats, still carefully studying the man's face. For his part, McDouglas took the examination with nary a sideways glance as he stared off into the distance.

"He's in shock," she said quietly, glancing sideways at Jason. "It's a miracle he's still able to verbalize anything."

"I'm okay," the president said with a firm shake of his head, though he made no attempt to shrug off her gentle grasp.

"Why don't you come with us?" She moved to the side and placed a hand under the man's left armpit, widening her stance.

Jason followed her lead and positioned himself on the other side, working with his wife to hoist the man to his unsteady feet.

"Eli, Sarah? Go make a spot on the floor in the living area of the RV. Find a pillow and blanket and set them up there. Start boiling up one of the cans of stew, too."

Eli nodded stiffly, still staring at the man with an odd expression. He took an unsteady step backwards, but Sarah grabbed him by the arm and yanked him toward her. She whispered urgently in his ear, and he nodded, both twins jogging back toward the RV and going back inside.

"Let's take this slowly, okay?" Samantha wedged herself close to the man at his left hip, pressing against him so he could use her as a crutch.

Jason cradled the small of his back with an outstretched arm, assisting his balance.

"Grab my rifle?" Samantha nodded toward the weapon that was still on the ground.

Jason released his grip on the President momentarily, lifting the rifle and clutching it with his right hand as he returned his left hand to the small of McDouglas' back. As the president limped onward, his rapidly blinking gaze drifted across the bodies of the three suited figures once more, lingering there for a handful of seconds.

"Everyone," he whispered, his head shaking. "All of them. Everyone is dead. Everyone around me, my family, the city, the whole blasted country, they're all dead!" His voice raised an octave as the words tumbled from his lips and tears glistened in his eyes, working tracks down his soot-stained face. "How did this happen? How could any of this happen?" He shook his head weakly as they all stumbled forward, his legs almost buckling beneath him.

"What did happen, Mr. President?" Samantha squeezed the man to her a bit more tightly. "What happened to *you?*"

"I don't know."

"But you survived. Somehow you survived."

"We... we came out of the convention center." There was a faraway echo to his voice, an almost silent tremble. "Those three, the ones who helped me. We came out of the convention center and saw the convoy, but we... we heard voices even before we reached it. Strange voices, a lot of them." The president lifted his right hand and wiped tears with the back of it. "Those three, I... I didn't even get their names. But they wanted to stash me away, to protect me, in case...."

"They did the right thing."

"Did they? I... but they died. Were they shot? I... I can't...."

They'd reached the RV and Samantha held the president back, nodding for Jason to go in first. He stepped ahead of them and turned, positioning himself on the stairs, reaching down and taking the president's wrists. They worked together to help him up the stairs, working in conjunction with each other to go up and inside the RV.

"Dead... they're all dead, every last one of them." His voice strangled again, and he tried to twist around and look back in the direction of the convention center.

Samantha gently pushed him forward, turning him left as she and Jason helped him navigate the narrow aisle of the RV and head back toward the living space.

"I don't even know what happened," he muttered, shaking his head, one knee wobbling to the point where it almost folded in upon itself, and Samantha maneuvered herself behind him, ensuring he'd stay upright.

"It's okay," she said, a more soothing tone in her voice. "You can finish your story later."

"Okay," McDouglas said quietly, his whole body shivering and trembling.

His nod quickly shifted into an uncertain shake as Jason and Samantha led him back toward the section of the living area. Eli and Sarah took a few steps backwards, making room, a stretch of empty floor set up with a pillow and the rumpled pile of a blanket, freshly removed from someone's bed.

"Let's get you on the floor, okay?"

"Wait - who are you? Why are you doing this to me?" The

President resisted for a moment, but Samantha and Jason gingerly overpowered him, lowering him to the ground.

"My name is Samantha O'Brian. I'm a former first sergeant in the Army and a field medic. I'm just trying to help you, okay?"

"Samantha." The president nodded unevenly, then looked at Jason. "Medic. Him too?"

"This is my husband, Jason. You're in good hands, Mr. President. Do you understand? You're safe now, I promise."

The President sat on the floor, back hunched and knees bent, resisting their efforts to fully lay him down.

"She's right," Eli said, speaking for the first time and drawing a quick shift of the President's attention. "Mom and Dad both used to be in the Army. They're good people, I promise."

"How's that beef stew, Eli?" Samantha inched around McDouglas and bunched up the pillow against the wall so he could sit partially upright.

"I'll go check." He hurried off, nearly stumbling in his haste to thread his way toward the kitchen.

"Are those your kids?" A fresh glisten of tears reflected the pale light of the RV's interior.

"They're ours, yes. Eli and Sarah. Thirteen year old twins. You're safe with us, okay?"

From the front of the RV, Kale whined as she watched the proceedings with wide, brown eyes, keeping perfectly still. "Kale," Eli whispered, "hush! Stay!"

"Dog?" The President looked at the German Shepherd, then at Samantha again.

"Also ours, yes. Her name is Kale." Samantha touched McDouglas' arm. "I really need you to lean back, or lay down. Can you do that for me?"

The president squeezed his eyes closed. More tears broke free, brimming at where his lids met before they tumbled loose, rolling in thin rivers down the contours of his face.

"Dead," the president whispered once more, his voice broken and ragged. "They're all dead."

Samantha's mouth eased open but she didn't speak. The president's eyes opened again, releasing another trickle of tears and he wiped them with the back of one hand.

"Sarah, can you grab me a bottle of water?" Samantha gestured toward one of the kitchen cabinets.

Snapping into action, Sarah launched herself forward, yanked open the cabinet and removed a bottle, cracking the lid open and returning to where the President was seated. Samantha nodded and mouthed a silent thanks, then tipped the bottle to the President's lips, her hand pushed to his back as she helped him drink some down. He coughed at first and sputtered a bit, but eventually swallowed down a few mouthfuls, his throat bobbing as he drained half of the bottle. Samantha lowered it and set it aside, pausing for a moment to let the man breathe. She pressed the back of her hand to his cheek once more, then took his pulse again, scrutinizing him closely.

"You seem to be doing a little better."

"I don't feel much better." He licked his chapped lips and grimaced, tucking his chin toward his chest.

"It's ready," Eli reported, standing at the stovetop, stirring the pot of stew.

Kale whined again from where she sat at the front of the RV, eliciting another shush from Eli. Her tail whipped rapidly across the floor, her ears lifted, and another soft, plaintive whine escaped her tightly pressed lips.

"Good girl," Samantha encouraged her, giving the dog a brief nod.

The affirming comment elicited a slightly louder, more elevated whine, but she remained seated where she was, her claws scratching at the floor as a demonstration of her impressive level of self-restraint.

"Put it in a small bowl. Even a mug if we have one." Samantha motioned toward Eli, who was already reaching into another cabinet. He pulled out a small soup bowl and began to ladle some of the stew into it, thin wisps of steam rising from the liquid. "Your pulse is a bit steadier," Samantha said, pulling her fingers from the president's throat, then she leaned in, examining his eyes. "Pupils looking a little less dilated as well. Skin's not so clammy."

"How do you feel? Anything in particular that's bothering you the most?" Jason asked, leaning in from where he was crouching a short distance away.

As Eli approached, Jason twisted around and took the bowl and spoon from his offered hands, cradling them as he inched toward the president once more.

"Tired," McDouglas replied in a whisper. "Really tired."

"Let's get some stew in you, then you need to get some sleep." Samantha propped him up with a hand to his back as Jason scooped out a steaming spoon of stew and offered it to him.

"I can feed myself." McDouglas shifted, lifting a hand as Samantha moved in closer to steady him.

Jason held in mid-feeding pose as McDouglas re-situated himself, taking the bowl in one hand and the spoon in the other. It took some effort, but he leaned over the bowl and began to spoon some of the stew into his mouth. He slurped mildly at first, testing the heat of the liquid with quiet, sucking sips, then ate more eagerly, spooning more and more stew in, chewing through the meat and vegetables, sucking it down until the bowl was empty.

He let out a languid breath and handed the bowl and spoon to Jason, his eyelids fluttering. His lips pursed again, searching for breath as Samantha backed up, lowering him toward the floor of the RV. She cradled him for a moment, easing him down until the back of his head rested against the pillow Eli had laid out. A moment later, she tucked the blanket over him and his head lolled to the side. Soft, breathy snores quickly filled the air and both

Samantha and Jason stood, stepping away from his prone form, silent stares lingering in disbelief.

"As if our lives couldn't get any stranger." Jason's head shook slowly in disbelief. "The honest-to-goodness President is lying on the floor of our RV."

Samantha scratched at the top of her head, still gaping down at the sleeping man in unfiltered bewilderment. "What," she finally whispered, turning toward Jason. "are we supposed to do now?"

---

The blanket shot upwards, yanked free of the president's once-still form as he jerked upright, mouth opened, a panicked shout caught within the tightness of his clenched throat. Kale lurched at the sudden movement, a woofing bark letting loose as the man scrambled to his feet, clawing at the nearby counter, tugging himself upright on unsteady knees.

"Where am I?" It was a ragged shout, laced with the sharp edges of anxiety, his body twisted frantically around in the living area of the RV. "What's going on?!"

Samantha was on her feet in an instant, pushing herself upright from the chair in the dining nook, hand outstretched.

"President McDouglas! It's okay! Calm down!" She crossed the threshold, strode through the kitchen and came to his side, pressing a comforting hand to his arm. "It's okay. You're safe."

His breath stabbed hard and fast as he slumped back against the counter, supporting himself with a palm pressed to its smooth edge. Bent slightly forward, he expelled a rush of air, gathered himself, then inhaled again, each frantic motion eventually slowing into a steady, smooth, rhythmic breathing. His gaze lifted, then shot left and right, color returning to the eggshell pallor of his cheeks.

"Do you remember us?" Samantha asked, keeping at arm's

length, just letting her fingers brush his shoulder. "I'm Samantha. That's Jason." She gestured toward where he sat in another chair at the dining nook. "Eli and Sarah." The twins lurked nearby, Sarah sitting in the passenger seat of the RV while Eli sat on the floor, arms wrapped around Kale's thick neck. "That's Kale."

McDouglas nodded stiffly with each spoken name. His breathing had steadied further, regulating, his back more rigid, his legs set wide and stable.

"The medic," he said quietly, his tense shoulders easing into relative relaxation. "Husband." He nodded toward Jason. "Twins. Dog." He drew in one more deep breath. "Sorry. It's been a trying day."

"It's okay," Samantha replied, "we can relate."

"I bet you can." He eyed the rifle leaning against the wall near where Samantha stood. "Have you had to use that?"

Samantha turned toward the weapon, her head shaking. "Not that one." McDouglas nodded knowingly and Samantha looked back at her son. "Is there still some stew left in that pot, Eli?"

Eli nodded and stood, releasing his grip on Kale. The dog eagerly moved forward a few paces, sniffing the air. McDouglas leaned a bit and scratched Kale on the head, and she responded with a more aggressive sideways sweep of her furry tail.

"Kale's taken a liking to you?" Samantha smiled. "That's not very common."

"Is she registered to vote? I could use all the help I can get."

Everyone chuckled, though the humor was quick to fade. Eli adjusted the dial of the stove top, reheating the stew and Sarah approached with the remainder of the bottle of water in hand.

"Here. Sit." Jason slid out of his seat and into the aisle, then took a step back, gesturing toward the place he'd been.

"Thank you." McDouglas slipped into the seat, pressing close to the table and set the water bottle down, leaning a bit back.

"How are you feeling?" Samantha asked.

"Better, I think. My brain's not so cloudy."

"You were dealing with a lot. I'm surprised you were still on your feet."

"Oh, sure, I managed to do that. Failed at everything else."

"I wouldn't assume you've failed anything, Mr. President."

"Call me Tim, please. And, yes, I certainly have failed. If the things I was being told right before everyone around me died are accurate, we're talking about the potential of millions of dead. That happened on my watch, so I'd say that constitutes a pretty significant failure."

Samantha stepped past Jason and slid into the chair across from the President. McDouglas took another drink of water and Eli set a freshly steaming bowl of stew in front of him. He dug back in, taking a few eager bites before he set the spoon in the bowl and stared across the table.

"Samantha and Jason O'Brian," he said. "Something tells me you weren't in the city on business, eh?" He gestured around at the RV and then at Eli and Sarah with his spoon.

"Nope. This was supposed to be a vacation. A relaxing drive up and down the Pacific Coast."

"Is there anything you can tell me?" He asked, leaning forward and taking another bite of the stew. "I'm in the dark on all of this. Literally. Been locked in either a closet or cowering in the back of a transport for most of it."

"The attack appears to me to be chemical in nature," Samantha replied. "We were heading up the freeway when it started and it's pure luck we managed to get up on an elevated highway, high enough in the air that we escaped the worst of it."

McDouglas nodded, focusing his attention on the stew for a moment.

"There's no indication of a ground zero." Jason continued. "I've never seen so many bodies in my life. Thousands – probably more. Very few survivors."

"How did you make it through? If what I saw of the outside of the convention center is any indication, the city has to be a parking lot."

"It's been interesting." Jason and Samantha exchanged a look. "We made a lot of progress in the old Los Angeles River basin and followed the drainage system for quite a ways. Ran into some friendly folks in one of the tent cities who helped guide us."

"Where are you trying to get to?" The President's demeanor continued to change, his back straightening, eyes brightening and voice growing stronger as he ate and drank. "Where's home?"

"It's... a long ways from here," Samantha replied. "But my parents live in Oregon. That's who we borrowed the RV from and are trying to get back to. Once we can get out of the city, that is."

"Sounds like a smart idea to me. Sorry if I got in the way of that."

"You didn't. We decided to come to the convention center since we inadvertently camped in one of the outer parking lots last night. We figured it might not be a bad idea to take a look around." Samantha leaned back in her chair.

"Still have that Army blood running in you, I'm guessing."

"You never quite lose it, even after retiring." Samantha shrugged.

"Don't let her fool you." Jason winked at his wife. "She's a medic, wilderness and emergency instructor several weeks a year. Not retired at all."

"Well, then thank you for your service. I owe you my life."

Samantha shrugged. "Nothing we wouldn't do for anyone else."

"Fair enough." McDouglas scraped the spoon against the bowl, gathering up more bits of stew and chewing them eagerly.

"Feel like telling us your story yet?" Jason crossed his arms and leaned back against the driver's seat. "You were pretty out of it when we ran into you; I'm not sure how you managed to survive when everyone else didn't. Well, except for the three guys in the suits who were shot."

"There's not too much to tell." McDouglas finished what was left in his bowl and set the spoon inside with a soft clatter, and Eli lifted it at once and carried it back to the sink without being asked. "I was at the convention. It was almost time to give my speech and I was reviewing it one final time as I was getting ready to get up on stage."

"Was there any hint at all that something was about to happen?" Samantha stood and crossed the narrow aisle of the kitchen and peered into the stew pot.

"Nope. Something happened, though, because the Secret Service suddenly appeared and ushered me into a secure storage room in the back of the convention center. It all happened so fast, I had no idea what was going on. Once they locked me in there, they gave me a mask and an oxygen tank and said something about a credible threat to the city of Los Angeles. That's what I kept hearing them say, time and time again. Credible threat, credible threat, credible threat." He scowled as he stared at the table.

"I wasn't in there very long, only a few minutes at the most, before there was all sorts of chaos outside. People running, shouts and screams, other..." his voice trailed off, the renewed color in his cheeks fading once more to pale white, and he cleared his throat. "Then the agents in the room with me died. I tried to help them, but there was nothing I could do. They died so, so fast. It took less than ten minutes before everything just went totally silent, like a tomb."

Samantha took the President's trembling hand in her own, squeezing it tight. "Deep breaths. We don't want you going into shock again."

McDouglas nodded, swallowed hard and continued speaking. "I tried to get out of the room after everything quieted down, but I couldn't. I was banging against it for... hours? Days? I'm honestly not sure. When my mask ran out of air I was sure I was going to die but I guess whatever killed everyone else in the room lost its potency." He sighed again. "I heard some noise at some point and three men – the three in those suits who were shot – pried the door open for me. They were from one of the office buildings – if it weren't for them, I would have died in there. They gave me some water and got me out of the building. When we opened that door and stepped outside..." he exhaled, looking toward the RV's ceiling. "It's a sight I'll never forget."

"It's awful out there."

"It's unspeakable."

"What happened after you got out of the building?"

"We exited near the convoy, and we decided to try and find a vehicle that was working. Bless those three – they wanted to get me somewhere safe. But... there were voices coming from nearby. I caught a quick glimpse of some men before the three told me to hide in the armored transport... said I'd be safe while they figured out if the voices were friendly or not."

"You caught a glimpse of these men, you said? The ones whose voices you'd heard?"

McDouglas nodded. "Yep. They were wearing red and white jackets. I remember they had this logo stenciled on their chest that looked like the Roman numeral five. Just a big, block-shaped 'V' right here." He tapped the chest pocket of his button-up shirt. "Like I said, though, it happened quickly. The three guys who found me basically forced me into one of the transports and told me to lock the door, then I heard shouting and gunshots. So many different gunshots, and I just... cowered inside. I just hid there while those men who'd saved my life got slaughtered."

"There was nothing you could have done," Samantha said from near the stove. "You would have been killed, or captured. I think the five-jacket thugs are part of some kind of gang." She'd scooped out a small pile of stew from the pan and ate some of it from a coffee mug as she spoke.

"She's right." Jason nodded toward her. "We ran into a couple of those groups already and they definitely have a shoot-first-ask-questions-later attitude."

"They're probably the ones who took all of the weapons from the convoy."

Samantha and Jason turned toward Sarah, who'd spoken for the first time in several minutes.

"What's that?" Samantha asked.

"You guys said something about missing weapons before. All the dead soldiers out there, none of them had their guns with them. Maybe those guys in the red jackets stole them?"

"You might be on to something." Samantha scraped the last of the stew from the mug and set it down. "If they're not done stirring up trouble, they'll want all the weapons they can get."

"Whoever they were and however it went down, I feel like I could have done something more. I should have done something more. Hiding in there while three innocent people – who saved my life – were gunned down? That'll never sit right with me."

"Not much I can say that'll make you feel less guilty." Samantha settled into the seat next to Jason. "So, it sounds like you have no idea where this all started?"

"I don't have the slightest idea. I've spent the better part of two days being locked up inside either a storage room or an armored truck. I probably know less about what's going on than you do."

Jason and Samantha sat in silence for a moment, though Jason twisted and raised his eyebrows expectantly. "You want to tell him your working theory?"

"It's not really a working theory," she replied. "Just what I've surmised based on evidence."

"Please. Tell me."

"Well, like I said before, the attacks are clearly chemical in nature, though I have no way of telling what sort of chemical was used. A nerve agent of some sort fits with how fast people died, though. Several of the dead soldiers we came across in this area were reaching for gas masks, though whatever it was, it hit hard and fast enough that they didn't even have time to put them on."

"That... tracks with what I saw in the storage room." He lowered his head and pressed his palms to his temples. "Secret Service was rambling about Los Angeles and Washington right before they all died around me. Tell me things aren't this bad in Washington, too?" His gaze lifted, hands slowly lowering.

"It's not just Los Angeles and Washington, Mr. President. We've heard snippets of radio chatter. Emergency broadcasts, things like that. It's a lot more widespread than just two cities."

"More widespread? How widespread?"

"Chicago, New York, Washington, Los Angeles... the context from the emergency broadcast indicated it was even worse than that. Major population centers everywhere have been hit."

President McDouglas pressed his eyes tightly closed, his white teeth clamping together, flexing his jaw beneath his pale flesh. His right foot tapped restlessly on the floor of the RV and his once-steady breath quickened once more.

"Is there any clue who might have done this, Mr. President? Any sort of chatter in the intelligence community?" Jason asked.

"There's been nothing," McDouglas replied in little more than a breathy whisper. "I mean, there's always something, but it hasn't been unusual. No signals or rumors that anything of this scale was going on. Whatever happened, this was clearly a significant, irredeemable intelligence breakdown at the highest levels. To not see something like this coming, that's an unforgivable failure at all stages." The president turned and stared out the window of the RV, his attention momentarily fixated on the smoke-filled skies of Los Angeles, a gray, penetrating haze painting a monochrome canvas of the city beyond.

Samantha gave Jason a quick, uncertain look, one eyebrow raised. He shrugged and shook his head, and she returned the gesture, her skepticism remaining unspoken.

"Whatever happened or whoever is behind this, our most immediate need remains getting out of the city." Jason stood from behind the table. Stepping out into the aisle, he bent slightly, looking over the front and out through the windshield.

"Mr. President?" Eli asked in a soft, tentative voice.

McDouglas twisted in his seat, tearing himself away from the remains of Los Angeles.

"Are you coming with us?"

The stoic, statuesque facade of President McDouglas' face cracked, the crevice of a smile forming in its rough, rugged surface.

"Well, I guess that depends on if I'm invited. I'm happy to get out and walk if you'd all prefer, but a ride would be nice."

"Of course. Don't be ridiculous." Samantha tussled Eli's hair, smiling at McDouglas. "You're the President of the United States. We can't leave you behind. Now, everyone buckle in. Let's get moving."

# CHAPTER 7

**CBRN Response Team**
**Denver, Colorado**

Major Sarah Hayes had seen chemical attacks before, from sarin in Syria to deadly chlorine gas in Iraq, but nothing had prepared her for downtown Denver, Colorado. Her six-person squad from the 8th Civil Support Team moved through the concrete canyon of 16th Street Mall, their boots crunching on broken glass. The normally bustling pedestrian thoroughfare was a graveyard – both of bodies, and of abandoned vehicles and scattered belongings. The Rocky Mountains loomed in the distance, their majestic silhouette obscured by thick smoke from uncontrolled fires burning in the LoDo district by Union Station while the iconic blue bear outside the nearby convention center stood sentinel over scores of fallen bodies.

Hayes checked her broad-spectrum analyzer for the hundredth time. Tech Sergeant Cooper and Lieutenant Winston flanked her, both carrying their own specialized detection equipment. Behind them, Master Sergeant Williams, their EOD expert, kept watch with Specialists Jiro and Clarkson. All six wore the latest generation of CBRN gear, but Hayes still proceeded with the epitome of caution, moving forward one slow, practiced step at a time, checking her analyzer frequently.

"Still no signs of life." Cooper's voice crackled through the comm. His hometown accent had all but vanished, replaced by clipped professionalism.

The spire of the familiar tower rose above the buildings ahead, its cream-colored stone stained by soot. A derailed light rail train blocked half the intersection and the analyzer's display flickered with numbers and symbols that she closely studied with her practiced, well-trained gaze.

"Command, this is Hayes," she keyed her radio, but only received static back in her headset. "Command, this is Major Hayes." There was still no response. Switching from long range communications to team comms, she clicked the radio again. "No response from Buckley." Standing upright, she turned in a slow, lazy circle, studying the large, towering buildings surrounding them. "Jiro. Bring that other radio up, would you? I want to see if we can get better range with that thing than we can with our personal comms."

"On it." Jiro stepped over the legs of a sprawled corpse and angled toward her, shrugging off his backpack and letting it dangle as he drew near.

Struggling a bit with its weight, he knelt in one of the few empty sections of body-strewn streets and unfastened his pack and dislodged the receiver, handing it over to Major Hayes as she approached, hand outstretched. Squinting at the radio, she held the receiver in front of her masked face, close to her filtered speaker. Static rippled from the radio, an undulating hiss of sound and she adjusted the dials, trying to find that sweet spot.

"Here, let me check." Jiro crouched alongside her, adjusting one of the channel settings and gave Hayes a nod.

"Command, this is Major Hayes, please respond."

There was nothing but the continued backdrop of static. Shaking her head within the translucent face shield, she attempted one more radio call, but once again, only static came through.

"Too many tall buildings around," Major Hayes said, handing the radio off to Jiro.

He steadily retracted the antenna and placed the radio communications gear back in the backpack, sealing the flap and shouldering the equipment again, balancing the heavy pack across both shoulders.

"Buckley wanted report-outs every ten minutes. What do you suggest, Major?"

"I suggest we do our job, Jiro. We keep moving through the city, see if we can figure out what killed millions of people."

Cooper approached, looking into her own analyzer, letting the scanner drift left-to-right, leaning in to check the screens. "Whatever it is, it didn't leave much trace."

"So we keep looking." Hayes signaled for the others to follow her and continued throughout the choked streets of Denver.

As they moved farther down Lincoln Street, their boots crunched across thicker, more denser layers of broken glass, the surrounding buildings marred with blackened storefronts, shattered windows, and doors yanked ajar. Contents from several of the small businesses they passed were torn asunder and littered the sidewalk and roadways. Plastic wrappers, crushed aluminum cans and fluttering paper coated the asphalt and pavement. The morning sun cast harsh shadows through the urban canyons, revealing a darkened, festering landscape ahead.

Bodies lay in stacks along the sidewalk and spilled into the lanes of travel. In some places, the charging riots of desperate evacuees had jumbled together into a mixed mass of arms, legs and torsos, making it impossible to tell where one corpse ended and the other began. Stopped vehicles choked both lanes, some of them having collided with each other, bumpers bent and twisted, metal compressed against metal, ragged fistfuls of buckled wreckage crunched together. Several vehicles were little more than blackened char, smoldering, charcoal skeletons where automobiles used to be, surrounding bodies fused and melted to the pavement beneath or inside, to what remained of the metal structure.

Along the right side of the street, a delivery truck had gone up in flames, melting to a congealed mass of blackened metal and liquified tires. An outward spread of burned corpses confirmed the source of the fire, nearly a dozen dead bodies reduced to little more than ashen skeletons. Hayes stopped short, head whipping to the right, a slight rustle of noise drawing her attention sharply from the carnage. Along the edge of a roof, a mass of feathery crows had gathered, lurking, waiting for the right time. Hayes held up a fist, halting the team's forward progress just as a cloud of dark birds darted forward and down, settling in a wide mass among the dead. Birds picked at burned and rotting flesh, peeled skin from tendon and bone with sharp claws, wings flapping as they feasted.

"Go on! Move!" Hayes shouted as she strode forward again, waving her arms, the crows calling their discontent as they launched themselves skyward.

A few stubborn birds remained, perched on the uneven bulge of shoulders, claws digging into bony skulls, beaks pecking hard and noisy against slack skin, taut muscle, and brittle bone. A block away the shrill call of a coyote erupted and once more Hayes signaled them all to stop with an upward clench of her fist. Her crew gathered around, halting as a pack of coyotes studied them from several feet away. A large crowd had been crossing an intersection, all dying at once, a carpet of corpses from one side of the road to the next. Coyotes waded deep within the bodies, two of them feeding hungrily while a third lifted its dark snout and peered suspiciously in their direction. Four dogs, mangy and without collars, gathered just beyond the three coyotes, one of them scattering away as it spotted the human interlopers.

Cooper cleared her throat and inched to the left, approaching the burned-out delivery truck, her multi-spectrum scanner settling on one of the nearest corpses. She stood with the scanner, playing it along the length of the dead body, but the screen showed nothing to indicate a hint of unexpected chemical or biological material.

"I'm not seeing anything yet, Major," Cooper reported, angling her face to look up toward Hayes.

"Lieutenant Winston?" Hayes turned toward Winston, who already had his scanner out and was making some adjustments as he pointed it toward a trio of bodies piled together at the curb of a nearby sidewalk.

One of them had been a mailman, slumped lifeless over a second man, his blue shirt and shorts caked with dark stains, ragged wounds on his left cheek where he'd been pecked by scavenging crows. There was another warning yelp from the nearby pack of coyotes, though Hayes ignored the creatures, tense in anticipation of Winston's report.

"Clean here, too, Major." Winston stood and shrugged. "Thirty minutes on the ground and nothing to show for it."

"Keep moving." Hayes strode forward, angling left to make her way around a crashed SUV.

The driver's side door was open, a middle-aged woman lying on the pavement, left arm extended, head tucked low, showing no sign of life. As Hayes drew closer, she leaned, examining the woman's face, her skin pale, tears of caked blood beneath her eyes and ears and a makeshift rust-colored mustache between her nose and mouth, and a reddened, crusted beard carpeting her chin. She used her own analyzer, letting it linger close to the corpse and ran it from head to toe, then back to head, muttering quietly as the screen stayed dim, its indicators normal. Wading through strewn bodies, they approached the intersection, coyotes still studying them as they drew near. Their white Level A suits stood out starkly against the gray backdrop, like astronauts hiking the surface of the moon.

"Sergeant Williams, draw your weapon. Just in case."

Williams didn't have to be told twice. He removed the Remington pump-action shotgun from its sheath and held it in two hands, one set of gloved fingers around the grip, the other resting along the pump. They approached the pack carefully, moving step by step, two of the coyotes sprinting away while another couple lingered, hackles slightly raised. The animals studied them intently, but didn't advance, huddled close to their meals, each movement of the intruders followed closely with a scrutinizing stare.

Passing through the intersection, they continued on, Master Sergeant Williams hanging back a bit, shotgun at the ready in case the coyotes decided to push their luck. Winston and Cooper stopped every few moments, running their scanners across the strewn heaps of corpses, shaking their heads softly in unison as both scanners registered nothing out of the ordinary. A burned-out Toyota was melted into the asphalt a short distance beyond the intersection, its aluminum wheels silver puddles, frozen mid-flow. Formerly unyielding pavement around the vehicle showed ripples like a frozen lake, the vehicle's interior a charred cavity, members of the CRBN team facing forward to avert looking too deeply into the remains of what was seated within.

A murder of crows watched the proceedings from power lines above, their harsh, cawing brays echoing off the storefronts of surrounding empty buildings. The birds followed the team's progress, hopping from wire to wire, some of them no doubt the same scavengers they'd chased from the bodies moments earlier. The analyzer remained silent as Cooper drew it over each cluster of victims they passed, Winston mirroring his movements on Hayes' right side. There were no indicator lights, no soft chirps, just the solemn hum of clean air surrounding city blocks of death and decay.

The team of six continued onward, navigating the terrain of corpses as they might the uneven rocks of a foreign planet. They passed a blown-out coffee shop on the right, ceiling fans still spinning lazily from within, propelled by the late morning breeze. Paper cups littered the sidewalk, small puddles of days-old coffee congealing on the rare empty sections. Inside, a half dozen bodies were visible, some of them blackened by char, the unknown source of the fire raging quick and scalding. Just outside, a businessman's briefcase lay splayed open, documents scattered across the street like autumn leaves. Not far away, a child's stuffed rabbit, pristine except for a light coating of ash, sat propped against a parking meter as if it had paid to be there.

As the team paused to run their scanners on the nearby bodies, a coyote darted from beyond a mail truck ahead, carrying something unknown in its jaws. The animal was gaunt, but moved with a clear, swift purpose, heading toward a nearby alleyway with its prize.

"We've got more over that way." Cooper stepped up alongside Major Hayes and pointed toward the next city block.

Two coyotes were working together, trying to free a part of a body from beneath a pile of others. There wasn't a hint of fear in the animals' movements, just fierce determination as they worked at the corpse, clamping its arm, tugging and pulling in unison. The six-member team stopped and stared, captivated by the grisly scene, the lack of life in the city giving the animals previously unknown courage. Williams threaded between Hayes and Jiro, shotgun in hand, taking the lead as they approached the pair of coyotes. One of them released its grip, the other shaking his head vigorously as he worked a bare, bloodied arm in his teeth. Neither coyote ran away, they just went about their business as the team made a wide arc around them, continuing to move through Denver's downtown. A short time later, they came across a city bus halfway on the sidewalk, its windshield starred with impact patterns. The driver sat in his seat, slumped over the steering wheel, passengers shoulder-to-shoulder in the seats behind him as if they'd all fallen simultaneously asleep.

Cooper hesitated by the side of the bus, running the scanner along its open door, though without registering a reading. Hayes followed her there, gingerly stepping over the outstretched arm of a dead teenager, her cell phone resting on the pavement a few inches from her hooked fingers. Taking a tentative step up the stairs leading to the bus, Cooper waved the scanner throughout, giving things a moment to register, then turned back toward Hayes, shaking her head.

"Clean. Again."

Hayes stepped back to make room for Cooper to exit, then they rejoined the group and continued onward, making their way through streets of death. As they rounded the corner, they came across a massive glass and concrete tower which rose from the corner of 19th and Broadway like a massive quartz crystal, gleaming sharply against the ashen gray backdrop of the ruined city. Modernist angles carved sharply against the organic horizon of the Rocky Mountains, its curved facade wrapped in reflective blue-green glass, which mirrored the surrounding devastation of the city.

The building's base featured a granite-clad lobby area, strewn with abandoned security posts and countless sheets of fluttering white papers. An angular crown which defined Denver's town served as a perch for more scavenging birds, a gathering of dark crows creeping along the upper level's perimeter like the creeping approach of dark storm clouds. Several windows on the lower floors were broken out, leaving dark holes in the otherwise seamless glass skin, like the missing teeth from a chrome-plated smile. Slowly they made their way past the towering structure at 1999 Broadway, moving in practiced coordination.

"Hold up!" Cooper's voice snatched in the silent air, drawing Hayes to an immediate halt, her shoulders jerking back.

As she wheeled left, Cooper's scanner emitted a distinctive chirp, its light brightening with the alert of trace indications of airborne pollutants.

"We've got something." Cooper lifted the scanner closer to her face mask, making some swift adjustments to its controls. "It's faint, but it's something."

"What is it?" Hayes strode cautiously toward Cooper, who continued studying her analyzer.

"I can't match it in our database. And the source is... it's not clear. There are traces of something, but I can't tell what and I can't tell where it's coming from."

"That's great, Coop. Real helpful." Williams lowered his shotgun and came toward them, leaning to get eyes on the meter.

"Go back to hunting coyotes, Williams, let the adults figure this out."

"That's cute, Cooper." William's voice was scratchy and metallic through the built-in speakers.

"Cut it out, both of you," Hayes snapped. "Focus up!"

"Trace elements are bit stronger over this way." Winston lifted a hand from several feet away, approaching the menacing spire of 1999 Broadway.

"Okay. Everyone partner up. Check each other's suits, make sure we're buttoned up nice and secure."

The group all fell into a circle, each individual taking up station next to their established "buddy," each of them closely examining the other's seals, air reserves and other key technical details. It took a few moments of coordination, but everyone signed off and spread out, fanning out around Major Hayes.

"Listen up! You all heard Cooper and Winston! We're getting some trace readings. It may be a false positive or we may be on to something here. We proceed with an abundance of caution, do you follow me?" Heads nodded all around, a few sets of fingers gripping their handheld scanners more tightly. "We are deviating from our planned route. Instead of continuing down Broadway, we're going to circle around to the backside of this building." She turned toward Specialist Jiro. "Any luck getting Buckley on comms?"

"Negative, Major." Jiro held out the handset, his head shaking.

"Command isn't going to like this." Williams shook his head, the shotgun held low, barrel pointing at the ground.

"They don't have to like it – it's not our fault that comms aren't working. We're following our noses, like we're trained for. Everyone on me. Let's go." Hayes spun on her booted heels and strode across the pavement, heading toward the looming tower of 1999 Broadway.

She veered right, offering silent hand-signals, which the rest of her team obeyed without question. Scattered papers fluttered beneath their footfalls, several dead bodies littered about. A few of them were broken upon the pavement, surrounded by an outward halo of broken glass. As Williams made his way around a well-dressed female, her body bent at an awkward angle, he shifted, gazing up toward the rows of windows high up the side of the skyscraper. Several of them had been broken out, dark, vacant squares standing out against the sheen of surrounding windows.

"Pretty sure this one swan dived," he said, turning slightly as he walked past.

"Have some respect, Sergeant," Hayes replied, not even looking back.

"What? Just pointing out a fact is all. Half of this gig is about observation, right?"

"Some observations you can keep to yourself." Hayes rounded the perimeter of the base of the building and made her way toward the rear.

On each side, both Cooper and Winston held up their scanners, painting the air with the readers, their screens chirping lightly, displaying a varied beacon of colored lights. Just beyond the far side of the building, cast within the shadow of the curved, glass-encased skyscraper, the Holy Ghost Church crouched in the shadow of 1999 Broadway like a defiant relic of another age. Its brick façade, darkened by decades of urban grime, stood in stark contrast to the sleek glass tower beside it. Where the skyscraper reached for the heavens with sterile precision, the church huddled close to earth, its gothic revival architecture speaking to older, darker times.

Ornate stone carvings adorned the entrance, saints and martyrs watching the street with hollow eyes. The marble inscription *CHURCH OF THE HOLY GHOST* floated above massive wooden doors, each panel carved with biblical scenes obscured by a fine layer of residue. Stained glass windows rose on either side, their colored panes casting sickly rainbows across bodies scattered on the steps. The two buildings created an architectural time capsule, the church's weathered spires and stone crosses competing with the skyscraper's clean lines and reflective surfaces. The morning sun caught both structures differently, the tower reflected it harshly, while the church's ancient stones absorbed the light, holding it like a secret. Between them, a small courtyard had become a killing field, dead bodies filling the empty spaces, limbs sprawled and entangled, a knee-high blanket of death the team made their way around.

Chirping alerts within the scanners intensified slightly, indicating higher levels of trace chemicals with each step they took toward the stone church. Cooper gingerly approached the body of a man dressed in a minister's robe, face-down, slung across the flight of stairs. Holding the scanner close to the corpses, she sidestepped to the right, paused for a moment, then swung to the left, the screen brightening sharply as she did so.

"We've got a positive trace," she reported, her voice echoing through the speaker with built-in air filter in her bunny suit.

"On the bodies?"

Winston confirmed the finding, crouching near an elderly

woman who rested prone, head lolling sideways down the same flight of stairs.

"Confirmed. Clear indications of trace elements of those same chemical agents we caught back on Broadway. A much stronger concentration here, but..."

"But what?" Major Hayes asked, checking her own scanner.

"Still too weak to do an effective cross-reference with our database. There's been enough decay in the past two days that we can't quite get a consistent picture."

"Jiro, can you check comms again? We're in a little more of a wide-open space here by the church. See if you can pick up a signal with that radio."

"On it, Major." Jiro stepped toward the street and once more lowered the backpack from his shoulders, the group slowly converging on him as he freed up the long range antenna and searched for the appropriate channel. Lifting the handset from its mount, he held it close to his facemask and verified the frequency of the radio call, using an encrypted channel back to Buckley Space Force base. "Buckley Command, please come in. This is response team Echo." Once more the attempted communication was greeted with nothing but static. "Repeat, Buckley Command, this is response team Echo, please come in."

Major Hayes shook her head, waving off Jiro. "Still not getting a clear signal out." She eyed the nearby skyscraper, looming tall and gleaming over the low-slung roof of the old, stone church. "Williams. How young are your legs feeling?"

"Excuse me, Major?"

"You're the hiker, right?"

"I like to get outside, sure." Sergeant Williams shrugged.

"Swap packs with Specialist Jiro. I need you to take his radio and get up to the top floor of that building, see if you can get a signal back to command."

"The top floor of *that* building?" Williams twisted, tilting back his head toward the rooftop levels of the nearby skyscraper.

"Yes, that building. The rest of us are going to head into the church, see if we can't dig up a stronger concentration of this crap. Meanwhile you'll get as high as you can in that skyscraper and try and get a signal out on Jiro's long-range radio."

"Why can't Jiro do it himself?" Williams jerked a nod toward the younger specialist.

"Jiro just finished his certification on the Ion Mobility Spectrometer. We need him to help do a deeper sweep of the church."

"I just think if you run into hostiles in the church, you're going to need my—"

Hayes turned toward Williams. "Sergeant, did I give you the impression that this was a debate? Remove your pack, swap it with Specialist Jiro and start climbing those stairs."

Sergeant Williams nodded curtly and wrestled one shoulder out of his backpack strap, then lowered it to the ground. Kneeling alongside it, he removed a pair of sealed pouches and set them on the ground, then handed the pack over to Jiro, who had already removed his radio pack. Jiro nodded apologetically and took Williams' pack, then shrugged it on as Williams set the pouches in a side compartment of Jiro's communications pack and lifted it, tugging it over his own broad shoulders. He picked the shotgun up again and faced the group.

"We're hoping we'll be able to maintain localized communication, but those stone walls are thick." Hayes nodded toward the church. "There's a possibility we might have an interruption in our short range comms. If so, just keep climbing as high as you can and try to get a signal out to command. Notify them of what we found and attempt to relay their communications to us, if possible. Can you do that?"

"I'm on it." Williams nodded curtly, then spun on his heels and began a stiff-legged march toward the looming tower of 1999 Broadway.

"Winston and Cooper, you're with me in the front. Jiro and Clarkson, you two bring up the rear. Jiro, are you five by five on that IMS?" Specialist Jiro gripped the spectrometer in his gloved hands and held it up. "Good. Let's go." Hayes led the team back toward the church and once more, they hesitated along the stairs, probing with their scanners, double-checking the readings from a few minutes earlier.

They scaled the short flight of steps and Hayes stood poised at the threshold, once more scanning the area around them.

"Readings are definitely higher here than anywhere else. Seems like the closer we get to the church, the taller the spikes we're seeing." Cooper held out the scanner so Hayes could see what she was seeing.

"Do you suppose this is where the chemical was released?" Winston asked, studying his own readouts. "Jiro, what are you seeing?"

"IMS is showing similar results," Jiro confirmed. "Traces of the chemical composites are much higher here than they even were about twenty feet that way." He gestured toward the nearby section of pavement where they'd entered from.

"If they released the chemical here, do you suppose they did in other churches, too? Could that be the vector they're using to launch these attacks?"

Major Hayes shook her head. "It's way too early to speculate anything like that. Let's do our jobs first. Figure out where the source is right here and then we can put together our informed opinion and communicate it up the chain." Other heads bobbed around her in unison. "Good. Let's move in." Hayes pressed her shoulder against the seam between the double doors and pushed her way in.

---

Master Sergeant Williams had stopped counting the flights ten minutes ago, but the numbers painted on the stairwell walls kept track for him. Sweat pooled inside his Level A suit, unable to evaporate, running down his back in rivulets, pooling in his boots and squelching beneath his feet. The radio gained ten pounds with each floor, the padded straps digging into his shoulders through the protective gear, dragging them into an uncomfortable arch. Ragged, uneven breathing echoed inside his mask, becoming more labored despite his regular and aggressive fitness routine.

Three years of 5AM workouts at Forward Operating Bases across Afghanistan hadn't prepared him for climbing stairs in what amounted to a personal sauna. The suit's cooling system wasn't designed for this kind of sustained exertion, and as if that wasn't bad enough, his hydration pack was running low. A droplet of sweat stung his right eye, but he couldn't wipe it away through the faceplate, and his jaw clenched, top and bottom teeth grinding together as he blinked the sweat away.

His exhalation fogged the inside of his faceplate momentarily as he rounded another bend and reached the thirty-fifth floor, emergency lighting casting everything in a sickly green glow, turning the institutional beige walls the color of scum riding the surface of the still waters of a pond. The stairwell was a snapshot of the larger evacuation itself, a dropped high heel here, a briefcase there, scattered like breadcrumbs up the concrete steps. A backpack leaned against one wall, a half-eaten sandwich spilling from its open zipper.

There had been a thick glut of dead bodies near the base of the stairs when he'd first entered the upward corridor. With each flight he climbed, the numbers had lessened, though as he curled around the corner and scaled another flight, two more bodies were slumped, heads down, one curled in a fetal position on the landing, the second strewn down a length of the stairs, one shoe missing, her purse a few steps beneath her splayed form. Shifting his shotgun to his other hand, Williams drew out his broad spectrum analyzer and scanned the woman's corpse, though the results were as clean as they'd been out on the street. He navigated around the dead woman and continued up the stairs, pushing through his stabbing breaths and pained legs.

The higher he climbed, the more the rubber seals of his suit chafed against his neck, and the fabric bunched uncomfortably behind his knees with each labored upward step. His technical manual called it "advanced polymer protective layering", but Williams called it torture. Reaching the thirty-fifth floor, he halted for a moment, letting his ragged breathing slow into a more natural rhythm. As the noise of his exhalation eased, a grinding creak of sound echoed throughout the narrow, upward stairwell. Williams clamped his lips shut and froze, turning an ear toward the stairwell he'd just ascended. The noise came again, somewhat softer, though more prolonged, a strange shifting of motion leaving traces of sound he couldn't properly identify.

Turning his head slightly, Williams clamped his teeth around the bite valve of his internal hydration system and gently sucked in a sip of water. The last time he'd checked, his water supply was down below a quarter tank, but he was leaking more fluids than he was bringing in and needed to refuel. Drawing a deep breath and shaking off the strange groaning sounds he'd heard, Williams continued to scale the steps, one at a time, grunting through the effort of hoisting the heavy pack along with him. Head lowered and legs burning with exertion, he scaled another flight and paused for another breather. Once more, the low, undulating creak emanated from within the tight confines of the stairwell, a shifting groan of motion loud enough to draw his head around, gaze scanning from within the translucent face shield. There was nothing within view aside from the scattered remains of a hasty exit.

Another corpse rested on the next landing, knees bent, lying on his right shoulder. Williams crouched next to him, examining the expensive business suit first before he finally withdrew his analyzer and began gathering data.

"That suit probably cost more than I make in a month," he

hissed through the tinny scratch of his speaker. "Whole lot of good that did you, buddy."

He ran the analyzer along the length of the dead man's body, shook his head at the negative readings, then slipped it back into its holster at his belt and returned both hands to the shotgun. Angling back up, he climbed another run of stairs, then slowed, rounding one more bend, his chest heaving, his fogged breath clearing through the climate-controlled facemask as he stared up the length of steps. At the top of the last run of stairs was a gate-like entrance, a darkened corridor continuing upward beyond it. A sign bolted to the wall to the right of the gate read *ROOF ACCESS*.

"Finally," he breathed, then continued onward, moving up the stairs two at a time until he came upon the gate.

Gripping its handle, he tried to lever it aside, but it caught, a secure lock holding the gate in place. Williams shook his head as he crouched, more closely examining the locking mechanism, then he reached around him for his backpack. As his fingers brushed the pack, he lifted his chin toward the ceiling.

"I gave Jiro my toolkit." He whispered the words incredulously to himself, the radio pack continuing to weigh down his shoulders, drawing them back painfully.

His gaze lingered on the locking mechanism, peering at it through the translucent shield. With the slightest twitch of motion, he transferred his attention from the lock itself to the shotgun resting on the landing at his feet. Smiling, he shouldered off the backpack and rested it on the other side of him, then unzippered a side pouch and removed one of the secondary sleeves he'd transferred from his pack to this one. Ripping the Velcro clasps open, he revealed a sleeve of shotgun shells, each one identified by a different colored band around the cylindrical shape of the shell.

Standard 00 buckshot provided too much risk of fragmentation in the confined space, so he thumbed through the rounds until he located the distinctive crimped end of a breaching slug. Lifting the shotgun, he ejected the chambered shell with practiced efficiency, then slipped it into the empty section of the sleeve where he removed the breaching slug. He pressed the slug into the shotgun with a solid click, then stepped back a couple of paces and angled the shotgun forty-five degrees toward the locking mechanism on the gate. Bracing himself in a wide, downward stance, he pulled the trigger, the sharp report echoing in a deafening boom throughout the stairwell.

His ears rang with the roar of the shotgun blast, but the powdered metal slug did its job, disintegrating on impact, but transferring its full kinetic energy into the lock. The mechanism burst apart, fragments of steel scattering across the concrete floor, even as the reverberating echo still rang in Williams' ears. He jacked the pump, ejecting the breaching shell casing which he placed back into a pocket on his backpack. Williams yanked the gate open and lifted the backpack over his shoulders once more, poised to advance. As the echo of the shotgun blast faded and as he strode further upward into the final section of darkened stairs, the lingering strain of the mysterious groaning sound still resonated from deeper within the stairwell.

# CHAPTER 8

**The Tills Family**
**Silverpine, Oregon**

Doug stared at the two small, white pills in his cupped hands and tilted his head back, tossing them into his opened mouth. Lifting a small bottle of water he took a brief swallow, gulping them down before he returned the water to the small fanny pack he wore. Benjamin studied the fanny pack with a single arched eyebrow, trying but failing to suppress the sardonic, crooked grin spreading across his face.

"Something funny?" Doug asked, twisting around to zip up the oversized pouch that rested along the small of his back.

"Not in the least." Benjamin wore a full-sized backpack strapped tight to his broad shoulders, though Darryl went without, relying on Benjamin to carry his supplies for him.

"I need easy access to my water and my pills. A whole big backpack seemed like overkill."

"Sheila get that for you?" Benjamin nodded toward the fanny pack, still with an upward turn of the corner of his mouth.

"That's Mrs. Tills to you, buddy." Doug couldn't help but smile himself, then bent down and lifted an old ski pole, using it to help lever him down the driveway and toward the vineyards beyond.

The bright glow of the sun warmed Doug's skin and brought out the rich tapestry of green color from the surrounding forest and plants, not to mention the rolling carpet of vibrant, emerald grass.

"It's hard to believe things are as bad as they say." Darryl peered across the wide expanse of coiling grape vines, thrusts of colorful fauna and the forests in the distance beyond. "It's just so doggone peaceful here."

"If I hadn't seen it with my own eyes on the road, I might agree with you." Doug leaned heavily on the ski pole as he hobbled after Darryl, making his way toward the nearby gravel path.

Both he and Darryl had bolt-action rifles slung to their shoulders, having removed the long guns and their respective magazines from the safe before heading out. Benjamin carried the shotgun in both hands and lingered behind, his gaze drifting slowly across the nearby driveway as if anticipating the inevitable return of the white panel van. They moved to the gravel walkway and angled left, walking around the perimeter of the vineyards and heading toward the barn where the solar batteries were being stored.

"Those batteries are pretty big and heavy," Benjamin warned from the rear of the trio, walking slow enough that even Doug was moving more quickly. "We'll need to use the tractor."

"What's the fuel status like?" Doug asked.

"I topped it off yesterday while you guys were on the road. Still plenty of diesel in the storage tank. We should be in okay shape for a little while." Benjamin walked faster, making his way around Doug and striding swiftly, closing the distance on Darryl.

As he came up alongside Darryl, he pointed toward an outbuilding near the barn to their left, a structure the size of a small, free-standing garage.

"I parked the tractor in there." He jerked his head toward it, then gestured for the others to follow.

Darryl gave Doug a tentative look over his left shoulder and Doug waved him on, using the ski pole to propel himself forward as quickly as his injured leg could muster. Wincing and favoring the injury, he half-limped and half-hopped toward the makeshift garage, reaching it as Benjamin unlocked the door and lifted it up on its rails, exposing the building's interior. As Benjamin had said, a mid-sized tractor was parked within the building, its faded green color worn by age and frequent use. Thick, knobbed tires lifted the rear of the tractor off the ground, a smaller set of equally rugged wheels mounted along the narrow front. Alongside the tractor was a wheeled cart with a squat rail that ran the perimeter of its rectangular shape.

Benjamin crawled up onto the bucket seat of the tractor and started it up, the engine snarling to immediate life, before settling into a comforting purr. He guided it out of the building, rolling over the uneven ground and parking it a short distance from the building's entrance before he killed the engine and dismounted. Together, he and Darryl lifted the hitch of the cart and maneuvered it around, securing it to the rear of the tractor with a locking mechanism.

"Is that going to be too bumpy for you, Mr. Tills?" Benjamin walked toward the tractor, nodding back in the direction of the trailer.

"It'll be fine."

Darryl folded down a ramp, then stood on the ground, offering a hand to assist Doug in climbing up into the trailer, but Doug ignored the offer and hobbled up on his own, then gripped the railing and settled into a seated position as Benjamin started the engine. Darryl folded the ramp back up into the trailer, narrowly avoiding Doug where he sat, then secured the rear gate and sat on the opposite wheel well, holding the railing as the tractor began to ease its way forward, bumping along the uneven terrain.

Doug pressed himself back against the railing, his arms slung from his side, each bump and jostle rippling a sharp stab of pain through his left leg. The ski pole rested on the base of the trailer, while Darryl sat across from him, hunched over on the wheel well, perfectly balanced. The tractor growled as Benjamin accelerated, closing on the large barn in the near distance, guiding the green farm vehicle left, so it merged from the gravel path to the stretch of mown lawn between them and the barn. They rolled up a slight incline, then pulled to a stop outside the barn door, the tractor engine elevating for a moment before it cut into rattling silence.

The old barn wore its age like a badge of honor, its weathered redwood siding having endured decades of Oregon winters. Back when the vineyard still ran sheep between the neat rows of pinot noir vines, the structure had been a chaos of bleating and wool, hay dust dancing in shafts of light that pierced through gaps in the roof slats. The eastern wall had featured a line of feeding troughs, their metal edges worn smooth by countless hungry mouths, while the western side housed neat rows of sheep pens that had filled the air with the sweet-musty scent of lanolin and straw.

The hayloft above had been a cathedral of golden bales stacked to the rafters, accessible by a ladder that listed slightly to the left, its rungs polished by generations of farmhands' boots. During lambing season, the upper level would slowly empty as winter progressed, the space growing cavernous while below, the pens filled with the tiny bodies of newborn lambs, their wobbly legs learning to navigate the straw-strewn floor.

But the sheep had been sold off three years earlier and the barn had undergone a transformation that would have likely bewildered the original builders. The feeding troughs were gone, replaced by metal racks housing rows of industrial battery banks, their LED indicators unlit and unpowered, the batteries lined up for storage purposes. The pens had been dismantled, making way for floor-to-ceiling shelving units that held spare parts for not just the solar array at the far edge of the property, but various other tools and vineyard equipment as well. The air no longer smelled of hay and animals, but of new oil, grease and the faint scent of fuel. An opened space in the center of the barn had been reserved for machinery repair, the concrete floor stained by spilled fluids.

Where hay bales once stood, neat rows of labeled bins contained everything from power inverters to backup components for complex grape picking and sorting apparatuses. The old ladder had been replaced by a sturdy steel version, clamped tightly to the loft, its treads covered in non-slip strips. For all its modernization, the barn hadn't completely surrendered its agricultural soul, though. The original hand-hewn beams still stretched overhead, their ancient wood supporting the roof as well as some concealed network cables that helped run the vineyard's wireless network. The massive sliding doors still rolled along their original track, the steel wheels singing the same deep note they had for decades. Even the traditional barn swallows hadn't abandoned their home – they'd simply adapted, building their mud nests in the eaves above the storage racks, their wings cutting through shafts of light just as they always had as they flew in and out of the structure through gaps in the upper walls.

In late morning, when the bright yellow sun painted the vineyard in gold and green, the barn stood as a bridge between eras. Its silhouette remained unchanged, a familiar landmark against the backdrop of surrounding forest, though its interior served another function entirely. The old timber frame embraced its new purpose with the same steadfast reliability it had shown for generations, proving that even in the heart of wine country, progress and tradition could coexist in harmonious balance.

Darryl stood, crossed the trailer and extended a hand, though Doug shrugged him off, instead pushing himself upright, hands pressed tight to the straight edge of the railing. Grunting, he rose to a one-legged crouch, then picked up the pole and used it to help himself stand, then hobbled toward the edge of the trailer where Darryl was already lowering the ramp to make his descent easier. Tentatively navigating the ramp, Doug allowed Darryl to help, and by the time he made it to the ground, Benjamin had already opened the barn door and was inside, silently scrutinizing the batteries where they'd been stored.

Doug limped in, leaning heavily on the ski pole and Benjamin turned toward him, waving a hand at the solar batteries. They were stacked up in the far corner of the barn, wedged like tin soldiers standing at attention, back-to-front and side-to-side.

"Figure if we use the trailer we can probably take two at a time. Ferry them across the vineyard to that outbuilding near the solar panels."

"Remind me which building that is?" Darryl said.

"Used to be the toolshed, though we moved a bunch of those tools to a few other buildings. I'd started prepping the batteries to go in there a month or so ago, but other jobs took priority while we were waiting for the inspectors to take their sweet time with the approval process."

"Is that outbuilding large enough?"

"Sure. It's about fifteen by fifteen. I'm pretty sure we measured before and figured that they'd all fit."

Doug studied the batteries, brow knitting above his penetrating stare, his right foot repeatedly tapping the ground. "They will," he finally said, "but if you remember, one of the items we were waiting for with the inspectors was their opinion on ground conduit."

Benjamin's eyebrows lifted slightly, and he nodded almost imperceptibly. "You got me there," he said. "Almost forgot about that."

"We've got about a hundred and fifty feet between that outbuilding and the panels. We'll need to run cable between the two to hook the batteries into the grid." Doug leaned heavily on the ski pole, draping both arms over it, using it to balance his weight. "And we can't just drop cable on the ground or bury it bare in the soil. Too much of a risk for it to get caught up under tires or impacted by the weather. It won't last a few months, let alone a year or more."

"Well, as far as digging goes, we've got the trencher somewhere around here. A hundred and fifty feet, we could dig that up in a few minutes."

"Most of it, anyway," Doug replied, "might need to do some clean up by hand, but the trencher will make that work a whole lot easier." He turned in a lazy circle while leaning on the pole, searching the interior of the barn. "I don't see it in here. Where is it?"

"I think I left it on the other side of the vineyard somewhere; we were using it for one of your wife's projects." Benjamin motioned to the opposite side of the property with a nudge of his head.

"Let's head on over there." Doug turned and limped back toward the trailer.

After Doug and Darryl climbed back in, Benjamin fired up the engine and accelerated, pulling away from the barn and back onto the gravel road that encircled the vineyard itself. They wound gradually around the sprawling acreage of twisting vegetation, circled to the other side, then rode along the edge, following the far pathway. Before they could pass the tasting stations, Benjamin pulled off to the side and drove along the sloping grass, taking a shortcut to get them to the outbuilding that was once their toolshed. Darryl helped Doug out of the trailer, then Benjamin dismounted and unhitched the trailer, resting it on the ground.

"You two open up that building if you would, give it a once-over, make sure it'll do the trick. I'm going to take the tractor up the path a piece, find that trencher and come right back."

"Sounds like a plan." Darryl stepped around the trailer and walked toward the outbuilding, fishing out a set of keys from his pocket and unlocking the padlock that secured the doors.

He peeled the doors open, revealing the interior of the shed, which had been mostly cleaned out as Benjamin had indicated. There was a smooth, concrete floor and plenty of wall space and Doug stood in the center of the shed, looking up and down and left and right across the space.

"What do you think? Benjamin right? You think they'll all fit?" Darryl tugged a flashlight from his thigh pocket and shined it throughout the interior.

"We already measured it before, but it wouldn't hurt to double check."

"I've got a tape. Hold this?" Darryl turned and handed the flashlight to Doug.

Darryl reached more deeply into another thigh pocket and pulled out a tape measure, then strode toward an empty section of wall, extending the tape as wide as it could go. He pressed it up against that same wall, hooked the edge into a narrow gap between boards, then drew it across, eyeing the numbers on the tape, softly whispering them to himself. Removing the tape, he then went vertical, measuring from ceiling to floor, crouching low while Doug held the flashlight on him, helping him see the small print as he lowered himself close to the concrete. Slipping the measuring tape back in his pocket, he pulled out a pad and a small pencil, then jotted down the numbers he'd just measured, slipping the pad back into his rear pocket.

"How much stuff do you have crammed in those jeans?"

"Just what I need most." Darryl grinned and shrugged, the same crooked grin that Doug had seen on Benjamin's face as they left the house. "I'm just glad I can fit it all in my pockets."

"Mhm." Doug rolled his eyes. "You best hold those comments about my fanny pack."

Darryl drew an imaginary zipper across his pursed lips as the low, undulating growl of the tractor approached once more. They stood outside as Benjamin drove the tractor toward them, the vehicle meandering over the rolling green hills. As it angled toward them, the trencher attachment on the rear came into view, a chainsaw-shaped attachment designed to dig narrow ditches in the earth at various depths. Benjamin had it slightly elevated as he transported it, a curved, metal shield held in place just above the blades. The tractor rolled down the final length of grass-covered slope, then came to a rest, the large teeth of the trencher flat matte against the emerging light of the late morning sun. Doug circled around the tractor, leaning on the pole as he approached, bending a bit to examine the trencher. Benjamin leaned back, twisting toward the rear of the tractor and gripped a control lever for the trencher, the tractor engine still idling.

"Hydraulics all set?" Doug shouted above the growling engine of the tractor.

Benjamin nodded and tapped the lever for the controls. "Ready to go! How deep are we looking to dig?"

"We need to run it through conduit, but even that'll need to go reasonably deep," Doug replied, "I think they suggest anywhere from twelve to eighteen inches. You good with that?"

Benjamin extended a thumb and steered the tractor closer, guiding it around and then parking it alongside the outbuilding, in an empty space between the building and the parking lot where the solar panels were mounted. He cut the engine and dismounted, walking forward, pacing off the distance between where he parked the tractor and the junction boxes along the exterior of the paved parking lot. Doug and Darryl stood by as he made his way back, nodding silently to himself.

"You were right on the money. Pretty close to a hundred and fifty feet." Walking around the tractor, he leaned toward the outbuilding. "We're not going to be able to get quite flush with the building, and I don't want to risk getting all up in those panels with it either." He walked to the tractor and reached alongside the seat, then removed a pair of shovels. "Sorry, we'll need a little elbow grease." He studied Doug and lifted a single eyebrow. "No offense, but I'm not sure how useful you'll be."

"Just give me one of the shovels; Darryl and I will figure it out."

"Your funeral." He handed the shovels to them, and Darryl gathered them both up before Doug could try and take one of them.

"Stand back a bit." Benjamin climbed up into the tractor, started the engine once more, then reached for the hydraulic controls.

He kicked off the PTO, which growled loudly, the blades on the chainsaw-shaped attachment starting their cranking rotation as the engine revved down momentarily in the face of the additional load. The blades moved slowly at first, following the oval shape of the trencher's track, then began moving more quickly, soon becoming a black blur as Benjamin throttled up, the engine snarling into a deafening, almost bestial roar. Benjamin twisted around and lifted up in the tractor seat, then gripped a lever to his right and slowly eased it forward, the blade of the trencher lowering inch by inch.

The whirring blades bit into the grass and dirt, the engine groaning with the newfound resistance. Blades hacked into the ground, soil spraying up into the downward angle of the lowered shield. A thick gouge ripped into the lawn, the trencher hewing through as Benjamin slowly accelerated, guiding the tractor forward. Doug and Darryl stood back as dirt sprayed and the tractor rolled forward, dragging the trencher through the ground in a straight line.

"He's pretty good at this." Darryl leaned toward Doug, lifting his chin at the rear of the tractor as it continued its straight-line path toward the nearby parking lot.

"Had plenty of practice. We never would have been able to open this place up without Benjamin on that tractor. He's a wizard with that thing and saved us a fortune not having to bring in professional contractors."

Darryl lifted one of the shovels and approached the near end of the trench, which was a few feet from the edge of the outbuilding. As Benjamin guided the tractor toward the lot with the panels, Darryl stabbed the shovel hard into the ground, working the blade back and forth to hack through grass and underlying soil. Doug limped over, still leaning heavily on his ski pole, then rested it against the outbuilding and picked up the second shovel.

"Are you sure you want to try that?" Darryl arched his eyebrows, looking up from where he'd bent over, shovel in his hands.

"I've got a twisted ankle and some bone bruises. No broken bones. I think I can manage." Doug hobbled toward the grass near where Darryl was digging and awkwardly hammered his own shovel into the hard earth.

Darryl's cautionary gaze lingered for a moment on Doug, but he eventually resumed his digging, the two men continuing the narrow, twelve-inch deep trench that Benjamin had started. By the time Benjamin ran the trencher all the way to where the panels were mounted, Darryl and Doug had extended the trench to the exterior wall of the outbuilding, though Darryl had done most of the work. Sweat streaming down his face, Doug picked up the ski pole again, then tugged his fanny pack around to the front and removed the bottle of over-the-counter pain relievers. Tapping out two pills, he downed them with another gulp of water, wincing visibly.

"I could have done that myself." Darryl watched Doug closely. "Mrs. Tills is going to be really upset if you get hurt."

"This is my place. I'm not going to stand back and watch everyone else do the work for me, bum leg or not."

"Fair enough."

"Shovel!" Benjamin held out a hand as he approached, and Darryl picked up one of the discarded shovels and jogged it over toward him.

Benjamin took it with a curt nod and walked back to where he'd parked the tractor, the trencher raised back up out of the ground at an elevated angle. With a muffled grunt, Benjamin started digging, using the trench as a starting point to extend it all the way to where the panels were, navigating more closely than the tractor would have allowed. Darryl grabbed the second shovel and sprinted over, working alongside Benjamin until the trench had been fully dug from point-to-point.

"Great work!" Doug cupped his hand to his mouth, still leaning against the outbuilding with most of his weight off of his bad leg.

Benjamin and Darryl worked together to unhitch the trencher, resting it on the grass before hooking up the three-point tow receiver back to the tractor. Once in the seat, Benjamin turned the tractor on and steered it to where they'd left the trailer, backing it up to the trailer's hitch, then all three of them lifted and dragged the trailer back in place. Benjamin tugged loose a handkerchief from one pocket and wiped the sheet of sweat from his brow, then glanced back over his shoulder toward the far end of the vineyard property.

"We got more tools in the barn?" he asked, still looking at something far away.

"There are some, I think, yeah. Why?"

"I left my favorite tool bag back at my house. Shame it's so far away, I need to think about moving it closer at some point. No offense, boss, but I like my own bed better than the guest rooms."

"No offense taken," Doug replied. "There is something to be

said about sleeping in your own bed." His voice trailed off and he sighed, looking off into the distance.

"What's eating at you?" Benjamin asked, stuffing the handkerchief back into a pocket.

"Just thinking of Samantha, Jason and the twins. Wondering how they're doing. That RV is pretty nice, but it's far from a luxury. I'm betting they're all missing their own beds right now."

"Don't dwell on it, all right? We'll get them back here. Might be as close to home as they get for a while, but better than those glorified cots in the RV." Benjamin gave Doug a gentle slap on the shoulder.

"Appreciate that, Benjamin. I hope you're right."

"Everyone in the trailer." Benjamin waved to the trailer, signaling for both Doug and Darryl to climb up inside.

After messing with the ramp once more, Darryl helped Doug in, collapsed the ramp, then climbed in himself and, moments later, the tractor was grumbling across the gravel path surrounding the vineyard, heading back toward the barn. Doug leaned back against the railing, the sprawling tangle of green vines and red and white fruit passing by as the tractor ambled along. A soft breeze blew through his trimmed hair, comforting his sweat-soaked skin. They followed the curve of the path, and soon the barn loomed before them, once more in view, the tractor nearing it.

Benjamin pulled the tractor along to the front of the barn, cut the engine, swung his leg off, then made his way to the barn door and slid it open. Once more they stood before the retooled barn interior, wooden stalls and the hayloft replaced by metal storage shelves, cabinets and racks. The batteries were where they were always kept, neatly stacked in the far left corner of the barn's interior, free of dust and hay, stacked on plastic sheeting away from where equipment maintenance typically took place.

"Darryl can you check the loft? One of those storage cabinets should have some of the cable we need to run between the panels and the batteries." Benjamin nodded toward the stainless steel ladder and Darryl did as he asked, quickly climbing up, his boots clanging on the metal steps.

Benjamin used the handkerchief again to wipe sweat from his forehead and walked out of the barn and back toward the tractor.

"Watch yourself, Mr. Tills!" He angled back from the tractor seat, shouting across the distance, and Doug listened, taking a few steps back from the opened barn door.

Benjamin started the engine of the tractor, twisted around to look behind him and began to reverse. He eased the old tractor backward, his calloused hand light on the steering wheel as the trailer's wheels crunched over the gravel. Years of working the land had taught him the exact angle needed to reverse through the barn's wide doors without so much as grazing the frame. The tractor's diesel engine grumbled low and steady, its dirty voice and occasional belch of smoke a counterpoint to the polished metal racks and relatively clean barn interior.

He killed the engine and climbed down from the cab, his knees protesting slightly as his boots hit the concrete floor. The new batteries waited in their shipping crates near the entrance, a dozen lithium iron phosphate units, each about the size of two suitcases stacked top-to-bottom. Their industrial gray casings were utilitarian rather than sleek, with heavy-duty handles on either end and warning labels clearly visible on their sides.

"Ain't exactly like loading hay bales," he muttered, examining the spec sheet attached to the first crate.

Doug limped his way toward him, grinding his teeth as he evened his stride, then leaned the ski pole against the interior wall and made a few labored steps toward where Benjamin stood.

"No use faking that you can walk. You're not in any shape to lift these bad boys. They're a few hundred pounds apiece."

"Benjamin!" A voice echoed from the former hay loft above, drawing both Doug and Benjamin's attention.

Darryl's silhouette stood alongside a row of shelves and cabinets, then slowly stepped back and turned, pressing up against a railing.

"We've got a problem."

"What kind of problem?"

"You said we had cable up here. We don't. No conduit either."

"It's gotta be up there somewhere," Benjamin called back. "We ordered it almost a month ago!"

"I don't see it."

Benjamin's gray eyebrows folded as he turned toward Doug, his thick arms crossing his broad chest. "You don't happen to remember anything coming through to the main building? A shipment of cable and conduit?"

Doug set his jaw, then gently ran his fingertips along the stubble on his chin. "I don't think so. I know we ordered it, but it's possible it hadn't come yet."

"There were some pretty significant shipping delays from that place," Darryl interjected from up on the loft, leaning over the railing. "Something about import restrictions or whatnot. It could have been caught up in some of that."

Benjamin shook his head and focused his attention once more on the batteries. "Come on down here, Darryl, and help me load these things up. We can take them two at a time, I think, and still have room for you and Doug in the trailer."

Darryl made his way toward the ladder and slowly descended. Once he reached the bottom, he approached, brushing his hands off on his pants. "If we don't have the cable and conduit, what are our options?"

"We could put the batteries in the main building, I suppose. Repurpose some of the existing wiring, just slot them into place." Benjamin crouched alongside the batteries, scratching his bearded chin.

"I'm not super comfortable with that," Doug grimaced. "I know they have safety features and all of that, but if there was a fire I'd rather it *not* be under where we're sleeping."

"Yeah and if there's any flooding for any reason, or some kind of electrical fault, that's not where we want it to happen." Benjamin began removing the protective packaging, his pocketknife making quick work of the industrial-grade cardboard and foam inserts. Each battery had mounting brackets attached and thick connection ports along one edge. They weren't much to look at, just robust, practical pieces of equipment designed for years of steady service.

Benjamin and Darryl worked together to hoist one of the batteries up, then side-step it toward the trailer, finally setting it inside and wedging it against the wheel well so it wouldn't slide around too much. Each unit weighed close to three hundred pounds and even with both men working together, the massive units nearly overwhelmed them on more than one occasion. They moved back toward the next battery in the stack and Benjamin cut away the protective covering again, then the two of them maneuvered it over to the trailer and set it in place.

"I remember when the heaviest things we moved in here were hay bales and sheep." Benjamin used his handkerchief to wipe the sweat from his face again. "At least these don't squirm on you."

The three of them shared a laugh, but the humor died somewhat quickly as they stood, staring at the batteries. "So, uh, not to beat an already dead horse, but what *are* we going to do about the cable and conduit? If there's no way to wire them up, what's the point of bringing them to that outbuilding?" Darryl used his sleeve to wipe his own sweat-soaked face.

Doug leaned heavily on his ski pole, his face contorted into a tight-lined, furrowed, thoughtful expression. "You think Greenberg's still at home?" Leaning on the pole, he glanced in Benjamin's direction.

"You mean Cliff Greenberg?"

"Yeah. Remember when we were first putting the wireless in here, we contracted with him to supply the network cables, and he even brought in some labor to help with the wiring. Only reason we didn't buy the solar panel supplies from him was because we needed a larger quantity of it."

"Oh yeah," Benjamin nodded, a look of realization softening his formerly confused expression. "Been a while since we've been out to his place."

"I can't imagine he'll have a bunch more customers clamoring for his conduit at this point. Might be worth paying him a visit, just to see what he's got. I doubt looters are trying to break into an electrical supply warehouse."

"You might be onto something there," Benjamin replied. "Hey, am I remembering right that he's by himself? His wife died like fifteen years ago and he never remarried. Don't think he's even got any kids, so he wouldn't have had anywhere to go." The more Benjamin spoke, the more assured he got until he was finally nodding in approval by the end.

Benjamin looked at Darryl and nodded. "What do you think? You and me head to Cliff's place?"

"How about you and me?" Doug interjected, gesturing between the two of them.

"I don't know, Mr. Tills. You're still a hurting unit. It might be better if you just laid low for a little while. Don't want you to hurt yourself even more."

"If we're going to get everything done that we want to get done, we'll need to multi-task." Doug stabbed a thumb in Darryl's direction. "Darryl can keep running the batteries back and forth between the barn and the outbuilding while you and I head to Greenberg's and see what he's got."

Benjamin tapped one booted foot on the hard floor as he shifted his weight from one leg to the other.

"Darryl, are you on board with that?" Doug turned toward him before Benjamin could convince him otherwise. "You'll have to use the forks on the tractor to lift them by yourself, but I figure you can manage. Just don't puncture the batteries themselves."

"Totally, I can do that. I'm down for whatever, Doug, you know that. All flexible like."

"Good. Then it's decided."

"All right." Benjamin grunted. "You and I will go to Greenberg's while Darryl keeps trucking the batteries back and forth." Benjamin nodded toward the stack of batteries that remained in their shipping sleeves. "You sure you can handle those by yourself?"

"Are you kidding?" Darryl grinned. "I'll probably be faster with the forks than with us loading and offloading them from the trailer. And I swear I won't puncture them, either."

"Fair enough." Benjamin placed his hands on his hips, then strode toward the barn door and peered outside. Sun shone through the barn door, drifting dark shadows from the surrounding trees. "It's getting pretty late already," he finally said, "what do you think about heading to the electrical store first thing in the morning?"

"I'm good with that plan."

"It's probably going to be best if we take the trailer with us." Benjamin grabbed the railing and stared down at the two batteries already stacked inside.

"Let me guess, you want to take these two batteries back out?" Doug snorted.

"Ayup. C'mon, Darryl." Benjamin and Darryl worked together to heft the batteries back out and rest them back on the stack with the others before disconnecting the trailer.

"I'm going to go grab the Jeep." Benjamin walked toward the open barn door. "If I've got permission to drive it."

"You fixed it, you can drive it," Doug replied.

Doug leaned against the ski pole as Benjamin walked across the grass and toward the gravel walkway, soon disappearing as he headed in the direction of the house.

"I'm going to park this tractor back in the garage next door."

Darryl looked at Doug as he stepped up into the tractor. "You okay here on your own?"

"I've got a bum leg," Doug replied with a crooked grin, "I'm not a child."

"Never said you were, Mr. Tills." Darryl added some extra emphasis on the final two words before climbing up onto the seat and starting the engine. Rolling forward, Darryl steered the tractor toward the small garage building, navigating it through the open door and killed the engine, then exited once more. Doug stood at the edge of the barn, still favoring his leg with the ski pole as Darryl made his way back.

"You've been a huge help, Darryl. Not just with all of this, but for a long time now. It's great having you around."

"It's all good, Mr. Tills. You all gave me a chance when nobody else would. Turns out some guy living in a van at a campground without much education or job experience doesn't attract a lot of suitors. Things were getting pretty hairy before you made me that offer."

"What were you going to do, Mr-can't-stand-to-call-me-by-my-first-name?"

Darryl shrugged. "Move to the coast, live on the beach? Start surfing? I don't know, I've never really bothered too much with structure. Still don't, except where it counts."

The Jeep's engine carried from the direction of the house, its familiar silhouette rolling down the gravel road from the parking lot, the tires kicking up dust.

"I struck you as being a slacker, didn't I?" Darryl continued, joining Doug in staring out at the direction of the Jeep.

"Not really. If I thought you were a slacker I wouldn't have offered you the job and Benjamin sure as hell wouldn't have let you stay on. You're... carefree. That doesn't mean you're a slacker. And, apparently, you're a world-class Judo champ which isn't half bad, either."

"Ah, come on, Mr. Tills, you don't have to keep bringing that up."

"Mhm. Just keep those hands ready, okay?"

Darryl grinned in spite of himself as the Jeep angled left from the gravel path and drove across the grass, heading in the direction of the barn. Benjamin hit the brakes, reversed, then navigated a three-point turn, eventually backing up toward the barn, trailer-hitch first.

Darryl stepped away from Doug and lifted a hand, positioning himself where Benjamin could see him in the rearview mirror. Waving and pointing, Darryl guided him toward the barn, inching the trailer hitch toward the trailer, until he finally showed his palm, telling Benjamin to stop. The brakes hit, tires grinding against gravel and by the time Benjamin extracted himself, Darryl had nearly lifted the trailer hitch in place all by himself. Benjamin helped him finish the job and Doug and Darryl climbed back into the trailer and the Jeep pulled them away.

Gravel spat from the spinning tires, a roiling gray and brown cloud of dust billowing in the Jeep's wake as it rolled onward toward the house. Soon it was scaling the hill, moving up and around, until it finally parked back in front of the building, the engine cutting to silence. The sun had continued to march its way toward setting while they'd been working, shadows growing thicker and darker, the green and gold fading into a muted shade of indigo. Darryl vaulted over the side of the trailer, his boots thudding down on gravel before he made his way toward the rear and lowered the ramp, helping Doug make his way down, step-by-step.

"Doing good, boss," he said affably when Doug finally reached the bottom, still heavily favoring his leg and using the ski pole for balance.

"Good timing!" Sheila stood in the opened doorway to the house, hands on hips. "We were about to call you all in for dinner!"

"Dinner? Sun hasn't even set yet."

"Well, you missed lunch. What do you want to call it? Whatever it is, you need to eat. Burning off all those calories." She stepped aside and ushered them in.

"I didn't burn off anything. I just limped around and watched a lot. Feeling pretty useless."

"Relax, Doug. You can only do so much."

The three men made their way through the hall and eventually into the large restaurant area. Sheila's hair was tied back in a practical bandana.

"You boys picked a good day to work yourselves half to death," she said. "The walk-in's starting to warm up – only having power for half the day isn't cutting it. We're going to lose those steaks soon, and the dairy's not far behind."

"Steaks? We can freeze the steaks, can't we?" Doug gripped his ski pole, putting a bit more weight on his injured leg.

"Eventually, yes. But, again, we can't expect the freezers to keep everything frozen when they don't get power but during daylight hours."

"Fair."

They made their way to what had been called "the chef's table" in better days, a broad wooden table near the kitchen where the staff had once tested new dishes and offered samples during dining events. The table was already set with mismatched plates that had once been part of various elegant place settings. Brandi pushed through the kitchen's swinging door carrying a large platter.

"We've got rib-eyes from the walk-in," she announced, setting down a plate of beautifully seared steaks, their surfaces crusty and brown. "They were meant for the spring wine-pairing menu, but they'll do better in your bellies than spoiling. Sheila found fingerling potatoes as well and roasted them with some olive oil and rosemary from the spices and herbs stocks."

Sheila ventured back into the kitchen, then emerged a moment later with another platter.

"The spring mix was starting to wilt, so we dressed it with the end of a bottle of champagne vinegar." She set down a third dish with a flourish. "The cream in the fridge wasn't going to last another day, so I made a sauce. Might as well enjoy it while we can."

The scent of peppered cream sauce mingled with the char of the steaks and the earthy smell of roasted potatoes. Through the window, they could see the last of the sunlight glinting off the solar panels in the distance. Soon the power would fade with the daylight, but for the moment, the gentle hum of the walk-in cooler provided a backdrop to their meal, along with the evening chorus of frogs from a nearby irrigation pond. Cool air drifted through an open window, carrying the rich scent of ripening grapes.

"Might not be able to save all the food," Doug said, somehow managing to pull out a chair for his wife while balancing the ski pole, "but at least those batteries we're setting up will keep the basics running after sunset." He looked at the spread before them, then at his dirty hands. "I suppose we should wash up first. Civilization might be crumbling, but I'm not letting your cooking get cold, honey."

Doug hobbled toward the kitchen with Darryl and Benjamin moving alongside him, the three of them going in and using the sinks to wash their hands. They returned a moment later to see Brandi and Sheila already seated, waiting patiently for their return. Each of them took a spot around the oversized rectangular table and began to use their utensils to carve into the seared steaks and potatoes.

"I know the portions are small, but we didn't want to dig into the meat we could freeze eventually. The due dates on these two steaks was a day or two ago, and they're not worth trying to preserve." Sheila forked a chunk of steak into her mouth, chewing eagerly.

Serrated steak knife blades bit through the meat, carving the already small sections into even smaller sections, the five of them methodically dipping meat in sauce, eating, then complementing the meat with forkfuls of potato. Conversation ceased for a few moments, the only sounds the gentle scraping of blade on plate, chewing, and the slurping sips of glasses of water. Brandi's gaze lingered on Darryl as they consumed their dinner, her attention focused on his profile. As he chewed through his fourth bite, he met her narrowed stare.

"What? I got something on my face?"

"I just can't get my head around it." Brandi said, her affable smile turning more serious as she put down her fork. "How you did what you did to that guy in the van."

"It wasn't that big a deal..."

"Yeah, it was." Brandi twisted her shoulders. "I saw it, Darryl, plain as day when I was watching out the window." Brandi's cheeks flushed with color. "You punched that guy right in the throat, Darryl. Slammed his head in the door, *twice*. You were a totally different person."

It was Darryl's turn to set down his fork, folding his hands over each other on the tabletop. "I'm not a different person," Darryl explained, his soft, typical smile firming into a straight-lined grimace.

"I wasn't insinuating that you were, just that you're normally so happy. Carefree, everything just sort of slides off your back. Then at the flip of a switch, suddenly you were... someone else."

The table fell into silence, Darryl's gaze downcast, his folded hands pressed atop each other. One finger twitched, and he placed others on top of it to keep it still.

"Brandi, let's drop the subject," Sheila said quietly, lifting a hand. "Clearly there's—"

"No. It's okay." Darryl swallowed hard. "I got into Judo during a pretty rough time in my life, honestly. I won't go into the details, but it really helped me. Gave me goals to work toward, something to focus my mental energy on. It was exactly what I needed at that time, and I'll always be grateful for that."

"How long did you do it?"

"A while. I trained rigorously. Seven days a week, nonstop. It came really naturally to me. My instructor was a seventh dan, essentially a seventh degree black belt. His family came to the United States shortly after World War II. Master Akihiko was like the father I never had at a time when I needed a father the most. He was also, let's just say, a lot more disciplined than anyone else I'd grown up around." A hint of a smile brushed Darryl's lips. "I spent a lot of time with Master Akihiko. He took me under his wing and eventually I became his prize pupil. It caused a few minor spats among his other students and a few of his peers, but he always had my back. Said there was no reason I couldn't be as great as anyone else, if I worked hard."

Darryl leaned back, stabbed his fork into a chunk of steak and dipped it into the cream sauce. Pinching the fork with his fingers, he lifted the meat slightly, his narrowed eyes fixated on it.

"He's the one who got me into competing. It wasn't my favorite aspect of Judo, at least not at first, but Master Akihiko made me understand its importance. He'd always tell me you can only push yourself so far. Eventually you have to be pushed by others, and in his mind, competition was the way to make that happen." Darryl ate his bite, then wiped his mouth with a napkin. "It took me a little bit to get a full appreciation for that, but once I did, it was off to the races."

"And you were a world champion?" Brandi leaned forward on her crossed arms.

Darryl shrugged. "Briefly. It was actually my first title defense at the World Judo Championships in Marrakesh where things went a little sideways for me."

"Marrakesh? Like...Morocco?" Brandi managed to lean forward even more.

"Morocco, yes. I didn't have a whole lot of time for sightseeing, unfortunately."

"So, what happened in Marrakesh?"

"Things started out like any other competition. It's not unusual during a world championship to go through four or five matches in a single day, each with a different opponent. They're single elimination, a bracket sort of system." Darryl scraped his fork along the plate and sighed, staring at the texture of the cream sauce pooled near the final chunk of steak. "I made it to the finals. It was a grueling trek, and I was feeling a lot more tired than I usually do. But I made it there and Master Akihiko was there to support me. As tired as I was, I was confident, too.

"The finals match was against Juba Shizuko, one of Japan's finest athletes. He'd been on the Olympic team, he already had a gold and silver medal and was one of the biggest names in the sport. If I was ever going to prove my worth as a world champion, it was against him." A smile played across Darryl's lips as his attention focused not on his plate, but on somewhere beyond, putting together the puzzle pieces of a memory. "The match started out perfectly. I was holding my own, answering his attacks, getting in a few good shots of my own. But as time went on, I could feel myself fading. I was getting tired, and it was feeling more and more like it wouldn't be my skill that beat me, but my endurance. I was outfighting Shizuko-San, but he was going to outlast me. So, I took a chance. I increased my aggression, fought harder in an effort to overcome my stamina.

"He attempted a two-handed shoulder throw, a pretty typical first volley, and there were plenty of counters. But I went for the kill, a rear throw, where you slip behind your opponent, go belly-to-back and throw them down."

"Like a suplex." Benjamin nodded.

"Like a suplex," Darryl replied. "But I was tired, over-aggressive, and I was sloppy. Shuziko-San landed wrong. He... broke his neck." Darryl cleared his throat. "*I* broke his neck."

The table fell into a shared silence, all gazes fixed on Darryl as he laced his fingers together, looking anywhere but in the eyes of those gathered around him. Darryl probed another chunk of meat with his fork, then finally stuck the tines in and lifted it to his mouth.

"In that one single moment, I paralyzed him. One over-aggressive move, one step too far in about a thirty second span of time and I ruined his life forever."

"That... can't be your fault. That's a risk of competing. Sometimes things happen." None of Brandi's exuberance remained as she set her fork down and leaned back, folding her hands in her lap.

"You're probably right, and that's what everyone told me, but I wasn't going to let it happen again. The moment I flew back home from Morocco, I gave Master Akihiko my regards and... I put that entire existence behind me. After so much fighting, I decided to embrace peace and joy wherever possible. Moved to the West coast for a little while and started living a more nomadic life. Eventually, I ended up here. End of story." Darryl shrugged and pushed his empty plate away, then lifted the glass and took a long drink.

"Can I ask you a stupid question?" Benjamin said, his voice losing a trace of its normal gruffness.

"Sure."

"Why'd you intervene? Doug had a gun, I was handling that punk decently enough. Isn't you stepping in, like, you going back to your old life somehow?"

Darryl nodded, a slow smile spreading. "Yeah, I guess. But the answer's simple, Benjamin," he replied with a shrug, "you people are my family. I can't *not* defend my family."

Benjamin's throat softly clenched, his Adam's apple bobbing up and down. Sheila's face brightened, her mouth extending into a long, slightly gapped smile, her fingers pressing to her lips. Doug nodded softly, reached over and placed a hand on Darryl's shoulder, squeezing his fingers along its contours. Brandi reached across the table and put her hands over Darryl's and nodded her silent appreciation.

"I speak for all of us when I say thank you for what you did," Sheila finally said. "I'm sure it wasn't easy for you."

"It was easier than I thought." Darryl shrugged again as Brandi gently released his hands, pulling hers back across the table. "Especially when it worked and sent them packing."

Benjamin continued to look at Darryl, gently stroking his broad, beard-littered chin, his normally hard and rigid features softened into a looser, more open expression laced with respect. "You're a good man, Darryl." Benjamin cleared his throat. "And – for the record – thank you for stepping in. Pretty sure I wouldn't have been able to handle that guy."

"Oh, I'm sure you would have figured something out. Grumped him to death, maybe?" Darryl smiled as Benjamin rolled his eyes and stood up from the table.

"Alright, smart guy. Moment's over. Let's get these dishes cleaned up, shall we? There's some more work to do to button things up before nightfall."

Everyone nodded their agreement and began gathering their dishes together, all standing as one and moving in unison toward the kitchen.

# CHAPTER 9

**The O'Brian Family**
**Los Angeles, California**

Jason flexed his fingers as they rested in his lap, his hands unaccustomed to the lack of steering wheel within the curve of his bent knuckles. Samantha sat next to him in the driver's seat, leaning over the wheel to better study the treacherous roadway ahead. Grimacing, she steered around a three-car pileup, then angled back, moving forward at a slow, but deliberate pace.

"It drives you crazy, doesn't it? Not driving."

"It's against the natural order of things." Jason fought against the urge to grind his teeth.

"I was going stir crazy, I needed something to occupy my attention."

"Well... there's plenty going on." Jason leaned forward, glancing toward the right side of the road where a gathering of crows lurked along the trailer of a delivery truck.

Wings flapped, a few heads raising, their echoing calls filling the momentary silence. A scattering of them launched into the air, hurtling upward in a flurry of spraying black feathers. Angling through another gap between stalled vehicles, Samantha grimaced as the front bumper thudded against a truck, scraping it across the street to make room for them to pass. It pushed gently sideways, then crunched against a light post where it remained as the RV continued onward. Jason grabbed the paper from the dashboard and spread it out to study, his head slightly cocked, fixated on the scrawled lines that etched its surface.

"How's it looking?"

"The magic map made by the homeless people? I'm not sure it's quite up to Rand McNally standards, but..."

"Who's Rand McNally?" A voice popped up from behind them.

Jason turned in his seat and lifted an eyebrow at Sarah, who sat in one of the kitchen seats, strapped in with a seatbelt next to Eli. Across the table from both twins sat President Timothy McDouglas, who was busy scratching Kale's head as she panted and wagged her tail happily.

"You kids never heard of Rand McNally?" the President asked. "All this time spent in an RV, and you never once looked at an atlas?"

"Is that one of those old map books?" Eli scrunched his forehead, then leaned over and pulled his phone from his pocket. "Why do we need that when we've got this?"

"Don't even bother trying to explain, Mr. President," Jason said from the front seat. "They've never known the joy of manhandling one of those huge books and frantically flipping the pages to find the closest exit on whatever highway you were on. The joy of closing the atlas on purpose and just driving, not even knowing where you were headed."

"That doesn't sound very fun to me." Eli shoved his phone back into his pocket.

President McDouglas stopped petting Kale for a moment and

Kale scowled at him, then lowered her head and shoved it into his right arm. She woofed softly, her tail darting back and forth.

"You'd think nobody patted you a day in your life." Jason shook his head as McDouglas went back to scratching Kale's ears and chin.

"I don't mind for a second," McDouglas said with a chuckle. "Reminds me of Hunter, my second dog back when I was with the senate years ago. Old Hunter got himself something of a reputation with the press corps. I swear that dog gained ten pounds during my second campaign, somehow convincing everyone he visited that he hadn't eaten in a week. The press started carrying pocketsful of dog treats with them. I almost had to issue an executive order to put that fat old hound on a diet."

"Don't tell me she reminds you of Hunter because she's fat." Samantha glanced up in the rear-view mirror. "I'm pretty sure that dog burns five thousand calories a day. We had to bump up her portions a few months ago because she was losing weight."

McDouglas ran his hands along her sides, scratching and petting her fur. "Nah, she's not fat. Just starved for attention is all, just like Hunter." He wrapped an arm around Kale's neck and squeezed gently. "I miss that dog something fierce. Back when a dog could just be a dog without being some sort of political figure." The President leaned over the table, lifting his chin in Jason's direction. "Did you say that map was given to you by homeless people?"

"It's a long story." Samantha offered a dry chuckle. "But yes. We ran into a tent city in the old Los Angeles River basin. Some surprisingly helpful people live there and made us a little map of the city. Some shortcuts, some places to avoid. We wouldn't have gotten this far without it."

She gripped the wheel more tightly in both hands and steered the RV to the right. They bumped up along a curb, scraped past a mailbox and another light pole, the RV grinding softly as they brushed past, her fingers tensing tight around the steering wheel.

"You still anxious about the damage to the RV?" Jason asked.

"My parents lent it to us in good faith. I don't want to return it all busted up."

"They're going to be so glad to see us, I don't think they'll care one bit about the state of their RV."

"I know. Still, it was – is – my dad's prized possession. They spent so many years saving up for this thing."

"You're all very fortunate to have it." McDouglas sat back a bit, looking around, absorbing his surroundings. "Bathroom, running water, the whole nine yards? Couldn't ask for more right now."

"It's been a life saver," Jason replied. "Things could have gone a lot worse without it." He leaned over and studied the fuel gauge on the dashboard. "It's a little bit of a gas guzzler, though."

"We went to Yosemite a couple of days ago," Eli said. "That was pretty fun."

"Stayed at a campground near there," Sarah said. "Lots of people had to be out in tents and stuff, but we got to lie right in here in the beds. A lot more room than in the tents."

"Maybe for you. Remember those people were setting off fireworks that first night? Kale slept with me, I barely had any room at all." Eli scowled good-naturedly and reached over the table, scratching Kale behind the ears.

"You said you were traveling the Pacific Coast Highway. How far were you planning on going?"

Jason and Samantha exchanged glances and Jason shrugged at McDouglas. "We didn't really plan that part out. Just figured we'd drive for a little while, then eventually turn around and drive back. We were playing it by ear."

"I wanted to go to Mexico," Eli said. "I've never been to Mexico."

"Mexico wasn't in the plans, buddy, we told you that."

"Besides," McDouglas said, "if you wanted to go to Mexico, I could think of some nicer places than Tijuana." He lowered his hand and leaned back again in his seat, ignoring Kale's quiet pleas for more attention.

"We'd purposefully decided to keep things open-ended," Samantha continued. "It's the first vacation we've had in a few years. Not that it's much of one anymore...."

"So, I take it your post-military careers have been a success?" McDouglas leaned forward, resting his arms on the table.

"I suppose so." Samantha still kept her attention fixed on the road ahead, navigating through obstacles as they continued through the city. "I run training exercises for wilderness survival, EMT training, stuff like that. Mostly focused on emergency medical techniques when a hospital isn't a phone call away. We just finished the latest exercise up in Oregon, where my parents live. After that was over, we grabbed their RV and headed south."

"What about you?" McDouglas nodded toward Jason.

"Logistics consultant. Work for myself. We've both been working really hard the past year, saving up some extra cash so we could take the next couple of months off. It's unusual that we have this much free time, but like Samantha said, we wanted to keep things somewhat stress free and off-schedule."

"So, you live out here somewhere? On the West coast?"

"Nope. We live in Grand Rapids," Elijah replied. "Out in Michigan."

"That's a long ways from here."

"It is," Samantha acknowledged, "but that's okay. My parents have very busy lives running their vineyard and we've got busy lives back in Michigan. We make a point to come out and visit whenever we can. It works out pretty well for everyone."

Samantha steered through a narrow intersection, pressing the RV through a gap between a passenger bus and an SUV a car length ahead. The door to the passenger bus had been accordioned open and a scatter of corpses were splayed across the pavement. The President turned, looking out through the window for a long, silent moment as they ambled past, shaking his head.

"Can't say I've been mentally prepared to see the city like this. Any city in the United States." Slowly, he faced front again. "This is what you've been seeing the past couple of days?"

"This and worse," Jason replied quickly. "Just be glad we're not forced to drive over them right now. The sounds they make... the stuff nightmares are made of."

Color drained from McDouglas' face and he cleared his throat, hooking a finger to tug gently at his collar. They continued driving along another city block, once more steering past dead bodies scattered across the nearby sidewalk and a clutch of storefronts, windows broken outward, the darkened forms of stores and businesses leaking tendrils of smoke.

"We have to stay alert," Samantha said. "Those guys in the red jackets have been in three separate locations... I don't want to run into them again."

"At least you're equipped to handle them if we do run across them. Two vets? I could be in much worse company."

"Well, I can't say as I have a whole lot of combat experience," Jason replied, still looking through the windshield. "I've mostly been on the paperwork side, though Samantha makes me keep on my toes. You never really forget your training."

They continued on in silence for a few more moments, the president finally leaning in to look at Sarah. "You've been pretty quiet. Everything okay with you?"

Sarah lifted her chin a bit. "You seem like a nice guy," she said quietly, "and Kale seems to like you."

"Well, thank you, I suppose." McDouglas chuckled. "Is that a bad thing?"

"I just feel bad," Sarah said quietly, her tentative glance darting toward the front where her parents sat.

"Feel bad? About what?"

"I think I know what's bugging her," Samantha chuckled, her eyebrows raising. "Jason and I... voted for the other guy."

Sarah nodded and McDouglas laughed loudly, leaning back in his seat. Kale whipped her head around, cocking it at angle, ears perked forward.

"Oh please!" He finally sputtered the words after his laughing had subsided. "I am a politician, it's true – you have to be to get to this point in my life, but I'm a person, too." He chuckled again, leaning forward a bit and running his fingers through his messy, dirty hair. "I'm very grateful to all of you, no matter who you voted for. And," McDouglas laughed again, "knowing that now, I *really* appreciate the fact that you haven't dumped me on the side of the road already."

"Hey now," Jason said, turning in his seat and draping his arm over the back, "the day's still young, right? No, seriously though, we get it – we all have to stick together in times like this."

"That's a fact," McDouglas replied, growing serious as he looked at each of them in turn. "Sometimes people in their political bubbles – me – can forget that. But you're exactly right. Working together is what made this country great. And it's the only thing that will help rebuild it."

"Rebuild it." Jason shook his head. "That's a scary thought."

"If the rest of the nation looks half as bad as Los Angeles...." All good humor was gone from the President's voice as he trailed off, looking out the window at the devastation surrounding them.

Up ahead, the next intersection was barricaded by a tour bus that promised drive-bys of celebrity homes. The bus had overturned in the middle of the intersection, blocking their path forward. Jason studied the paper map on the dashboard in front of him and pointed toward a side street to their right.

"If you take that street over to the next block then follow it north, I think we can maneuver around this intersection."

Samantha tapped on the gas again, steering to the right, thudding across the extended curb. The front bumper of the RV struck a trashcan and knocked it over, then transitioned onto the pavement beyond, angling around a pair of stopped vehicles. There was a ragged scraping from the left, the exterior of the vehicle crunching against the brickwork facade of the next building. Samantha grimaced as she touched the accelerator a bit more, speeding up to get to the next road. The scrape increased in volume and pitch, the RV lagging for a moment before it tore itself free and catapulted onward.

Samantha hit the brakes and swerved left, the large, cumbersome vehicle slewing slightly as it bumped a garbage truck that had been caught in traffic. They pushed past and continued north, once more pushing past a wealth of stopped vehicles, the size of the RV giving them an edge over the dozens of smaller cars and trucks. Ahead of them, a crosswalk spanned the next intersection, would-be pedestrians fanned about, arms spread, bodies twisted, a blockade of corpses separating them from the next street over.

"I would cover your ears if I were you," Samantha warned, then pressed the gas, picking up speed.

Tires tore through bone and burst limbs, the distinctive jostling crunch of rolling over bodies both familiar and sickening. McDouglas stiffened, his gaze widening as he pressed the back of his hand to his mouth.

"You get used to it," Eli spoke in a soft voice, though his complexion turned a sickly green. "Mostly."

"Sorry," Samantha whispered to Jason, "if there was any way around it—"

"You're doing great." Jason reached over and gripped his wife's forearm. "Best thing is to just keep going."

"We've got plenty of water," Samantha said, lifting her gaze momentarily to the rearview mirror to eye the trio at the kitchen table. "If anyone needs to get sick, go use the bathroom and make sure to flush."

The President lurched to his feet and pushed past Kale, stumbling out into the narrow hallway. He swayed momentarily as he navigated the aisle, then vanished into the small bathroom, sliding the door firmly closed in his wake.

"The most powerful man in the world is puking in our toilet." Jason shook his head steadily from side to side.

"This trip has turned from awful to surreal."

"Tell me about it."

Samantha paused for a beat. "Do you think he still is?"

"What?"

"The most powerful man in the world?"

"That's... a thought. Yeesh. Does anyone even know he's alive?"

"Who'd take over for him?" Samantha twisted her shoulders slightly, glancing at Jason. "I think I saw the VP's face on those signs at the convention center."

"Who knows at this point? DC got hit as well, so who knows what happened to everyone else." Samantha drove forward, the tires crunching across another section of splintered bone. "If the President barely survived by sheer luck, though, you've got to figure that a whole lot of people down the chain are dead, too."

Samantha gritted her teeth, steered left, and angled the RV back to another crossroads so she could traverse the connecting street and reach the same path they'd been traveling all along. They bumped along another section of curb until they reached the street north of the tour bus crash, then continued onward. The bathroom door slid open and McDouglas levered himself out, gripping each wall with splayed fingers as he came back out into the narrow hallway.

"Sorry," he muttered, a hand over his stomach as he managed to lope back to the kitchen and slide in past Kale and into his window seat.

"All good," Jason replied. "It's gnarly out here, to say the least."

Jason clutched the paper in his hand, drawing it closer as he squinted down at the lines sketched throughout. Samantha continued driving, the surrounding buildings falling away as the road opened up, which made navigation easier for the time being. Up ahead, a tangled cloverleaf of twisting, intersecting roads, overpasses and ramps clutched together, an indecipherable maze of angled pavement directly ahead.

"Jason?" Samantha's voice carried an upward tilt. "Which one do we take?"

"Uhhh, we've got a problem." Jason continued staring down at the paper.

"What?"

"This is as far as the map goes."

"*What?*"

"This is it." Jason spread the paper across the dashboard and tapped his finger at the top of it. "This is as far as the tent city people got us. It stops right here."

Samantha hit the brakes, the RV screeching slightly as it came to an abrupt halt in the middle of the multi-lane road heading toward the mass of interstates and highways.

"Where are we supposed to go?"

"There's an onramp over there," Jason instructed, pointing toward a raised section of pavement surprisingly empty of other vehicles. "That'll get us to the freeway over there, which I think heads north." He leaned right and gestured toward the left, at a raised section of highway that crossed over the roadway before them.

"You sure you want to take that onramp?" Samantha raised an eyebrow.

"Abso-freaking-lutely not," Jason snorted, "but we've got to figure something out."

"You don't want to take the freeway?" McDouglas pointed at the road. "It looks like a pretty short jaunt from the onramp to the northbound highway over there."

"It involves going on an overpass," Jason replied flatly. "We had a bad experience with that at the beginning of this whole adventure."

"Ahh, yes." McDouglas stood and made his way toward the front of the RV, crouching to look through the windshield. "I guess I can understand that."

Jason folded up the paper map on the dashboard, then stuffed it into one of his pockets and turned to look at Eli and Sarah. "What do you guys think? The road continues north straight ahead. We can keep going the way we're going without getting on the freeway, but I'm not sure how far this road goes."

Sarah had already pulled her phone from her pocket and had it powered on. She stared down at it, a furrowed scowl on her face.

"This thing is useless now. No satellite connection, no cell service, nothing."

"Dashboard navigation crapped the bed, too," Jason pointed out. "We've got to do this seat of our pants."

"If we keep on this road," Samantha said, "we'll end up in the San Fernando valley. Going that way should keep us moving north until we're out of the city."

"Are you sure about that?"

"About as sure as I can be."

"Then lead the way, Commander O'Brian."

"If you think I won't smack you in front of the President of the United States, think again." Samantha grinned crookedly, then started the engine once more.

McDouglas stood and back-pedaled to the kitchen, then returned to his seat, pausing momentarily to once again pay Kale some much-needed attention. The street opened up ahead, traffic thinning, most of it converging on various other transitions to the highways. Samantha accelerated, the RV picking up speed as it moved forward.

"So your parents have a vineyard in Oregon, eh?"

"Yep. A small town outside Salem. But we can take you anywhere you want to go along the way, as long as it's safe." Samantha peered at him from the reflection in the rearview mirror.

"Oregon sounds fine to me. I just need to find a way to get in touch with the government and let them know I'm alive and figure out where I can get transport back to... well, wherever the new C&C is set up. We could stop in Sacramento, if it's still standing."

"Who's the president right now?" Eli asked.

"Yeah," Sarah continued, "have they sworn someone else in?"

"Absolutely they have," McDouglas replied. "That would have been one of the first things they did once they assumed I was dead. I can't blame them for that, either. The guys who found me didn't indicate that they ran across any other survivors in the convention center."

"What happens to you?" Sarah leaned forward, her arms propped on the table. "Once you get back, I mean."

"The power will transfer back to me once they find out I'm alive; I just need to let them know where I am, and they'll come to get me."

Another twisting cloverleaf of intersecting roads emerged ahead, more sets of onramps lifting to elevated highways, a multi-lane freeway crossing above them in another overpass. Jason twisted around in his seat to face Eli and Sarah. Before he could speak, a sudden screeching of tires filled the RV's interior, the vehicle lurching to a jolting, sliding stop. It careened left as the brakes squealed, the entire vehicle lurching as if it might suddenly capsize, almost throwing Jason from his seat. Eli and Sarah gasped, pressing their palms against the edge of the table and Kale leaped from her seat, landing on the floor, tail sunk between her legs, ears flat against her head.

"Sorry!" Samantha pushed back from the steering wheel, arms locked.

The RV had taken a sharp right-hand turn to navigate the bend in the road as it passed beneath the elevated cloverleaf. Beneath the tangle of intersecting overpasses above them, another military convoy filled the lanes, a ravaged and wrecked line of armored vehicles strewn across the entire swath of pavement ahead. The convoy stretched across all lanes of the freeway underpass, the shadows of the elevated cloverleaf casting strange patterns across the wreckage. Three M35 cargo trucks formed the core of the column, their olive drab paint blackened and peeling from intense heat. The lead truck lay on its side, its front cab crushed where it had impacted the concrete barrier, the windshield imploded, remaining sections of glass starred and shattered. Dark fluid, oil or blood, or a mix of both, had leaked in a wide pool beneath it.

Between the trucks, two Humvees were positioned defensively, their doors hanging open while spent brass casings littered the ground around them, glinting dully in the filtered sunlight. A gunner still slumped over his .50 Cal mount, his helmet askew while others lay scattered behind and throughout the vehicles. Like at the convention center, several others were slumped on the pavement, reaching for protective gas masks or other hazardous materials gear that they'd been too slow to put on. Equipment lay scattered across the scene, rucksacks and communications gear mostly, though with no sign of any of the convoy's weapons. While the .50 caliber mount was intact in the roof turret of one of the Humvees, the weapon itself was missing. The air held the acrid smell of burned rubber and diesel fuel, mixed with the sour stench of death and the coppery edge of spilled blood.

The last truck in the convoy had jackknifed across the lanes, its cargo bed split open. Olive drab containers spilled across the pavement, some crushed, others intact. Yellow HAZMAT placards were visible on their sides, the numbers and symbols partially obscured by soot and settled smoke. Tattered camouflage netting hung from the vehicles like Spanish moss, swaying slightly in the hot breeze that whistled through the underpass. Broken glass glittered like kernels of quartz on a beach, littering the pavement before them in a wide cross-section surrounding the scene of the crash and ensuing violence. The president stood and stepped out into the aisle, then marched forward, standing just behind the two front seats. Looking at the remains of the convoy ahead, he shook his head and tucked his chin low, his eyes closed as he mouthed a silent prayer for the dead.

"So much for taking this route." Samantha shifted the gear into reverse, checked a back-up camera and slowly began to ease the RV backwards from the wreck.

As she inched away from the ruined convoy, a scattering of noise from the roof drew Jason's upward gaze. There was a pitter-patter of something striking above them, like a sudden shower of hail, though the overpass still shadowed their surroundings. Eli inched closer to the window, bending sharply to look outside. Thick chunks of concrete tumbled, a sudden springtime rain-storm of thick, gray stone. It struck the ground to their left and thudded loudly on the roofs of the battered convoy ahead, trails of clouded dust following along.

"Mom! Dad! There are cracks in the overpass! I think it's falling apart!"

"He's right!" Sarah swept around the table into the opposite chair and pressed her face tight to the glass. "The entire road above us is crumbling! We need to move *right now*!"

# CHAPTER 10

**The Tills Family**
**Silverpine, Oregon**

They'd purposefully saved some of the steak from the previous night and had eaten it for breakfast, accompanied with a few more fresh eggs and some of the leftover cream sauce. The sauce wasn't quite hollandaise, and they hadn't broken out the English muffins, but it had been about as close to Eggs Benedict as they were likely to get for a while and Doug relished every bite. The rich taste of the sauce still lingered on his tongue as he popped two more pain relievers into his mouth and chased them down his throat with a swallow of hot coffee. From where they stood, Doug could see the sprawling vineyard beyond the lower level parking lot, rolling fields of rich green beneath the bright shine of morning sun.

Long shadows painted the vineyard, the sun catching crystalline dew drops that transformed each grape leaf into nature's own glinting prism. The grand main building, with its carefully maintained gingerbread trim and sweeping rows of windows, stood sentinel over the rolling hills of vines that stretched toward the distant mountains. Doug's fingers were firmly hooked through the handle of his favorite coffee mug, the liquid inside still steaming, locally roasted beans that added their own aromatic complexity to the morning. His fingers were worn and weathered, decades of vineyard work had left their mark in the deep creases and callouses, but those same hands could detect the subtlest differences in soil composition or grape ripeness.

Benjamin stood beside him, showing similar signs of a life lived working the land, both men standing astride the Jeep, their faces warm under the yellow sun. Doug lingered on the gravel, his attention still focused on the endless twisting tails of grape vines. Before everything had started, the Cabernet Sauvignon had shown the first hints of veraison, small patches of purple beginning to mottle the green grapes. In another few weeks, the entire vineyard would undergo its dramatic transformation, rolling waves of deep purple replacing the uniform green. The morning air carried the sweet perfume of grape blossoms mixed with the earthy scent of the cover crops planted between the rows, nitrogen-fixing clover and drought-resistant native grasses that maintained the soil's delicate balance.

Doug leaned against the ski pole and flexed his injured left leg, moving his limb more easily than he had the previous day. His knee bent freely, his lower leg swinging out, holding its outward extension, then flexing back once more. Each movement came smoother and with less pain than the previous day and Sheila watched him move, her gardening gloves clenched in a bunch of fabric within one hand. Brandi and Sheila had both already donned their wide-brimmed gardening hats, protection against the Oregon sun that would soon enough turn fierce. Above them, a pair of red-tailed hawks rode the morning thermals, their lazy circles drawing ever-higher as the warming air created invisible elevators to the sky. From somewhere in the old oak grove beyond the last row of vines, a California quail called its distinctive morning greeting.

The fog that had blanketed the valley floor at dawn was retreating to the distant hills, burning off in wispy tendrils that caught the strengthening sunlight. The day's future was unknown, but for the moment, the air held onto its morning crispness, carrying the complex bouquet of soil, vine, flower and a touch of freshly brewed coffee. Doug checked his watch, the keys to his truck jingling in his pocket. Benjamin swallowed down his last gulp of coffee, then he and Doug set their mugs down on the stoop outside the front door and made their way back to the Jeep.

"And you're sure about this?" Sheila asked. "You think Cliff will help you? Do you think he's even still there?"

"I don't think he's got anywhere else to go," Doug replied, limping mildly toward the passenger side of the Jeep. He used the ski pole less, purposefully walking without it, unless an unexpected shooting pain forced him to rely on it.

"Shouldn't Darryl go instead of you?" Sheila nodded to Darryl, who stood in the shadows of the main vineyard building, his arms crossed.

"I can do that. Whatever's best." Darryl took a step forward, but Doug held out his hand.

"It's like we said yesterday, we need someone here to move those batteries. I'm going to be much more capable of sweet-talking Cliff than I will be getting off and on the tractor nonstop while working with those batteries."

"You think so?" Sheila lifted one eyebrow. "Sweet talking has never been one of your strong suits."

"I sweet-talked you well enough." Doug flashed her a wink and Sheila's cheeks brushed pink.

"Darryl's also better equipped to defend the place if he needs to," Benjamin said, his gaze darting toward Doug. "No offense."

"None taken. Besides, the conduit isn't very heavy. We'll manage that job just fine. Everyone needs to do their part, and this is mine."

Sheila walked toward Doug, cupped his face in her hands and gave him a kiss on the corner of his mouth. "Stay safe. The roads are—"

"I know," Doug replied in gentle interruption.

"Those batteries aren't going to do us a bit of good if we can't get our hands on some cable and conduit to connect them to the panels. Quicker we get to Greenbergs, the quicker we'll be back." Benjamin eased the door open.

"You could just say 'hurry your butt up' instead, you know." Doug smirked.

"Yeah, well, I'm trying not to be *too* disrespectful, Mr. Tills." Benjamin paused for a second. "But, yeah. Hurry your butt up."

The women's garden cart was already loaded with morning tools like pruning shears, twine, harvest baskets, plus a number of smaller trowels and other odds and ends. A distant wind chime caught a breath of morning breeze, its deep tones carrying across the property like meditation bells. Sheila turned in the direction of the methodical chime, the conversation falling silent as the sound of morning carried through. Doug's fingers gripped the ski pole as he stood next to the Jeep, slowly opening the passenger side door. Stillness froze the air, the gentle morning breeze easing into soft nothing. Barely controlled chaos normally swarmed the vineyards at that hour of the morning, a converged combination of customers and employees, a flurry of restless activity that propelled them toward afternoon and into evening. That morning, the world was preternaturally still and quiet, only the soft and faded interruption of birdsong to remind Doug that life still carried on.

He stepped into the passenger's side of the Jeep and dragged the ski pole with him, twisting around to put it in back. Benjamin hammered his own door closed, perched behind the steering wheel, gripping it firmly with both hands. Doug shut his own door but rolled down his window and leaned out.

"You seem to be moving a little better at least." Sheila nodded toward the rear of the Jeep where Doug had placed the ski pole. "Don't need that thing quite so much."

"I'm doing better. Still limping, but I think I'm already on the mend. Good thing, too; last thing we want is to deal with a major injury right now."

Benjamin started the engine and gunned the accelerator gently, turning one ear toward the sound. He'd given the Jeep another once-over that morning, checking its fluids and tire pressure, once again gathering some spare fuel in the jerry cans in back.

"We'll be back." He nodded toward Sheila as the Jeep accelerated, making a wide turn as it navigated with the trailer they'd hitched to the rear.

Moments later, the Jeep was heading up the gravel driveway, throwing clouds of billowing dust in its wake, tires spitting small bits of gravel and then both the sight and the sound of the vehicle were gone, leaving Sheila, Brandi and Darryl in silence.

"Looks like you ladies have a plan?" Darryl took a few steps toward them, studying the cart that was loaded with gardening supplies.

"We sure do," Sheila replied. "There's a spot on the other side of the house where we want to set up a garden. We've got a decent supply of food inside, which will be even better once we can run those freezers full-time, but that food won't last forever. We'll need to grow our own, too."

"Sounds like a fine idea." He eyed the house near the front entrance where a double-barrel shotgun rested against the exterior wall. "Benjamin and Doug took the other shotty, I didn't realize there was a second one."

"To be honest, we almost forgot about it. Doug and I were looking for a few of the long guns and came across it downstairs. I think it's been in Doug's family for a while, but probably best if you carry it with you just in case." She lifted the shotgun from where it leaned and handed it to Darryl, who took it and gripped it in two hands.

"Where we're working on this garden," Sheila continued, "we'll have a full view of the road." She patted the radio hooked to her belt. "These are all charged and ready to go so we'll give you a shout if we see anything. You can focus on moving those batteries and we'll keep on eye on things up here."

"Are you sure about that?" Darryl turned toward the driveway and shielded his eyes.

"We're sure. We can handle watch duty okay, can't we, Brandi?"

"We did fine yesterday." Brandi affirmed.

"All right, if you say so. I'm going to get that tractor started up and find the pallet forks wherever Benjamin left them last."

"Take as long as you need. I'm betting Doug and Benjamin will be gone for a while."

Darryl tipped a non-existent cap to the women and began to walk down the slope leading to the lower parking lot.

"All things considered, we're pretty fortunate out here." Sheila gave Brandi a gentle pat on the back, then turned and made her way back toward the front door of the house.

Brandi followed as Sheila hesitated for a moment, then stared down at the empty coffee mugs resting near the front stoop.

"Those boys, I swear. I'll be picking up after them until the day I die." She bent over and hooked her fingers through the handles of the mugs, then stood, both of them going inside.

After a quick pit stop to the kitchen to deposit the mugs, Sheila made her way toward a set of stairs leading down to the lower level, the basement area where the loading dock and food storage section of the restaurant was.

"I have a confession to make," Brandi said as they neared the top of the stairs.

Sheila held at the first step, turning back toward her. "What's that?"

"I've never really gardened before."

Sheila laughed. "You're about to get a crash course. Come on down to the basement with me, rookie." Sheila descended the stairs quickly, almost jogging down them with Brandi clinging close to her heels.

The wide concrete stairs led down into the vineyard's basement, each step worn smooth from decades of use. At the bottom, Sheila flipped a nearby light switch, industrial lighting casting a bright, clean glow across the space, which stretched the full footprint of the house above. The air held the complex scents of wine storage mixed with produce and the earthiness of stored root vegetables. To the left, the loading dock's heavy steel door was flanked by commercial refrigerators, their motors humming steadily. Prep tables lined the wall, immaculate stainless steel ready for restaurant deliveries that would no longer arrive. Boxes of produce sat staged nearby - local lettuce, heirloom tomatoes, and seasonal vegetables awaiting their journey upstairs. Several of the boxes were without their lids, Sheila and Brandi using as many of the vegetables as they possibly could before they spoiled.

"Refrigerators are on again," Brandi said, taking a few steps toward the nearby unit encased in stainless steel.

She pressed her palm to the door, the low, undulating hum vibrating against her skin.

"Best we keep them closed as much as we possibly can. I can't wait for them to get those batteries installed; having power twenty-four hours a day will change our lives for the better."

The center of the basement housed both the vineyard's and Tills family's extensive storage. Floor-to-ceiling metal shelving units created narrow aisles, each section meticulously organized. Cases of water, tomato sauce, condiments and other restaurant supplies were stacked and organized neatly along the various shelves, marked with alphabetical labels. A section of spices nearby filled the air with a potpourri of rosemary, sage and lavender. Sheila led Brandi toward the far right corner where several plastic totes were stacked neatly against a far wall, bins protecting different varieties of seeds, each labeled with Sheila's precise handwriting. Stacks of terra cotta pots stood ready for transplanting, while bags of specialty soil and organic fertilizers were neatly arranged on even more heavy-duty shelves. Garden tools hung from a pegboard wall, their handles worn smooth from years of use.

In another back corner of the basement, a climate-controlled wine room stood out against the more rustic backdrop, its glass walls revealing rows of family vintages dating back decades. The sealed environment kept the temperature and humidity perfect for long-term storage, the bottles resting in custom-built racks that showed off their distinctive Tills Winery & Vineyard labels. The floor sloped subtly toward central drains, the polished concrete bearing scuff marks from countless dollies and hand trucks. Despite being beneath the main building, the space was open and welcoming, a working testament to the family's dedication to both their vineyard and their restaurant.

"Let's grab some of these seeds first." Sheila gestured toward the stacked plastic bins and Brandi nodded, trailing along behind her.

Hooking her fingers into recessed handles in the bin's lid, she eased the top off, revealing neat rows of packaged seeds inside, stacked side-by-side, dozens of boxes of varying types of plant, fruit, and vegetable. Sheila and Brandi worked together, lifting the entire bin and carrying it in clumsy unison through the storage room and back out to the loading dock area. They set the bin down just inside the door, then Sheila unlatched the door from the inside and eased it open, revealing the bright shock of morning color just outside.

"Oh good, it's still here." The side-by-side utility vehicle remained parked in the grass just outside the loading dock door where it had been left earlier. "If it wasn't here, I wasn't sure where we'd find it. We'd be radioing Darryl already for help and we don't want that."

"We're strong, independent women!" Brandi exclaimed with a mocking pump of her fist.

"Darn right." Sheila chuckled and slapped her lightly on the back of her shoulder, giving her a wink. "That, and I want those batteries hooked up sooner rather than later."

With the door open, the drifting scent of various flowers and ripening grapes filled the basement interior, the organic smells contrasting sharply with the concrete and stainless steel that made up the floor and lined storage shelves. Sheila crouched and unhooked the lid from the plastic bin, lifting it off to expose the boxes of various seeds contained within. Filing through the boxes, she lifted a few out, turned them over in her hands, then placed them in the rear bed of the side-by-side. Removing several of the seed pouches from the boxes, she returned the rest to the bin, then she and Brandi hoisted the tote and moved it back to the rear corner, setting it in the darkened shadows where they'd picked it up.

Walking to the pegboard, Sheila lifted off a pair of hoes and nodded toward a pair of shovels that Brandi retrieved, the two women carrying the gardening implements back toward the side-by-side. As they set them in the rear bed of the utility vehicle, Sheila's radio crackled with static, the faint sound of Darryl's voice coming through the tinny speaker.

"You there, Mrs. Tills?"

"Darryl?" Sheila lifted the radio to her mouth. "What's up?"

"I'm keeping an eye on the road while you're loading that utility vehicle. Coast is clear so far, just wanted to be sure you knew."

Sheila silently shook her head. "Thanks for looking out for us, Darryl. I didn't think about that while we were down here in the basement."

"It's no problem. We're not exactly professionals at this."

They exchanged a few farewell pleasantries and clicked the radios off, Sheila hooking hers back on her belt.

"Rookie mistake."

"To be fair, we *are* rookies." Brandi shrugged. "Even us powerful, independent women can make mistakes sometimes."

Sheila chuckled. "Let's keep getting this thing loaded. Grab some of those stakes and some of that pink ribbon. We've got twine in the cart up near the front door, but that ribbon would be useful." Sheila circled around Brandi, who was loading the supplies into an empty crate and made her way toward a small, wheeled device with a long, chrome handle.

She tipped the handle down, tilting the gas-powered tiller up on two wheels, then dragged it behind her as she marched in Brandi's wake, both of them heading back toward the UTV.

"Help me lift this in?" Sheila gestured toward the gas-powered tiller as Brandi set the crate of ribbon and other supplies into the rear of the vehicle.

Together, they both bent low and hoisted it up, keeping it upright as they levered it into the rear of the utility vehicle, wedging it against one side. Sheila walked around the other side of the vehicle and opened a metal storage compartment just behind the front seats, then removed a ratchet strap, coming back around so she could secure the tiller to the vehicle's rear without risk of it tipping over. She wrapped the thick, canvas strap around the tiller, secured it to a few mount points on the side-by-side's exterior, then ratcheted it tight, locking the upright tiller in place.

"Let's run up and grab that cart." Sheila stepped up behind the steering wheel of the side-by-side and started it up as Brandi made her way into the passenger seat.

Driving forward, Sheila steered left, bringing the vehicle around and toward the nearby parking lot, which she crossed and eventually climbed the gradual slope heading toward the front of the house. She pulled up alongside the abandoned cart and tapped the brakes, halting the utility vehicle just ahead of where the cart sat. Hopping quickly out of the seat, she grabbed the handle of the cart, folded it down and hooked it onto a trailer hitch, tugging on it to make sure it stayed securely fastened. She double-checked all of the supplies inside the cart, then turned and compared them to what she'd loaded in the side-by-side and nodded, satisfied, as she returned to the driver's seat. Starting the engine once more, she drove around the front of the house, then pulled along a section of grass on the other side, separating the main building itself from an outward section of sprawling forest.

"Let's start off with some of those stakes. Can you grab a handful for me?"

Brandi reached into the rear of the side-by-side and pulled out a handful of stakes, walking them over to Sheila and handing them to her. Sheila tucked the stakes under her arm and shielded her eyes with the blade of her hand, searching the long stretch of grass that extended before them.

"Grab that roll of twine, would you? I'm going to start planting these stakes. I want you to tie them together with that twine; we're going to section off a big area here."

Brandi nodded and obediently retrieved the twine as Sheila paced off several feet, stopping every few moments to push a stake into the ground. She had Brandi run back to the vehicle and grab more stakes as she ran out, carefully measuring each stride until she'd reached a hundred feet from end-to-end. She pushed one final stake into the grass, then turned toward Brandi, only to see she was already heading back at a jog, more stakes bundled in her arms. Sheila paced off another thirty feet, one step at a time, staking the grass every two yards or so. After hitting the other corner, she turned left again and paced off another hundred feet, mirroring her stake placement from the other side until she closed in the rectangle, measuring approximately three thousand square feet for planting.

"This is it!" She stood in the center of the roped-off area and spread her arms wide. "This is going to be our garden. We've got a couple of months of good growing season left and we need to make the most of it." She lowered her arms and strode back toward the side-by-side. "We pulled out some cucumber seeds, carrots, lettuce, arugula, beets, a bunch more."

She reached the utility vehicle and made her way around to the left side for a better angle on the gas-powered tiller. Grabbing the ratchet, she pushed it back and forth, loosening the grip of the straps and by the time she freed them, Brandi had arrived, the two of them hoisting the heavy tiller together and setting it down on the grass-covered ground. Sheila wiped sweat from her forehead and planted one fist on her left hip, staring down at the machine.

"This is usually Benjamin and Doug's job. We'll see how this goes." She approached the tiller, opened the gas cap, then used its attached stick to check the level of the fuel that was inside.

"You mind grabbing a jerry can from the utility room?" Sheila gestured toward a single side door. "I think we've got a few in there that already have some gas in them. Benjamin didn't steal them all when he took off in the Jeep."

"Sure!" Brandi replied cheerfully and strode to the side door, opening it up and entering the utility room.

Sheila leaned back the tiller on two wheels, then pushed it forward, rolling it across the grass and to the edge of the garden. Untying the twine for a moment, she pushed the tiller through and left the twine untied so she could pull it back out again afterwards. With a grunt, she muscled the tiller up and over to the near corner of the roped-off rectangle, then positioned it so it was facing the far end of the garden's perimeter. The tiller was more or less a beefy 2-stroke engine mounted above a horizontal shield which sat perched above a trio of thick blades designed to dig through grass and dirt, churning it up to prepare it for planting. Her experience with one had been limited to watching Doug operate it, but she confidently tilted it back and pressed the rubber ignition switch, which gave with a slight click.

Brandi emerged from the door to the utility room with a can of gas gripped in one hand as Sheila gave a few tugs on the starter cord, the engine roaring to life on the tiller, the blades slowly starting their forward rotation. The engine revved as Sheila gently squeezed the throttle, then she slowly tilted the tiller forward, gritting her teeth as she fought to ease it toward the grass without letting it drop. Whirling blades blurred, the tiller vibrating heavily within her grip, her palms turning numb with the repeated thrum of the machine. Lowering it gingerly, she braced herself as the blades bit into grass, grinding and revving loudly as green chewed and shot up, spattering the inside of the gradually curved shield resting over the spinning tillers. For a moment, the ground fought back, gripping the tiller and holding it firm, forcing Sheila to bend her knees and lean into the machine, squeezing tightly as she pushed forward.

The tiller groaned and moved, the blades hacking angrily through the ground, spitting grass and dirt, revealing a ragged rectangle of brown soil beneath. Sheila wrestled with the growling beast, pushing it in a straight line along the interior of the right-side border of stakes and twine. It was a long, arduous process, moving step by step, gripping tightly to force the tiller under her control. By the time she reached the far end of the roped-off rectangle, her arms and hands were tingling with the sensation of persistent vibrations, her back and legs sore from leaning into the machinery. She cut the engine as she turned and stared back toward the other end, sweat flowing freely, dampening the fabric beneath her arms.

"Let me help!" Brandi jogged the length of the garden and Sheila nodded as she caught her stabbing breath, giving Brandi room to position herself behind the handlebars.

Sheila showed her the ignition switch and how to use the pull start, the engine snarling to aggressive life and nearly dying when she released the throttle too fast. After a brief lesson from Sheila, Brandi started marching forward, leaning sharply into the handlebars as the tiller roared through the soft ground, eviscerating grass and the top levels of soil. She made her way back to the other end of the garden, then managed to pull back, rotate the tiller and start back again, her skin glistening with sweat, her long hair clinging to the back of her skull. Several minutes later, Brandi had made two more passes before she finally asked for a break, stepping away from the tiller and wiping sheets of sweat from her face.

Rested since the first path, Sheila took over, topping the gas tank off with some of the fuel from the can, then starting up the tiller and taking over where Brandi left off. It was hard work they had to accomplish together, but after a long exhausting stretch, they'd successfully carved up the entire rectangle, pummeling the grass and topsoil into an evenly shaped bed of lightly-colored brown dirt mixed with green and brown pieces of grass. Sheila, who had made the final pass on the far edge of the garden, killed the engine, tilted it back, and wheeled it out through an opening in the twine perimeter, resting it near the utility vehicle. Her breath coming in fits and gasps, she bent over and placed her palms on her knees, shoulders heaving as she exhaled.

"Are you okay?" Brandi approached, bending slightly to get a better look at Sheila's face. "You're breathing pretty hard."

"Oh, I'm fine," Sheila replied, forcing a lip-quivering smile. "I just thought I was in decent shape for an old bird, but I guess not."

"You're not an old bird."

"Old enough to be your mother." Sheila drew back, looking crookedly at her. "Maybe even your grandmother, if I got started early enough."

"Sheila!" Brandi gasped, drawing back, a sly smile curling her lip.

"Oh, relax you prude." Sheila grinned and winked at the

younger girl, then straightened up and walked toward the tiller once more. "Help me lift this in." They worked together to heave the tiller back up into the utility vehicle, then Sheila grabbed a pair of hoes and handed one to Brandi, keeping the other for herself. "You know what to do with these?" Sheila lifted the hoe slightly as she crossed the space where the twine had been undone and rested in the grass.

"Make the furrows, right? For the seeds?"

"Right the first time." Sheila positioned herself a few inches from the far edge of the garden and began to walk backwards, digging at the fresh dirt with the hoe, carving out a narrow furrow.

Brandi spent a few moments watching her work, then began mirroring the same movements. They worked in concert with each other, dragging the blades of the hoes, digging straight-lined furrows in the dirt one at a time until they were evenly spaced throughout the rectangle of dirt they'd tilled. The work done, Brandi and Sheila returned the hoes to the back of the utility vehicle and Sheila grabbed a few more stakes, handing some to Brandi and keeping others for herself. She also dug through the crate Brandi had loaded and located a small, black marker, which she tugged the cap off of with clenched teeth.

"We're going to place these stakes at the beginning of every row and use this marker to identify which seeds we're planting. That way we can keep track of exactly what we're planting where."

"Ooo, clever. I like it!"

They walked each row, shoving stakes in the ground at the head of each lined furrow they'd dug with the hoe. Crouching near the front stake, Sheila wrote *LETTUCE* in large, thick, black letters, then moved on to the next row, shoving another stake in place and writing *ARUGULA* in the same blocky text. Standing, she eyeballed the row she'd just marked and then wandered to where Brandi had stuck the next stake and marked that with another batch of seeds they'd pulled out from the basement. Sheila and Brandi conversed along the way, talking back and forth about what they might plant and where, coming to a consensus as they each marked the rows with stakes and labeled them with the seeds they were planning to plant.

"Now, the magic begins." Sheila gave Brandi a playful pat on the shoulder and walked past her, back toward the side-by-side, then began lifting the seeds from where she'd stashed them.

Brandi followed Sheila over as she approached one of the furrows they'd dug with the hoes, and Sheila knelt in the dirt, her knee pressing into the finely tilled ground. She carried a trowel with her.

"Lettuce needs loose, rich soil," she explained, running her fingers through the dark earth. "See how it crumbles? That's perfect."

She used the fine tip of her trowel to push the soil around a bit. "You want these about six inches apart. Not too deep, though; lettuce seeds are tiny." She tipped a few seeds into her palm, showing Brandi the small, oval shapes. "Watch," Sheila demonstrated, pinching three seeds between thumb and forefinger, dropping them along the furrow with practiced precision. "Better to plant extra and thin them out later." Her weathered hands moved methodically down the row, evenly spacing the seeds apart, sprinkling them little by little into the furrows they'd dug.

It took a few minutes for her to make her way down the entirety of the row, glancing up once in a while. When she reached the end, she lifted her trowel and held it up for Brandi to see.

"Now cover them gently, just a whisper of soil." Delicately, she dipped the trowel into the surrounding soil and dusted it over the seeds, making her way back up the entirety of the row, covering every small batch of seeds she'd dropped into the furrow. "Enough to protect them from the birds, but not so much that they'll struggle to break free."

"We'll have to water them, right? This whole garden?"

"Of course. Thankfully we have power, the well and we've got several sets of sprinklers. Our built-in irrigation system doesn't reach up here; who knew we'd need it?" She stood and made her way back toward the utility vehicle, trowel hanging at her hip.

One by one, Sheila gave Brandi instructions for each of the batches of seeds they'd gathered from the basement. Once Brandi caught on, she took over, working shoulder-to-shoulder with Sheila in the stark, yellow heat of the sun, sweat running in rivulets down their faces, sticking their shirts to their back and leaving tiny wet spots in the dirt along the way. They stood at the far side of the garden, having just planted a row of carrots and cucumbers, and Sheila stared toward the road, beneath the cover of her flattened hand. A figure emerged around the corner, circling the house and walking toward them, little more than a darkened silhouette against the daylight's backdrop.

"Looks like you're working awfully hard out here!"

Sheila's taut shoulders loosened as she stood, lowering her hand. "Gotta do what we gotta do, Darryl!"

She and Brandi were careful to walk between rows, filing their way toward Darryl who came to the edge of the garden, carrying a pair of water glasses in his hands. Brandi reached him first, eagerly taking the glass from his left hand and drinking a few desperate gulps. Sheila took the second glass and drank just as eagerly.

"That hits the spot, thanks, Darryl."

"Things are looking good. Anything I can do to help?"

Sheila placed a hand on Brandi's shoulder and shook her head. "I don't think so. We've got things under control here. How's the battery project going?"

"I can only do so much with the tractor, so I'm having to muscle them by hand a fair amount, too. It's slow and heavy, but it's going pretty well."

Sheila drained the last of her water in a long, thirsty swallow.

"We've got things well in hand here. Thanks very much for the water, Darryl, but feel free to keep moving those batteries. Plenty of work to go around."

"Yes, ma'am." He offered a slight forward bow, crossing his legs as he angled downward and spread his left arm out.

Brandi and Sheila shared a whispered snicker as he turned and walked away, leaving them to their gardening.

# CHAPTER 11

**Jane Simmons**
**An Undisclosed Location in New England**

Jane pauses at the intersection between hallways, one shoulder touching the wall, ear directed toward the next corridor. Whispered voices carry throughout the aisles of dark mahogany and rich, maroon-colored carpet, getting louder with each approaching step. She takes a tentative step back, placing herself in the shadow of an unlit side hallway, her eyes alert as a pair of well-dressed men cross ahead and vanish down the next leg beyond the intersection. Their heads are turned, hands lifted in silent gestures of urgency as they walk away and once more the hallway falls into silence. She stalks forward, twisting left around the corner and walks a few more paces before she comes to the familiar wooden door to her left. Thick oak, lined with ornate, decorative panels and a gleaming brass knob, it resembles any number of other doors in the well-concealed government facility.

Her fingers brush the smooth, cool metal of the knob and she twists, pushing the door open, a swift step between the narrow separation of door and frame. She closes it quickly, though holds the knob tight to make sure it clicks softly closed rather than slams. The room wraps her in mahogany and velvet the moment she closes the heavy door behind her. Light filters through leaded glass windows, casting diamond patterns across a Persian rug in deep burgundy and navy as the air holds the scent of old books and leather, with undertones of lemon oil furniture polish.

A massive desk dominates one end, its surface gleaming beneath a green-shaded banker's lamp. Behind it, built-in bookshelves climb to the coffered ceiling, their contents a mix of leather-bound classics and government binders, almost apologetic for their institutional presence among such elegance. Two wing chairs, upholstered in worn leather the color of good cognac, face a fireplace where logs wait unburned behind a brass screen. Above the carved marble mantel, an oil portrait of some long-dead sea captain stares sternly across the room, his fierce expression at odds with the peace she seeks. Lush wallpaper is deep green damask, its pattern barely visible in the dim light but rich with texture. Brass wall sconces cast pools of warm light that reflect off picture frames and the curved glass front of a Chippendale secretary as a grandfather clock marks time in the corner, its steady heartbeat a counterpoint to the chaos outside.

Modern intrusions are few but jarring, which include a secure phone on the desk, a tablet charging station disguised in a wooden box, the subtle blue light of a Wi-Fi router blinking from behind a Chinese screen, all reminders that even here, she hasn't truly escaped. On a side table, another modern amenity, a coffee maker sits burbling, filling the air with the rich, earthy scents of freshly ground beans.

"You made it."

Jane turns and smiles as her husband crosses the room from her left, pausing momentarily to rest a hand on her back and kiss her cheek. Her three daughters sit around a brightly polished, oval-shaped table a short distance behind him, wrapped in the soft shadows of the dimly lit room. They each have a plate of eggs sitting on the rich, dark wood before them, forks in hand, the underlying smells complementing the coffee in a way that makes Jane's belly gurgle in anticipation. Charles Simmons lifts the coffee maker from the warming plate and pours a mug for his wife, then hands it to her, Jane eagerly wrapping her palms around its warm surface.

"Do I want to know how many cups of that you've had today? You've been awake since before sunrise."

"It doesn't matter. I'll treat this one like my first." Jane lowers her chin and smells the coffee, then takes a long sip, heat biting her lips.

Ramona, Jane's eldest daughter, leans against one of the bookshelves, arms crossed, watching her youngest sister Pearl fidget with an ornate chess piece from the nearby table.

"Put that down before you break it," she says, her voice carrying a familiar eldest-sister authority.

"I'm not going to break it," Pearl protests, but sets the carved queen back in its place. "I just hate being stuck in here all day. There's nothing to do."

"Better than being out there." Lucile doesn't look up from her phone, though it's useless; there hasn't been cell service in days.

It's just a matter of habit, muscle memory of a normal teenage life. Jane watches them from the doorway, coffee forgotten in her hand. Her girls, Pearl with her restless energy at thirteen, Lucile lost in her own world at sixteen, and Ramona, trying so hard to be the adult at twenty. The room is suddenly smaller, more confined, and Jane fights the urge to throw open the windows, to let them run free across the manor's grounds. But there are snipers on the roof, motion sensors in the gardens, and somewhere beyond the property's walls, a nation in chaos.

"We could at least go outside," Pearl continues, moving to the window. "Just in the garden?"

"No," Jane and Ramona say simultaneously, then exchange a look, Ramona apologetic and Jane proud despite herself.

"Your sister's right," Jane adds, finally moving to join them. "The Secret Service has enough to worry about without having to reorganize the perimeter. We stay inside."

"But Mom—"

"Pearl." Jane's voice carries the weight of command, the tone she's been using more and more in briefing rooms and crisis meetings, but she catches herself and softens it. "Come here, all of you."

The girls gather around her, even Lucile setting down her phone to make her way over. Jane pulls them close, breathing in the familiar scents of their shampoo and the fabric softener Charles demanded their escorts bring with them. There is a strange, almost pained familiarity swirling within the tight confines of the ornately decorated former office, a small slice of home wedged into the alien terrain of dark, rich wood, and portraits of famous people they didn't know. Instead of the signs of her young family, a stray field hockey stick, a few pairs of abandoned sneakers and the white board schedule that was never accurate, Jane faces hand-carved ivory chess sets, solid glass decanters, and intricately sculpted wainscoting. But she smells her daughters' hair, she feels their touch, and in that moment, all is whole.

"I know this is hard," she begins, but Ramona cuts her off.

"You don't have to explain, Mom. We understand."

"Do you? Because sometimes I don't." Jane's laugh is hollow. "I've had countless debriefings and meetings with government agencies about cities I've never even visited, but I haven't helped Pearl with her algebra in weeks, or heard about Lucile's story she was writing, or talked to you about college."

"College isn't exactly a priority anymore," Ramona says quietly.

"It should be. All of it should be. You should be worried about boys and grades and what to wear to parties. Not..." Jane gestures vaguely around the room.

"We're okay, Mom," Lucile speaks up, surprising them all. "Really. And you're doing important things."

"More important than being your mother?"

Pearl wraps her arms around Jane's waist. "You're doing both. You're like a superhero."

"Superheroes don't hide in manor houses," Jane murmurs into her youngest's hair.

"No," Ramona agrees, "but they do what needs to be done. Even when it's hard."

Rapid footsteps thud from a distance in the hallway, and Jane's shoulders tense. Another crisis, another decision, another moment stolen from her children.

"Mom?" Lucille steps back and lifts her chin to look more closely at her mother. "That story I was writing? It's about a president. A woman president. I started it before all of this happened. But I'm still working on it. I could show you when you have time?"

Jane's vision blurs. "I'd love that, sweetheart. Tonight, after the briefings? We could all have dinner together, and you could read it to us?" Untangling from her children, she accepts the mug of coffee she'd handed to Charles and gives him an apologetic smile.

His eyes are glistening, and he touches her arm with the briefest brush of his fingertips.

"What's going on, Mom? Have you learned anything more?" Ramona walks to the coffee maker and pours herself her own cup.

"Nothing I can share, unfortunately," Jane replies.

"Are you going to get in trouble for being here?" Pearl asks and looks conspiratorially toward the door.

"I'm the president, dear, I can do whatever I want."

"You know that's not true," Charles replies with a hoarse scoff.

"If anything, your most important duty is to basically do whatever everyone else asks."

"Tell me about it." Jane sips at her mug and allows the tension in her shoulders to slowly leak away.

A sudden thudding drumbeat of footfalls crashes overhead, drawing her gaze sharply upward. Her grip on her coffee falters, but she slaps her second hand around the mug and barely keeps it from falling. More shuddering slams of stalking feet echo from the hallway alongside the once-quiet room, closer than it was, then the noise ceases, pausing momentarily just outside the wooden door. Jane braces herself but doesn't have to wait for long as the rapid rabbit-punch of fist knocks hammer at the door a second later.

"Madame President?" A muffled voice comes from beyond the oaken door.

"How did they know you were here?" Pearl asks.

"They always know where I am." Jane smiles weakly, takes another sip of her coffee and hands the mug over to Charles. "Sorry I couldn't stay longer."

"The world needs you." Charles takes the cup and lifts it to his lips, drinking the coffee inside as Jane turns and puts her hand on the door.

Jane squeezes Lucile's hand, kisses Pearl's forehead, touches Ramona's cheek. "Watch after your sisters?" she asks, as always.

"Always," Ramona promises, as she always does.

Jane stares at her three daughters, her gaze tracking the contours of their faces, the drape of their clothes, their posture and their mannerisms. She carves that into stone within her mind, memorizing the look, the feel, the touch and the weight. Jane lingers there for a moment, turning around slowly, peeling herself from their gathered group until she faces the door once more. She reaches toward the knob and opens the door, straightening her slackened posture, clearing her throat, and making a series of subtle transformations from mother to president.

A man stands framed within the opened doorway, dressed like the day after a particularly rowdy wedding, his black pants wrinkled, his once-pristine white shirt faded with eggshell stains of sweat and untucked at the belt. There is no tie anymore, the top two buttons unfastened to reveal a pale sliver of chest, dusted with dark hair. Two Secret Service agents are stationed just behind him, standing against the far wall of the corridor, looking straight ahead at nothing.

"My apologies, Madame President. The plan you requested is ready."

"An hour early. I applaud your punctuality." Jane sighs and turns back to the room.

Charles drains her coffee and sets it down on the nearby table, then approaches, a light kiss pecks her cheek. She accepts brief embraces, one at a time from her three daughters in ascending age order, then hesitates as Ramona starts to pull away. Jane places her palm against the twenty-year-old's cheek.

"Sorry I have to run."

Ramona nods and then Jane whisks herself away, moving back out into the hallway, the door closing in her wake. She finds herself consumed within a hustling group, drawn down the hallway like a fish in a strong current, bodies pressed tightly together moving in unison.

"What's the latest from our advance teams in the cities? Any luck landing on a source of the chemical attack?"

The young man with the sweat-stained shirt shakes his head firmly. "Most teams are reporting either finding no information to speak of, or..." his voice trails off.

"Or what?"

"Or they've gone dark completely."

"Do we know why they've gone dark?"

"Most likely because they've ventured into areas that are blocking radio or satellite signals. Cell tower backup power has been exhausted at this point as well, ma'am. All teams are expected to check in within the next three hours, so we're hoping to have a better update for you by then."

"Good enough."

The rich wood of the wainscoting blurs past them as they stride rapidly through the hallway, footfalls softening upon the thick, dark carpet that lines each corridor. They navigate a series of twists and turns, Jane trailing along with the momentum of the people surrounding her. Finally, as they round one more right-turn corner, the area looks familiar and the group heads directly toward a set of double doors separating them from the briefing room. Two Secret Service agents flank the set of doors, and one of them reaches across his body to open it as Jane files in.

"I hear we've got a plan?" She says as they push through the conference room doors.

All around the long, rectangular table, people scramble to their feet as she enters, but she waves her hand at them, silently gesturing for them to sit back down, which they do. The only immediate response to her question is the unsettled scraping of chair legs and the swish of fabric as they all stand, then sit again, repositioning themselves in their high-back chairs. The briefing room is the same one she's visited countless times since being dragged to the secret government facility, the faces sitting around it mostly the same.

"We've spent long enough trying to figure out who attacked us and planning on how to bring them down. How about we focus some of our attention on helping our people?" She leans back at the head of the table and looks around the room. "What do we have?"

Sterile light from recessed fixtures in the ceiling cast everyone in the same sickly, artificial shade. Faces around the table are drawn, sullen and haggard, thick bags colored beneath dim, weary eyes. Colonel Drake is the first to speak, turning slightly to face President Simmons.

"We've managed to gather up enough pilots to get most of the

C-130's in the air so we can start dropping supplies to impacted areas. But it's not a simple, straight-forward operation. We've got some choices to make."

"Don't we always?" Jane asks. "What choices?"

"We've had our analytics folks running a few computer models. If we focus on dropping supplies where the models show the highest likelihood of survivors, it's going to take close to a week to complete the first round of drops. They're spread far out and they're more difficult to reach. If we consolidate our supply drops to just outside major cities, that will reduce the time to complete the drops to around forty-eight hours at the most, but we may not reach the largest numbers of survivors."

Jane folds her hands on the table in front of her, taking just a moment to consider the alternatives.

"There are no doubt survivors in the cities," she says, "and they matter just as much as anyone else." She sighs and leans back, separating her hands and gently tapping her fingers on the polished surface of the table. "But we're playing a numbers game here. The needs of the many must outweigh the needs of the few."

"Understood. What are you proposing, Madame President?" Colonel Drake leans forward in his chair.

"Let's put ninety percent of our available resources into the rural supply drops. Get the biggest bang for our buck that we can. Whatever these computer models say, hit the largest numbers first and work your way down."

"Understood."

"The remaining ten percent can focus on the major cities, again, the bigger the better. I want us to get these critical supplies to as many Americans as we possibly can."

Colonel Drake twists a bit and meets the gaze of Agent Provost to his right, both of them nodding to each other in silent acknowledgement.

"We'll have to run a few more models," Provost says, "just to evaluate the effect of what you're proposing. But from my side of things, I'm on board with this."

Colonel Drake nods as well, and his affirmative gesture is echoed by others scattered around the table. Some of the sullen expressions soften, a bit of brightness coming to several sets of eyes around the table, the tension in the room easing, malleable like dough, softening into something easier to work with.

"Good. I'm glad we're all on the same page. Does anyone have any counterpoints to offer?"

A young woman raises her hand, her throat clears.

"Joy? Concerns?"

"No concerns, Madame President. I just wasn't sure if you wanted the latest numbers."

"Numbers?"

"We have some updated casualty counts," Colonel Grady says as he leans over from beyond where Joy, the presidential aide, sits.

Jane's throat tightens, her fingers curling against the smooth table and says nothing.

"Latest estimates are close to two hundred million, Madame President in the United States alone."

The numbers startle Jane, her only response a rapid blinking of her eyelids. If her nails were sharp, they would dig into the varnish on the table, but they're chewed and ragged, so her tips simply squeak as she slowly clenches her fists.

"Over half of our population," she says in a quiet whisper.

"We believe those numbers might be..." Colonel Grady speaks softly, chewing the words like a tough piece of steak. "They might be low, Madame President."

Jane lets the slightest breath escape between her clenched teeth. "And they're only going to get worse the longer things get before we start dropping these supplies."

"That is our fear, yes. But we have to be very clear, this is based purely on computer models that may or may not be accurate. It's just a little bit better than a best guess."

"It's the best we have," Jane says, slumping back into her chair.

"Okay, everyone." Colonel Drake speaks loudly and pushes his chair back, bolting upright. "We have our orders. Let's give the president a brief break and then we'll reconvene."

Voices murmur from around the table, heads nod and turn, quiet, whispered conversations pass between gently leaning heads. Jane pushes back from the table, her chair moving across the carpeted floor. She rises as if in a trance, her muscles following only the most basic of commands. The room smears into a mottled pattern of color and shapes, her eyes try to focus on anything and somehow manage to focus on nothing. She leans slightly, resting her closed knuckles on the table, head dipped until a gentle hand guides her from the room and back out into the hallway. Joy O'Hara is at her side as she always is, leaning close, her whispered voice low in Jane's ear.

"Are you okay, Madame President?"

Jane nods and forces an uneven smile as they walk down the corridor, two members of Secret Service falling in behind them.

"We'll get you back with Charles and the girls. Let you refill your family tank."

"What about yours?" Jane turns, glancing beneath a single arched eyebrow.

"My what?"

"Your family?"

"Oh." Joy clears her throat, stares straight ahead, her legs scissoring in a swift, slicing motion. "My two sisters are okay, last I heard. Neither of them live near any of the impacted areas. My brother..." her voice trails off and she glances away for a moment, tracing the left wall, various famous men staring back from painted portraits. "My brother is an investment banker in Chicago. I... haven't heard from him." Her pace remains steady. "My parents were on a cruise, it took off from Miami four days ago. I haven't heard anything from them either."

"Joy." Jane stops and gently touches her arm, drawing her to an unsteady halt. "Why haven't you said anything?"

"It's not important, Madame President. Everyone in this building has family members unaccounted for. Most of us, anyway."

"Certainly there's something we can do."

"I don't want you to." Joy shakes her head, a narrow slice of white teeth biting down on her lower lip. "It's like you said, it's a numbers game. We can't devote resources to finding three of my family members when those same resources could air drop supplies for hundreds, if not thousands."

Jane's nostrils slowly flare, a brimming, hot surge of frustration swirls within her. She is at once the most powerful person in the world and also somehow useless as well. It's a dichotomy she struggles with, frozen in that hallway, face-to-face with Joy O'Hara and without answers.

"Come on." Joy nods down the corridor, then twists away, resuming her walk.

Jane hesitates at first, but catches up quickly, shaking loose her previous cobwebs of concern and uselessness. They match stride-for-stride for a few minutes, navigating the corridors until they approach an intersection where a neatly dressed, middle-aged woman emerges, turning toward them.

"President Simmons! Just who I was looking for."

Jane draws to a halt, almost backpedaling to avoid running straight into the woman, whose ruler-straight locks of jet-black hair extend from her scalp in thick iron shoots like bamboo tipped in tar.

"I didn't mean to startle you. Monica Leary. I was a senior advisor to President McDouglas. I apologize it took me a little extra time to get here, but I wanted to introduce myself." The woman, who appears constructed from granite relief extends a hand, her elbow sharply bent, palm extended, her every movement filled with purpose, every word run through a finely tuned internal filter, her gray-hued eyes bright and alert.

"Monica." Jane nods and presses her palm against the cool, dry skin, the two women exchanging their firm greeting.

"I know you expressed an interest in taking an hour break with your family, and the last thing I want to do is get in the way of that."

"What can I do for you, Monica?"

"I've been working alongside Colonel Drake on coordinating advance team operations. I believe he mentioned during that last meeting that some of those teams have gone dark."

"He did. He also mentioned we'd wait for their next check-in three hours from now before we raised the alarm."

"I heard that." Monica clears her throat and turns her head to look down the hall, then back in the other direction. "Colonel Drake is compartmentalizing, which is a good plan, but I wanted you to be in the loop on exactly what we're dealing with."

"And that is?"

"One of the teams that went dark was based out of Houston. A six-person CRBN team, similar to what we're running in Washington, Denver and other places. Boots on the ground, they were sweeping the city, using broad-spectrum analyzers to try and detect any traces of the chemical that did this."

"I understand what these teams are doing, Monica. What's so special about the team in Houston?"

"We actually received a signal from them shortly before they went dark. A brief squelch, three seconds, no more."

Jane crosses her arms, folding them tight over each other, her head tilts slightly to one side, inquisitively.

"It was nothing more than... gurgled screams is the best way to describe it, unfortunately. We ran it through some advanced algorithms to try and isolate the vocal track, but all we could hear were screams."

A cold streak runs the length of Jane's spine, trailing icicle fingernails, gooseflesh shoots throughout her arms and prickles the nape of her neck. The air temperature drops by six full degrees and her crossed arms become more of a warming embrace.

"That doesn't sound good," she says, her voice a low whisper.

"Colonel Drake agrees. I agree. But with your focus so intently on supply drops for survivors, we were hesitant to..."

"Stop hesitating. Whatever is going on here has to take an equal priority. If something is still going on out there, if these attacks are not done..." her voice trails off and Monica nods firmly.

"I appreciate your sentiments. Colonel Drake was hesitant to bring this up with the larger group, that's why he asked me to meet you more privately." Monica's steel-blue glare darts toward Joy, locks there for a moment, then swings back toward Jane.

"I agree with Colonel Drake, we don't want to raise an alarm. But we have to figure out what's going on. Keep me apprised."

"Understood." Monica nods sharply, takes one step back, then another, and then turns and vanishes down the side hallway, chased by the echoing tap of her high-heeled shoes.

# CHAPTER 12

**Doug and Benjamin**
**Silverpine, Oregon**

The trees that gave Silverpine its name rose in tall, spear-tipped spires along each side of the narrow road, which wound its way through the Oregon wilderness. Benjamin slowed, watching the path of an oncoming vehicle. A dark-colored SUV approached from around the corner, moving slowly, a pair of silhouettes in the front seat, one huddled close to the wheel, the other staring out of the passenger side window. The two vehicles came abreast, stark, white eyes staring out at Benjamin as the SUV slowed to a crawl, its driver closely scrutinizing the two men in the Jeep. Benjamin eased the accelerator down, sped up, and left the SUV behind them as he turned the vehicle along the sharp bend in the road.

"A nice reminder that we're not the only ones left alive around here." Doug twisted in his seat as the rear of the SUV vanished beyond the outward curve of trees.

"Uh huh. Last time we ran into other alive people, they tried to start trouble. I'd rather stay away from other alive people if we can help it." Benjamin gripped the wheel, following another bend through the quiet, nearly empty road.

Ahead of them, a pickup truck was parked at an angle across the narrow shoulder, the front of the vehicle resting in the grass, its driver's side tire flat. There was no sign of its driver or any passengers, just the lone, abandoned vehicle, a landmark against the backdrop of trees and green grass. The sky above the nearby treetops was blue and peppered with white clouds, a few tendrils of gray smoke rising like smeared pencil marks against a sheet of flat, cyan paper. Inside the Jeep, the air thickened with acrid smoke and Benjamin leaned forward, closing the vents and coughing.

"Did you go into town when you and Sheila headed out last time?"

"No. We took as direct a route to the highway as possible."

"Judging by that smell, I'm not sure we'll like what we see."

"Is there any way to get to Greenberg's place without going through town? I'm not crazy about driving through any population centers, even ones as small as downtown Silverpine."

"I suppose we could, it would just take us an extra hour or two to get there. Is that something you're willing to entertain?"

"No. Just go through town. It'll be fine." Doug instinctively touched the pump-action shotgun that rested between his legs.

As they rounded the next corner, another abandoned vehicle came into view, parked on the opposite shoulder. From the outside there wasn't anything of note, though the driver's side door stood open, and the interior of the vehicle was empty. A soft breeze fluttered scattered trash across both lanes of travel, lifting a stray piece of paper and sweeping it across the pavement until it rested along the shoulder near where the vehicle was parked.

The Jeep sped through another scattering of refuse, trash swirling out from each side as they neared the initial cluster of familiar buildings. Benjamin eased off the gas as they approached downtown Silverpine, the truck's tires crunching over even more scattered debris. Fog and lingering smoke clung to the valley, drifting in from somewhere beyond Main Street. Doug sat rigid in the passenger seat, his shotgun leaned against the interior of his right knee. Grimacing, he maneuvered his left leg, the stiffness stabbing at his knee joint, the pain throughout his shin and calf more of a dull, penetrating ache than sharp agony. Reaching into his pocket, he fished out a small bottle of over-the-counter pain medicine and unscrewed the cap to study its interior. He twisted the cap back on without shaking any out, then returned the bottle.

"You doing all right?"

"Leg's stiff and a little sore, but not sore enough to waste pain meds we might need later."

"Suit yourself." They crept forward, the tall pine trees giving way to shorter clusters of oaks and maple, interspersed among the more frequent placement of buildings. "Looks quiet."

The Jeep crawled past the Silverpine Diner, its windows intact but dusty, a neon "OPEN" sign hanging dark and lifeless, and last week's special of Meatloaf with Mashed Potatoes still decorating the chalkboard outside. A red Subaru sat abandoned in front of Tracy's Hair Design, parked at an angle that suggested its driver had left in a hurry, one door hanging open. The salon's front window displayed a spray of spider-web cracks, several points of unknown impact fracturing the pane, though not totally breaking through it. Saying nothing, they continued down Main Street, past the post office with its flag still raised but hanging limp in the stagnant air. The local credit union's time and temperature display was dim and unlit, the lack of power reducing it to blackness.

A few cars were visible within the confines of downtown, slotted into angled parking spaces, their drivers nowhere to be seen, but even more of Main Street parking had been vacated.

The town bore more resemblance to a last century ghost town than a town decimated by recent calamity. If Doug hadn't known better, he might have assumed most people just up and left, headed for greener pastures. There remained a few more signs of potential trouble, the side door to the credit union hanging open, a shower of shattered glass sprayed along the asphalt walkway.

Papers and other items from within the credit union rustled in the wind along the pock-marked pavement parking lot, the cavern of the building dark and impenetrable from the road where they traveled.

"Silverpine was always a nice little town." Doug leaned over a bit to stare through the driver's side in the direction of the credit union.

Bits of metal glittered in the sun along the pavement just outside the credit union, sharper and brighter than the surrounding glass. Chunks of broken brickwork littered the pavement as well, holes dotting the wall in a ragged, uneven upward and downward slope.

"Things change when folks get desperate. Or when folks think law enforcement's got bigger things to worry about. Silverpine isn't a whole lot different than anywhere else as far as that's concerned."

"I'd like to think it was."

"You might be fooling yourself, Doug."

"I'm just a hopeless optimist."

Smoke thickened as they approached the center of town. Near Ruby's Books & Coffee, a small fire smoldered in a metal trash can, thick columns of charcoal-gray smoke rising from whatever burned within. Shattered windows stood along the coffee shop's exterior, spilling fractured glass fragments onto the parking lot separating the storefront from the sidewalk. Even through the closed vents, telltale pungent odors of smoke twisted with overdone coffee beans and Benjamin accelerated, the two men exchanging glances as they kept moving.

The bookstore and coffee shop's window displayed a cheerful *Summer Reading Program* banner that stood stark, colorful and unusually decorative against the stoic, utilitarian gray of the smoke-filled world. They continued driving in silence down Main Street, Benjamin's fingers curled tightly around the steering wheel, Doug's face pressed close to the glass, searching their surroundings. Without realizing it, he'd closed his grip around the pump of the shotgun and pulled it up into his lap, cradling it there in anticipation.

The town hall stood sentinel at the end of Main Street, its brick facade blackened on one side from a fire that had burned itself out. Two more vehicles blocked the intersection, one of them a Silverpine police cruiser with its driver's side door hanging open, the second a delivery van for Portland Bakery Supply that had jumped the curb and crashed into a bench.

"Turn left at the Grocery Outlet," Doug instructed, adjusting his grip on the shotgun.

"I remember the way."

The store's parking lot was eerily empty except for a single shopping cart that rolled lazily in the breeze, its wheel squeaking a lonely rhythm. A pair of shadowed forms rested at the far edge of the parking lot, indistinct from where they traveled. Doug's mind played tricks, envisioning them as a pair of dead bodies who had been locked in mortal combat over the contents of the small market. As Benjamin made the turn, the forced-open glass front doors of the store came into view, a slumped body wedged between them, the interior of the store a mangled mass of toppled shelves and spilled contents.

The smoke was heaviest throughout that section of town, though no cause was visible, the air was simply clouded in all directions, the world a clotted, coiling churn of gray hues. Through gaps in the haze, they navigated another stretch of side road, the outskirts of downtown Silverpine peeling away, growing sparser and falling behind them as they were once again surrounded by the familiar structure of evergreen trees.

A single car sat askew on the other side of the road and Benjamin's gaze passed over it as they drove by, studying the darkened interior. As they drove by, Doug took over scrutinizing the vehicle so Benjamin could watch the road, the white Toyota Camry parked half on the shoulder with a bumper sticker that read *My Child is an Honor Student at Silverpine Middle*.

"I didn't even know there was a Silverpine Middle School." Doug turned back around in his seat. "By the time we moved out here, Samantha was all grown up."

"Elementary and middle schools are in the same building. High schoolers have to travel out to Great Heron."

"Did you grow up here, Benjamin?"

Benjamin nodded, his face a stoic mask, jaw slightly clenched, the tendons standing out against the sides of his thick neck.

"Graduated with Ruby James, the woman who owned that salon. Hoping she's okay." He kept his gaze fixed through the windshield, guiding the Jeep along the meandering path.

The Jeep's engine was unnaturally loud in the surrounding stillness of the world and as they passed by an outward clutch of trees, a flock of birds hurtled into the air, calling wildly, wings fluttering as they spread out into a cloud of dark against the blue sky.

"Sorry you had to see that." Doug nodded back toward downtown.

"I was expecting worse, honestly." Benjamin glanced in the rear-view mirror. "What I want to know is what's burning."

The sun shone brighter, burning off the lingering fog and smoke, the air clearing as they drove further from downtown. Ruts thudded beneath the wheels of the Jeep, the neatly paved downtown street shifting to unkept pavement, riddled with potholes and the heaved remains of winter chill. For a few minutes they continued through the encroaching Oregon wilderness, the smoke clearing further, the abandoned cars vanishing and for a brief moment, Doug allowed his tense shoulders to relax, his coiled grip on the shotgun loosening. Benjamin accelerated, bringing the Jeep close to forty miles per hour before he tapped the brake, rounding another unanticipated bend in the narrow road.

Just ahead, in the gap between flanking walls of evergreens a patch of dirt broke through the pavement, carving an uneven gash in the forest, and Benjamin pointed the hood of the Jeep toward that gap, slowing further. Benjamin hit the brakes and brought the Jeep to a halt just off the patch of dirt.

"Are we still sure about this?" He turned slightly in the driver's seat, grip curled tight around the steering wheel.

"We didn't drive all this way out here for nothing." Doug peered through the window to his right, searching the trees. "And it's been quiet the whole way through. I say we do it."

Benjamin nodded and hit the gas, the Jeep crunching across the loose stone as it transitioned to the dirt road leading into the trees. Just a short distance from the road, the path opened up into a wide, sparse clearing, the single-floor structure coming into clear view ahead of them, surrounded by a poorly maintained gravel parking lot and a perimeter of a long scrabble of grass and weeds. A white pickup truck was parked in the lot, a faded logo reading *Greenberg Supply* on its passenger door. Jeep tires crunched over gravel and Benjamin parked just behind the pickup truck, though he left the engine running, staring intently at the darkened windows of the white building ahead.

Greenberg Supply sat in a natural clearing among towering Douglas firs and Ponderosa pines, their branches creating a sheltering canopy around the property. The main building, a practical structure with white aluminum siding, dominated the one-acre lot. Its facade featured a simple sign in bold blue lettering, weathered but readable against the white background. The pickup truck was a white F-150, carefully maintained despite its age, the faded logo its only sign of wear and tear.

The gravel parking lot, large enough for several vehicles, was a mix of local river rock and crushed granite. Two metal shipping containers, converted for additional storage, flanked the main building's sides, their blue paint faded by years of Oregon weather. A chain-link fence encircled the commercial area, separating it from the more private residential section of the property. Behind the store, connected by a well-worn dirt path, stood the owner's house, a single-story ranch style home with cedar siding and a metal roof. Between the house and store, a workshop occupied its own outbuilding, its large rolling door visible from the parking area.

Through the store's front windows, shadowy shapes of industrial shelving were barely visible in the dim interior. A CLOSED sign hung crooked on the front door, which was closed tight. Doug handed the shotgun over to Benjamin and tugged on the door handle, pulling back, then pushing his door slowly open. Teeth clenched, Doug eased his way out of the passenger seat, still favoring his leg, then paused for a moment just outside the door, gently bending his knee and flexing. Benjamin started to open the door, his opposite hand gripped around the pump of the shotgun.

"Stay. I've got this." Doug lifted a hand, gently waving Benjamin off.

"What are you talking about?"

"I've got this."

"What are you planning to do? How are you going to play this?"

"How am I going to play it? What are you on? I'm planning to walk up to his front door and knock."

"You're sure that's a good idea?"

Perched alongside the open door, Doug turned and searched the front of the house, his head swiveling to the left, then right. The front of the commercial space was empty, a soft breeze shifting the needles of the nearby trees. Somewhere in the distance, the shrill cry of birds rippled throughout the surrounding forest.

"It's Cliff, Benjamin. Ease up on the paranoia just a tad?"

Benjamin sighed but stayed still, repositioning the shotgun on his lap, leaning a bit forward to get a better look at the front of Greenberg Supply.

"Tell you what. Go knock on the door, do what you want to do." Benjamin gently pushed his door open and withdrew, sheltering himself behind the Jeep. "I'm going to remain out of sight, shotgun within easy reach. Just in case."

"Uh huh." Doug rolled his eyes, then shut the passenger door and took a step toward the building.

Glancing over his shoulder, he peered across the roof of the Jeep, nothing but the trees beyond within view, the white F-150 parked just ahead of his own vehicle. Doug strode toward the front door, his limp less pronounced but still present, a slightly oblong stride giving him a crooked gait as he made his way toward the door. Doug grabbed the knob of the front door and turned, the mechanism clicking softly after a quarter turn, unable to go any farther due to the lock being engaged.

Pausing, Doug turned his ear toward the door, but no sound came from beyond it, the commercial building as empty and silent as it had first appeared. He closed his fist, angled close to the door and knocked, driving the side of his hand into the wood a few times before lowering it again.

"Cliff?" Doug asked, his voice only slightly elevated, though no response came from within.

Doug lifted his hand once more and drove it hard into the door three times, then four, then finally a fifth, each hammering knock coming harder than the one before.

"Cliff!" His voice boomed across the front yard, its echo trapped within the surrounding forest. "It's Doug! It's Doug Tills! You alive in there, old man?"

Doug took a step back when a shift of sliding fabric caught his eye, a half-drawn curtain moving along one of the front-facing windows.

"Cliff?" Doug asked, lowering his voice and leaning toward the window.

The man's face clarified at the other end of the glass, one palm pressed against the window, his stern, sculpted expression softening almost at once. "Doug? Is that you?"

"Darn right it is."

The man's face vanished from the window as the curtain slid back into place, then the metallic clack of a disengaging deadbolt rattled from the other side of the door. After a soft rustle of movement, the doorknob turned and the door drew open as movement caught in the periphery of Doug's vision. Benjamin was approaching from his left just as the front door opened all the way, Cliff smiling widely from the other side.

"Doug, it's so great to see you. I wasn't expecting visitors." His friendly demeanor faltered, his head turning slightly as Benjamin sidled up next to Doug, shotgun in hand. "Is that..." His gaze narrowed and lowered, fixed on the weapon Benjamin rested along his shoulder. "Benjamin? The hell are you doing skulking around out there with that cannon?"

"Believe me, we'd rather not be toting it around," Doug replied, apologetically, "but we're taking every precaution these days."

"I can't blame you for that." Cliff took a step onto the stoop and leaned out between them, looking out into the parking lot and beyond. "After all the craziness in town, I've just been locked down in here, hoping to ride this thing out."

Doug glanced anxiously across the front yard himself, eyeing the sliver of road through the nearby trees. "Speaking of which," he said, "unfortunately, we're not here for a social call."

Cliff nodded absently, then stepped aside. "Didn't figure as much. Come in, both of you." He ushered them both inside, then stepped forward, closing the front door in their wake. "Sorry I didn't hear you knocking at first. Like I said, I wasn't really expecting visitors."

The interior of Greenberg Supply resonated with the quiet efficiency of a well-maintained establishment. Metal shelving units lined the walls and created neat aisles throughout the space, stocked with an impressive array of electrical components. Spools of wire in various gauges sat on rotating racks, their copper gleaming in the faint light of overhead fluorescents which still glowed softly throughout the business' interior.

A solid oak counter dominated the front of the store, its surface marked by years of contractors leaning on it while writing orders. Behind it, pegboards displayed an array of specialty tools, wire strippers, multimeters, and heavy-duty crimpers, all neatly sorted by tool type and size. A glass display case beneath the counter housed high-end testing equipment, each piece in its designated spot and labeled with printed adhesive strips.

Near the rear, a door marked "Employees Only" led to a storage area, while to its left, a workbench held a bench vise and measuring equipment. A rack of electrical conduit stood in one corner, their galvanized surfaces reflecting the pale glow of the various battery-powered lights. The ceiling was a maze of exposed metal trusses, with chains hanging down at intervals for securing larger spools of wire.

Unlike the chaos they'd seen in town, Greenberg Supply remained orderly and a clipboard hung near the counter with precise inventory notes in Cliff's neat handwriting. Though the store showed signs of recent activity - some empty spaces on shelves where emergency supplies had been opened and stacked - it retained its usual organization. The air held the distinctive scent of rubber insulation, cardboard, and machine oil, familiar and almost comforting in its normalcy.

"It's good to see you both. Friendly faces are always welcome in times like this." Cliff checked and double-checked the interior deadbolts, then peeled the curtain back and stared out into the front yard once more.

"Have you seen many unfriendly faces?" Benjamin asked, lowering the shotgun from his shoulder, but still gripping it tightly in one hand.

"Not here, thankfully. I made the mistake of going into town yesterday, just to see what was happening. I walked through the trees and was able to get back here without being spotted. Glad I didn't take my truck."

"That bad?" Doug asked, the imagery of the circular impact craters and the glittering brass of possible shell casings outside the credit union fresh in his mind.

"I didn't stick around long enough to find out. Heard some people shouting, smelled some smoke, heard some smashing glass and I turned right around and came back here." He leaned by the oak counter and crossed his arms, studying both Benjamin and Doug in turn.

"How about the two of you? How's that wife of yours, Doug? She okay with all this going on?"

"We're holding together. All things concerned, we're probably doing better than most. The vineyard's in decent shape, turns out it's an okay place to hole up during a crisis. Benjamin here is sticking around, we've got a couple of other people helping out, too. What about you? Besides that scary foray into town, things been okay?"

"I guess that depends on your definition of okay. I've got food reserves, I've got a well and the water's been fine. As you can see I've got power, too, though I try and use it sparingly if I can. I'm a little worried that the glow of lights in the trees might attract unwanted visitors, especially judging by what I heard in town yesterday."

"Smart man." Benjamin held the shotgun at his right hip and took a slow walk around the open section of Greenberg Supply.

"You've probably seen more of downtown than I have." Cliff stepped away from the counter and made his way around it, bending low and disappearing from view.

There was the low suction of a refrigerator door opening and he emerged a second later, three brown bottles clenched within his hooked fingers.

"Beer?" He held them out.

Doug and Benjamin simultaneously held up their hands. "None for us, thanks," Doug smiled.

Cliff nodded and ducked down again, the clatter of glass and opening, then closing of the mini-fridge following.

"Didn't you have an employee or two who worked for you?" Doug angled to look behind the counter.

"I did. Haven't seen either of them since this started. I was working on my own that first day, Buck had the day off and Ronnie called in sick." Cliff laughed and looked down at the bottle in his hand. "More like called in hungover. That was happening more and more often recently." He took another sip, oblivious to the irony of his words and actions. "Just as well, I guess. Keeping myself upright, fed and sheltered is difficult enough, I wouldn't want to think I'm responsible for a couple of others. Give you credit, Doug, you and your wife both."

"Believe me, the folks at the vineyard have earned it. We're all working pretty hard together up there. Needed all hands on deck."

"Nice to hear stories of folks coming together. All the movies and books about this sort of thing, everyone wants to kill each other right from the get-go."

"There's some of that, too," Benjamin replied, then lifted his shotgun slightly. "We're not carrying this thing around as a fashion accessory."

Cliff took another swallow of beer and set the bottle on the oak counter. "You said you all needed something?"

"We do. Wish it was safe enough to just come over to say hi, but unfortunately, yeah, we need something." Doug gestured toward a few spools of wire mounted on one of the nearby walls. "Hoping maybe you have some two gauge and some conduit. We thought we had some, but it turns out the delivery never arrived before everything went belly-up."

"You want two gauge?" Cliff's brow bunched, forming creases along his forehead. "This for those solar panels you guys were installing?"

"Exactly," Benjamin replied before Doug could. "The panels are down, and we've got no power. Rotten food in the freezers, the whole nine yards. We think the wire underground between the panels and the house is messed up. Not sure when we might get them back up and running, but some fresh cable might help."

Doug gave him a brief sideways glance, but only for a moment.

"That's no good." Cliff shook his head. "That's no good at all. This is the exact sort of reason you want panels like that in the first place. Are you all doing okay? Managing without power the past few days must be tough." Cliff shook his head and took another long drink. "I've been taking my power for granted, I wouldn't want to be in your situation, no way, no how."

"Things could be a lot worse." Benjamin drew his broad shoulders into a shrug. "We're making out okay. But we really could use some of that cable, just to help figure out what's going on. If we can get a panel or three up, we might could get some running water going."

"Happy to help," Cliff replied. "My roof panels have got me more than covered, and I've got plenty of what you need. Happy to get you some two gauge, and I'll recommend some ten, just in case your panel-to-panel connections are faulty."

"That would be much appreciated, Cliff." Doug reached into his pocket, fumbling inside for a moment, then retrieved a thick wad of folded bills. Holding the cash in one hand, he began to leaf through it with the other, silently counting it off. "We always kept a bit of cash at the vineyard, just in case, but I'm afraid this is all I've got. It's definitely not enough for all of what we need, but..." Doug held out the cash and Cliff accepted it, not even counting it before he shoved it in his own pocket.

"Don't be ridiculous. I know you're good for it, Doug. How long have we known each other, after all? Besides, I know where you live." He flashed Benjamin an affable wink. "Though if you're walking around with that twelve-gauge, maybe I won't come looking for the rest after all."

The three men shared a laugh and Cliff drank down the rest of the bottle of beer, setting the empty back on the counter.

"Sure I can't trouble you for one of these?" He lifted the empty. "I don't have many left, but the last thing I need is to get blind drunk, anyway. Probably best if I share the wealth. This thing will be past us in a few weeks and the stores'll be opening right back up."

"We're okay, Cliff, but I appreciate the sentiment."

"Suit yourself." His beer finished, Cliff walked around the nearby oak counter and grunted as he struggled with something. "You doing okay, Doug? That limp ain't nothin' serious, right?" He asked the question without looking over, still focused on his work.

"I'll be fine. Just a little mishap at the vineyard, nothing serious."

"Glad to hear it. You'll tell Sheila I said hello?"

"Of course. She'll be happy to hear from you."

With a clunk and a muttered grunt, Cliff back-pedaled from behind the counter, wheeling a portable cable reel stand in his wake. It rolled freely on two wheels, tipped slightly back as Cliff maneuvered it into position beneath the spool of two gauge cable mounted on the wall rack. The metal frame of the jack was shaped like an "H" with a pair of sturdy support arms extending upward, designed to cradle the heavy, wooden reel. He turned the jack's hand crank, the gears clicking as the support arms rose. The threaded spindle that ran through the center rotated smoothly, lifting the support assembly.

"This beauty can handle up to five thousand pounds," Cliff said, positioning the support arms just beneath the cable reel. "That boy Ronnie still needed my help to operate it when he needed it. Been working here for six years and couldn't even run a cable jack. I swear, maybe I'm better off without him." Cliff laughed heartily, then coughed and thumped on his chest. "Excuse me." He continued cranking until the weight transferred from the wall mount to the stand. "See how this works? Keeps the spool at the perfect height and lets it rotate freely when we pull the cable."

He released the wall mount's locking pin and guided the reel onto the stand's spindle. The spool settled with a solid thunk, balanced perfectly on the rotating support arms and Cliff gave it an experimental spin with his palm. "How many feet you boys need?" He produced a measuring tape from his belt.

"What do you think, Benjamin?" Doug asked.

Benjamin was already chewing his lower lip, deep in thought. "Can you spare three hundred? Better to have extra we can cut down rather than ending up not having enough."

"That's probably a good number. You start getting higher than that, the cable gets a little unwieldy. As it is, we'll need a dolly to load it in that trailer of yours. You have one at home you can use to unload it?"

"We'll manage with the tractor forks," Benjamin replied.

"Measuring tape isn't going to help much if we're talking about three hundred feet." He hooked it back onto his belt and returned to the counter.

Reaching behind it, he emerged once more a moment later with a mechanical footage counter, which he clamped to the edge of the cable stand. There was a spring-loaded wheel built within the counter that pressed against the cable, a faint digital display counting the feet as the cable moved past it. Cliff zeroed out the display, then began to pull, the counter ticking up as he did so. Its wheel spun steadily, its rubber surface gripping the cable's black insulation and Cliff continued pulling until the measurement read 310 feet.

"Always measure just a little extra." Cliff vanished behind the counter again and returned a moment later with a set of heavy-duty cable cutters, gripping the long handles and prying open the curved, serrated blades.

He positioned the serrated blades on either side of the stark, black cable, then threw his weight into the handles, compressing them together, the cable parting with a satisfying snick. Cliff flipped the release on the footage counter and retrieved a metal coiling frame from nearby, a simple stand with four pegs forming a square.

"This'll keep the loops uniform," he explained, beginning to guide the heavy cable around the pegs in careful circles.

He moved methodically, each loop of the thick, insulated wire laying neatly against the last, building up layers of three-foot diameter coils. Every few loops, he threaded heavy-duty zip ties through the bundle, securing the layers together. The cable's natural memory helped it hold the circular shape and when the full length was coiled, Cliff added three more zip ties, spaced evenly around the circle. He then crossed the bundle with nylon strapping in a figure-eight pattern, cinching it tight with a ratcheting buckle. The finished coil was about eight inches thick, secured against unraveling during transport.

"This baby will weigh just over two hundred pounds, so like I said, we'll want a dolly to load it into your trailer and you'll need more than the two of you to get it out."

"We'll be fine," Benjamin assured him. "Can't thank you enough for this, Cliff."

"Trust me, I'm happy to help. I was starting to wonder if I'd never see another friendly face ever again. Sure am glad you guys are doing okay." He stood and dusted off his palms. "Now for your conduit." He led them down an aisle where gray PVC pipe stood in neat and even rows. "Schedule 40, since you're burying it. That'll protect against any rocks in the soil." Crossing his arms, he stepped back, studying the rows of varied lengths of PVC conduit. "How long is your trailer?" Cliff glanced briefly over his right shoulder.

"Twenty-four feet."

"Tandem axel? How much weight?"

"Plenty," Benjamin replied with a curt nod. "Five tons, more than enough for a spool and some PVC."

"Good. Sounds good." Cliff patted a stacked row of tall lengths of conduit. "These are measured off at twenty feet apiece. For three hundred feet, we need fifteen. I've got twelve here and probably thirty more in the back, so we should have more than enough."

"I hate to use up your whole supply."

"Honestly, Doug, what else am I going to use it for? Even if I run into some trouble out here, you're leaving me enough to work with. And I know where the distribution warehouse is. If things go that far down the crapper, I can take a drive to Salem and get more."

"It may not be as easy as that," Doug warned.

"Oh?" Cliff didn't bother to turn his head, still staring at the PVC as he counted on his fingers and in his head.

Benjamin coughed lightly, catching Doug's eye, and shook his head while mouthing 'no,' and Doug nodded. "At least from what I heard. Someone passed by at the vineyard, said the road between here and Salem was in rough shape. Abandoned vehicles, a big crash that clogged traffic."

"Well that sucks. I'll figure something out, but come on, like I'll need more of this crap anytime soon. Come on, help me with it, would you?"

The three men worked together, counting off fifteen lengths of twenty-foot PVC conduit, then threaded it through the shop, out the front door and into the trailer behind the Jeep. Doug stood and watched mostly, his weight on his right foot, tensed in uneasy anticipation.

"Let me help with the next load," he said, stepping forward as Benjamin and Cliff came back inside, Cliff dabbing at his sweat-glistened forehead with the back of his hand.

"You need to keep weight off that leg." Benjamin said in his usual sternness. "I know you're my boss, but Sheila's *your* boss and her orders were pretty clear."

Doug blew out an exasperated breath, then stepped out of the way as Benjamin and Cliff continued loading the conduit. A few moments later, they'd stacked and strapped down fifteen full lengths of twenty-foot conduit, wedging it along the left side of the trailer, leaving enough room for the coil of three-hundred feet of wire. Cliff retrieved a dolly and wheeled it out from the back room, then positioned it alongside the coil of cable, extending the reinforced platform so it was long enough to carry the thick bundle of coiled cable.

"Lift that up just a bit." He pointed toward the wire and Benjamin crouched low, wedging his gloved hands beneath the wire and lifting it just enough for Cliff to slide the platform beneath it.

The two men walked around to the other side of the zip-tied cable and grunted as they struggled to lift it, muttering between themselves. Doug limped over and crouched alongside them, bending to put most of his weight on his right leg. Benjamin turned toward him, but Doug shook him off.

"Don't bother. I'm helping whether you like it or not."

Benjamin ground his teeth, the three men working together to lift the coil and rest it back against the dolly. Breathing hard, Cliff wiped some more sweat from his brow, then tipped the dolly up, walking it toward the rear of the store instead of the front.

"We'll have to take this out through the loading dock in back, it won't fit through the front door."

Doug limped down one of the wide aisles and pushed open the double doors marked Employees Only, revealing the neatly organized back storage room, each thick, metal shelf lined and marked in Cliff's same neat handwriting. A corrugated steel door at the rear stood between them and the outside, and Benjamin hurried to it, unlatching and lifting it to reveal a concrete slab in the rear of the building. Together, the three men took turns wheeling the dolly out and around, following an asphalt walkway until they came back around to the front. Once they lowered the ramp to the trailer, it took some effort and coordination to push and pull the dolly up the slope, but they got the job done, resting the coil of wire in the trailer alongside the fifteen lengths of PVC conduit. Without the wire on the dolly, they were able to wheel it back through the front door and into the shop.

"Well, that's my workout for the week," Cliff said with a laugh.

Once more, he vanished around the counter and emerged with a bottle of beer. He raised his eyebrows at Doug and Benjamin, but they echoed their polite decline, and Cliff cracked the bottle open, taking a long gulp. He exhaled afterwards and set the bottle on the counter.

"I'm assuming that's not all you guys need." Cliff walked toward the glass display case, then unlocked it and removed a set of heavy-duty wire strippers with long, compound action handles and hardened steel blades. "These'll handle anything up to 250 MCM. I'll throw in some smaller ones too, for when you're making your connections."

He made several more trips to the display case, coming back with terminals, heat shrink tubing and electrical tape. "Want some PVC cement for the conduit? Got the purple primer too."

"Better grab it all," Benjamin said. "Rather have it and not need it."

Cliff produced the cans of cement and primer, then paused.

"Almost forgot – you'll need these." He grabbed a bag of conduit spacers and set those on the counter alongside the rest. "These will keep it all aligned underground. And some pull string to run through before you put the cable in." He tossed some of that onto the counter, too. "What else do you need?"

"Cliff, honestly, this is above and beyond." Doug shook his head as he surveyed everything on the counter.

"You never know, I might need your help down the road. Consider this a down-payment in case that ever comes up." Cliff gathered the remaining supplies into a bag and handed it to Doug. Benjamin held the shotgun in his right, gripping the pump action as the two men walked toward the front door.

"Honestly, it's just great to see you both," Cliff said, a note of joviality in his voice.

He lifted the bottle he'd taken from the counter and took another long swallow, then stood at the opened door while Doug and Benjamin headed for the Jeep. Doug paused by the passenger side door as Benjamin slid behind the wheel, then tossed a wave toward Cliff and climbed in, slamming the door in his wake. It wasn't until they were both inside the vehicle and Benjamin had started the engine when Doug looked over, brow furrowed.

"What was up with that?"

"With what?" Benjamin shifted into gear and accelerated, turning the Jeep around in the gravel lot, then headed back toward the road through the gap in the trees.

"You lied to him. Or at least you didn't tell him the full truth. Why didn't you tell him what we really needed the wire for? He bent over backwards for us just then."

"I've got no problem with Cliff. You're right, he is a good guy. But did you hear him rambling on? He told us all about his own solar panels, the supplies he's got. The guy's got loose lips and he drinks a little more beer than he should. I trust him, but he's not the kind of guy I want to entrust with our own secrets. Who knows who else might stop by this place? People he knows, people he doesn't? I don't want us to be victimized by his loose lips." Benjamin pulled out onto the street and turned left, heading back toward downtown.

"Don't you think that's a little melodramatic?"

"Not at all. Look, I didn't like lying to him, Doug. It's just that, in times like this, when the world is so dangerous, we should keep as much information close to our vest as possible."

Doug nodded, peering through the passenger's side window at the seemingly endless scroll of evergreen trees along the far side of the road. "I understand," Doug finally replied. "I don't like it, but I understand. And I guess I agree, too."

Moments later they were entering downtown Silverpine once more, passing the same familiar landmarks only in reverse order. As he had earlier, Doug studied the parking lot and the exterior of the credit union, focusing even more attention on it coming from the opposite direction. The longer his gaze was held on the brick-work exterior, the more certain he became that the small holes dotting the outside of the building were in fact bullet holes and the glitters of metallic reflection were brass shell casings. He kept staring as they drove by, his head turning back and back and back some more as the Jeep continued ahead.

"You're thinking what I'm thinking." Benjamin steered around the next corner, the building falling out of sight.

"There was a gunfight there."

Benjamin nodded. "Bad one, too. Dead body in the entrance."

"I saw it."

Doug sighed, his grip tightening around the shotgun as he lifted it and draped it across his thighs. Once more the buildings thinned out around them, structures gradually replaced by trees until there was nothing around but forests of tall, pointed green arrows. Benjamin accelerated more quickly, eager to put downtown Silverpine in the rearview mirror.

Both of them were so relieved to have left the town, neither one even glanced at the small dirt section off the right shoulder of the road where a white panel van was parked. Both men faced forward, intent on the road ahead, unaware of the sets of eyes within the panel van following their movements, not hearing the rattling growl of the van starting up, and not seeing as it slowly pulled out, merged onto the road, then ambled after them as they made their way back toward the vineyard.

# CHAPTER 13

**CBRN Response Team**
**Denver, Colorado**

A faint rectangle of light surrounded Major Hayes as she advanced into the stone church, one hand resting near her holstered pistol, the second arm extended, her fingers clasped around the contoured handle of the spectrum analyzer. She took two strides forward, then hesitated, the silence of the church's interior a veritable wall against the outside world. Together, the entire CBRN team paused just inside the heavy wooden doors of the Church of the Holy Ghost, their Type A protective suits friction-rubbing with each movement. Afternoon light filtered through the stained glass windows above, casting rainbow patterns across the church's ornate interior. Major Hayes raised her fist, the universal signal to hold, while Tech Sergeant Cooper swept his broad-spectrum analyzer across the entrance.

As Hayes held her post, she changed her elevated fist to a forward jerk of two fingers and the rest of the team fanned out around her.

Five sets of boots softly scraped along the wooden floor as the team moved into the building, shadowed against the light from the sun at their backs. For a long moment, the team stood spread and separated throughout the main entrance, then Clarkson released the door, and it hammered closed, its booming echo jolting Hayes where she stood.

"Warn me when you're going to do that," she hissed, peering back over her right shoulder.

"Sorry, Major."

To Hayes' left, Cooper and Jiro advanced into the building while Winston and Clarkson passed to her right. Each of them held a different device in one hand, three of them with broad spectrum analyzers while Jiro clutched a more advanced Ion Mobility Spectrometer. They moved throughout the dimly lit interior of the church, pausing every so often as they collected and collated the data.

"Readings are definitely elevated here," Cooper reported through his mask's comm system, "Showing similar trace elements that we saw outside, but parts per million are climbing."

"Understood," Hayes replied. "Lieutenant Winston, take point with detection gear. Jiro, keep a close eye on that IMS. See if it's noticing anything the broad spectrums aren't."

They strode further into the narthex, boots echoing on the marble floor, the sound dulled by their protective gear. Motes danced and fluttered within the colored sunlight through stained glass, a sickly pale glow slung across dormant holy water fonts. The vestibule opened into the main sanctuary, and even through their protective masks the space weighed on them, solid, heavy and overpowering in its grandeur. Soaring Gothic arches disappeared into shadow above and brass chandeliers hung like silent sentinels. Stained glass windows lined both walls - saints and martyrs staring down at the intruders with expressions more accusatory than beatific in the dim light.

Winston moved forward, her detection equipment humming.

"Getting even stronger readings here, Major. Whatever we're looking for, we're getting closer to where it started."

The nave stretched before them, row upon row of wooden pews leading to the distant altar. Papers littered the center aisle along with hymnals, bulletins, a child's coloring book and a woman's shoe lying on its side, its owner lying face-down two rows up.

"Jiro?" Hayes spoke through clenched teeth.

"I'm seeing a lot of the same, Major. Elevated readings, detection spikes the farther in we move."

The team advanced slowly toward the center aisle, their instruments casting dancing shadows across the pews. Each step brought new readings, new data points that painted a grim picture. Cooper's analyzer chirped steadily, its display showing rising levels of the unknown compound. A hymn board still displayed last Sunday's songs, its white plastic numbers stark against the black felt. Below it, a table held a stack of donation envelopes, weighed down by an empty offering plate.

"Clarkson, holster that analyzer. Use local comms, see if you can reach Williams. I'd like to see how his trek up Broadway is going."

Clarkson nodded and hesitated, slowing his forward stride. He slipped the spectrometer in a holstered sleeve on one hip and unhooked a walkie talkie from his belt alongside it. After a quick channel check, he thumbed the call button.

"Williams, this is Clarkson, Major Hayes looking for a status check, please report." Clarkson released the talk button, static filling the speaker once more.

A few seconds of static stretched out into a minute, and then two minutes, Clarkson eyeing Hayes through their translucent helmets.

"Give it another try."

Clarkson followed the major's orders, initiating another call to

Sergeant Williams, but like before, nothing returned over the speaker except for mottled, unsteady static.

"I don't think we're getting a signal. Stone walls are too thick, like you thought they might be."

Major Hayes nodded and Clarkson swapped his radio back out for the analyzer. "Cooper, Winston," Hayes said, approaching the other two, "full spectrum analysis of every row of pews leading to the altar. Jiro, keep that IMS going, tell me if you see something we're missing."

They made their way toward the rows of pews. Cooper froze just inside the first bench, glancing to the right. A dead body was slumped on the bench, resting on its right shoulder, a left arm draped over its chest, dangling over the edge of the seat. A second body was a few feet deeper, on the floor, wedged tightly between the two rows of benches. Hymnals were scattered about, some on the seats, others on the floor, dropped when the parishioners made their hasty exits. An outstretched hand reached from between two more rows, fingers grasping for something Hayes couldn't see. A bible was open on the floor nearby, an elderly woman lying in a fetal position behind another row of pews, clutching something to her chest. Dried blood was caked to her face in frozen tears, her head tilted over a bony shoulder.

In the center aisle, a man in minister's garb was lying face down, arms splayed, a few more scattered bodies within view between the altar and where the team stood a short distance away. None of them spoke, the only noises their rasping breaths from within their ventilators and the steady, trilling chirp of their analyzers, all moving in careful concert. Cooper halted near the elderly woman, dropping to a crouch, using the scanner to closely examine her body. Winston made his way to the minister, performing the same analysis, pausing to slightly adjust some of the dials to capture the data they needed to bring back.

"Each step forward the readings tick higher and higher."

Winston craned his neck around, fingers still clamped around the handle of his instrument.

"Then we keep moving and we keep scanning," Major Hayes replied.

The group did as ordered, converging, advancing, then spreading out again, using their instruments to examine whatever bodies they came across. There were six of them wedged in various rows as they drew nearer to the altar, and the CRBN team checked each one, tracking their readings. Their footsteps echoed off the vaulted ceiling as they approached the chancel. The carved wooden altar stood silent, its brass cross reflecting the pale, rainbow lights through the stained glass windows. Behind it, the pipe organ's massive tubes stretched upward, silent witnesses to whatever horror had unfolded.

Winston's detector emitted a sharp tone as they approached the altar. "Another spike in our readings here. Unmistakable."

"Team, converge. On me, here at the altar."

The other members of the team closed ranks, approaching from the side aisles where they'd been performing more of their own analysis. Moments later, the group gathered together in the shadows of the altar, staring up at the cross and the pipe organ beyond. Everyone stared at the miniature screens, tracking the scrolls of data, each one nodding softly at similar readings. Pale, green light reflected from translucent masks, the late afternoon sun streaming through the west windows, turning the saints' faces blood red.

"We need to keep moving. Past the altar, into the rear of the church. It looks tight back in there but you know the routine, slow and steady."

Heads nodded all around. Major Hayes' chest ached, a steady, rapid thrum, her heart pounding in her ears, shooting an unsettling flutter through her chest. She battled through the urge to breathe more deeply and more quickly, forced herself to keep her inhalations and exhalations consistent and steady. To her right, the uneven rhythmic hiss of someone's ragged breathing turned her head.

"Clarkson? You okay?"

Clarkson bobbed his head up and down, still focused on the analyzer in his hand. "We're close, Major," he replied in a breathy, metallic whisper. "Readings are still climbing." his voice broke off at the end of the sentence.

"Focus, Clarkson." Hayes' reached out and grabbed his arm, her voice laced with warmth and compassion. "You can do this."

In the young man's hand the analyzer shook, trembling left to right, the pale, green screen jostling. Clarkson wrapped his other hand around the first, gripping the analyzer like a pistol, but it still shifted unsteadily in his grasp.

"We're going to go past the altar, okay? Walk toward the rear of the church." Hayes leaned back toward Cooper. "Cooper, can you check the retrochoir?"

"The retro *what*?"

"It's the space behind the high altar. There." Hayes gestured with her own measuring implement. "Just run a few high level checks. Then we're heading to the ambulatory." She pointed toward a tall set of doors at the rear wall just beyond the main altar.

Brass candlesticks flanked the high altar, unlit and tarnished in the dim light while behind it, the reredos stretched upward, carved figures of saints and angels disappearing into encroaching shadow. The pipe organ's massive tubes loomed above, their polished surfaces reflecting the colored light filtered through the stained glass windows in dull, crimson gleams.

"Readings are climbing," Cooper reported, his analyzer's display showing steadily increasing numbers. "Back here behind the high altar, numbers are definitely still elevated."

Hayes nodded, then gestured for Cooper to come back and he did so, hesitating for a moment alongside Clarkson. Cooper whispered a few quiet encouragements to the man and slowly, the device in his grip slowed its sideways jostling and remained steady.

"You with us, Clarkson?" Hayes asked.

"I think so." Clarkson nodded, his face softly illuminated by interior lights within the translucent face shield. "I'm sorry."

"No need. Just focus and do your job – that's all you need to worry about."

Whether it was a trick of the light or truly the young man's complexion, his face was stark white, the color of the unused linen. Hayes chewed her lip, glancing back toward the entrance of the large church, beyond the sprawled bodies, the faint rays of colored light through the windows and the even rows of pews. For a moment, she considered sending Clarkson back out to give him some time and space to work through whatever he was going through, but she bit back the urge and waited for him and Cooper to rejoin the group.

Together the team all pushed through the tall doors and entered the ambulatory where the curved walkway wrapped behind the apse. Smaller, enclosed chapels opened to their left, each room dedicated to different saints. Their helmeted heads turned methodically, sweeping every corner, each of them triggering helmet mounted flashlights, which cast an eerie pale glow throughout the dimly lit corridor, littered with abandoned devotional candles and prayer cards.

Winston's detector chirped more urgently. "Major, these levels are still rising."

The ambulatory's vaulted ceiling curved overhead, its ribbed arches meeting at carved bosses while even more stained glass windows lined the outer wall, their colors muted in the failing daylight. A statue of Mary stood in an alcove, her outstretched hands more plaintive than welcoming. Before them, a trio of corpses were sprawled about the passage, each one nearly on top of each other, all three heaped like discarded trash just before a doorway leading to a large storeroom beyond. Inside, through the opened doorway, metal cabinets lined the walls, their surfaces dulled with a fine powder that absorbed the light. They approached the bodies carefully, each of them still moving their analyzers through the faded light of the corridor, steady undulating alerts signaling levels of contaminants.

Cooper's analyzer screamed a warning. "Whoa. Readings just flew off the charts."

"I'm seeing it, too," Clarkson reported, his voice stronger, but still thready.

"Confirmed," Jiro reported. "IMS is the same."

"Winston?" Hayes asked, staring at her own elevated readings.

"Same thing here, Major. It's unanimous."

"Any hits in the database yet?" Major Hayes took a few more steps toward Cooper, whose analyzer was running through the familiar process of cross-referencing known chemical agents and comparing those to what was in the air.

"No hits, but it's churning on something right now. Gotta let it do its voodoo."

Hayes took the lead, stepping over one of the sprawled bodies and advancing on the door to the storage room. Winston fanned left while Cooper fanned right, the two of them moving around the bodies while Jiro and Clarkson brought up the rear. They converged on the storage room entrance, then filed into it together, pressing through the narrow doorway. The team's lights played across the cabinets and storage shelves, the faint residue of something catching their light that should never have been there at all. The storage room seemed smaller with five people in protective suits, but they moved with practiced efficiency. A table sat in the center of the room alongside a row of shelves pressed up against the far wall. Beyond it, a small office set up with a desk and a swivel chair stood darkened by shadow, rows of filing cabinets along the wall. To the left, several stacks of boxed supplies lined another wall; paper towels and napkins, plastic dishware, and other odds and ends that didn't capture much of Hayes' attention.

"Set up the scanner," Hayes ordered, gesturing toward the nearby table in the center of the room.

Cooper disengaged from the group and made his way over, cautious step by cautious step, finally coming to a halt as he set the scanner where Major Hayes had indicated.

"Major? Can you take a look at this?"

Hayes turned toward him, the intersection of their helmet lights falling upon a trio of cylinders which stood on the table.

"What are those?" She slowly advanced, moving gingerly, head tilted as she scrutinized the oddly shaped packages.

"Label says they're AquaGuard water filters. But... I've got an AquaGuard pitcher at home and those don't look like any AquaGuard filters I've ever seen." Cooper lowered himself on bent knees, his light glowing even more brightly against the wrapped cylinders.

"Maybe they're some sort of commercial version?" Lieutenant Winston stood just behind Cooper.

"Nah, look at the label. That doesn't even look like the right logo."

Hayes reached out, grabbed one of the cylinders in a gloved hand and lifted it, turning it slightly as she studied it through her translucent face shield. She lifted the scanner from the table and ran it briefly along the length of the cylinder, nearly dropping both objects as the scanner screamed a sudden, shrill chorus of warning bleats.

"We've got active chemical agents on this cylinder." Major Hayes took several deep breaths in rapid succession, but didn't release her grip on the item.

"It's way taller than any water filter I've seen," Cooper continued, still staring intently at the cylinder even with the scanner's scream of warning in the background. "And look, the white paper filter stuff on the outside is just a shell. The interior is metal.

What kind of water filter has *metal* on the inside? None of this makes sense, Major."

Clarkson made his way around Major Hayes' left, angling around to the opposite side of the table where other cylinders stood. He slipped his scanner into a holster at his hip and leaned forward, gripping one of the other cylinders and lifting it for a closer look.

"So this is what we've been looking for, huh? Are these the deployment devices, then? Disguised as water filters?"

Across the table, Clarkson lifted the cylinder upward, turning it over to get a better look. As Hayes gave Cooper and Winston a rundown of instructions, Clarkson lowered the cylinder and examined one of the rounded ends. He spread his gloved fingers around a circular cap at the end of the cylinder and gently began to twist, squinting through the backlit shield covering his face.

"Major," he said quietly, finally drawing Hayes' attention. "I think this one might be intact still."

As she looked at him, he twisted the cap one more rotation to the left, a muffled ratchet and click signaling the adjustment of the cylinder.

"Clarkson! Don't!" Hayes reached across the table, her outstretched hands a few inches from where Clarkson stood, but it might as well have been miles.

The cylinder released another muffled clack, and a spring-loaded mechanism activated, the ends of the device suddenly erupting outward. Both caps punched free, launching a volley of hair-thin glass needles in a three hundred and sixty degree arc, a sudden and violent burst, like a crystal porcupine launching its quills. The entire storeroom was filled with the outward burst of glass shards as the needles crashed against the interior of the confined room, shattering on impact and releasing their contents. All at once, vapor erupted from the points of impact, billowing out from where the glass needles exploded. Major Hayes and the others in the room recoiled, screaming in agony as the glass needles ripped through their suits, penetrating straight through the Type A fabric and protective gear. The sudden, unexpected volley of piercing glass needles slashed through the protective suits of all five members of the CRBN team.

The air inside the storeroom – and the interior of their suits – filled with a sudden billowing eruption of pale-colored haze as the contents of the thin pieces of glass were released from their confinement. The fog swirled and churned like a living thing, a vacuous creature unleashed from the depths, filling all the empty space within the storeroom in a sudden surge of foul, penetrating death. Major Hayes gasped, stumbling backwards, looking down at her suit as another wave of pain lanced throughout her arms, torso and legs. Jerking her head upwards, she stared at Clarkson who watched back in wide-eyed horror, his face no longer pale but almost colorless. His suit had been totally ravaged from being in such close proximity to the device, his chest, stomach and thighs a tangled mass of shredded white and quickly spreading blood.

"I didn't..." his voice choked, his expression obscured beyond a swirling cloud of vapor that was releasing from inside his suit. "I didn't..." he dropped the cylinder with a clatter and clawed at his face, a ragged, lung-tearing chorus of coughs suddenly gripping him.

Cooper screamed, throwing himself backwards, away from the detonated cylinder, but his back pounded hard against the row of storage shelves with nowhere to go. Jiro threw the IMS down and wheeled around, but before he could take two steps, his knees buckled and he went to the ground, his voice a ragged scream. Winston slumped back against the wall, staring blankly as she gasped a weeping, desperate plea, her back sliding down until she was seated on the floor, slumped, blood already beginning to flow from her mouth and eyes as she whimpered helplessly.

Static crackled from nearby, Hayes' walkie-talkie coming to life. She clawed at the radio, her lungs straining, already nearly unresponsive to her desperate attempts to breathe. Grasping at the radio, she desperately tugged it free, her throat an impossibly narrow pinhole, refusing to allow any more air through. She gripped it in both hands, her vision clouded, her throat raw and lungs on fire. Her fingers trembled around the walkie talkie as she fumbled with the talk button, trying to respond to the hissing voice through the static that was suddenly so far away. The radio slipped from her fingers and clattered noisily to the hard ground and a moment later, Hayes joined it, her limbs no longer working, her internal organs releasing their fluids, her entire existence consumed by a flood of agony and then the blessed respite of darkness.

---

Master Sergeant David Williams paused on the scant landing, his suited left hand gripping the railing while his right held fast to the shotgun. Within his face shield, sweat trickled down his temple, the stairwell turning his Type A gear into a personal sauna. Jiro's large, heavy radio pack dug into his shoulders, and the shotgun was heavier and heavier with each upward floor. The silence within the stairwell was pervasive, his hissing breath and thudding bootsteps the only backdrop, his only grounding point between the darkened world and reality beyond. His breath stilled and somewhere below him, a rattling thunk drew his downward gaze, a whisper of noise passing through the darkness that almost sounded like a voice. It had been three days since he'd last heard Emma's voice. Three days of silence from Aurora, while reports of death tolls nationwide climbed into the millions. He'd tried her mother's landline, cell phone, even called the neighbors, but got nothing but dead air.

The steep incline of stairs reminded him of his last climb up Mount Elbert two months ago, Emma matching his pace step for step. She'd gotten so strong, no longer the little girl who needed carrying on trails.

"Just like wrestling practice, Dad," she'd said, powering through the thin air at fourteen thousand feet. "One more round." Sergeant Williams had smiled broadly at the back of his daughter's head, the warmth of his love doing little to melt the block of ice that surrounded his heart, forged by the divorce from her mother that had forced their separation.

He adjusted the radio pack's straps and started up again, step by step. Forty-two was a lot older in hazmat gear than it was on mountain trails, even during the steepest of hikes. The pale glow from his helmet-mounted flashlight cast everything in sickly green, his shadow stretching grotesque and distorted against the concrete walls. His boots echoed in the enclosed space, each step a deliberate push against gravity.

That day on Elbert, they'd watched a storm roll in across the valleys, purple clouds building like the crushing waves of an incoming tsunami. Emma had snapped photos with her new cell phone while he pointed out landmarks: Leadville, Mount Massive, the Arkansas River Valley far below. He clung to that memory as he climbed through artificial twilight, radio bending along his spine, one gloved hand wrapped around the body of the shotgun, the other pulling himself upward on the railing. Somewhere out there, Aurora lay silent, his daughter's fate unknown, potentially just another statistic, a single tick mark in a field of millions.

Beyond the narrow sliver of a landing, the last flight toward roof access loomed ahead, faintly illuminated by the glow from his helmet's flashlight. His analyzer's display glowed a soft green, its readings steady, showing no signs of contamination. Lowering his head, he continued onward, just like those last few hundred feet on a fourteener, one foot in front of the other, steady pace, controlled breathing. The difference was that mountain summits didn't have steel security doors between the climber and the view.

He'd been on Mount Evans when the first attacks hit Kansas City. His phone had lit up with emergency alerts while other hikers gathered around their cars at Summit Lake, faces pale as reports rolled in. He'd made it home in record time, just as his emergency beeper was going off, calling him to Fort Buckley to form a response team. Sergeant Williams had made it to Buckley in record time and been in one of the first teams sent into action, boots on the ground in Denver. No place he'd rather be, except for perhaps the summit, staring down across the valley beneath the purple clouds of approaching dark.

Another sign was bolted to the wall to his left, identifying ROOF ACCESS ahead, an upward sloping arrow pointing into the gathering darkness. Finally he reached the top landing, his breath heavy and sour in his mask, rasping out through built-in filters. The door ahead revealed itself among the outward spray of his flashlight, three-inch layered steel, thick, reinforced hinges and a multi-layered electronic locking mechanism with an internal battery, glowing softly red to indicate it was securely fastened. A metal sign on the door read ROOF ACCESS but when Williams reached out and tested the door, it didn't budge. Crouching slightly, he rested the shotgun on the stairs, leaning it against the nearby wall and closely examined the keypad, searching for any sign of a manual override or an access panel he could use to bypass it.

Williams unslung the radio pack next, setting it carefully against the wall opposite the shotgun, his hands groping at the door, searching for any potential weak spots. The hinges were external, a poor design choice normally, but with their thick, reinforced cylinders, he had his doubts about their vulnerability. Constructed of three solid pins, hardened steel fastened the door to its perimeter frame, and though the hinges were worn from years of use, they showed no evident signs of weakness.

"Let's give my lock pick another shot." Williams grasped the shotgun, gathering it up into two hands and he took a partial step back, pointing the barrel at the middle hinge of the door.

He scanned his surroundings, illuminating the darkness with the sweeping glow of his helmet light, side-to-side, then up in a broad arc and down again. He was in a tightly confined space, the corridor closed in around him like a narrowed throat. Williams took another step back and aimed the shotgun at the center hinge, bracing himself sideways, swallowing down the surging thrum of his heart. He counted off one second, then two, then ejected the buckshot shell and dug out another breaching round, feeding it into the chamber and pumping it home. Bracing, he aimed the barrel at the hinge, then pulled the trigger. An eruption of light and sound was blinding and deafening all at once, the weapon exploding with an all-encompassing roar within the tight confines of the corridor. Sparks blasted from the center hinge, a full-on sheet of projectile fire striking that area and scattering back in a wide, spraying arc. Williams swung around recoiling as the ricochet sprayed, breach fragments pelting the surrounding walls.

Williams took another step back and down, re-centered the shotgun and loaded another breaching shell. The second time he aimed at the locking mechanism and not the hinges, then he pumped, lowered his head and fired again, the power of the weapon kicking it in his tight grasp. Once more it blasted into the door lock, then splashed back in a sudden sparking rebound. The swirling hum of ricocheting fragments buzzed just past the side of his head, clattering against the wall to his left, the blinding light of the shotgun blast shrinking back into shadow. His ears rang and his eyes danced with orbs of brightness against the darkness that returned in the wake of the blast.

"Well, crap." He lowered the weapon and stared at the door, still illuminated by his headlamp.

The steel was barely scuffed, both at the hinge and the lock, a couple of tiny indentations the only evidence of the shotgun blasts. The damage was superficial and did nothing to release the lock or free the door, leaving Williams standing on the upward slope of stairs, the shotgun held at his side. More sweat wormed its way into his right eye, thickening cool dampness on the nape of his neck, the heat and acrid stink filling the insides of his hermetically sealed helmet. Williams fought back his rapid breathing, forcing the hammer of his heart to slow into a more even rhythm. Lowering the shotgun, Williams turned and settled into place, taking a seat at the narrow shelf of a top landing just before the roof access door. He bent, resting his arms over his thighs.

Emma would have been waiting at her mom's place in Aurora, working on her science project. Williams promised to help her with it this weekend, his weekend, one of the two weekends per month he most looked forward to waking up in the morning. His ears continued to ring from the echo of the shotgun blasts, his gloved hands thrumming from the vibrations. At the outskirts of his distorted hearing, his ex-wife's voice came to him through the phone, that last twenty second, static-filled call as everything burned. He'd told her not to worry, told her to tell Emma not to worry, everything was going to be okay. She'd asked him if he'd heard anything 'through the grapevine' but at that point he hadn't. He hadn't warned them to seek higher ground, he hadn't warned them to shelter in place, and in fact his ex-wife had already decided to head to her mother's place with Emma in tow. Williams had started to voice his displeasure as static ripped through the phone, and his ex-wife had taken his concern for anger. She'd hung up on him at that moment and he'd never reached her again.

At his hip, the holstered analyzer chirped again, and he tugged it free, searching the screen, which read clearer than it had since they'd touched down in Denver. There were no signs of anything up near the top level of the tower. Turning, he looked in the direction of the church in the skyscraper's shadow, trying to picture what might be going on with the rest of the team down below. Voices scratched in his ears, low and faint, ghosts from his previous life, fading echoes from the nonfunctional radio. There was another sound alongside them, the same odd creaking groan from the depths of the narrow stairwell, the building continuing its creaking settle.

He stared at the radio pack, but rather than get the long-range gear out, he freed his short range local-channel walkie talkie and pressed the talk button, double-checking the frequency. "Major Hayes, this is Sergeant Williams. Hayes, are you there?" Releasing the button, static filled the speaker.

Somewhere, the voices continued, but not from the speakers, from somewhere else, most likely from his unstable mind. He pressed the button again, lifted the radio and called to the team a second time, but once more got no response. Surrounded by the shadowed darkness, perched on the top step in the narrow corridor leading to the roof of 1999 Broadway, he was as alone as he'd ever been. Leaning, he rested the back of his helmeted head against the sturdy door at the top of the stairs, then slipped his radio into its sleeve and reached over, clawing the radio pack toward him. Accessing the long-range radio pack, Williams extended the antenna and disengaged the handset, gripping it in his hand and double-checked the channel.

"Buckley Command, this is Response Team Echo. Master Sergeant Williams from Response Team Echo, please come in." Static came back through the handset, an undulating crackle of sound obscuring any voice that might have come along with it. "Buckley Command, this is Team Echo." Williams rested back against the door, the metal smooth against his spine and the back of his covered head.

Still no response came from the radio, the walls of 1999 Broadway muffling the signal. Williams blew out a long breath, its metallic hiss filling the narrow corridor as he returned the handset to its place and bundled the radio back into its pack, his chin lowered toward his chest. Shadows thickened, darkness clawing around him, the tunnel of light formed by his headlamp insufficient to light the entire stairwell. For quite some time he sat on the top step, working through the options in his mind, the pain in his legs easing to a dull ache, his back further stiffening the longer he sat on the stairs. Whispered voices came and went, too low and indistinct, causing Williams to glance around in the creeping darkness.

"I'm hearing things." He shook his head and pressed his palm to the wall to his right, using it to push himself up.

Shifting his stance, he balanced on the stairs and froze for a moment, directing his ears down the stairs toward the darkness beyond. Whispers fell silent, the corridor returning to its quiet darkness, and his ramrodding heart slowed in response. He looked around the stairwell, his brow furrowed in pensive thought as he shrugged the backpack on his shoulders once more and lifted the shotgun back into his two hands.

Altitude was one part of the puzzle they were after in their attempt to reach Buckley, but it was about more than altitude. Turning left, he rapped on the nearby wall, the thick, rigid concrete echoing back at him, cracking his knuckles. It wasn't the resonating rebound of a hollow wall, just the dull, boney thud of solid concrete and steel.

"No wonder I can't get a signal through here." He eyed the stairs and slowly began to descend, leaning a bit as he traversed.

Taking one step at a time, the thick soles of his boots pounded dully in the darkness and silence, creeping down, one soft stride after the next. Reaching a narrow landing, he paused for just a second, then continued down the next flight, moving the opposite way the arrow was pointed for roof access. A moment later, he reached the next level, Floor 43 labeled on a sign bolted to the thick concrete wall. If the roof wasn't going to work, perhaps the penthouse was the next best thing, and he angled toward the door, turned the knob and pushed it open. Within the translucent face shield, Williams grinned long and wide as he neared a series of doors leading to various offices, including an executive suite of the penthouse businesses.

In mid-stride, he paused once more, turning as he heard more strange sounds in the background. No whispered voices, but a low, undulating creak, the soft, grinding groan from somewhere not beneath him, but around him. For a moment, the floor swayed beneath his feet, rocking back and forth, but he held out his hand, shifting his weight and then shook off the sensation, the building growing still once more.

"Get a grip, Williams," he hissed to himself, the echo of his boots covering up the strange creaking and tapping sounds that were present moments earlier.

The helmet-mounted flashlight created a maze of shadows in the 43rd-floor hallway as Williams moved carefully, the weight of his suit and gear making each step deliberate. His shotgun swept the corridor methodically, muscle memory from countless building clearances. Elaborate mahogany wood paneling lined the walls, dulled by age, shining pale and bland against the reflection of his light. Brass nameplates marked closed doors, law offices, investment firms, the ghosts of Denver's financial elite. The sound came again, a strange, unsettled creaking noise that didn't belong among steel and glass, the floor once more seemingly swaying beneath his feet. It echoed from somewhere ahead, where the hallway opened into the northwest corner suite.

The carpet muffled his footsteps, thick pile that probably cost more than his monthly mortgage and he approached double doors ahead, heavy oak with frosted glass panels. Through them, the sound came again, a groan mixed with rhythmic tapping, like a large rodent skittering through an attic that wasn't there. Nearest to him, a nameplate read "Geoffrey Lancaster, Managing Partner." The brass had been polished so recently he could see his suited reflection, distorted and alien and the analyzer's display ticked softly as he approached the doors, still showing no sign of whatever had ravaged the city of Denver. His hand found the door handle and he pushed it open. Through his facepiece the Denver mountains came into view beyond floor-to-ceiling windows, the afternoon sun painting them blood-red.

The corner office sprawled across the northwest edge of the building, downtown Denver's amber sunset flooding through cavernous windows. Williams stepped inside the suite, sweeping his shotgun across the breadth of the space, pointed at nothing but wall-sized glass and ornate, expensive furnishings. Williams advanced, staring through the far windows, the sky beyond shifting slightly, moving with the wind, the sense of the swaying floor beneath him more pronounced than ever. The city beyond was moving slightly, the wind buffeting the upper levels of the skyscraper, making it feel like the structure was moving left and right.

In the executive suite, a massive desk dominated the room, a single slab of polished walnut wider than some cars, cluttered with scattered papers, a few abandoned laptops and a couple of office chairs that had been upended, resting on their backs, wheels pointed up like the legs of dead insects. Behind the desk, a half-empty highball glass sat on a marble-topped credenza, amber liquid catching the dying light. Another creak stretched along, just over the silence, drawing a swift turn of Williams' head. Lifting his hand, he killed the switch for his helmet-mounted flashlight, the exterior light of the fading sun providing all the illumination he needed within the suite of paneled wood and elaborate decor.

Three separate seating areas filled the vast space, a formal conference setting in the middle where the desk and toppled chairs stood with a more casual arrangement of modern sofas around a glass coffee table to the right. A private meeting nook was tucked into the opposite corner with an almost panoramic view of the Front Range. The walls wore sophisticated gray grass cloth where they weren't glass, interrupted by abstract paintings in thick gold frames. A private bathroom and wet bar occupied one corner, its door slightly ajar, the bar's mirrored backsplash reflecting the room in fragments, making the space seem even larger. A collection of crystal decanters glinted on glass shelves, their contents untouched.

Technology mixed with luxury throughout, a vast flat screen dominating one wall, while discrete speakers were built into the coffered ceiling. A multi-screened terminal had toppled over on a side desk, its multiple screens displaying nothing but dull black. Brass art deco sconces would have provided soft uplighting had the power been on, but the only illumination was faded crimson from the exterior sunset. The sound came a bit more clearly for a moment, the groaning creak, the repeated tapping, no hint of whispered voices, but more regular and insistent to the point where Williams turned in the middle of the suite and examined the darkened corners, anticipating company. Once more he peered through the windows, the world outside gently swaying and he clutched his breath behind clenched teeth.

"It's just the building," he tried to tell himself in a quiet, insistent whisper. "Just creaking in the wind."

Windows covered all sides of the suite, and he immediately advanced toward the north, making his way around the meeting nook. Gripping his shotgun, he faced the wall-sized sheet of translucent glass and stared out into the sprawling city of downtown Denver beyond. The darkness and the silence of the city was not unlike a camera view on an abandoned planet, alien structures sitting dormant for centuries. Normally Denver would have been a carpet of twinkling lights as the sunset approached, a scattering blanket of terrestrial stars coming on as the natural light faded. There was none of that, just a geometric puzzle of shadowed shapes, rectangles of various sizes spread throughout the city like building blocks in a toddler's playroom after lights out.

They weren't far from Denver International, yet no planes flew in the skies, no telltale twinkles of moving lights in the sky indicating travel. Clouds churned and gathered, the sky's color shifted and faded as the sun marched inevitably to the west. Williams approached the north-facing windows and tightened his grip around the shotgun. Inching forward, he peered through the north-facing window, inching up in his stance.

"I've had a lot of dumb ideas in my life," he whispered in a low voice, speaking to himself, "but this might just be the dumbest." Without giving himself a moment to question his next move, he re-centered the barrel of the shotgun and pulled the trigger.

It exploded with an outward burst of light and smoke, buckshot erupting from the darkened cylinder. At close range, the barrage hammered into the north window and splintered it immediately, blasting through the glass and blowing it out into the dusk-lit sky. A sudden shower of glinting shards caught the faint, red hue of sunset, seemingly frozen momentarily in time, then fell away as the smoke cleared, a sudden surge of wind slicing through the space where the window had once been. Williams took a step back, tensed his legs, bracing himself for the sudden gust. There was another preening creak, though the persistent tapping had stopped, the building's gentle sway easing into an unsettled shift.

Giving it a moment for the glass to finish falling away, Williams shrugged off his radio pack and strode gingerly toward the shattered section of wall where the window once was. Serrated shards of intact class lined the perimeter of the broken window like the fangs of a wide-open beast. He extended the long-range antenna and powered on the radio once more, removing the handset and placing it close to his shielded face.

"Buckley Command, this is Master Sergeant Williams from Response Team Echo. I repeat, this is response team Echo, do you read?"

Static hissed through the radio speaker and his gloved fingers tightened around the handset, the plastic housing rigid against the added pressure of his grip.

"Buckley Command, please come in."

Wind whipped through the window, and he swayed slightly as he knelt on one knee, bracing himself against the wall separating him from the small meeting nook next to him. A whistling howl swept through the broken window and battered him, but he remained upright for a few moments, the whisper of static his only conversation partner.

Williams shook his head and stood upright, keeping the antenna extended, but wrestling the pack on one shoulder, his shotgun clutched in the other hand. He muttered to himself as he stalked away from the north-facing window and walked toward the western edge of the executive suite. There were a few more windows there, overlooking another sprawling section of darkened Denver downtown, a geometric gathering of shadowed shapes far beneath the 43rd floor of 1999 Broadway. Williams went through the motions again, placing his pack on the floor, chambering a fresh round in the shotgun, then he braced himself and fired, another deafening boom ringing in his ears and filling the air within the suite.

Windows blew outward once more, a vomit of broken glass purging out into cool Denver air. Shards rained down on the street below, the shimmering vibration of glass replaced by a knife of swift wind hitting Williams in the chest. Once more he knelt by his radio pack, bracing himself against a nearby wall and called out to Buckley Space Force base.

"Buckley Command, this is response team Echo. Please respond!" His voice was firm and insistent, his tight grip clenched around the handset.

Static resonated from the small, square-shaped speaker, a low hiss. Then somewhere underneath the noise, there was something else... a whisper of faint sound mixed with the static, a sound almost like a voice speaking.

"Buckley Command? Are you there? This is Team Echo, I repeat, this is Team Echo! Please come in!" He leaned in close, fingers pressing even more tightly around the handset. "Buckley Command! Come in!" He loosened his grip, staring down at the silent radio cradled in his palm.

Williams fought the urge to cock his shoulder back and chuck the handset through the shattered window, instead hammering it back into place alongside the radio pack and then lifted the pack onto one shoulder. He blew out an exasperated breath, air hissing through his respirator as he stormed away from the western windows, back toward the center of the expansive executive suite.

As he reached the center of the elaborately decorated suite, wind buffeting him from the north and the west, Williams froze, his boots skidding softly in the plush carpet. From somewhere nearby, the low creaking came again, but it was clearer and more distinct and from a very specific location. Williams swung around to his right, bringing his shotgun up in his practiced two-hand grip. As he did, another distinct noise echoed throughout the suite, a clattering bang, the sound of a door closing.

"Hello?" He shouted, the echo of his own inquiry coming back at him amid the slicing wind. "Is anyone there?"

Just like with the radio, the only reply he received was whispers, coming from the wind and not from static in the radio speakers. Williams moved faster, striding toward the south-facing windows, already pumping the action of the shotgun to load another round. Beneath his type-A suit, his skin prickled, claws of ice raking up the length of his spine, a blanket of gooseflesh draped across his body. Crashing footfalls echoed from beyond the wall, the door leading to the hallway practically shuddering within its frame. Voices rose in earnest, a chorus of them, not just one random whisper, but a crowd rippling throughout the area beyond the wall.

"Hello?" He shouted again, two feet from the southern windows, his breath coming fast and hard, his heart blocking his airway.

His jaw clenched beneath the translucent face shield, his frantic breath clouding the clear material. He turned back toward the window and fired the shotgun again, jerking away with the kickback. Another set of large windows exploded, the singular pane of glass detonating into thousands of smaller, jagged fragments. The door swung open to the suite, whipping inward, pounding hard against the far wall, and people were there, not just filling the emptiness where the door had been, but filling the hallway beyond.

"I'm here to help!" Williams shouted, frozen for a moment, though the contorted looks on his visitors' faces told him the help they were looking for wasn't help he could provide. "Stop!" One of them took a tentative step inward, others pushing from behind him, funneling into the suite, teeth bared in angry snarls.

Williams wheeled left and sprinted toward the eastern windows, running as fast as his aching legs and stiff, sore back could propel him. He was already jacking the pump of the shotgun and loading another round as he approached the windows, the rippling murmur of the angry crowd closing in from behind. Pulling the trigger, the shotgun roared again, blasting glass out into the world beyond, releasing another gust of high-altitude wind which swarmed in and over him, forcing him to take a step back.

He pumped the shotgun again, loading another round and spun toward the approaching crowd, not just a crowd but a mob, a thrumming surge of fury, a dozen people, more than a dozen, forcing their way through the narrow doorway, then spreading apart, filling the expanse of the executive suite. Williams pointed the barrel of his shotgun at the approaching horde, fumbling for his short-range radio at his hip, and barely tugged it loose as the group converged, suddenly charging straight at him.

"Major Hayes! Team Echo, this is Sergeant Williams! Need an extraction from floor 43 of 1999 Broadway ASAP! Repeat, need an immediate extraction—" his thumb slipped from the call button, opening the two-way communications to the rest of Team Echo.

Static-laced screams filled the executive suite, a shrill and preening chorus of agony squelching from the radio, so swift and sudden that Williams gasped, yanking his hand back as if the radio had turned white hot. It clattered to the ground and Williams jerked his head up, the crowd of a dozen angry people closing on him at speed.

"Stop! Don't! I'm here to help!"

They came at him in a fury and by pure reflex, he pulled the trigger of the shotgun. It was away and to the right, the blast of buckshot screaming through empty air, blasting out chunks of overhead tile, raining plaster down as the crowd kept coming, swarming at him, then over him. Williams turned away, bending down, screaming into the void of his useless radio, back arched and limbs tensed, bracing himself against the clutches, grabs and punches of his sudden attackers.

They slammed him at first, then clawed at him, grappled with his arm, wrenched his shotgun free and tossed it away, leaving him defenseless and broken. Then there was an object, the leg of a chair or some sort of club, and it hammered him in the collarbone, shooting a lightning bolt of pain throughout his chest and back. A second unknown truncheon blasted the side of his head, hitting so hard, his translucent facemask starred with the impact, obscuring his already hindered vision. Fists and clubs pounded and hammer, his knees buckling. The metallic tang of blood filled his mouth as he went down, both knees pounding the carpet, the wave of attackers piling on him, groping at him, punching, kicking and battering him with blunt objects.

Williams opened his mouth wide to scream, but no noise would come out, a blistering explosion of pain erupting within the darkness of his vision. Blood filled his mouth and slipped from between pursed lips, the sour taste curdling his guts. He bent over, his arms buckling as a frenetic drumbeat of impacts pounded down on his spine, shoulders and back. His lips parted, his teeth separating just enough to speak one word.

"Emma..." was the only ragged, whispered gasp he uttered before blackness swallowed him whole.

# CHAPTER 14

**The O'Brian Family**
**Los Angeles, California**

A fine mist of concrete dust drifted down like toxic snow, coating the broad hood of their RV in pale gray powder. Eli pressed his face against the rear window near the kitchen, squinting at the massive concrete structure looming above them. The entire underpass was choked with military vehicles, Humvees and transport trucks jackknifed across all lanes, creating an impassable barrier of twisted metal.

"We need to back up," Samantha said, her knuckles white on the steering wheel. "Jason, can you—"

A deep, resonating crack cut through the air like a gunshot and Sarah screamed from near the kitchen table. More dust showered down, and pebble-sized chunks of concrete clattered against the roof like thick stones of hail.

"Mom!" Eli's voice cracked with panic. "The whole thing is—"

"I see it," Samantha said, jamming the gear shift into reverse.

Before she could move the cumbersome vehicle, President McDouglas called out from where he sat at the small dinette behind the driver's seat. "Wait," he ordered, his usual confident, commanding tone tinged with fear. "Look behind us!"

Jason twisted around, peering all the way back through the rear windows. More debris rained down behind them, thick, ragged chunks of overpass concrete hammering into the roadway, smashing into scattered fragments as they impacted the pavement and the roofs of a few stray abandoned vehicles. Another louder crack erupted above them, an even louder rifle shot than the one before as the overpass fragmented. Kale whined from the kitchen chair next to President McDouglas, her nails clicking against the plastic as she sat, bolt upright, alert, barely muzzling her own terror. A larger chunk of concrete smashed against the windshield, leaving a spiderweb of cracks across the glass, eliciting a muffled shout of surprise from Sarah and Eli both.

"We're trapped," Sarah whispered, twisting around to look at the concrete slabs behind them.

"We're not trapped!" Jason's gaze met Samantha's in silent desperation, their options vanishing as quickly as the structural integrity of the overpass. "I think you can—"

Before Jason even finished, Samantha slammed the gearshift into reverse, hitting it hard enough to send a reverberating thump throughout the RV's interior. Heads twisted back around to face the front seats, and the president leaned over, grabbing onto the edges of the table. The ground shuddered beneath them as a section of the overpass gave way thirty yards ahead, crushing two of the military vehicles in a thunderous cascade of concrete and rebar. The shock wave rocked the RV and set off a chorus of car alarms in abandoned vehicles gathered throughout the scene.

"Now or never!" Samantha cranked the wheel hard to the left and hammered the accelerator, the RV lumbering backwards.

Its bumper scraped along a box truck behind it, shoving the vehicle aside as she twisted the wheel the other way. Steel groaned against steel as she threaded backwards past the truck, the passenger's side tires bumping up over sections of broken concrete as they moved.

Eli pressed himself back in his seat, fingers clawing the chair, his pale face taut and mouth tightly pursed. Sarah mouthed words nobody else could hear and even Kale had fallen silent. Another section of overpass collapsed behind them, the concussion powerful enough to cave in the hood of a sedan left by the side of the road. The roof, windshield and front of the vehicle were all but obliterated by the fallen tonnage, smashed into a mangled ruin, lingering smoke and dust residue coating the air. McDouglas ducked and winced as concrete shrapnel peppered the back of their vehicle and continued raining hard against the roof.

"Keep going!" Jason shouted, though Samantha needed no encouragement.

She was entirely focused on the treacherous path behind them, steering by inches through the maze of wreckage as more of the structure came down. The RV's rear wheels suddenly lost traction, spinning in a layer of pulverized concrete. The engine roared as Samantha fought to maintain their backwards momentum, forcing the RV in reverse, crunching past another car and narrowly weaving between fallen chunks of broken overpass. Another shower of debris rained down, small, peppering pebbles at first, thwacking the hood, leaving tiny, but unimpactful dents throughout. Another crack roared from just above them, a sudden shadow swallowing the entire front of the RV and the section of empty pavement ahead.

"Samantha!"

"I see it!" She hammered the gas, throwing the RV swiftly backwards as a massive section of concrete slammed down on the windshield.

It had already been weakened by a smaller chunk before, and the larger chunk nearly caved it in entirely, carving ragged spiderwebs throughout whatever small sections of gummy safety glass had remained intact. The chunk broke apart, sliding down the sloped hood and hitting the road as the RV continued its swift, but uneven path backwards. A tire struck another section of fallen overpass and the RV leaped up momentarily, grabbed traction and lumbered over the wreckage, continuing on. Dust billowed out from ahead and around them, the overpass letting loose, a firestorm of falling concrete hammering down all around.

Just behind them, a truck fell from the collapsing overpass, nose-first, shooting down toward the pavement. Its hood struck the road and caved in, folding in upon itself as the windshield exploded outward, the truck toppling over into the roadway. Another, smaller vehicle chased it down, slamming hard into the prone pickup, then toppled the other way, landing hard on its roof, blowing out both side windows as it did.

"We're not going to make it!" Eli tensed his shoulders, pulling them close to his ears, recoiling as if the concrete was raining down on him, not the surrounding vehicle.

"Yes we are!" Samantha growled.

She gunned the engine, and the RV lurched backward, finding purchase enough to send them shooting through a final gap, slamming aside the fallen pickup and careening backwards just as the remainder of the overpass collapsed, unleashing a wall of debris and dust which chased them backwards into the sunlight. Samantha didn't stop until they were well clear of the destruction, the RV's engine straining from the effort. When she finally hit the brakes, the vehicle rocked and creaked on its suspension as they all sat in stunned silence, listening to the settling of concrete ahead and their own ragged breathing.

Kale broke the spell, barking sharply as if to hurry them along and McDouglas let out a shaky, uncertain laugh. "I think," he said, breathing hard, "that your dog has the right idea. We should keep moving."

Jason stood and circled the passenger seat, walking back to

where the kids and the president were sitting. He crouched and gently squeezed Sarah's knee.

"You okay, sweetheart?"

Sarah nodded unevenly, the color still vacated from her panicked expression. Reaching past Sarah, he gripped Eli's arm, firmly, yet with a gentle squeeze of reassurance.

"Eli?"

"I'm okay, Dad." His voice was thready, as if he was re-learning how to speak.

"I kept my eyes closed," Sarah continued, "tried to imagine we were going through a car wash." She bit her lip, and the people seated at the kitchen table chuckled softly.

"Smart girl," Samantha checked the rearview mirror, then turned back ahead, leaning right to try and peer through the cavernous remains of the broken windshield, not to mention the massive chunk of debris that still stood in her field of vision.

The overpass was nothing but a mountain of rubble, cutting off any advance, their entire path forward obscured by a wall of broken concrete, bones of rebar and the crumpled remains of a few vehicles that had been on top.

"Everyone still in one piece?"

They did a quick inventory of the RV's passengers, revealing little more than rattled nerves. The RV had clearly sustained some damage, but the engine still ran steadily as Jason and Samantha spoke to McDouglas, Eli and Sarah in turn.

"We're all in one piece," Samantha finally said, having turned off the engine before standing in front of the group. "That's the best we can hope for." Turning to face the windshield again, she silently assessed the massive chunk of concrete that had caved it in and rested near the top of the RV's hood. "You all stay in here, Jason and I are going to go see how the RV made out, okay?"

"Oh no, not this again." Eli inched forward on his seat. "I don't want to be stuck in here any longer."

"Okay, okay." Samantha lifted a calming hand. "Let's all step outside for a few minutes. Mr. President?"

"Timothy. Or Tim. I won't answer to anything else."

"Fine. Timothy? Would you mind taking Kale and see if she'll do her business?"

"Not at all."

"Thank you. Kids, stretch your legs while your dad and I give the RV a walkaround." Everyone began to move toward the door when Samantha gave one last bit of advice. "Keep your eyes open, okay? Watch for... well, you know. Anything."

McDouglas, Eli, and Sarah nodded and Eli retrieved Kale's harness and leash for McDouglas, who got her all hooked up and ready to go outside. Samantha lifted the rifle from where it leaned against the RV's dashboard and clutched it in two hands, leading the way out of the vehicle. Upon stepping out into the dust-filled world, she rotated right, then left, rifle elevated, searching their surroundings for potential threats.

"We're clear," she said, nodding back in Jason's direction, and he ushered the rest of them out, his own hand resting near the holstered weapon at his hip.

Eli and Sarah wandered toward the nearby shoulder as Kale tugged at the leash in the President's hand, glancing back unhappily at the tether she was unaccustomed to wearing. The twins talked among themselves as they stood off on their own, looking relieved to be out of the cramped confines of the RV for a breather.

"First things first," Jason said, taking a walk around the hood of the RV, craning his neck for a better look at the chunk of broken concrete. "Let's get that piece off." He stepped up onto a running board and levered himself up, then reached with two hands, clawing at the chunk of broken concrete and rebar.

Grunting, he heaved on it, scraping it across the hood, moving it only a few centimeters from where it had fallen. "Hold on, muscle man." Samantha slung the rifle over her back and used the opposite running board to climb her way up onto the hood.

She slid carefully across it, distributing her weight as evenly as possible so as not to cave it in, then reached out and the two of them worked together to wrestle free the chunk of concrete and slide it across the hood, letting it thud onto the roadway. Stepping down from the running board, Jason circled back around the hood as Samantha descended, then opened the door and stepped back inside the vehicle.

Samantha stood alongside the hood of the RV outside, looking at him through the windshield as he slipped into the driver's seat and leaned back, bringing his knees up into his chest. He thrust out with both feet simultaneously, hammering the heels of his boots into the starred and partially caved-in windshield. Adhesive along the edge of the windshield tore free, the slab of fractured safety glass peeling loose from the surrounding metal. Samantha climbed back up onto the hood as Jason drew his legs toward his chest, then kicked out again, knocking another section of windshield loose.

Samantha positioned herself near the partially separated windshield and gripped it, helping Jason try and wrench the gummy, mostly broken windshield free, though some of the stubborn adhesive refused to give.

"Kick here!" She pointed toward an attached section at the far edge and Jason moved to the passenger seat, then pounded it as instructed, only separating it slightly.

"Can I help?" McDouglas had approached the side of the RV, shielding his face from the sun. "Your son took Kale and I need a new job to do."

"There's a crowbar in the side compartment over there." Samantha knelt on the hood and pointed toward the far side of the vehicle. "Can you grab it and bring it to me?"

"Sure thing." McDouglas nodded and made his way toward the side of the RV, moving slowly and gingerly.

He vanished from view and Samantha inched forward, leaning close to Jason to whisper through what remained of the windshield.

"Did I really just tell the President of the United States to get me a crowbar?" She shook her head. "Reality has become surreal."

Jason nodded, staring back at his wife, her face shattered into a refraction of splintered safety glass. "I'm having trouble figuring out what's reality and what's not these days, myself."

"The weirder it is, the more real it is, I've decided." Samantha shrugged as McDouglas scuffled back toward her, lifting the crowbar. "Thank you, Mr.—" She stopped herself as she leaned over, grabbing the tool from his outstretched hand.

"Nuh-uh. Don't you even." McDouglas raised his eyebrows good-naturedly.

"Sorry. *Tim*. Thank you."

Samantha gripped the crowbar and hammered the narrow end into the seam alongside the windshield. It scraped against the metal frame and pushed a section of glass outward, flecks of gummy adhesive tearing loose. For a few minutes, she and Jason worked together, kicking and levering, pulling and pushing until finally they'd torn what was left of the windshield away, leaving the front of the RV exposed to the air. Lingering smoke and dust floated aimlessly between them and the collapsed overpass, the mass of fractured concrete and mangled vehicles heaped before them, across all lanes of travel.

Slipping from his seat, Jason reached into the nearby glove compartment and pulled out his flashlight, tucking it into a thigh pocket as he descended the stairs and walked back out. The air was choking with heat and particulates that floated like dust motes in the glow of sun through parted curtains. Around them, the entire world was clad in gray, swirling billows of smoke rising from within and beneath the pummeled overpass. Jason made his way toward Samantha as she whistled softly, staring at the RV, her head shaking.

Jason craned his neck around as they both surveyed the vehicle from a distance. Several scrapes and runs of peeled paint marred the RV's exterior, thick, discolored gouges of buckled metal, massive slices of color torn away from the outside of the vehicle from fallen concrete. A layer of pale dust coated the majority of the RV and Jason sighed, throwing his hands in the air.

"Yeaaaaah..." Jason said. "Your dad's going to strangle me."

"Look on the bright side," Samantha put an arm around his waist. "He's probably going to strangle *me*, too."

Jason chortled then lowered himself onto the pavement, reaching beneath the RV and pulling himself forward, scraping along the rough concrete until he was partially beneath the large vehicle. Worming to squeeze deeper, he pushed his arm over his chest and shone the flashlight throughout the darkness beneath the large vehicle.

"I don't see any wet spots on the pavement!" His voice echoed from within the tight confines beneath the RV. "I don't think anything is leaking!"

"There's one bright spot, I guess," Samantha replied, and Jason slid himself back out, using the RV to help him stand.

Samantha and McDouglas stood along the exterior of the vehicle, and she gently wiped away some of the concrete dust, wincing as her fingers traced a series of dents and deep gouges. The once-pristine white fiberglass was a battlefield of scrapes and dents, with gray concrete dust settled into every new crevice. A thick, caved-in dent malformed the rear of the roof, buckling it severely enough to be visible from ground level. The passenger-side mirror dangled by a few wires, swaying gently in the hot breeze. Above it, a long streak of yellow paint from the box truck created an uneven racing stripe down the length of the vehicle, ending at a crumpled back corner where they'd caught the edge of a fallen truck during their escape.

Jason crouched by the rear tires, examining several scrapes

along the sidewall. "It's a miracle we don't have a flat. I was sure the way we were running over those concrete chunks that a tire was going to pop."

"I hope that's not some sort of commentary about my driving." Samantha stood on her tip-toes examining another section of buckled exterior.

"We're all alive. That makes you an expert in my book." Jason stood and made his way along the side of the RV, crouching to check the rear tire as he had the front.

Samantha crawled up a half-ladder bolted to the rear of the RV, using it to access the roof, perched upon it and stared across the top. The roof had taken the worst of it, by far, with the possible exception of the windshield. A cargo container was completely gone, leaving only mounting brackets behind, and the air conditioning unit looked like it had been beaten with a sledgehammer. A separate storage rack had partially collapsed, hanging off the opposite side like a chrome-plated broken wing. Crawling down the ladder, she crouched near the rear and extended her hand.

"Let me see that flashlight? I know you said the engine was okay, I want to check and see if the gray water tank is leaking."

Jason pressed the flashlight into Samantha's palm, and she lowered to her left shoulder, squeezing beneath the RV, shining the beam of light at the tank.

"The water tank still seems to be intact. It's a mess under here, probably more from running over bodies than the overpass, but...." she pushed herself out, rose to her knees and delivered the flashlight back to Jason.

She straightened up and wiped her dusty hands on her jeans as Jason walked around to the other side of the vehicle and made a few more checks of the tires.

"It's not pretty, but it should still get us out of the city." Samantha elevated her voice so Jason could hear her from the other side. "This thing looks like it drove through a war zone."

"We did," Jason replied grimly, coming back around from the front of the vehicle. "We absolutely did."

Eli and Sarah returned with Kale, everyone gathered together near the front of the RV, silently assessing the vehicle.

"We need to find another path north," Samantha said, crossing her arms.

"What about the windshield?" Eli leaned to look around his mother at the wreckage of the front of the RV.

"We can live without a windshield."

"Agreed," Jason affirmed with a swift nod of his head. "Getting out of the city is our first priority. We can deal with a bit of fresh air."

Samantha walked toward the front door and eased it open, gesturing for everyone to head back inside. "You hanging in there, Tim?"

McDouglas walked slowly, hesitating for a moment and letting Eli, Sarah and Kale swing past him. "I'm doing okay. Sorry, a little shellshocked, I guess. The accumulation of everything is just piling up."

"One step at a time, one bite at a time and all that. We'll stay focused on getting out of here first and foremost, then figure out what comes next."

"I count my blessings every time I talk to you and your husband, or watch you and your kids snap into action. It makes me proud to see such fine examples of veterans and citizens pitching in to help during the most challenging times." McDouglas climbed the stairs and Samantha and Jason exchanged skeptical, eye-rolling looks.

"I'm not trying to butter you up," McDouglas half-shouted back down the stairs. "Just making an observation is all."

"Uh huh. Whatever you say, Mr. President."

"Call me Tim, dammit!"

Samantha and Jason made their way up into the RV, stifling

chuckles, and Samantha once more took her spot behind the steering wheel.

"You still up for driving? Or do you want me to take over for a bit?" Jason asked as he sat next to her in the passenger seat.

She drummed her fingers along its rounded, vinyl-covered perimeter. "I've got it under control, I think. Yeah. Yeah, I'm good."

"Never doubted it for a second." Jason placed a hand on Samantha's shoulder and squeezed, as she crossed her arm over her chest and rested her hand on his.

For a long moment they sat there, hands touching, staring out through the empty window toward the crushed remains of the overpass ahead. Crumpled vehicles and shattered concrete had been slammed together into an abstract art style sculpture of mass destruction and gray smoke lingered, a scant snowfall of concrete dust coating everything before them.

"Everyone buckled in?" Samantha adjusted her rear-view mirror, eyeing Eli, Sarah and the president as they settled back into the seats near the built-in kitchen table.

"All set," Eli replied, and Sarah echoed.

"Tim?"

"Yes, mother." He chuckled dryly as he clicked his seatbelt in place.

"Thank you. Last thing I need is the Secret Service on my butt because you wouldn't put on your seatbelt." Samantha flashed him a wink.

"Duly noted."

Samantha shifted into reverse and once more backed the RV slowly away from the toppled overpass. She steered left, guiding the large, cumbersome vehicle into a wide backwards turn, then began driving again, backtracking the path they'd taken to get there.

"Try that way." Jason reached across Samantha, pointing toward a side street they'd traveled by earlier.

Samantha steered left and threaded the large RV down the narrow street, which had been divided into two lanes, but in reality was more like a lane and a half. Metal scraped against metal as she eased the RV past a line of stalled traffic, though there was still enough room to squeeze the large vehicle through. They rolled and bumped along for a few minutes until another road to their left emerged, just beyond the continued line of stopped cars.

"I think if we take that road there, it'll end up connecting back to the path that was blocked by the overpass. Regardless, though, it's heading north which is where we want to be."

"Sounds like a plan." Jason affirmed.

"Hold on tight, everyone." Samantha steered left, gradually at first, then accelerated more severely, wedging the front of the RV into an area where two bumpers were about a foot apart.

There was a muffled thud of impact as the RV struck the two vehicles then pushed them slowly apart, grinding themselves a path through the traffic. A moment later and they were through and on a three-lane northbound roadway, accelerating as they moved parallel to their previous track. Wind buffeted them from the front, slicing through the gaping hole in the front of the RV, slightly stinging their eyes and biting their faces as they picked up speed. The road bent slowly right and Samantha followed it until they came upon the smashed wreckage of the overpass several yards to their left. It was a broken and battered mass of rubble slowly consumed by thickening swirls of smoke, which rose in broad columns toward the gray sky above. Eventually, the road bent back around to the left and they rejoined the main northbound route beyond where the convoy had wrecked and previously blocked their way.

Samantha squinted through the empty section that had once been their windshield, her throat raw and dry, her chest thick as she tried to suppress a cough. The already-gray sky had darkened further, and more encroaching smoke seeped across the horizon in all directions. The way north was clouded in sheets of churning gray, the air temperature rising moment by moment as they continued to drive. Once more they found themselves moving through the outskirts of the city, a sprawling, thickly congested business district, buildings lining both sides of the street.

Jason wiped glistening sweat from his forehead and coughed, then dug a knuckle into his stinging eyes. They drove through the darkening sky and through the billowing gray smoke, a warm breeze becoming a hot wind, sending swirls of trash scattering across their lanes of travel. Samantha was forced to slow, navigating around even more halted traffic, but the gaps were wide enough for the RV to at least squeeze through without them having to get out of the vehicle.

"That smoke is getting thick." Jason's voice was hoarse as he leaned forward, peering out through the rush of wind in his face. "Hot, too. There are fires somewhere close by."

"You think the city's burning?"

Jason coughed loudly, turning away as the gray smoke leaked into the RV through the shattered void of their windshield. "I'd almost... I'd almost guarantee it." It was getting harder and harder to speak, each breath an inhalation of hot razor blades.

Samantha guided the RV past another intersection, and the more north they traveled, the less comfortable it became, smoke lingering within the RV itself. Eli, Sarah and McDouglas all started coughing and even Kale sneezed a few times in discomfort.

"Watch out," Jason warned, pointing toward the right, just beyond the next intersection. "We've got some bodies there."

"I see them." Samantha coughed, then cleared her throat. "I think we need to stop. We need to figure something out; I can't keep driving like this."

Jason shielded his stinging eyes, tears streaming freely down his cheeks. "Agreed."

"Look. We've got an office park over there. Looks like we've got enough room to park the RV."

"What did you have in mind?" Jason turned toward Samantha.

"I don't know. Let's stop and look around, see if we're hit with any ideas." She drove past a line of corpses which clogged a pedestrian walkway to their right.

Dozens of bodies in business suits were littered about on the ground, having vacated the multi-level office buildings just in time to be stricken down as they walked. Samantha drove past the rows of bodies, then approached the office park, swinging right before she slotted the large vehicle into an empty loading dock area where a delivery truck might park. The air was thick and clouded with smoke, tears streamed down everyone's faces, only seconds passing between coughing fits.

"We need breathing protection, and we need eye protection." Samantha killed the engine and stood, facing away from the absent windshield. "Eli, how many T-shirts did you bring?"

"I don't know." Eli shrugged.

"Tons as usual," Sarah choked out, her watering eyes rolling. "He always packs hundreds of T-shirts."

"I like my T-shirts."

"Hate to break it to you, Eli, but we're going to need one or two of those shirts, if you've got extras."

"What?"

"Two of your least favorites."

"I only brought my favorites. Those are the ones I like to wear."

"Eli," Jason said, the edge of his voice sharpening. "We don't have time to debate this. Shirts, dude, now."

"Okay, okay, hold on." Eli unfastened his harness and slipped past Sarah, giving her a bitter glower as he did.

President McDouglas struggled to suppress a grin and another round of coughs as Eli stalked back toward the rear of the RV to retrieve his shirts. There was a rustling sound followed by a zipper as Eli crouched near his bag and started rummaging through his prized collection. Jason stepped around the president and made his way through the RV, approaching his son. The shirt in Eli's hand bore a familiar logo, though Jason couldn't immediately place it. His son's shoulders were deeply slumped, his gaze directed toward the floor of the RV as the rumpled pile of shirts was exposed within the unzipped flaps of the bag like the internal organs of a bloated corpse.

"Eli, buddy. What's wrong?" Jason crouched next to Eli, putting a hand on his shoulder.

"You know how Grandma has her photo albums?" Eli asked in a quiet croak.

"Sure."

"These are my photo albums." He lifted one of the shirts. "They're ways for me to remember events in our life. This one is from that escape room we went to in Grand Rapids last year. We all went together, it was so much fun, do you remember?"

"Of course I remember."

"I picked it out at first, thinking we could just cut it up, but I started to remember how fun it was. Then I thought about how we'll never be able to go to an escape room again. That makes these even more important, doesn't it?"

"Your memories are still there, Eli. You can still remember those great times without having a piece of fabric to remind you. Not having a shirt doesn't take away from the fun we had."

Eli nodded.

"Here." Jason shifted onto his left knee and pulled his phone from his pocket where it had been, almost forgotten, for the past day or so.

He held the power button down and the screen lit up, showing less than half of its battery life and the familiar array of icons that no longer worked without an active internet connection. His finger tapped the photo icon and brought up the camera and he took the shirt from Eli's hand and spread it out on the floor near the unzipped bag.

"I know it's not the same, and I hate that we're taking these from you. But you brought a lot of extra shirts, buddy. The rest of us don't have enough spare clothes."

"It's okay, Dad. Really."

Jason adjusted the position of his phone and snapped a quick photo of the t-shirt, then created a separate album on his phone and named it Eli's Shirts. He saved the photo there and held up his device.

"Here we go. Created a new album for all your shirts. We can keep taking pictures, so you have something to remember the shirts by."

"And what happens when the batteries die in all of our phones? What happens when we have no other way to charge them?"

"Let's not dwell on that right now." Jason cleared his throat again, barely muffling a cough. Even as far back in the RV as they were, the air was acrid and stale, vision blurry with the lingering sting of smoke. "Are you sure you're okay with us using this shirt? You don't want to use another one?"

"It's fine, Dad." Eli cleared his own throat, bringing his back up straighter and pushing his shoulders out.

Jason and Eli stood together, with Jason gathering up the shirt and carrying it over to the kitchen. Samantha had already pulled a pair of scissors from a narrow drawer and a few bottles of water were stacked on the nearby counter. Stepping past Jason, Samantha placed her hand gingerly on Eli's cheek.

"You okay?"

"He's good," Jason replied and mussed his hair.

"I'm fine, Mom. Just having a moment, that's all."

"It's okay to have a moment, Eli," Samantha replied, "we all do, and we all will."

Jason handed her the shirt and she spread it across the kitchen table, drawing back to get a better look. She drew the scissors along the seams, cutting up the side, then spread it out lengthwise and began to cut the cotton in several equally wide lengthwise strips. As she worked, Samantha stopped a few times to turn and cough into her fist, her chest burning with each lung-inflamed hack.

"Sarah, hand me one of those bottles of water, would you?" Samantha gestured toward the counter.

Sarah handed her mother the water and Samantha began pouring a small amount over the cotton, then lifted the strip and bound it around her nose and mouth, tying it off at the base of her skull. They took turns, going through the process for everyone until they all had ragged strips of Eli's old t-shirt around their nose and mouth.

"What about Kale?" Sarah knelt next to Kale, stroking her fur, her voice muffled through the soaked cotton.

"I'm not sure we can rig her up something like this." Samantha gestured to her own face covering. "She's always hated muzzles, so this is going to drive her crazy. Once we start driving, we can always put her in the bathroom with the vent closed. That work?"

"Yeah, I guess," Sarah replied.

"Sorry hon. I wish I had a perfect answer for you."

"What about our eyes?" Eli squinted over the mask, tears brimming, one thin line of moisture trickling down his left cheek. "Not having the windshield *sucks*."

Samantha made her way toward the front of the RV, leaning down a bit, staring out through the empty hole in the front of the cabin. They were parked in the loading dock alongside an office park, dozens of dead bodies scattered about, corpses spread out in a wide fan along the sidewalk, between buildings, and filling the nearby parking lot itself. She leaned down a bit, looking at various surrounding buildings.

"Looks like mostly commercial," Jason said, coming up behind Samantha. "Not much retail space."

Samantha eyed a young woman's body, sprawled across the nearby curb and wearing an expensive looking suitcoat and pencil skirt. Hair was fanned out beneath her head, her face pale, though her eyes were obscured by an oversized pair of stylish sunglasses. Squinting through the smoke, Samantha scanned the rest of the bodies, nodding to herself.

"Everyone all masked up?" She took a step toward the door to the RV, looking back toward the others. "I think I have a plan."

McDouglas turned, looking at Eli and Sarah who stared back, all of them wearing the wet fabric around their noses and mouths.

"Eli and Sarah? The two of you can stay inside if you want."

"Nah," Sarah said. "I want to get out of here for a bit."

"Same."

Samantha nodded. "We've got to move quickly." She stepped out and down the stairs and over a sprawled corpse, giving the others some room to follow.

They gathered in a small group, Sarah placing a hand on her stomach as she gazed upon the gathered bodies around her. The late afternoon sun cast long shadows through the nearby office park's glass towers but failed to soften the horror of what lay before them. Bodies carpeted the wide plaza like fallen leaves after an autumn storm, their business attire wrinkled and stained. Some had collapsed mid-stride, while others appeared to have slowly crumpled against planters or benches, as if finally giving in to overwhelming fatigue. Flies were buzzing incessantly around all of them, and the stiff breeze and copious amounts of smoke failed to fully mask the stench of death.

Samantha stepped carefully around a young woman in a blue blazer, her laptop bag still clutched in rigid fingers. People had been heading to meetings, planning lunch dates, worried about deadlines but were instead part of a vast, open-air morgue that stretched for blocks in every direction.

"Should we check the buildings?" Jason asked. "See if we can't figure out something to protect our eyes, or at least give us a break from the smoke?"

A crow landed on a nearby bus stop shelter, its feathers beating as it eyed them warily before hopping down to investigate something they couldn't see. More birds circled overhead, not just crows, but larger shapes as turkey vultures and California condors normally reserved to the surrounding wilderness had found their way into the city. The air hung thick and stagnant, heavy with the crimson copper smell of death and the lingering chemical taint that made their eyes water. Even through their handmade masks, the stench was impossible to ignore. It clung to their clothes, their skin, their hair, as persistent as the memory of what they were seeing.

"See that woman there?" Samantha pointed toward the well-dressed corpse strewn over the curb. "We need to look for as many bodies with glasses as we can find. The larger the better."

Jason shrugged. "You're the boss. Everybody, spread out. Grab as many sets of glasses as we can find."

"Will do." McDouglas cleared his throat and drew a deep, rasping breath.

Gathering himself together, he continued walking forward, wading through the piles of surrounding bodies. Samantha eased her way between a pair of well-dressed businessmen, narrowly avoiding a colored stain on the sidewalk next to a lifeless body. She approached the dead woman, bent down and lifted the glasses from her corpse, gingerly pinching the corners of the eyepieces. Lifting them free, she folded them up and slipped them into a pocket, then turned to search another nearby body. Even though the makeshift mask, the pungent, rancid aroma filled her nostrils, souring the contents of her stomach.

To her right, Jason strode long over a face-down body, then drew up alongside an overweight man in a long, beige-colored trench coat. His face was slightly turned, a pair of glasses crooked on his face, half resting on the sidewalk. Jason crouched down, grasped the man's shoulder and heaved slightly, rolling him over and freeing the glasses, which he slipped free, folded, and slipped into his own pocket. Samantha pulled her shirt collar up over her mask, a futile gesture against the overwhelming stench. The baking sun had accelerated the rot of the bodies, adding a new layer of horror to an already unbearable task. She envisioned them as mannequins, just store displays tipped over in their business casual attire, but the illusion wouldn't hold.

"I'm sorry," she whispered to a middle-aged man in a charcoal suit as she gently lifted his head.

His glasses had slipped down his nose in death, but they were intact, wire-rimmed and professional, the kind an accountant might wear. The man's face was purple and blotchy, his eyes clouded, but his expression was almost peaceful compared to others. She worked the glasses free as carefully as she could, trying not to think about how his skin had already begun to change texture. They went into her pocket along with the regular pair and the set of stylish sunglasses she'd gathered so far.

"Found some sunglasses," Jason called from nearby. He was searching a row of bodies near a coffee cart, where people had been waiting in line for their morning lattes. "Wrap-arounds."

"Great! Grab whatever you find. I've got three sets already."

Samantha forced herself to keep moving, scanning the ground methodically. A woman in yoga clothes, probably headed to or from a morning workout, still wore sports sunglasses with yellow lenses.

"I'm borrowing these," Samantha murmured. "You don't need them anymore, and my kids do."

The sound of shifting cloth and rustling papers accompanied her movements. Overhead, the crows had grown bolder, no longer retreating when humans drew near. One watched her from atop a parking meter, its head cocked as if trying to understand what she was searching for among its future meals.

Near a toppled bike-share rack, there was a young college student, his laptop bag still slung across his chest. The thick-framed glasses he wore drew her gaze immediately, stark against his pale face and powder blue UCLA sweatshirt. Samantha added them to her pocket, noting how each pair carried a fragment of its former owner's personality; tortoiseshell for the fashionable, titanium for the practical, bright colors for the bold. For a few other minutes, she, her family and the President rummaged through the bodies, folding each pair, sliding them away before moving on to the next.

"That should be enough," she called to the others, unable to bear another minute of this grim harvest. Not only was the rancid stink overwhelming, but the needling sting of smoke continued digging at her eyes.

The rest of the family had already pushed up into the RV when Samantha approached, Jason lingering long enough to give her a silent assessment. "I'm okay." Samantha nodded toward her husband, gesturing for him to head inside.

She followed him, closing the door behind her, though the air inside was still gray and spoiled with smoke and the putrid stink of death, somehow still palpable even through their makeshift masks. She reached into her pocket and gestured toward the kitchen dining nook.

"Toss them all on that table. How many did we get?"

Eli pulled out two pairs from his pocket and set them down, while Sarah removed three and playfully extended her tongue in her brother's direction. Jason dropped three in a pile, McDouglas set down a pair, and Samantha tossed her three in the pile as well.

"Thirteen. That's not a good number." McDouglas leaned back on the counter, his arms crossed.

"You want to run out and grab another? Make it an even fourteen?" Jason gestured toward the door, a crooked smile on his face.

"Thirteen is a fine number," McDouglas replied. "What I'm really wondering is what we're doing with all of these. I get we need eye protection, but glasses? Those aren't going to cut it on their own."

Samantha lifted the pair of stylish sunglasses she'd found on the dead businesswoman. She pulled out a pocketknife and extended the narrow blade, settling into one of the kitchen chairs.

"Jason, can you grab me that roll of plastic wrap from the middle drawer?"

"Uh, sure," Jason replied, his voice lifting in a note of inquiry.

Samantha focused her attention on the sunglasses, working the blade of the knife into the spot where the lens met the frame. She poked and prodded, moving the blade back and forth, until it slipped in by about a centimeter. With a twist and flick of her wrist, the blade went down and the lens popped out, freed from the frame and clattering loosely to the tabletop. She repeated the process with the second lens and soon had the stylish frame in her fingers, the darkened lenses resting loosely on the table. Samantha turned the frames around, angling her neck back and forth as Jason dropped the rectangular box of plastic wrap on the table alongside the pile of remaining glasses.

All eyes on her, Samantha peeled off a small section of plastic wrap, tore it along the serrated cutting edge, then wrapped it around one of the empty spots where the lens had been. A moment later, she'd finished the second side, then hooked her finger in Sarah's direction.

"These had your name all over them," Samantha joked, holding the frames up. "You like them?"

"They're okay, I guess." Sarah shrugged.

"Put them on."

Sarah did as she was asked, hooking the earpieces above her ears and resting the empty frames on the bridge of her nose.

"Is that plastic wrap tight enough? Can you see through it?"

"Kind of," Sarah replied. "A little foggy, but I can see okay."

"Good. Come here and have a seat." Samantha slid over one seat and patted the chair where she'd been.

Sarah was hesitant, but took tentative steps forward and sat down, giving her mother an almost mistrustful side-eye. Samantha was already peeling plastic wrap from the roll which only earned a more narrowed, apprehensive glower.

"This isn't going to hurt."

"What exactly is it going to do?"

"Just hold still." With a plastic wrap sheet stretched between her hands, Samantha leaned forward, tugged the plastic across the pair of glasses Sarah was wearing, then pulled it tightly around the sides of her head.

"Ouch ouch," Sarah protested, scowling. "You're pulling the frame against my face. It's tight."

"It needs to be tight. The idea is to keep the smoke out. That's not going to happen unless it's tight."

"Okay." Sarah's jaw tensed, her back rigid as Samantha continued wrapping the plastic wrap around the glasses, then pressed it tight against the sides of Sarah's head.

Samantha continued working on it for a moment until she was finally satisfied, leaning back to study her daughter.

"How does that feel? Are your eyes still bothering you?"

Sarah blinked rapidly, a crease forming between her eyebrows. Her eyelids fluttered, then slowed and she nodded her head gently.

"That's better, actually. The smoke doesn't sting nearly as much."

"There you go."

Eli barely muffled a snicker as he stared down at Sarah, snorting loudly as he pressed the back of his hand against his mouth.

"Laugh it up, you're next." Samantha gestured toward Eli, who stopped chuckling. "This isn't just for Sarah's sake."

"Are you serious about this?" Eli lifted an eyebrow. "She looks ridiculous. Her head looks like a deli sandwich or something."

"You really think we need to worry about looks right now? Come on over here. I'll do you next, then the adults will all take their turns."

Eli blew out an exasperated breath and tipped his head back.

"You heard her. Your turn." Sarah stepped aside and waved a hand toward the seat.

Eli grumbled under his breath, but sat down in the chair and held still as Samantha dug out a pair of lenses out of a second pair of glasses.

"You wanted the bright yellow ones, right?"

"No!" Eli twisted around.

"Just kidding." Samantha held up a relatively plain pair of wire-rim glasses, lifting the corner of her mouth in a knowing smile.

"Not funny."

Samantha tossed Jason her pocketknife. "While I wrap him up, why don't you remove a few more lenses? Get a pair set up for you and the president."

"On it." Jason snatched the pocketknife out of mid-air and walked to the table studying the scattered pairs that remained.

As Samantha measured out some of the plastic wrap, Jason immediately went to work on two of the pairs of glasses. He turned and whispered a quiet question to McDouglas, who shared an inquisitive look with him, then Jason pulled two sets aside and began to use the knife to pop out each lens.

"How long are we going to have to wear these?" Eli sat, back pressed against the chair, one foot restlessly tapping the floor.

"Just until the smoke clears. Hopefully not long. Or if you *want* to have your eyes stinging and burning, I guess you can remove them whenever you want." Samantha clutched his shoulder, lowering her voice so that only he could hear her. "You're doing great, Eli, okay? I'm very proud of you." Samantha tugged free smaller pieces of plastic wrap and began to twist them around the empty lenses, pulling them as tight as possible to eliminate wrinkles.

Eli nodded as Samantha handed him the glasses, dragged the plastic wrap out, and sawed a piece off with the built-in cutter. Eli placed the glasses on his face, blinking through the plastic wrap and Samantha leaned in, pulling the wrap around the glasses, and tugging it tight over his ears and around the back of his head. She worked at it for long enough that Jason had popped out all four lenses and was waiting for her to finish.

"This should be enough," she said, her attention still focused on Eli, and Jason grabbed the plastic wrap, going through the same process she had.

Taking the box with him, he stood and walked to the bathroom, the familiar zip of pulling wrap audible from within the quiet confines of the small alcove. Kale was perched on the floor nearby, her head tilted one way, then another, taking in all the strange happenings. Ears perked in confusion, her front paws were outstretched as she twisted and stared at each member of her family. Samantha added some finishing touches to the wrap around Eli's head, then grabbed his shoulders and turned him partially toward her.

"How's that?"

"Glasses are hurting me a little bit, but my eyes aren't stinging as much."

"Good. Hopefully we can get clear of all of this mess soon." She reached up and tugged on a small section of the wrap, unfolding it, then smoothed it out a bit with her palm.

Samantha stood and stepped past Eli, moving out into the kitchen as Jason emerged from the bathroom shaking his head. He'd found a set of very professional glasses, the accountant's, a set Samantha had found but scowled and ran his fingers along the wrap.

"Can you double check this for me, Samantha?" He handed McDouglas the box of plastic wrap and McDouglas took it, shaking his head, almost in disbelief, as he walked to the bathroom.

Samantha gave Jason a once-over, turning him around and

examining the coverage of the plastic wrap. "You did a pretty good job."

"At making myself look ridiculous."

"It's better than not being able to see." Samantha rubbed at her own eyes, which still stung and generated tears that moistened her cheeks.

She grabbed some paper towels off a nearby counter and dabbed at her eyes with one, drying them. Walking to the table, she rifled through the remaining glasses and lifted up a pair of round, retro looking sunglasses, then took Jason's knife and began to poke and prod at the lenses. By the time she freed them both, McDouglas had extracted himself from the bathroom, stumbling slightly as he navigated the narrow hallway leading to the kitchen.

"I've never looked so silly in my entire life." McDouglas shook his head incredulously. "My press secretary would have retired on the spot rather than let me go out in public looking like this." He laughed, then sneezed through the t-shirt fabric.

"We should get these masks moistened again before we go too far. I'm hoping once we start driving we don't have to stop until we're clear of the smoke." Samantha freed the second lens, then took the plastic wrap from McDouglas and went to work.

"We don't even know what's burning. Impossible to see what with these surrounding buildings." Jason sat in one of the chairs and watched Samantha finish wrapping the glasses, then place them on the bridge of her nose.

She worked quickly, easing open the plastic wrap box and pulling out a long sheet before tearing it off and wrapping it around her own face. It took her a few quick-moving minutes, and while she did it, the others were adding a bit more water to their makeshift masks. Samantha finished binding the glasses to her face, scowling in discomfort as she completed the work, then refreshed her own mask. With everyone equipped to deal with the smoke, she stood before them all, each of them turning to face her.

"Anyone who needs a bathroom break should take one now. Otherwise, I'm going to get Kale situated."

When no one moved, Samantha ushered Kale inside, the dog's tail tucked between her legs, her head lowered. "I know, girl. It's okay. You're a good girl." Samantha slid the bathroom door closed and returned to the front seat.

"Last chance to have me take over," Jason said, perched behind the passenger seat.

"I've got it. Thanks, though." Samantha slid into the driver's seat and gave everyone a moment to get settled, then started the engine, gunning the RV to life while the soft clack of seat belts fastening came from behind her.

She accelerated, steering the RV away from the loading dock and swerving it widely around the scatter of bodies that tumbled from the sidewalk, spilling out into the street. They followed the road north, the traffic around them thinning as they continued moving out of the gridlock of downtown Los Angeles. The smoke still thickened the air, swirling past them on gusts of wind as the RV picked up speed, the buildings blurring on either side. Samantha had to slow from time to time to navigate through some tighter spaces, but the traveling got a bit easier as they approached a long stretch of pavement which angled uphill through some sparse clutches of buildings, both commercial and residential.

Samantha hit the gas as they approached the upward slope, the RV climbing the hill at speed, delicately weaving through a few stalled sections of abandoned vehicles. Bodies were still strewn about, but few enough in number that they could move around them instead of over them, and moments later, the RV approached the top crest of the long, meandering hill. Samantha's grip around the wheel tightened as they reached the summit, the sprawling acreage of the San Fernando Valley stretching out ahead and below. She immediately killed the engine, bringing the RV to a halt along the side of the road as swirling clouds of smoke rose in the distance.

"Oh... oh no." The words were barely audible as Samantha unhitched her belt, hands and feet fumbling to get her out of her seat as her eyes were locked on the scene to the North.

"Sweet merciful father...." McDouglas whispered, slowly standing from his seat at the kitchen table. He, Jason, Eli and Sarah followed Samantha to the door, everyone vacating the RV to stand next to it, stunned into silence.

The San Fernando Valley was an ocean of fire that stretched from horizon to horizon. Sheets of flames rolled across neighborhoods, leaping from rooftop to rooftop, a plume of smoke towered above all, a massive dark column that blotted out the sun, its top spreading outward like a mushroom cloud. Through gaps in the smoke, the mall at Sherman Oaks was outlined in orange, its vast parking lots reflecting the boiling inferno. Further north, a collection of buildings in an office complex blazed like a torch while swirling fire tornados, some hundreds of feet tall, spun across Van Nuys, their bases hidden in the general conflagration, but turning tops visible above the layers of smoke.

The heat somehow, impossibly, reached them where they stood, a physical force that prickled their skin and brought thick dampness to their underarms and the small of their backs. It radiated over them, washing across their exposed skin like scalding water with each shift and change in the wind. The sound was overwhelming, a constant roar like a massive blowtorch, punctuated by the sharp cracks of exploding transformers and the deeper booms of rupturing gas lines. Palm trees went up like giant matches, their fronds creating brief fountains of sparks that rained down on the structures below.

The elevated sections of the 405 stood out against the flames like black ribbons, choked with even more abandoned vehicles that were themselves catching fire. In the distance, a row of high-tension power lines collapsed one after another, their towers folding slowly into the inferno as the eastern front of the firestorm moved steadily south toward them, consuming everything in its path with methodical fury.

"That heat, it's intense." Jason turned slightly away from the blaze ahead, holding up a hand. "I can't believe we can feel it from so far away."

"Mom? Dad?" Eli asked, his voice rising in panic. "The heat's not just coming from there!" Eli looked back behind where they'd driven from in the RV.

Samantha and Jason both turned, looking toward the collection of brickwork structures no more than thirty feet away. Smoke churned, the windows glowing from raging flames within. A sudden surge of hot hair pushed toward them from the fire, clawing fingers of white-hot flame gripping at the angled walls of the building. A quiet groan rippled throughout the neighborhood beyond, one of the buildings giving way beneath the strain of the fire, tumbling from view in a shower and spilling bricks and a renewed surge of rolling flames.

"Oh no," Samantha gasped, drawing away from the sight as a wall of flame twisted up from within the neighborhood just to their right, throwing embers high into the air, scattering them about like a thousand daytime fireflies. "Everyone back in right now!"

A scalding wind sliced through at them from the apartment complex, hacking through the brick buildings like a scythe. The sudden surge stole Samantha's breath even through her makeshift mask and she staggered at its raw force. Eli and Sarah were already sprinting back up the stairs, McDouglas close behind them. Jason wheeled toward Samantha, grabbed her forearm and yanked her toward him, the two of them moving in concert back toward the RV. Heat, smoke and fire was suddenly upon them, pushing through the buildings like a petulant demon, reaching toward them with roiling talons.

"Buckle up!" Samantha screamed as she slammed the door

behind her and raced up into the RV, throwing herself into the driver's seat.

Everyone hurriedly dropped into their seats, grabbing for their seatbelts, gripping the table and their chairs. A twisting arm of fire snaked across the road ahead, its accompanying hot wind and ash unfiltered by the windshield that wasn't there. Embers swept across the hood and went inside the RV, Samantha squinting against them as she gunned the engine into starting. Suddenly the fires were everywhere, pockets of heat and white flame erupting through the neighborhood around them, another fuel tank in the valley rupturing, the entire world swallowed into the belly of a furnace.

Samantha hammered the RV into reverse, backing it away from the flames, then twisted the wheel, bringing the RV around in a nauseating, tilted rotation. The rear corner of the vehicle struck a parked sedan with a muffled crunch, though the RV's momentum barely faltered. She hit the gas and turned the wheel, completing the uneven turnaround then accelerated back down the hill, the roaring beast close on their heels.

# CHAPTER 15

**The Tills Family**
**Silverpine, Oregon**

Though the sun was in full retreat, the heat of the day had settled throughout the freshly tilled soil. Sweat coated Sheila's neck and back, her shirt clinging to her body like a second skin. Rich, fragrant scents intertwined, an organic bouquet of dirt, soil, seed and the nearby aroma of ripening grapes and lavender. Sheila closed her eyes as she stood, lifting her face to the setting sun, the gentle warmth a soothing bath across her dirt-caked skin. She was coated from head to toe with the remains of the soil they'd been working in throughout much of the day, thick swaths of brown and black painting her flesh and crusting thick on her sweat-stained shirt. Her footsteps left slight impressions in the loose earth as she approached the prepared bed, its borders neatly marked with twine and stakes. Sheila knelt beside the plot, pushing her hand into the soil.

"Make sure we've gotten this tilled up twelve inches deep at least." She turned back toward Brandi, who was a few feet away, her arm pushed into the soil, almost to her elbow. "Carrots need that depth to grow straight and long." She withdrew her arm, freshly coated with dirt and gestured for Brandi to come over. "Feel how loose it is?"

Brandi knelt alongside Sheila and buried her hands in the soil, nodding. A thick smudge of brown painted her right cheek and her hair was matted with sweat and dirt. There was a weariness to her movements, which had become slow and plodding as the hours went on, each step, each bend and each thrust of her hands carefully calculated, her energy reserves tested.

"These furrows are nicely spaced." Sheila dragged her finger through the soil in a straight line, about half an inch deep. "This will be our first row; we'll try and space them a few inches apart."

Working together, they created parallel furrows in the tilled soil bed. Sheila stood as Brandi continued working, walking back to the side-by-side and lifting the seed container from the tub they'd carried from the basement. The vast majority of the tilled garden had been marked and tied off, many of the various seeds already planted. They'd worked long and hard that day and had only moved more quickly as they approached late afternoon and evening.

She returned to where Brandi finished making the smaller furrows and cracked open the seed container, showing Brandi the tiny brown seeds. "Carrots are small, easy to overseed. Watch." She demonstrated, pinching a few seeds between thumb and forefinger, dropping them along the furrows, two inches apart.

"Is it better to plant a few extra?"

"Yes. We can always thin them later when they sprout. Setting them about two inches apart now, but they'll need four inches of space to fully mature." Sheila continued down her row, the tiny seeds falling from her fingers with practiced precision. "If they're too close together, they might twist around each other."

They worked in silence for a time, moving quickly and efficiently, despite their aching muscles and tired minds. Row by row, the seeds disappeared into the dark soil. Occasionally, Sheila would pause to check Brandi's spacing or demonstrate the proper depth again.

"Don't cover them too deeply," Sheila cautioned as they began filling in the furrows. "Quarter inch of soil at most. They'll struggle to push through more than that." She demonstrated the gentle brushing motion, barely disturbing the soil as she covered the seeds.

The entire bed took shape under their careful attention, and Sheila sat back on her heels, surveying their work. Ahead of her, the bed appeared barely disturbed, giving no indication of the hundreds of seeds waiting beneath the surface.

"Great job. We need to keep going, okay?" Sheila grunted as she stood, wincing, a hand pressing against the small of her back. "I'd like to finish planting today if possible. We're running short on daylight, but we're so close to being done."

Brandi nodded as she slowly worked her way to her feet, moving wearily, but with determination. She turned as Sheila lifted something from her pocket and stared down at it, the strange device carried in both hands.

"Is that the tracker?" Brandi took a couple of steps toward Sheila, angling her neck for a better view.

"Yes." Sheila scowled down at the screen, her eyebrows bunching.

The small dot indicating the position of their borrowed RV had been moving north, but as she watched, it appeared to be going south again, deeper into the city.

"They're still moving, but..." her voice trailed off.

"I haven't seen you look at it much since you guys got back." Brandi wiped the back of her hand across her sweat and dirt-streaked forehead as she approached the utility vehicle and lifted a half-empty water bottle from one of the cupholders, unscrewed the cap and took a long swallow.

"I've been keeping it with me at all times. I just try hard not to obsess over it; I get way too worked up the more I look at it." She sighed and thrust the device back into a pocket of her work pants.

"I'm sure they're okay. If they're moving, then that's a good thing!"

"They're still moving. I suppose that's all that matters." Sheila walked past Brandi and back toward the rectangle of tilled soil, marked with several stakes and twine borders. "Once we're done seeding, there's still a lot of work to do." Sheila changed the subject. "Tomorrow we'll need to lay down a light layer of straw and water everything thoroughly. We also have some fertilizer we normally use for the grapevines... we should put some of that down, too, given how late in the season we're planting."

"When do you think things will start growing?"

"I figure we'll start seeing shoots in as little as a few days. Harvest is probably still anywhere from a month or two from now, depending on the weather." She lifted her head toward the sky.

Despite the penetrating heat of the afternoon, the skies were clad in a gunmetal gray thanks to a persistent layer of clouds hanging low across the horizon. The faded orb of the sun glowed down through the thickening haze.

"The skies have been grayer than usual, probably from the fires, but hopefully that will pass before too long." Sheila wiped her sweaty hands on the thighs of her pants and strode forward, moving toward the last empty section of garden. "For this last bed we're going to do a mixture of beets and radishes." She knelt by the tilled bed and gestured for Brandi to come join her.

Brandi nodded wearily but made her way over, lowering herself down tentatively, resting on one knee.

"Beets need six inches of loose soil," Sheila said, pushing her hand into the earth, "we can plant the radishes between the beet rows, they'll be ready to harvest before the beets need the space."

Sheila marked the rows and went through creating the small furrows, then let Brandi take over as she stood and walked back to the utility vehicle to retrieve the seeds.

Brandi was more or less done when Sheila returned and she crouched next to her, opening the seed containers, one marked 'Detroit Dark Red' while the other was marked 'Cherry Belle Radishes'.

"These are beet clusters." She showed Brandi the rough, corky seeds. "Each one contains several individual seeds." Sheila placed them about four inches apart along the furrow. "Don't separate them, they'll grow in little groups and like the carrots, we'll thin them later."

"Got it."

In the spaces between the beet rows, they created shallow trenches for the radishes.

"The radish seeds are smaller," Sheila continued, sprinkling them about two inches apart. "They should start sprouting in just a few days and help mark the rows."

They moved methodically throughout the final bed, alternating beet and radish rows, working together until the seed containers were significantly depleted. When finished, they covered the seeds with soil, gently patting it firm.

"Radishes should be ready in about a month." Sheila stood and brushed the dirt from her gloves. "Just in time for the beets to need a little room to develop. They work well together."

Sheila stared out at the expanse of the large garden, her breath coming in rough, uneven gasps. Sweat cooled her skin, her muscles thick, heavy and weary, her hair plastered to her head. Brandi stood alongside her, tugging off her gloves and using the hem of her shirt to wipe sweat from her face.

"Talk about a good day's work." Sheila patted Brandi on the back. "You did a great job with this."

"*We* did a great job. It was mostly you telling me what to do."

"No, don't sell yourself short there. Even when you're used to this kind of work, it sucks your energy out. For someone new to it? You did fantastic."

From somewhere close by, the rattling snarl of an approaching engine cut through their talking and Sheila immediately dropped her hand from Brandi's back.

"Someone's coming." She grabbed one of the long guns she'd stashed in the rear of the utility vehicle, her opposite hand moving to the radio at her hip.

She tugged the radio loose just as the familiar outline of the Jeep rounded the bend, kicking up clouds of dust as it approached, dragging the trailer behind it. Sheila let out a breath of relief, yet lifted the radio to her mouth just the same.

"Darryl? Doug and Benjamin are back." She released the call button and Darryl immediately replied.

"Be right there."

Sheila returned the radio to her belt and slung the rifle strap over her shoulder as she walked toward the approaching vehicle.

"Brandi, can you just finish up here real quick? I want to make sure everything's okay with Doug and Benjamin."

"Of course. I'll get things cleaned up."

The Jeep came near, then swung around, parking alongside the front of the main house. A second engine roared from beyond the Jeep and as Sheila approached, Darryl appeared in the near distance riding the tractor, making a beeline for where Benjamin had parked the Jeep. The trailer was filled with a coil of cable, several bundles of PVC piping and a few other assorted items, all strapped down and neatly organized. As Darryl swung around and approached with the tractor, the Jeep stopped and the doors opened, Benjamin stepping out of the driver's side while Doug emerged from the passenger's.

"Good to see you boys!" Sheila called out and waved, still walking toward them, her sore legs moving more slowly than normal. "Looks like your trip was a success?" She nodded toward the trailer as Darryl stepped off the tractor, cutting its engine as well.

"It was. Cliff was only too eager to help. He was way more generous than I thought he'd be."

"Cliff's a good guy. Always has been." Sheila walked toward the trailer and looked across the gathered supplies. "Wow."

"Yeah, right? I paid him cash we had left, but most of this stuff he just gave us on credit."

"He didn't want anything in trade?"

Doug shrugged. "He did seem pretty interested in how the vineyard was holding up, but he has his own solar panels, said he had plenty of food."

"We ended up with a decent amount extra," Benjamin piped in, "I overestimated what we might need by a little bit. Figured that would give us some spare supplies in case anything goes wrong."

Darryl stood at the side of the trailer, peering over it at the coils of thick cable.

"Yeah, that will do nicely," he said with a nod.

"How... were things in town?" The question came hesitantly.

"Bad," Doug replied. "Not as bad as when we tried to drive south, but bad enough. Pretty sure someone robbed the credit union and there was a body on the ground."

"According to Cliff the town market got raided, too." Benjamin snorted. "I think it's safe to assume we're pretty much on our own out here."

"No police? Fire? Anything like that?"

"Not that we saw." Doug shrugged. "But we didn't spend a whole lot of time looking. We buzzed through, quick as we could."

"But Cliff was okay?" Sheila asked.

"Seemed to be," Benjamin replied. "As good as he ever is, out there on his own."

"So how much did you get?" Darryl asked, standing along the

other side of the trailer, running his fingers along the lengths of PVC.

"Three hundred feet. About twice what we need."

"Wow. Yeah this'll be perfect."

"Cliff was surprisingly amenable to it." Benjamin walked around the trailer, eying the supplies. "Guess he's figuring he won't need it."

"I think he's also figuring he might need friends down the line. Whatever the reason, we should just be grateful we've got it." Doug looked Sheila up and down, grinning as he wiped a smudge of dirt from the tip of Sheila's nose. "You look like you've been rolling around in the dirt. I take it things are going well?"

"We dug out the perimeter of the garden." Sheila twisted around and pointed toward the section of grass visible alongside the main building. Tilled soil extended from beyond, lined with stakes and twine, each row and group labeled with separate shafts of wood and letters drawn in thick marker. "We've gotten more or less everything planted that we wanted to. We grabbed a wide assortment of seeds from basement storage and in the next month or two we should start seeing things blooming. I think we're going to be in pretty good shape."

"You dug, tilled and planted that whole garden today?" Doug's brows elevated. "How many square feet?"

"Three thousand, give or take."

"Wow. Just you and Brandi?"

"Yep. We still need to lay the straw and start watering, but that's tomorrow's job." Sheila exhaled. "We're pretty beat."

Brandi approached from the direction of the garden, brushing her gloves together to shake off the dirt. Her face was beet red beneath the layer of dirt, her hair thick and slung tightly to the curve of her head. She approached them in a slow, somewhat labored gait, breathing hard with each measured step.

"How about the batteries?" Benjamin turned toward Darryl.

"I was just finishing that up when you guys pulled in. I got them all moved into that outbuilding and put 'em where we drew those chalk outlines a while back."

"All of them? By yourself?" Doug crossed his arms and drew back in mock surprise.

Darryl lifted one arm and flexed his bicep, smiling crookedly down at his own narrow arm. "You doubt my strength?"

"Nope, not when you've got that tractor to handle most of it." Doug chuckled. "Sounds like it was a productive day all around. You all should be very proud. That was a lot of hard work. Almost seems like we got off easy, huh?" He turned toward Benjamin, who scowled back at him.

"You forget how heavy that cable was? Just about blew my back out."

Doug groaned, rolling his eyes. "Oh quit your whining. We'll use the tractor to unload it all."

"We'll help with the side-by-side, too." Sheila stabbed a thumb in the direction of the garden. "Just need to get it cleared out first."

"Fantastic." Doug reached back into the Jeep and withdrew the ski pole he'd been using, then leaned on it as he made his way slowly toward the house. "But I think we've all just about hit our limit for the day. Let's eat, get a good night's sleep and get back to it first thing in the morning."

"So... what're we making for dinner?" Darryl asked. "I've worked up a bit of an appetite."

"Just so happens we run a restaurant here," Sheila smiled at him, looking back from the front of the group. "I was thinking a bunch of pasta with red sauce? Keep it simple and filling? We've even got the perfect Chianti to go with it."

"That sounds just about perfect," Doug replied.

As a group, they all filed together and headed inside the main house for a break and some much-needed food.

"Are you sweating already? This is the easy job." Benjamin jerked his chin toward Darryl who'd removed a handkerchief from his pocket and was wiping the glistening sweat from his forehead.

The morning sun beamed with a dull, amber glow through the gray skies above, the fresh morning's light bringing a long list of jobs that needed doing.

"Pfft, I must be working harder than you," Darryl replied, folding his damp handkerchief back up and stuffing it into a pocket.

They stood alongside the thick trench they'd dug earlier as Benjamin gestured toward a few pieces of long PVC that were resting on the ground not far away.

"Just hush up and help me grab that conduit, will you? I want to get this finished."

Darryl walked over to Benjamin, and the two men hoisted up the last length of conduit then walked it back toward the trench and lowered it in toward the threaded end of the previous length.

"Hand me the primer and cement?" Benjamin called up to Darryl who retrieved the purple liquid primer and the container of cement, bringing them over to Benjamin.

He applied the primer first, both to the pipe end and the fitting, coating each surface with cement a few moments later. Once the primer and cement was added, he pushed the sections of conduit together, then gave them a quick quarter-turn, locking them in place. He held them that way for thirty more seconds, then stood and gave the primer and cement back to Darryl, who returned them to the nearby utility vehicle.

"Mrs. Tills, can I grab that shovel?" Benjamin walked toward Sheila, who was standing nearby with Doug, both of them holding shovels.

She handed it to Benjamin, and he took it, walking back toward the trench where they'd just laid the PVC conduit. He walked over toward the solar panel array and stopped near the end of the trench they'd dug, which nearly butted up against the combiner box, which was bolted to a free-standing mount with connectivity to each of the panels. Digging and pushing around in the dirt, he extended the trench just a bit, revealing a section of the mounting post which held the combiner box nearby.

"Grab me that 'L'?"

Darryl went back to the utility vehicle and retrieved an L-shaped section of conduit, bringing the primer and cement with him once more. Benjamin went through the steps again, applying the primer and the cement, then wedging the L-shaped conduit into place, giving it a tight quarter-turn so the wire would go from horizontal to vertical in order to reach up to the box.

"Perfect." Benjamin rested on the shovel and sweat turned his vision blurry before he retrieved his handkerchief and wiped it away.

"We almost ready to start burying the conduit?" Sheila asked. "Brandi's going to be wondering where I am."

"You'll be freed up in just a second, I promise." Benjamin waved a hand toward her. "Ready for the next part?" He nodded toward Darryl as he walked past him, heading from the solar array to the outbuilding ahead.

"Ready as I'll ever be."

They both walked to the outbuilding where Darryl had set the batteries, moving quickly despite the early morning heat and the soreness already present in their muscles.

"How much did you actually sleep last night, anyway?" Darryl called after Benjamin as he quickened his pace forward.

"I didn't count."

"How early were you up?"

"I've been getting up at dawn for darn near thirty years. Nothing any different these days."

"I was up at dawn this morning. You were already awake."

"Someone had to keep watch."

"I thought that was Doug's shift this morning?"

Benjamin drew his shoulders up in a shrug, still only facing forward as he walked toward the outbuilding.

"He needs to rest up. Get his leg feeling better. Won't be much good to us until he's got two decent wheels."

"Aw, you're a big softie after all, aren't you?"

Benjamin stopped short and Darryl nearly ran into him, a crooked grin still on his face.

"Keep poking me, and I'll show you how soft I am, kid. I don't care about that kung fu you know." He waved a dismissive hand at Darryl, though the crinkles around his eyes betrayed his good-natured humor.

Darryl failed at muffling a laugh, then the two men entered the outbuilding. The long coil of cable they'd procured from Cliff's was in the center of the floor, taking up a section of the building's interior. Batteries had been stacked up and aligned with the chalk outlines and a recently mounted junction box stood bolted on the far wall. A thick hole had been drilled into the wall and a section of conduit was extended through the hole, insulation foam sprayed and drying around it. One of the L-shaped ends had already been cemented in place, pointing upward toward the base of the junction box.

"First course of action is to feed the wire through the conduit and toward the panels. We need to crimp the ends and put the connectors on so this end can hook into that interface. Cable first; this crap is pretty thick and heavy." Benjamin lifted one end of the coiled wire and began to unspool it, feeding it down through the L-shaped end and into the conduit. "But it being thick means I can push it along the length on my own once I get it started. I need you on the other side to let me know when it's through. It's a straight shot, pretty short, so it should be quick." Benjamin started feeding the wire in, and Darryl exited the outbuilding, jogging along the length of the conduit.

Sheila and Doug each held a shovel and approached the conduit, patiently waiting for the word to come. Darryl reached the far end of the as the thick wire began to poke through, moving as Benjamin pushed it from his end. Darryl snatched the radio from his belt and opened the channel.

"Wire's through!"

"Good. Make sure there's plenty of slack so we can connect it to the terminal lugs. I'm not going to cut it until we're good on that end." There was a moment of quiet, then static crackled again. "Come on back here, would you? Just want to show you something."

Darryl rested the length of cable along the other side of the conduit and walked back toward the outbuilding. "We should be good to bury." He gave a thumbs up to Sheila and Doug, who approached the conduit and began to push dirt back over it.

"What's up?" Darryl returned to the outbuilding and leaned in to check on Benjamin.

"I've gotta wire these batteries up. This stuff is thick enough it'll work fine for that, too."

"Okay."

"Just wanted to make sure you knew what I was doing because if something happens, someone else is going to have to know how all of this works."

"Got it, yeah I'll pay attention."

Benjamin went to the opposite end of the coil of wire and used a set of heavy-duty snippers that Cliff had given them to cut off a long section of the cable. He went to work stripping, crimping and then plugging in the positive and negative terminals, wiring the two cables back to the junction box. Darryl's radio crackled loudly, and Sheila's voice broke through the static.

"Conduit's buried. Brandi is going a little stir crazy just standing watch. She feels like she's not doing anything."

"She's keeping us safe," Benjamin growled.

Doug eased his way into the outbuilding and limped up alongside Darryl to get a better look at what Benjamin was doing.

"Oh, I've got an audience now. Great."

"Maybe this is better," Darryl said. "You and Doug can work together on getting everything hooked up while I grab the tractor and start moving some straw bales up to the garden? That way they can start laying it down and make Brandi a little less anxious."

"I'm more worried about getting power going than Brandi's anxiety." Benjamin rolled his eyes. "But go ahead." He waved a dismissive hand toward Darryl, who nodded and backed out of the building.

"Doug and Benjamin are going to work on getting the wires crimped and plugged into the terminals." Darryl called over to Sheila. "I'm going to take the tractor and run to the barn to grab a few straw bales for your garden."

"Sounds good!" Sheila walked over to the side-by-side, slipped behind the steering wheel and started it up. "I'll see you up there?"

Darryl flashed her a thumbs up and took a quick look at the ground where they'd laid the conduit. Dirt had been placed back over and patted into place. If it wasn't for the missing grass along that narrow strip of dirt, it would have been difficult to tell that anything had been disturbed. Darryl approached the tractor and hopped on, then started it up and began rolling toward the distant barn.

Benjamin peered out from the outbuilding at Darryl's retreating form. "Come on." He nodded toward Doug, who grabbed his ski pole and went after Benjamin, the two of them walking the length of the buried conduit. Benjamin carried a tool bag over his shoulder and walked slowly, giving Doug the opportunity to keep up with him.

"You didn't have to let me sleep last night."

"I woulda been up anyway. Too wound up to sleep. Figured one of us might as well get some shut-eye."

"You can't keep burning the candle at both ends, Benjamin. We need you."

"Appreciate the sentiment, Mr. Tills, but I'm all right."

Doug nodded, gripping his ski pole as he labored forward, still favoring his left leg, though far less severely than the day before. A few moments later, they reached the far end of the conduit, where the wire extended from wall, hanging loose with plenty of slack.

"Good work, Darryl," Benjamin whispered approvingly and knelt alongside the wire, opening his tool bag and retrieving some of the wiring gear that Cliff had given them.

He and Doug worked together on stripping the cable, placing the terminal on the end and crimping it tightly, then fitted the plug into the lugs, tightening them down. Doug watched him work, studying him closely, the two men working swiftly and silently. Soon enough, they were walking back along the length of buried conduit toward the outbuilding.

A short distance away, Darryl drove the tractor, guiding it up the slope from the lower parking lot to the upper one, a trailer pulling behind him loaded with several bales of straw he'd recovered from one of the barns. Sheila's utility vehicle was already parked alongside the new garden, both her and Brandi talking animatedly as Darryl pulled up and parked the trailer alongside the freshly tilled patch of land.

"Tell you what," Darryl said, sliding from the seat of the tractor, "I'll keep watch for a while so you ladies can focus your attention on getting the straw down. Does that work?"

"Sounds great." Together, Sheila and Brandi hauled the first straw bale from the trailer and let it drop to the ground with a thud.

Sheila used a pocketknife to cut through the string and the straw fell loose, spreading apart as the string was cut free. She and Brandi grabbed handfuls of straw and walked toward the garden, tossing it down and spreading it out. They burned through every bale, covering the entire section of tilled ground, placing down a full layer of the dried grass. Sheila had gathered up some bags of fertilizer and placed them next to the garden and she and Brandi worked together, using scoops to retrieve the dark-colored material and spread it throughout the straw.

Brandi wrinkled her nose as she worked, trying to pull her shirt up over her face, but failing to keep it there. "Ugh."

"Smells great, huh?"

"Not so much. Reminds me of my uncle's farm. I hated the way it smelled."

"Get used to it. We'll be elbow deep in manure for the long haul."

"Oh, great. I can't tell you how happy that makes me." Brandi returned to the edge of the garden, the pungent, acid stink of fertilizer thick in the air. "Did you figure what to do about the water situation yet? Long hoses and sprinklers or something?"

Sheila folded her hands and looked toward the gray-hued sky, the pale sun filtered through the haze. "I'm hoping for rain in the next couple of days because it's been so cloudy. But if it doesn't, we may have to get Darryl to use a tank to haul some water up in the tractor."

"We'll figure it out one way or the other." Brandi returned her scoop to the bag of fertilizer, then she and Sheila were once more spreading it out across the fallen straw.

In the outbuilding, Benjamin walked Doug through the last connection points from the batteries to the combination box, then finally crimped one end on the main cable and threaded it into one of the lugs underneath.

"You ready for this?" Benjamin asked.

"Ready as I can be. You want to do the honors?"

"You're the boss, Mr. Tills. You get to flip the switches."

Benjamin took a long step back, holding his breath as Doug went to each battery in turn, flipping the power switch on the side of each of the units. One at a time, small LED indicators came alight on each battery, a slow trickle of incoming power starting a long and arduous charging process.

"Well, what do you know? It works." Benjamin laughed flatly and crossed his arms, staring at the batteries in disbelief. "Hopefully it'll move a little quicker if we can get some actual sunshine. Those gray skies, smoke and clouds aren't helping things much. Charging could be a long effort."

"Yeah, well, at least we've gotten somewhere, and once we—"

Doug's radio crackled, the static breaking free before he could finish his sentence. "Doug! Benjamin! It's Sheila, up by the garden!" Her voice was a hissing whisper of urgency. Doug yanked the radio from his hip and was about to talk into it. "It's the van!" Sheila shouted before Doug could even answer. "It's back!"

"Son of a..." Benjamin growled and moved past Doug, throwing open the door of the outbuilding.

Doug grabbed his ski pole and charged after him, using it to propel himself forward as fast as he could, though he still lagged behind, his injured leg slowing his progress. As they neared the rear of the main building, Darryl was already sprinting toward them, the pump shotgun clutched in his hand. He held it aloft as he neared, thrusting it into Benjamin's open grip.

"Take this," he gasped. "I need to get something really quick."

"What?" Benjamin shook his head in confusion, but Darryl had already launched himself back toward the main building, running at a dead sprint.

"I'll be right back!" he shouted, then vanished inside.

Benjamin and Doug spared a brief second to exchange a confused look, then the two men trundled onward, moving as quickly as they could, up toward the garden.

# CHAPTER 16

**The O'Brian Family**
**Los Angeles, California**

The inferno surrounded them, a raging wall of all-encompassing fire closing in from all sides as a plume of gray-black smoke rose overhead that turned afternoon into twilight. Samantha's knuckles whitened on the steering wheel as the RV's headlights strobed through the murk ahead. The president gripped the kitchen table, his makeshift mask of wet cotton doing little against the acrid air pouring in through the gaping hole where the windshield had once been.

"There!" Jason pointed through the plastic-wrapped frames perched on his nose. "Side street, right!"

Samantha cranked the wheel, the RV's suspension groaning as they left the main road. Heat pressed against the windows like a living thing, squirming along the exterior, surging through the broken windshield, filling the RV with a dragon's breath of heat. Through gaps in the smoke the fire front advanced, a churning orange tidal wave consuming buildings and trees with methodical fury. The RV's engine roared as Samantha navigated through a maze of abandoned vehicles strewn about the roadways. Smoke reduced visibility to yards, fingers of flame creating a disorientating dance of yellow and white through the haze. She weaved between vehicles, sometimes with only inches to spare, the RV's bulk scraping paint and crumpling side mirrors.

An explosion rocked the street ahead as a gas station went up, its fireball punching violently through the smoke ceiling. Samantha yanked the wheel left and they went down a residential street, palm trees lining the road like burning torches, their fronds shooting embers into the wind. They emerged onto a wider street beyond, but the smoke was thicker, Samantha slowing as she squinted through the converging churn. Shapes loomed and vanished; parked cars, fallen trees, buildings swarmed in violent flame, other things she couldn't identify. There was a second, closer explosion, the shock wave rocking the RV, and warning lights flashed on the dashboard.

The smoke parted briefly, revealing a city transforming into hell, fire tornadoes dancing between buildings, an incredible rush of suffocating heat blistering Samantha's face. Inside the RV, plastic components smelled hot, the air conditioning struggling and rattling loudly as they continued their rapid surge through the burning city.

Eli pointed through the vacant windshield. "Fire truck!"

An abandoned fire engine blocked the intersection ahead, its red paint dulled by ash. Samantha steered around it, nearly catching the extended ladder on the top of the fire engine, but missing just in the nick of time. The RV's engine stuttered again, but Samantha pressed the accelerator, willing it to keep running. The smoke pressed closer, the temperature kept climbing and somewhere in the inferno behind them, another explosion lit up the sky.

Jason leaned forward against the dashboard, squinting through layers of plastic wrap and smoke. "Watch out!"

A cluster of fallen bodies filled the road ahead, wedged between groups of abandoned vehicles and Samantha grimaced, tightening her grip around the steering wheel.

"Hold on!" she shouted, Eli and Sarah immediately clapping their hands over their ears while the President looked around, bewildered.

They crunched through the layer of bodies, bones snapping, bloated bodies bursting beneath the spinning crush of their wheels. McDouglas' face turned pale as he visibly recoiled, wincing as if struck in the face.

"Sorry," Samantha hissed, swerving left once there was enough road to do so, the RV leaning as it navigated a turn around an upended delivery truck.

The front corner of the RV cracked into a light post on the left side of the road, a violent shudder rocking the vehicle as she desperately corrected, only to clip an SUV on the opposite side of the street. The impact managed to throw her back to a straight trajectory as the RV hewed its way through clogged freeways and smoke-littered alleys.

"Are we still headed south?" Jason turned toward her.

"I hope so! I'm trying!" Samantha leaned forward, squinting through the smoke. "I can't even see the sun to orient myself!"

Samantha wheeled right, navigating a side street to work her way around a makeshift traffic jam ahead. The RV's tires rolled jerkily over a few more corpses strewn throughout a brickwork pedestrian walkway, then she twisted the wheel left, heading back in the same general direction. Smoke surged down the road, a boiling wall of gray soot and ash and she pushed the gas to the floorboards, desperate to stay ahead of the flames. They propelled themselves down the next length of smoke-smeared street, banging alongside a row of stalled traffic to the right and Samantha wrestled the large vehicle under control despite the jostling of impact as they continued south. Up ahead, a sudden flare erupted, peeling through a cloud of smoke, bright against the setting sun.

"Did you see that?" Jason leaned to the right for a better view. "I think the fire's in front of us!"

"Are you sure?"

"Samantha! Look out!" McDouglas shouted from the kitchen nook, and Samantha's gaze snapped back ahead.

A congested heap of piled traffic filled both lanes, barricading the roadways in a mass of crumpled steel, smashed glass and distorted plastic.

"Turn left! There!" Jason stabbed a finger toward a gap in the buildings.

"That's the direction of those flames!"

"There's no other choice!"

Samantha gritted her teeth, tapped the brakes and swung left, the RV heaving as it navigated the unexpected turn. The passenger side of the vehicle banged hard against another light post, the entire RV shuddering, then scraping as they continued down the street, rubbing against the building. Flames roared ahead of them, a scorching hurricane of blown embers tearing through the wall of smoke. Heat permeated the entire RV, an undulating wave of violent warmth that sucked the air from Samantha's lungs in spite of her makeshift mask.

"Get down!" she screamed, pressing herself close to the wheel as they bore down on the sudden surge of fire.

Jason threw himself to the floorboards, McDouglas, Eli and Sarah ripping free their safety harnesses and leaping down as well. Samantha accelerated into the belly of fire, a sudden clawing inferno raking throughout the vehicle, impaling her with spears of white-hot ash and coal. She gasped as an eternal flame consumed them, a wild, untamed beast constructed of pure magma, the RV racing through as fast as she could possibly go. By some miracle, they roared through the other side, a sudden break opening up into the smoke-filled street, fire racing through the surrounding buildings but no longer enveloping the RV. A sudden groan of sound shook the earth itself and just ahead, a six-story tenement building collapsed upon itself, brickwork folding into splintered rubble. It dropped, the base erupting outward in a shower of debris as the entire apartment building went down.

Samantha hauled the wheel left again, slamming up over the curb, careening against a nearby dumpster as she veered around the sudden avalanche of broken brick, stone, and billowing dust. For a moment the clouds further obscured her vision, and she drove blind, though she didn't slow with the fire licking at their heels. The RV slewed left, then right, hammering against lines of nearby vehicles, almost tearing itself from her control. Somehow, she retained her grip, and the RV surged as it wobbled unsteadily. Jason crawled up from the floorboards, back into the passenger seat, McDouglas and the twins trying to find their own footing again.

"Smell that?" Jason scrunched his nose, which had freed itself of the mask he was wearing, his voice hoarse from smoke and stress.

"Smell what?" Samantha spoke through clenched teeth.

"I think it's our tires."

As if on cue, the RV jostled even further, shaking violently as a sudden wave of familiar, pungent stink wafted through the cabin, unhindered by the missing windshield.

"I smell it, too," Samantha spoke through gritted teeth. "That might explain why I can barely steer this hunk of junk."

The RV thundered forward, rattling more with each passing second, the steering wheel vibrating within the tight grasp of Samantha's clenched fingers. Her teeth ached as the vehicle shuddered, an even more powerful stink of burning rubber stinging her nostrils and eyes. Lifting her fingers, she checked the plastic wrap around her glasses and found it peeling away.

"Mr. President!" she shouted without looking backwards. "Timothy! Can you grab Kale from the bathroom?"

"Huh?"

"Grab Kale from the bathroom!" Her voice rose as she struggled to maintain control of the vehicle. "Eli and Sarah, pack up whatever you can. Food, water, grab the guns and equipment we took from the police car, too!"

"Are we leaving the RV?"

"Sarah, honey, I just need you to do it! No questions right now!"

McDouglas made his way toward the bathroom as Eli raced toward the back of the RV, stumbling then catching himself on the wall. Sarah took off after him, the two of them disappearing into the back for a moment before they came back out, duffels and backpacks in hand.

"How much further can we make it?" Jason had partially stood, taking a few steps toward the bathroom as McDouglas retrieved Kale.

"I'm not sure. Another half-mile? Twenty feet? The tires are going to blow sooner or later and that'll be the end for us!"

Jason took a step back toward the dashboard, leaning over the seat and pointing out through the front hole where the windshield used to be. The wind had whipped up, briefly clearing the smoke out from in front of them.

"Is that water? Right there? A lake or a reservoir or something?" He gestured toward a murky spot of water further south of them. "That might be our best shot out of this."

"I think you're right."

Kale whined as she paced about, free of the bathroom, her tail tucked low, ears flat, head darting left to right in confusion. McDouglas bent alongside Eli, helping him pull several boxes of food from the cabinets and loading them into the duffel bag. Bottles of water came next, stuffed inside, then Sarah stood and darted toward the bathroom herself. She returned with the first aid kit and slipped that inside as well.

"Don't forget about that IFAK!" Jason shouted, turning toward them, using the back of the seat for balance. He pushed off and made his way toward them, angling toward a black pouch near the cupboards to the left.

"The what?" Eli asked.

"It's the medical kit we pulled out of the trunk of the police car." Jason lifted the black pouch and stuffed it inside one of the backpacks, which was already starting to fill up.

"If there's any room at all after we load up the food and stuff, grab some spare clothes. Grab whatever you can!"

"Dad! Are we..."

"Just grab it, Eli, okay?"

Eli nodded, biting his lower lip as he stood and darted back toward the bedroom. Jason worked with McDouglas to stuff the AR-15 into the bag, then hooked the holstered service weapon to his belt, going through a swift double-check to make sure other critical items had been packed away. McDouglas stood and made his way back toward the bathroom.

"I saw some medications in here, too."

A loud bang shattered the dull roar of flames and RV engine, sharp and echoing, and McDouglas fell to the floor, grunting as he hit chest-first. The RV suddenly swerved left, Samantha hissing as she battled against its lack of control. A loud, repetitive *thumpthumpthump* came from the front of the vehicle, the RV jostling even more wildly than it had been earlier.

"Tire blew!" Samantha screamed from the driver's seat, wrestling with every bit of strength in her being to keep them from veering off course.

"Everyone grab any last items you can!" Jason stood and shouted through the chaos. The RV shook and clattered, rolling unevenly down the street, swarmed by smoke inside and out. "We need to be ready to bail out! Right now! Come on, come on, let's go, get by the door!" He gestured wildly for everyone to return to the front of the RV.

Bending down, he shouldered the duffel, grunting as he hoisted it from the floor, its canvas weighed down by food, weapons, and water. Back on his feet, McDouglas handed off a backpack to Eli, then helped Sarah with a second one, then shouldered a third himself. Samantha huddled against the steering wheel, the world outside the RV a swirling mass of gray and orange, flames roaring all around them. From somewhere to their right, something detonated, a sudden sharp bang echoing loudly, too close for comfort. Instinctively, Samantha steered left, away from the sound, then struggled to correct, aiming the front of the RV toward an incline ahead.

"It's everywhere," she hissed, and Jason's hand pressed her shoulder.

"You're doing great. Just get us to that water."

"I'm trying... it should be right up here...."

They reached the crest of a hill, moving at speed, the RV barreling through a pair of cars, knocking both askew as she forced her way through, somehow still operating on one less tire than earlier. The RV slewed left, she battled it right, then managed to further accelerate. Down the slope of the other side of the hill, a large park sprawled ahead, its parking lot filled with abandoned vehicles. A few dead bodies fell into view, scattered across the grass, creeping walls of smoke swarming everything around it.

"There! The lake!" Samantha floored the gas again, picking up speed as the cumbersome vehicle raced downhill, showing no intention of slowing down.

Smoke and surrounding buildings blurred into smudges on either side, the entirety of the city swallowed by rapidly increasing flames as the RV rocketed toward the nearby parking lot, approaching the park. There was another flat clap of a bang nearby and the RV jerked, the steering wheel tugging against Samantha's practiced grip.

"Another tire! Everyone brace yourselves!" Samantha floored the gas, the RV screaming, barely under control as the park expanded before them. It revealed itself through the smoke, the shimmering surface of the lake separated from the parking lot by formerly well-manicured sections of ash-littered lawn and the slope of a rolling, green hill.

Samantha suddenly hammered the brakes, guiding them toward the parking lot as the RV screeched, its back-end slewing right. Somehow she regained control, pushing the vehicle straight forward, braking wildly as they converged on the clusters of vehicles still parked in the parking lot. The RV smashed through a perimeter fence, hammering slats of wood, exploding splinters as they tore through, rolling over grass as they approached the parking lot. She hit the brakes again, jerking the wheel as the RV hammered into the vehicles, already slowing and sliding as metal struck metal in a cacophony of crumpling impact. Plastic bent and twisted, metal buckled, and windows exploded in the surrounding vehicles as the RV slammed to a halt, swerving and upending, nearly tipping over, its passengers stumbling, desperate to keep their balance.

McDouglas slammed hard into a nearby cabinet, buckling the door and letting loose a gasp of surprise and pain. Eli lurched, hitting the chair nestled within the kitchen nook, but somehow remained standing, while Sarah spread her legs, and navigated the crash with the grace of a surfer in strong tides. Jason stumbled forward against the dash, the chaos of the impact already lessening as the RV's engine groaned into gasping silence.

"Masks. Everyone, masks!" Samantha gasped as she stood, pushing herself away from the steering wheel.

Her fingers clawed at the moist cotton around her nose and mouth, tugged it slightly, then readjusted it. She snatched another bottle of water free and used it to dampen the fabric, then handed it off to Eli who did the same, as the rest of them adjusted their face coverings.

"My glasses..." Sarah shook her head as her glasses had worked their way free, peeling the plastic wrap from her temples.

"They're all coming apart." Samantha tore hers off her face and tossed them aside, plastic wrap and all. "Masks are going to have to be good enough for now." She turned toward the empty windshield and pointed over the gathered roofs of surrounding vehicles that had stopped their uncontrolled forward progress. "See the water? That's where we're going! Everyone with me?"

Heads nodded throughout the RV as the group finished adjusting their masks, settling them over nose and mouth, dampening them with more water. Jason grunted as he adjusted the strap of the heavy duffel slung over his shoulder and Samantha grabbed one of the larger backpacks, her shoulders sagging. Kale darted left and right, claws clicking, head whipping back and forth, her ears sharply perked.

"We need to move right now! The fire's not going to wait, let's go, let's go!" Samantha sprinted toward the door and pushed it open, the group funneling outside, still adjusting their masks, blinking hard against the encroaching smoke.

"Down the hill! Toward the water!" Samantha waved them on, swarming flames roaring from just beyond the RV, reaching over and around the fence that lined the park's perimeter.

Jason hobbled forward, moving slowly with the large duffle as Samantha tightened the straps of her backpack. Eli, Sarah and McDouglas darted forward, moving around them and running toward the hill, Kale leaping across the grass in their wake.

"In the water! It'll be safest in the water!" She ran forward, her shoulders and legs aching, the air temperature sharply elevated.

They quickly caught up to the kids and started to pass, and Samantha twisted around to face Eli. "Make sure Kale and the president don't get left behind! You and Sarah both! We're all in this together!"

They continued running, loping and lunging down the slope, the weight of their bags threatening to throw them off-balance.

"Look!" Jason shouted, stabbing a gesture toward a curved section of the kidney-shaped pond ahead. "There's a dock over there!"

Sweat clung to Samantha's arms and legs which were thick and heavy with exertion. Breath stabbed hard, pulsing through the fabric that was stretched across her nose and mouth. Crackling flames rippled nearby, groping toward the park, the grass alight to their left, trailing smoke adding to the underlying gray.

Jason and Samantha altered their path, sprinting toward the covered dock and Samantha waved for Eli, Sarah and McDouglas to follow. The president nodded as he ran, checking briefly to ensure Kale was still with them as she sprinted past, and darted toward the head of the group. Eli and Sarah kept pace, legs and arms pumping, their cheeks red, but still they ran swiftly. The group made its way around the right curve of the pond and as they approached the covered dock, a line of paddleboats came into view, all tethered to the dock, bobbing up and down gently on mostly still waters.

"Paddleboats?!" Jason came to a stumbling halt as they neared the water.

"It's that, or treading water or staying here with *that*!" Samantha waved a hand toward the swarming orange wall only a short distance away, black smoke belching up from within its depths. "Come! Get in! Get in now, throw your bags! Just get in the water!" She frantically waved to the rest, gesturing wildly toward the floating plastic ducks, swans and other cartoonish creatures that had been fashioned into plasticine boats.

She took a lumbering stride toward a nearby duckling and shrugged off her backpack as McDouglas neared. "I'll take that!" He yanked the bag from her hands and ushered Kale toward her. "Get Kale inside!"

Samantha patted Kale's side and gently guided her toward the dock. "In! Get in! Kale, come on, girl! In the boat!" Samantha elevated her voice at the end and Kale got the message, bounding from the dock and landing inside the duckling, the boat bobbing gently under the dog's sprawling impact.

Jason approached a nearby swan, levering his duffel bag inside as he waved Eli and Sarah to come closer. They obeyed, tossing one of their backpacks into another duck as President McDouglas slowly approached a flamingo with a long, pink neck. Samantha descended upon Sarah, gently moving her toward a nearby paddle-boat as Jason did the same for Eli. Both children were soon inside as Jason and Samantha furiously untied the ropes attaching them to the dock. Tugging them loose, the boats began to drift out into the water.

"Use the pedals!" Jason inched up alongside the dock, the back of his neck hot with a rush of steaming air fueled by the nearby fires.

Eli fumbled for a moment, but soon figured it out, pedaling his legs, guiding the boat in a lazy turn as it began to head out into open water. "It's like a bike!" he shouted toward Sarah, and she followed his lead while McDouglas clumsily straddled the dock and the flamingo, his arms outstretched.

"You need help?" Samantha took a step toward him, but he shook her off, waving her away as he almost fell into the pink-colored boat, quickly correcting himself.

Jason waited for Samantha to get in alongside Kale, then maneuvered himself into his own white swan, wedging himself tight to the duffel bag. Samantha was already starting to move away from the shore, as McDouglas was doing a short distance away, the colorful boats dipping gently as they cut through the shimmering surface of the lake. Together, the boats moved toward the center of the water, putting as much distance between them and the shore as possible. Jason maneuvered his pedals, turning his swan as Samantha did the same with her duck, both bending toward each other until they bumped softly, wing-on-wing.

Jason reached out from within his boat, extending his hand and Samantha gently took it, the two of them lacing their fingers together, intertwining them. They gripped tight and held each other's hands and the hands of their children as the motley collection of boats came around, pointing them back in the direction they'd come. Thick columns of ink black smoke smeared across the sky, the RV in the parking lot a darkened shadow beneath the rippling glow of roaring flames. They stared up at the RV, fire creeping throughout the parking lot, peeling away at its exterior, swallowing it piece by piece. Soon the RV itself was fully engulfed in flames, nearly invisible within the opened maw of primal heat.

"Your dad's going to kill me." Jason whispered.

"And me, too." Samantha squeezed his hand tighter, tears streaming down her face as they watched their home burn before their very eyes. "Oh, Jason... what are we going to do?"

There was no answer forthcoming, just the spiraling smoke, the churning flames and a city burning to embers.

# CHAPTER 17

**The Tills Family**
**Silverpine, Oregon**

The all-too-familiar white panel van halted, its engine still running as the driver's side door eased open. Benjamin gripped the double-barreled shotgun in two hands, the weapon held toward the van as Doug and Sheila lumbered up alongside him. Brandi stood a short distance away, her expression slack and face pale, one hand pressed to her sternum, keeping her distance. With a grunt, the driver peeled himself out from behind the wheel and inched left, keeping the opened door between him and the double-barrel shotgun, both hands raised high.

"Take it easy," he said, his voice gruff and hoarse, an impossibly wide smile showing off his discolored teeth. An adhesive bandage clung to his forehead, purple bruises coloring the skin at his throat. "We weren't trying to scare you, all right? We get it, you're protective of your place. I ain't even mad about the guy who punched me in the throat."

"He could have done a lot worse," Benjamin replied, then gently moved his shotgun. "Or I could have."

"You wanna shoot a guy just for asking for help? Look, I'm really sorry about the way that went down. It wasn't supposed to go like that."

"How was it supposed to go? We roll over and show you our bellies? Let you take what you want?" Benjamin shook his head. "Nuh uh."

Through the sunlight reflecting off the windshield, the van's passenger shifted, the face of the woman falling briefly into view, her hair slung across her face and draped along her left shoulder.

"We just want a little help – and, hey, we're willing to trade. Eager to trade! You've got a big place here, you could use a lot of help. We can work. Do manual labor, pick grapes, do whatever you need. All we're asking for is a little gas, maybe some water, a place to rest our heads that isn't the seats of this old piece a junk." He nodded toward the van, offering a wry smile that Benjamin didn't return.

"There are plenty of abandoned cars out there. Plenty of gas you could siphon."

"We've tried siphoning. Those new cars there've all got tanks with screens that get in the way. It's not as easy as you're making it out to be."

Gravel crunched behind Benjamin, and he allowed himself the briefest of backward glances as Darryl slowly approached, his face sculpted into a facade of sternness. His rigid jawline drew taut, his eyes narrow, lips pressed into a thin line, any sense of humor and easy-going-ness melted away.

"Come on. You guys are the owners right?" The driver took a step in Doug and Sheila's direction, his hands lifted. "All we want is a few lousy gallons of gas. Just a few. If you give us that, we'll move on, we'll drive away, and you'll never see us again. I'm sure you've got plenty to spare. We've seen your Jeep out and about; a few gallons is really all we want."

Sheila turned toward the man, about to speak when Benjamin interrupted, striding forward, placing himself between Sheila and the van's driver. "What did you say?"

"Huh?"

"What did you just say?" Benjamin's voice was a growl, and he took a long stride forward, forcing the man to backpedal in the face of the raised shotgun. "You saw the Jeep out and about? Where exactly did you see the Jeep?"

"Hey, man. Take it easy. We just saw it is all." He held up his hands, his head shaking.

"Have you been spying on us? Have you been following us around?" Benjamin hissed through gritted teeth, the shotgun raised.

"Eddie!" A shrill voice echoed from within the van, complimented by the sudden chorus of yapping barks from the chihuahua, a deafening orchestra of preening racket from within the vehicle. "Just get back in the van!"

"No, Eddie," Benjamin said, taking another step forward, shotgun still clenched tightly. "Don't get back in the van. I want answers - where have you seen us? How do you know we've been out and about?"

"It doesn't matter, okay? It's not important. All we're looking for is a little gas..."

Before he could finish his sentence, the rear doors of the white van shot open, hinges squealing, doors banging loudly as they swung ajar. A man leaped free, landing on the gravel and quickly rose, a tire iron clenched tightly in one hand. Denim-clad, a second young man jumped free, a single-bladed hatchet with a wooden handle clamped in his tight fist, circling around the first man, heading toward Benjamin as a third appeared wielding a crowbar.

"We asked you nice," the driver hissed and lunged at Sheila.

Sheila gasped, recoiling from his grip, and he slammed into

her, knocking her back and she twisted and struck the ground hard on her left hip.

"Sheila!" Doug shouted, spittle flying as he lumbered toward the driver.

Despite his off-balance limp, Doug threw his left fist forward, hammering a swift punch into the bridge of the driver's nose. There was a sharp impact, a sudden whiplash of sound and motion as the driver's head snapped back, sending him staggering back toward the van. Benjamin fired the shotgun without hesitation, pointing it at the three men in back, a blast of light and smoke roaring from both barrels. The man in the lead was flung back, twisting wildly as blood spattered from his arm, a spray of buckshot swarming across him and pelting the exterior of the van in a drumbeat of metallic ricochets. He screamed, the tire iron fell free and he hit the van back-first, clutching at his bloodied arm with his opposite hand.

With a scream, the man dressed in denim sprinted past, angling around Benjamin and charged toward Doug, hatchet at the ready. Doug wheeled toward him and faltered as the axe-wielding man descended upon him. Darryl was at his side in an instant, though, swinging open his jacket and yanking a paintball gun free from where he'd concealed it. In a matter of seconds, he'd lifted the weapon and pulled the trigger, launching a trio of paintballs at Doug's attacker. The first round hammered the axe-wielding man high in the face, drilling into his left cheek bone, eliciting a primal howl of agony. Stumbling away, the man jerked as Darryl fired again, the second shot pounding hard into the back of the man's skull.

His axe fell to the ground as he stumbled forward, knees buckled, both hands clawing at his face, his shout of pain descending into a ragged, gasping scream. He wobbled left, then right, one hand extended, almost losing his balance as he shambled away, one palm pressed to his cheek, his voice muffled.

The driver turned toward Benjamin, who was in the middle of

reloading the shotgun, and charged, a fresh river of blood streaming from his broken nose. Benjamin tensed, shoving the shells into place, taking a step back, the driver already too close for the shotgun to come around. A paintball drove hard into the driver's chest, kicking like a stone, halting the driver's forward progress, his shoes kicking up gravel as he was propelled backwards once more.

Two more thuds of paintball fire came again, two more rounds driving hard into the driver's torso, pummeling him with rapid fire punches of impact. The paintballs fragmented as they hit the man, landing with dull *thuds* instead of wet splatters of paint, and Benjamin caught a glimpse of frozen pieces of the paintballs exploding out from the impact points. Eddie's hip struck the grill of the van and he spilled left, stumbling back toward the driver's side as Benjamin finished reloading and trailed him with the shotgun. He fired both barrels, twin rounds exploding into the grill and windshield of the van, sending a spider-web of cracks throughout the sloped safety glass.

The van's engine rattled and coughed, whining as it barely clung to life, the driver yanking the door open and throwing himself back behind the steering wheel. Darryl fired another paintball, the thick projectile rebounding from the hood with a muffled thunk. The disoriented man in denim who'd been wielding a hatchet stumbled back toward the van, Darryl firing another pair of paintballs at him, hurrying him as he ran clumsily across the grass. The third man helped the first, whose arm hung limp at his side, flesh ravaged with buckshot, blood flowing freely and spattered onto the grass at his feet.

The back door slammed as the men retreated and the engine's whine rose in pitch, rattling once more as the driver pounded the gearshift into reverse. Deep within the vehicle, the chihuahua was a deafening chorus of screaming yaps, and for a brief second its tooth-filled grimace appeared from the shadows, barking in unfiltered rage.

"Shut that dog up!" the driver screamed and a moment later, the van lurched backwards, kicking up gravel, the vehicle swerving wildly back and forth as they reversed up the driveway once more.

Benjamin hammered home another pair of shells and strode forward, launching another volley of buckshot at them as they finally vanished around the corner, the failing engine of the van growing faint until it silenced completely.

"Sheila! Sheila, are you okay?"

Doug knelt next to his wife, hand pressed to her back to help her sit fully upward, Brandi already having gotten to her first to get her up off of her side.

"I'm fine, I'm fine." Sheila waved them away, shaking her head. "I'm okay, he just knocked me over, that's all."

"Doug?" Brandi held out her hand but Doug waved her away, inching to his feet. "We're both okay," he said, "thanks to Benjamin. And thanks to Darryl. What in the world did you shoot them with?" Doug looked down at the paintball gun in Darryl's hand.

"It's what Benjamin was making fun of me for." Darryl grinned, his demeanor completely changed back to his normal self. "I threw a can of paintballs in the freezer last night, froze them solid. That's what I ran inside the house to grab." Darryl turned the paintball gun over in his hand. "It's like being shot with ball bearings. If the guy I shot in the head survives, he might end up with brain damage." Darryl's grin faded, his grip of the weapon loosening as he lowered it gently, pointing the barrel toward the ground at his feet.

"Smart thinking." Benjamin nodded his approval. "Looks like I owe you an apology."

Turning, Benjamin stared toward the gravel where the van had been, thick tire tracks visible in the loose stone and dirt. Spatters of blood, pellets of buckshot and pieces of slowly melting paintballs littered the ground, the only evidence of the chaos that had taken place.

"Like it or not," Benjamin continued, "this is a pretty high-profile location. People are going to keep coming and we need to figure out what to do."

"There are good people out there, though, I'm sure of it," Sheila said, wiping sweat from her brow. "If we can help people, I'd like to."

"But we've got to protect ourselves first and foremost." Doug slung his arm around his wife's shoulder, giving her a gentle, one-armed embrace.

"Protecting ourselves needs to be the *top* priority." Benjamin still stared toward the driveway. "I know you want to help people, but the more we make ourselves available to do that, the easier it will be to get taken advantage of."

"What are you saying?"

"First thing we need to do is build out some sort of gate or barricade. It's going to be almost impossible to prevent people from getting to us if they really want to, but we need to make it as difficult as possible."

"And we should all stay in the main house at all times." Sheila gave Benjamin a pointed look.

"Understood," Benjamin agreed. "Maybe patrols, too. Having someone always standing watch is well and good, but active patrols might be better."

"I don't like this, Doug." Sheila shook her head, leaning slightly to rest it on Doug's shoulder. "This is a lot for basically one group who were driven off."

"Don't assume they won't be back." Benjamin scowled. "I think it's very likely they *will* be back. They're obviously not the type to take no for an answer."

"Even with a few dozen pellets of buckshot in them?" Sheila asked.

"Even so. People get desperate enough, they'll do whatever

they think they need to. And even if it's not them it will be someone else."

Sheila slumped slightly against Doug, then brightened momentarily, straightening up as she reached for her pocket. Her happiness faded immediately, though, as she yanked something free from her pocket and held it in her hands, staring down at it in disbelief. It was the tracker for the RV, the lifeline that connected her to her daughter and her daughter's family, sitting in her palm, cracked and broken, splintered by the impact of her hip on the gravel.

"No," she whispered, her trembling fingers coiling around the handle of the tracker. "Please, no." Tears broke loose, tracking along her cheeks as Doug tightened his grip around her shoulders.

"Oh, hon. I'm so sorry." Doug whispered, inching close to Sheila's ear, "But they're tough and they're strong. You have to know they're okay. I promise you, they're okay."

Sheila collapsed into his chest, her sobs coming more freely as she, her husband and their friends stood together in the driveway of their home, the whole weight of the world bearing down upon them.

## READ THE NEXT BOOK IN THE SERIES

**FOLIANT Book 3**

**Available Here**
**books.to/foliant3**

Made in United States
Troutdale, OR
08/26/2025

33978589R00201